"Exceptional . . . Another fabulous book by uber-talented Amanda Scott . . . She fills our senses with the sights, sounds, smells, touch, and taste of the great lands and castles of Scotland."

—SingleTitles.com

"Fast-paced . . . An exciting Border romance with plenty of action . . . A terrific historical gender war."

—*Midwest Book Review*

"It was hard to put this one down . . . A pleasure to read."

—ReadingRomanceBooks.com

"The love story is funny, honest, and flares with both friendship and desire . . . Simon and Sibylla are outstandingly detailed and complex characters."

—TheRomanceReader.com

BORDER LASS

"5 Stars! A thrilling tale, rife with villains and notorious plots . . . Scott demonstrates again her expertise in the realm of medieval Scotland."

—FallenAngelReviews.com

"4½ Stars! TOP PICK! Readers will be thrilled . . . a tautly written, deeply emotional love story steeped in the rich history of the Borders."

—*Romantic Times BOOKreviews Magazine*

more . . .

"Wonderful . . . full of adventure and history . . . Scott is obviously well-versed on life in the fourteenth century, and she brings her knowledge to the page . . . an excellent story for both the romance reader and the history buff. I'm anxious to read others by Scott in the future."

—*Midwest Book Review*

"Scott's vivid attention to details makes you feel as if you are indeed visiting Scotland each and every time you pick up her delightful book."

—**ArmchairInterviews.com**

"A winner . . . Few authors do medieval romances as consistently excellent as Amanda Scott's."

—**HarrietKlausner.wwwi.com**

KING OF STORMS

"4 Stars! An exhilarating novel . . . with a lively love story . . . Scott brings the memorable characters from her previous novels together in an exciting adventure romance."

—*Romantic Times BOOKreviews Magazine*

"Passionate and breathtaking . . . Amanda Scott's *King of Storms* keeps the tension moving as she continues her powerful saga of the Macleod sisters."

—**NovelTalk.com**

"Intrigue and danger . . . Readers will enjoy the adventures and sweet romance."

—**RomRevToday.com**

more . . .

"A terrific tale starring two interesting lead characters who fight, fuss, and fall in love . . . Rich in history and romance, fans will enjoy the search for the Templar treasure and the Stone of Scone."

—Midwest Book Review

"Enchanting . . . a thrilling adventure . . . a *must* read . . . *King of Storms* is a page-turner. A sensual, action-packed romance sure to satisfy every heart."

—FreshFiction.com

KNIGHT'S TREASURE

"If you are a fan of historical romance with a touch of suspense, you don't want to miss this book."

—LoveRomanceAndMore.com

"Filled with tension, deceptions, and newly awakened passions. Scott gets better and better."

—NovelTalk.com

LADY'S CHOICE

"Terrific . . . with an exhilarating climax."

—Midwest Book Review

"A page-turner . . . her characters are a joy to read . . . sure to delight medieval historical fans."

—Romance Reviews Today

"Plenty of suspense and action and a delightful developing love story . . . Another excellent story from Scott."
—RomanceReviewsMag.com

PRINCE OF DANGER

"Phenomenal."
—*Romantic Times BOOKreviews Magazine*

"RITA Award–winning Scott has a flair for colorful, convincing characterization."
—*Publishers Weekly*

"Exhilarating . . . fabulous . . . action-packed . . . Fans of fast-paced historical tales . . . will want to read Amanda Scott's latest."
—*Midwest Book Review*

LORD OF THE ISLES

"Scott pits her strong characters against one another and fate. She delves into their motivations, bringing insight into them and the thrilling era in which they live."
—*Romantic Times BOOKreviews Magazine*

"Scott's storytelling is amazing . . . a captivating tale of intrigue . . . This is a definite keeper."
—**CoffeeTimeRomance.com**

more . . .

HIGHLAND PRINCESS

"Delightful historical starring two fabulously intelligent lead characters . . . Grips the audience from the onset and never [lets] go."
                              —*Affaire de Coeur*

"Perfect for readers who enjoy romances with a rich sense of history."
                              —*Booklist*

"A fabulous medieval Scottish romance."
                              —*Midwest Book Review*

SEDUCED BY A
ROGUE

AMANDA SCOTT

SEDUCED BY A ROGUE

FOREVER

NEW YORK   BOSTON

Copyright © 2009 by Lynne Scott-Drennan
Excerpt from *Tempted by a Warrior* copyright © 2009 by Lynne Scott-Drennan

Cover design by Claire Brown

Forever
Hachette Book Group
237 Park Avenue
New York, NY 10017
Visit our website at www.HachetteBookGroup.com.

Forever is an imprint of Grand Central Publishing. The Forever name and logo is a trademark of Hachette Book Group, Inc.

Printed in the United States of America

First Printing: January 2010

10 9 8 7 6 5 4 3 2 1

ATTENTION CORPORATIONS AND ORGANIZATIONS:
Most HACHETTE BOOK GROUP books are available at quantity discounts with bulk purchase for educational, business, or sales promotional use. For information, please call or write:

Special Markets Department, Hachette Book Group
237 Park Avenue, New York, NY 10017
Telephone: 1-800-222-6747 Fax: 1-800-477-5925

Dedicated
with many thanks to Jim and Jen
for their unwitting suggestion of a wonderful plot device
and for our amazing Cameron Scott,
born 6 October 2008

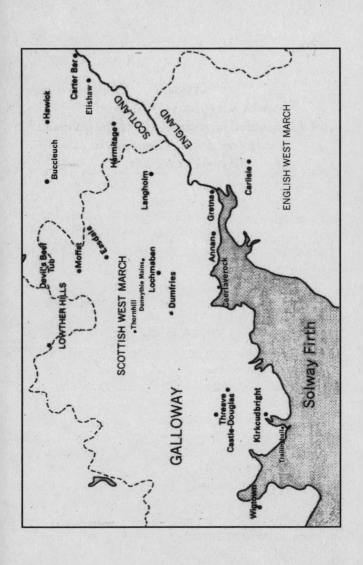

Author's Note _____

For the reader's convenience, the author offers the following aids:

Caerlaverock = Car LAV rock

Dunwythie Hall = "the Hall," the fortified house at Dunwythie Mains

Ebb tide = falling or receding tide

Flood tide = incoming or rising tide

Forbye = besides, also

"Herself" = in this book, Arabella Carlyle (née Bruce), Lady Kelso

Kirkcudbright = Kirk COO bree

Low tide (or low water) = lowest point of the ebb

Mains = the primary seat of a lord (from "demesne"), as in Dunwythie Mains

Neap tide = minimum tide, tide of minimum rise, when rise and fall show least change; occurs generally during first and third quarters of the moon

Nithsdale = NEETHS dale

Spring tide = tide occurring at or shortly after the new or full moon; tide of maximum rise, occurs twice a month

Stem up = begin to flood (at Annan, about three hours before high water; at Kirkcudbright Bay, about five hours before)

Thole = busy

Tocher = Scottish term for dowry

Chapter 1 _____

Dunwythie Mains, Annandale, 8 March 1375

Peering through new green foliage into a large field that the surrounding woodland sheltered from winds that could roar up the dale from Solway Firth, Will Jardine said, "What if Dunwythie catches us here?"

"He won't," twenty-five-year-old Robert Maxwell, Laird of Trailinghail, replied as they dismounted in the dense woods. "My lads saw his lordship ride north with ten men just after dawn." Looping his reins over a handy branch, he added, "He will be gone till at least midday, Will. And we have every right to be here."

The younger man's eyebrows shot upward. "Have we?" he said dryly. "Most Annandale folk would dispute that, including me own da, were ye daft enough to put your brother's impertinent demands to *him*."

"Alex's demands are hardly impertinent, since he is Sheriff of Dumfries."

"Aye, but *only* o' Dumfries," Will retorted. "Nae one here in Annandale heeds or needs the man, least of all Lord Dunwythie."

Unable to deny Annandale's defiance or Dunwythie's, Rob kept silent. He was watching where he put his feet as he and Will strode across the field toward a dozen or so men working on the far side. It would not do to give the recalcitrant Dunwythie more cause for complaint by trampling his tender young shoots.

"God bethankit for His gifts!" Will exclaimed. "What d'ye think can ha' brought the two o' *them* here?"

Rob looked up.

Emerging from woods north of them onto a narrow path down the center of the field were two riders. Although they were nearly a quarter mile away, their gowns, fur-lined cloaks, and fluttering white veils proclaimed them noblewomen. Their figures and their supple dexterity with their horses declared them youthful.

As they drew nearer, Rob saw that one was so fair that her hair looked white against her dark green cloak. The other was dark-haired, and both wore their hair in long plaits that bobbed enticingly on their breasts as they rode. They were watching the workers, and he was sure neither had yet realized that he and Will—in their leather breeks, jacks, and boots—were not simply two more of them.

A few puffy white clouds floated overhead but did little to block the sun. Its light glistened on the dewy green field and gilded the fair rider's plaits.

"I'm glad I came with ye," Will murmured with a wicked gleam in his eyes.

"They are noblewomen, you lecherous ruffian."

"Hoots, what noblewomen would ride alone here as those two are doing?"

"Dunwythie's daughters would do so on their father's

land, a mile from his castle, amidst his own loyal work-men," Rob said. "Behave yourself now."

"I've nae wish to frighten off such tasty morsels," Will retorted, chuckling.

Rob grimaced, knowing his friend's reputation with women. Glancing back at the two riders, he saw the fair one frown.

Clearly, she had realized they were intruders.

"We'll go to meet them," he told Will. "And you *will* behave."

"Aye, sure. Wi' such toothsome lassies, I'll behave right charmingly."

Rob sighed and altered his course to meet the two, hoping he could avoid trouble with Will. Old Jardine being the Maxwells' only ally in Annandale, Rob could not afford to anger the man's best-favored and sole remaining son. But neither would he let Will make free and easy with Dunwythie's daughters.

"Who are those two men?" the lady Fiona Dunwythie asked, pushing a dark curl away from one long-lashed blue eye to tuck it back under her veil.

"I don't know," nineteen-year-old Mairi Dunwythie replied. Wishing—not for the first time—that she knew more people in the area near her father's largest estate, she added, "They stride toward us like men aware of their worth."

"Then where are their horses?" Fiona demanded. "In my experience, men who know their worth rarely walk far."

"Doubtless they left them in the woods behind them," Mairi said.

"Then they'll have come from the south," Fiona said thoughtfully. "I wonder if they might be Jardines."

That the two strangers might be members of that obstreperous family had already occurred to Mairi. However, although she had begun her life at Dunwythie Mains, she knew few of its neighbors by sight.

Three years after the lady Elspeth, her mother, had died at Mairi's birth, Mairi's father had married the lady Phaeline Douglas. Learning soon after their marriage that the Jardines to the south of them and the Johnstones to the north were engaged in longstanding, nearly continuous warfare, Phaeline had demanded that her husband remove his family to the house near Annan town that represented the primary part of her tocher, or dowry.

At the time, Phaeline had been pregnant with Fiona, so her lord had readily complied. Thus, Fiona was born at Annan House, near the mouth of the river, and Mairi had lived there from the age of four, with only occasional brief visits upriver to Dunwythie Mains.

Whether the two men striding to meet them were Jardines or not, Mairi knew her father would expect her to welcome them, albeit with no more than cool civility.

Discerning eagerness now in her sister's posture, she said in her usual quiet way, "Prithee, dearling, do not be making much of these men. If they *are* Jardines, our lord father will not want us to encourage more such visits."

Tossing her head, Fiona said, "Certes, Mairi, Father would not want us to be discourteous, either. And they are both gey handsome."

Mairi had noted that fact as well. Both were large, dark-haired men with well-formed features. The one in the lead was narrow through hips and waist, had powerful-looking thighs and shoulders, and stood inches taller than his companion.

He also looked five or six years older and displayed a demeanor that suggested he was accustomed to command, and to doing as he pleased. He had worn his leather breeks and boots often enough that they molded themselves snugly to his form. The shirt showing beneath his dark green jack was snowy white.

As they drew nearer, she saw that his boots were of expensive tanned leather, not rawhide. He also wore a fan brooch of three short reddish-brown feathers pinned with a small but brightly sparkling emerald in the soft folds of his hat. Sunbeams painted similar reddish highlights in his dark brown hair.

The younger man had black hair, a lankier body, and looked nearer her own age. He was eyeing Fiona in a way that made Mairi think of a hawk eyeing a tasty-looking rabbit.

Clearly oblivious to the predatory look, Fiona smiled flirtatiously enough to make her sister yearn to scold her. But Mairi held her tongue and shifted her gaze back to the two visitors.

"Well met, my ladies," the younger one said as the women drew rein. "What are two such bonnie lasses doing, riding amongst these rough field men?"

Stiffening, Mairi put up a hand to silence Fiona just as the older man clamped a hand to the brash one's shoulder. Her own gesture failed of its aim, for Fiona said pertly and with an arch look at the younger one, "But who are *you*, sir, to address us so rudely? And *what* are you doing in our barley field?"

"Pray, forgive us, my lady," the larger man said, looking

at Mairi with long-lashed eyes of such a clear ice-blue that she could almost see her reflection in them. His voice was deep and of a nature to send strange sensations through her, as if its gentle vibrations touched every nerve in her body.

Still looking right at her, he said, "I am Robert Maxwell of Trailinghail. This unmannerly chuff with me is William Jardine of Applegarth. I expect you must be Dunwythie's daughters, are you not?"

Mairi nodded, touching Fiona's arm as she did in a hope that the gesture would silence her, at least briefly. Then she said, "You must know that you are on my father's land, sir. Have you reason to be?"

"Good reason, my lady," he replied. "I am Sheriff Alexander Maxwell's brother, here today as his sheriff-substitute."

For a wonder, Fiona kept silent, perhaps as captivated by the man's low, purring voice as Mairi was.

"But why do you come here?" Mairi asked, although she could guess. Her father had spoken often of the sheriff.

"Why, to determine the exact amount your lord father will owe the Crown in taxes this year," he said. "Sithee, one determines the figure by counting everyone on the estate, measuring its size, and estimating its likely crop yield."

Mairi knew that. Her father had recently been teaching both of his daughters about running his estates, as protection against the possibility that his lady wife might fail to give him a son to inherit them. Phaeline had been pregnant many times during their sixteen-year marriage, but so far, she had produced only Fiona.

Dunwythie had long agreed with his lady that, in due time, God would grant them a son. But, at last, urged by Phaeline's elder brother, he had decided to teach his daughters what each would need to know if she should inherit his estates.

The estates' crops being a primary source of his lordship's wealth in a region where few men had any, he had brought Mairi and Fiona to Dunwythie Mains to observe the progress of the early plantings there.

Despite her recently acquired knowledge, Mairi was reluctant to cross words with the sheriff's brother. Just meeting his gaze made her feel dangerously vulnerable, as if without effort he had melted her defenses and would as easily demolish any position she might take in trying to persuade him to leave.

As she sought tactful words to tell the two men they would have to wait and deal directly with her father, her outspoken sister said, "Surely, the two of you should not be prowling here for *any* reason without my lord father's consent."

"Did ye no hear him, lass?" William Jardine said, leering. "Rob acts for the sheriff. And the sheriff, as even such a bonnie lass must know, has vast powers."

Tossing her head again, Fiona said, "Even so, William Jardine, that does not explain what right *you* have to trespass on our land."

"I go where I please, lassie. And as I'm thinking I shall soon give your wee, winsome self good cause to ken me fine, ye should call me Will. Nae one calls me William except me da when he's crabbit or cross."

"Enough, Will," Maxwell said as he met Mairi's gaze with a rueful look in his distractingly clear eyes.

Despite her certainty that he would soon clash with her father, Mairi's heart beat faster, radiating heat all the way to her cheeks.

Robert Maxwell smiled, revealing strong white teeth. His eyes twinkled, too, as if he sensed the inexplicable attraction she felt toward him.

Was he as arrogant and sure of himself, then, as his friend Will Jardine was?

⁓

Noting her reddening cheeks and the quizzical look in her gray eyes, Rob felt an immediate and unusually powerful reaction that he could not readily define.

She looked so small and fragile on her horse, and so extraordinarily fair that the light dusting of freckles across her nose and cheeks seemed out of place, as if she had been more often in the sun than usual. But as he returned her disturbingly steady gaze, he sensed serenity and an inner strength that warned him to tread lightly. It also made him glad that he had made the effort to silence Will.

She seemed oddly familiar, as though he knew how she would move and what she might say next, as if he had recognized the soft, throaty nature of her voice, even the confident way she held both reins in one smoothly gloved hand.

Despite his having met her just minutes before, the feeling was, he thought, the sort a man might have if she had occupied his thoughts before, and often. He realized he was smiling—as if he were delighted to be meeting her at last.

That notion being plainly daft, he tried to dismiss it. He saw then that her light blushes had deepened to a painful-looking red spreading to the roots of her hair.

Hastily, and without looking at Will, Rob said, "I hope

you can forgive the lad's impudence, and mine own, my lady. Is there aught else you would ask of me?"

"You are kind to explain things," she said. "But as we are only women"—Rob saw the younger lass cast an astonished look at her—"you would be wiser and would accomplish more, I am sure, by explaining yourself instead to our lord father."

He would speak to Dunwythie later. Now, though, he smiled again, ignoring instinct that warned him he might be making a mistake to press her. "You can save us much time if you will just tell us how large your estates are," he said. "Men talk often of the size and value of their holdings, do they not?"

The serene gray eyes flashed, but her voice remained calm.

"Not to their womenfolk, sir," she said. "I doubt you would take my word for their size if I *could* tell you. My father will return this afternoon. You can talk with him then. Come, dearling," she said to her sister. "We must go."

With a nudge of heel and a twitch of reins, she turned her horse and rode back the way she had come.

Her sister followed, reluctantly and only after a last twinkling smile for Will.

Rob watched the two young women until they vanished into the woods.

"Sakes, Rob, ha' ye lost your wits? Ye stared at that lass like a right dafty."

"Unless you want me to teach you manners, Will Jardine, keep silent until you have something worth hearing to say to me."

"Och, aye, I'm mute," Will said, looking warily at Rob's hands.

Realizing he had clenched both into fists, Rob drew a breath, let it out slowly, and relaxed them.

"Aye, that's better," Will said with relief. "What now?"

"We get our horses and view the other fields," Rob said, fighting an urge to look again at the place where the women had gone into the woods.

What on earth was wrong with him, he wondered, that he could let one young female affect him so?

~

"I do think you might have been more helpful, Mairi. '*Only* women,' indeed!"

Grateful that Fiona had at least waited until they were beyond earshot of their visitors before commenting, Mairi forced a strong image of the disquieting Robert Maxwell from her mind as she gravely eyed her sister.

When his image threatened to return, she said more forcefully than she had intended, "You flirted dreadfully with William Jardine, Fiona! You must not! You *know* Father wants us to keep clear of *all* Jardines."

"Pish tush," Fiona said without remorse. "I do not understand how anyone can imagine that such a handsome, charming gentleman as Will Jardine can be aught but a friend to us."

"He may be handsome, but he was not charming," Mairi said. "He was cheeky and rude. And he behaved as if he thought he had every right to treat you disrespectfully. You should never respond to such behavior as you did."

"A fine one *you* are to say such a thing! You blushed at every word Robert Maxwell said to you."

"I did not," Mairi said, hoping she spoke the truth. Even now, his powerful image intruded.

Catching Fiona's shrewd gaze on her, she added quickly, "If I did blush, I will not do so again. He wants to help the sheriff extend his authority into Annandale, so he is no friend to us. Neither the Maxwells nor the Jardines are our friends, Fiona. We must both remember that."

"Aye, well, I think we should *make* them our friends," Fiona said with a teasing look. "Surely, making friends is better than going on as enemies."

"It is not as easy to do that as to suggest it," Mairi said. "Recall that our father told us the troubles between the Jardines and the other Annandale noblemen began long ago, in the days of Annandale's own Robert the Bruce. The Maxwells and Jardines sided with England, against the Bruce becoming King of Scots."

"Pooh," Fiona said. "That's just history and too long ago to matter to anyone. This is *now*, Mairi, and Will Jardine is one of the handsomest men I've ever seen."

"Fiona—"

"The truth is you've gone so long without an eligible suitor that you should welcome attentions from a man as handsome as Robert Maxwell. To be sure, he is old . . . at least five-and-twenty . . . and not nearly as good-looking as Will Jardine. But you are only six years younger, Mairi! And Robert Maxwell *is* handsome. Moreover, you cannot deny that he intrigued you enough to make you blush."

Mairi did not try to deny it. Instead, repressively, she said, "His brother is abusing the power of his office to extort money from the lairds of Annandale. We lie outside his jurisdiction, Fiona. And as your would-be friend William Jardine is clearly abetting the Maxwells, we have no more to discuss about *him*."

Fiona gave her a speaking look but did not otherwise reply.

Sakes, Mairi thought as the image of Robert Maxwell filled her mind again, the man had been much too sure of himself in a place he had no right to be. Despite his confidence, though, her father would certainly send him on his way.

And after he did, she would not see Maxwell again. That thought, although it failed to cheer her, assured her that forgetting him was the only sensible thing to do.

Thus it was with astonishment and tingling trepidation that she found herself confronting him again unexpectedly that very afternoon.

Rob had not expected his visit to go smoothly, because as Will had pointed out, every Annandale laird took a certain pride in defying the Sheriff of Dumfries.

However, before Rob had left Dumfries, Alexander Maxwell had said in the stern, fatherly tone he used whenever he lectured his much younger brother, "No less than the power and reputation of Clan Maxwell are at stake in this matter, Rob. Dunwythie is clearly their leader, so your duty to the clan is plain. If we are ever to regain our power, you *must* make him understand the vast powers I command as hereditary sheriff, and put an end to the man's defiance."

Rob was well aware that the Maxwells' power had waned for twenty years, since their loss of Caerlaverock

Castle, the once mighty guardian of southwest Scotland. He knew, too, that Alex wanted above all else to reestablish that power.

Although fiercely loyal to his clan, and understanding his duty to his immediate family as well, Rob had not hesitated to express his doubt that anything less than a Maxwell army would impress the lairds of Annandale.

"Bless us, we don't want war," Alex retorted. "Use your head for once, lad!"

So, although he would have preferred to use his good right arm and a sword, Rob had racked his brain for another way to persuade Dunwythie to submit.

Thus far, none had occurred to him.

Sakes, he told himself now, Alex himself had already tried several times and failed. So much for the power of his office!

Aware that the impudent Will Jardine would be an unwanted distraction in any discussion with Dunwythie, Rob sent him back to Applegarth. Then, collecting the half dozen of his own men who had been watching his lordship, Rob headed for Dunwythie Mains with them that afternoon.

Approaching Dunwythie Mains from the south, as Rob and Will had earlier, Rob had seen only the estate's extensive fields and woodlands. Dunwythie Hall was even more impressive. One would not be wrong to call it a castle.

Well fortified and strategically placed atop a wooded hill with the river Annan flowing in a sharp, protective bend below, the four-story keep loomed formidably above the stone walls of the bailey and its tall, ironbound gates. Rob noted that the ramparts commanded a view that must include a long stretch of the centuries-old Roman road that lay half a mile to the east. It ran much of the length of Annandale.

"Mayhap ye should leave two of our lads out here, laird," the captain of his escort suggested as they neared the gates. "If we dinna come out again, they can report our capture to the sher—"

"Nay, for I come on official business and will meet no danger. You can all be of use to me, though, for I want each of you to learn what you can from anyone willing to talk. We need to know as much about this place and its owner as we can."

Having no reason to refuse entrance to such a small party and doubtless aware that no reinforcements were in sight, men opened the gate at Rob's shout.

Inside the bailey, he dismounted and assured gillies who came running that his men would see to their own horses. Then, taking off his sword belt and handing it to one of his men, to make plain that his visit was peaceful, he followed a young gillie of Dunwythie's to the ironbound timber door of the keep.

The lad pushed the door open without ceremony, revealing a heavy iron yett against the wall behind it, ready to swing shut if attack threatened. The entryway was just a stair landing with stone steps leading up on Rob's left and down to his right. The gillie turned Rob over to the porter, who told him that his lordship would receive him in the great hall.

"I'll just be a-telling him your name when I take ye in, sir, if ye please."

Rob gave his name as they mounted the stairs to an archway. Beyond it lay a great hall with colorful arras cloths hanging at the far end, framing a raised dais. A cheerful fire crackled in the large fireplace.

Seated at the central position behind the long table on the dais was a middle-aged man that Rob knew must be Dunwythie himself.

As Rob strode toward him, a door near the left end of the dais opened, and Dunwythie's fair-haired daughter walked gracefully from the doorway to the dais. Lifting her skirts with her left hand as she stepped onto it, she had eyes only for her father as she approached him with a loving smile.

Dunwythie kept his gaze on Rob.

The lass, realizing that her father's attention had fixed elsewhere, shifted her gaze accordingly. As it fell upon Rob, he anticipated a reaction. But, other than a slight pause, he saw none—not so much as the lifting of one fair eyebrow.

Amused by what he believed was rigid composure but admiring it, too, Rob returned his attention to his host.

The porter said, "Me lord, this be Robert Maxwell, Laird o' Trailinghail and brother o' yon vexatious Sheriff o' Dumfries."

The lass reacted then, biting her lower lip as she flicked a glance at Rob.

Meeting that twinkling look, he felt a reaction that shot to his toes and touched all points in between.

Chapter 2 _____

Mairi was dismayed to find as she entered the hall that Robert Maxwell had chosen that moment to beard her father there. She managed to keep her composure only until the porter, Jeb Logan, identified him as brother to the "vexatious sheriff."

Meeting Maxwell's gaze, she knew she had let her amusement show.

The devilish man was frowning. So either he disapproved of her reaction or there was another, unknown cause. However, he continued to look at her almost as if he were challenging her. What the challenge might be, she did not know. But that look was as disturbing as others had been when they first met.

Only when he walked right into Jeb Logan, still standing at the foot of the dais with his back to him, did a chuckle escape her.

It was just as well that Jeb *had* stopped there, she decided, or Maxwell might have tripped over the raised dais and fallen flat on his face.

His frown deepened as he collected himself, so perhaps he had heard her chuckle or seen her smile. This time, his frown sent a shiver up her spine. He was clearly a man one would be wise not to challenge.

Since she had come only to ask her father if he had duties for her to attend, she had no good reason to stay when he had a visitor. Normally submissive to her parents and quick to anticipate their wishes, she hesitated despite her certainty that Dunwythie would deem her presence unnecessary.

Rob saw no sign that the lass meant to leave.

Inwardly cursing his clumsiness but wanting to get to the purpose of his visit, he used the few brief moments before Dunwythie acknowledged the porter's introduction to size up his host.

His lordship looked to be about fifty. His once-dark hair had nearly all grayed, doubtless the natural result of raising two such comely, still unwed daughters.

His clothing looked expensive but unfashionable, for he apparently favored the nobleman's black robes of earlier days. He had dignity, though, and he clearly did not mean to let Rob intimidate him.

In a voice that carried easily throughout the great hall, Dunwythie said, "My forebears were stewards of Annandale. Did ye know that?"

"Aye, my lord. But they are gone and times have changed."

"They havena changed so much," Dunwythie said. "We Annandale men still mind our estates well on our own, and look after our own people, until we pass into God's keeping. Likewise do we still pay our Crown taxes through our steward. Ye're wasting your time, lad. Your sheriff is powerless here."

"A sheriff's power to collect taxes extends throughout his shire, my lord. And whatever else Annandale may be, it is still part of Dumfriesshire."

"Faugh," Dunwythie retorted. "We do as we have always done. Your brother just wants to extend his power to places that have never before acknowledged it."

Honesty forbidding that he deny that statement outright, Rob let his gaze drift to the lass again as he tried to think of a more persuasive argument.

She had not moved but stood listening to them, doubtless hoping his lordship would remain blind to her presence. She must have changed her dress, Rob mused. He was sure she had worn something blue beneath her furlined cloak that morning. Now she wore a form-clinging pale green kirtle.

The snowy, ruffled edging of her shift peeked above its low-cut neckline, delightfully framing her pillowing, creamy white breasts.

"Well, have ye nowt more to say?" his lordship demanded, abruptly ending Rob's brief reverie. "Because, if so, I have—"

"Prithee, my lord," said a softly plump, beautiful woman who bustled in through the doorway the lass had used earlier. "Have you seen— Oh, forgive me!" she exclaimed when she saw Rob. "No one told me my lord husband had a guest."

Lady Dunwythie—for so Rob supposed she was— looked but ten or fifteen years older than his lordship's daughter. A youthful pink and white chaplet concealed her hair, and ruthless plucking had produced a fashionably high, bare forehead. She wore a loose, rose-colored surcoat with two vertical slits known as fitchets that allowed her to reach keys or other trinkets that he could hear clinking beneath it.

"Mairi," she said to the lass, "why do you stand here like a post?"

"One did not like to interrupt, madam," she said, sweeping her a curtsy.

"This gentleman is Maxwell of Trailinghail," Dunwythie said to his wife. "He is also brother to the Sheriff of Dumfries, who has apparently forgotten that I act as steward in Annandale, as mine ancestors did, and collect the taxes here."

" 'Tis a great privilege to meet you, madam," Rob said, making his bow. Then, turning back to his lordship, he said bluntly, "You would do well, my lord, to hand over to me any gelt you have collected from the others, to take to the sheriff. Mayhap you do not realize it, but he can seize the estates of any landowner who fails to submit to his authority. I warn you, he will wield that power if he must."

Dunwythie raised his eyebrows. "Alexander Maxwell had better examine his conscience well before he tries wielding such power outside Nithsdale." His voice hardened as he added, "As to your warning, I'll tell ye flat that anyone coming here with such grievous intent will put himself in mortal peril. Now, if ye want to take supper with us, ye're welcome. If not . . ." He made a gentle, dismissive gesture.

"I will take my leave," Rob said through gritted teeth. He was frustrated and angry, but he could see nothing to gain by further discussion. Even so, he kept his dignity with greater ease than he might have expected.

He had learned that her name was Mairi, and it suited her.

Bowing to Lady Dunwythie, he said, "'Tis an honor to have met your ladyship. And you, my lady," he added, looking into the lass's calm gray eyes again.

She gazed steadily back, whereupon Lady Dunwythie said curtly, "You had no business to come into this hall without your sister or another female to bear you company, Mairi. I wonder that your father did not take you to task for it."

Flushing deeply, the lass looked away.

Feeling his temper stir again, Rob called himself to order and abruptly took his leave.

~

Watching their guest depart, aware that he was angry, Mairi felt an inexplicable sense of loss.

Something about Robert Maxwell let her feel his frustration, even understand it. She was sure that he acted at the sheriff's behest, because the sheriff had been trying for a year to persuade the lords of Annandale to pay their taxes through him.

Having spent her own life trying to please those in authority over her, if only to keep the peace, Mairi thought she understood why Robert Maxwell was irritated.

Just then, Phaeline said, "In faith, my lord, why would the Sheriff of Dumfries even care who collects the Crown taxes? A most tiresome task I am sure! One would expect him to be glad that someone else saves him the trouble."

"Bless ye, my love, he cares because collecting them would not only increase *his* power over Annandale but also that of Clan Maxwell. It would also allow him to demand fees from us *and* from his grace, the King, for that service. Sithee, he would thereby considerably increase the contents of his own purse."

"Do you not also collect a fee?"

"Aye, sure, I receive a bit from each to defray my cost in conveying the gelt to Stirling each year. But I'd have nowt but ill will to gain by increasing such fees at a whim, as the sheriff could. I must depend on those others to support me in times of trouble, as I support them. Sithee, if we had to wait for a Maxwell to protect us, we'd wait a gey long time. But never mind all that now. How are ye feeling today?"

Hastily excusing herself before her stepmother could launch into one of her interminable, much-too-detailed descriptions of exactly how she felt, Mairi went up to her own bedchamber.

Dunwythie's explanation of the sheriff's likely motives had discomfited her, if only because it had reminded her yet again of her tenuous position in her family.

Although her father had railed against the sheriff many times over the past year, he had not explained the man's motives so clearly before. So the explanation itself had also made it clear that she still had much to learn.

Eldest sons learned all about such things from childhood, she was sure, because everyone knew they would inherit their fathers' lands, titles, and responsibilities. But, because a man could sire a son at any age, particularly if—like Phaeline—his wife was years younger than he was, surely most men without sons kept their hopes of producing one right to the brinks of their graves if not until they tumbled into them.

Dunwythie, encouraged by his lady wife, was just such a man.

Most of them also delayed teaching their daughters about their estates, just as Dunwythie had done. No need to teach a daughter if one was going to have a son!

The problem was, of course, that if one did *not* have a son, the daughter inherited without knowing much about her inheritance.

Mairi was in just such a position. She would inherit her father's estates as a baroness in her own right if she survived him and he had no son. But if Phaeline gave him one, Mairi would have only an elder daughter's portion to offer a husband. Consequently, at the ripe age of nineteen, she was still unwed.

Fiona had been right to say that Mairi needed an eligible suitor. But a man wanted to know what a woman would bring to a marriage *before* he pursued her.

Quietly opening the door to the bedchamber she shared with her half-sister, Mairi found Fiona reclining with her stitchery against a pile of cushions in the window embrasure. Not that she was stitching. Cloth, needle, and thread rested in her lap while she stared idly at the ceiling.

Shutting the door with a snap, Mairi chuckled when Fiona bolted upright.

"Fortunately, it is only I, dearling, not your mother."

"I did not hear you until you shut the door," Fiona said. "That latch makes almost no noise at all now."

"Shall I order someone to make it squeak again? An efficient gillie must have oiled it in the foolish belief that he'd be doing us a favor."

"Mock me all you like," Fiona said with a grimace. "*You* did not have to listen to a lecture about idleness only a half-hour ago! And just because my lady mother saw that I had stopped stitching for a moment to think."

"Prithee, what grave matter occupied your thoughts so completely that you let Phaeline catch you dreaming?" Mairi asked.

Fiona's blushes answered her question.

"Good sakes, it was that cheeky Jardine!"

"He is not cheeky," Fiona countered. "He is charming and delightful, not to mention good looking enough to make anyone stare. Be honest, Mairi. You were as taken with Robert Maxwell if only you could bring yourself to admit it."

"Don't be absurd," Mairi said. "Even if I'd had such a thought, I would have banished it. Neither our father nor your mother will countenance such connections for either of us. You must know that, Fiona. 'Tis rash to think otherwise. They are not suitable for us!"

"Aye, so you told me, but I care even less for your opinion now than I did then!" Hunching a shoulder, Fiona shoved her needlework off her lap.

"You are being childish," Mairi said. "What if I told you that, just a short time ago, Robert Maxwell was in the great hall with our father?"

Fiona's frown vanished and she jumped to her feet. "Was *he* with him?"

"No *he* was not. Even a Maxwell could not be foolish enough to bring that insolent lad with him on such an errand."

"Why not?"

"Because Father would dislike such insolence and Maxwell is now trying to persuade him to hand over *any* taxes he collects to the sheriff."

Fiona said thoughtfully, "The Maxwells are powerful, are they not? Mayhap Father should be more conciliating."

"If you paid more heed, Fee, you would know the very point in refusing to do so is that the more their power increases, the more they can affect what becomes of *us*. If we simply submit to each decree, they will just demand more. Cousin Jenny says it is important to understand all things that affect one's life or property. And surely, you realize by now that she knows more than we do about such things."

"Jenny and you need to know those things, aye. But I do not," Fiona said. "I'll be glad to see her when we visit Thornhill for Easter, and we can talk about anything you like with her then. But she is already a baroness in her own right, and you may become one. I am unlikely *ever* to do so."

Mairi sighed. "One cannot know the future, Fee. I do wish, though, that our father had seen fit to teach us as much as Jenny's father taught her. If Father should die without a son, I doubt I shall know enough to run everything properly."

"Aye, your lot is a hard one," Fiona agreed with a grimace.

Mairi looked narrowly at her, suspecting sarcasm.

Catching the look, Fiona said hastily, "I mean that, Mairi, for it *is* hard. It would be gey easier for all of us if my mother and our father would stop trying to make a son and Father would name you his heir. Think about *me*!"

Mairi did not try to conceal her amusement at the rider. "You think that your lot is even harder?"

"Aye, sure, it is! Sithee, you will inherit Father's title and all his estates. I shall inherit only Mam's tocher."

"Only our beautiful Annan House, its lands, and a generous sum to support it," Mairi said. "Poor Fee! But whatever happens, no good can come from encouraging the likes of William Jardine."

"But we never meet any *eligible* young men, and I *like* Will Jardine!"

Gathering patience, Mairi said, "Dearest one, we talk of a man whose entire family is untrustworthy. The Jardines have a long history of collaborating with the English against us. Now they simply accept English occupation of Lochmaben, the ancient seat of the Bruces and the most impregnable castle in Annandale."

"So do the Maxwells!"

"Aye, they do. But recall how Will Jardine treated you. Could you truly care for a man so insensitive to your rank and to the respect due to a noblewoman . . . to any woman? Faith, he treated you with extraordinary incivility!"

"I don't *care* about civility. I thought he was amusing and charming. And he is quite the handsomest man I have ever seen."

Mairi might have debated that point, because she thought Robert Maxwell was better looking. However, comparing the two men in any way being clearly unwise then, she said only, "Mayhap so, but I warrant William will look just like his father one day. Men frequently do, you know. Have you ever seen Old Jardine?"

Fiona frowned. "I never saw any Jardine before today."

"He came here once to raise some sort of grievance when I was about twelve. I remember that he had a bulbous red nose, tiny eyes, and he was fat. He was angry, though, which may account for the redness but not for his piggy eyes or vast girth."

"Mercy, I would not allow any husband of mine to grow fat," Fiona declared. "Why was Old Jardine angry?"

"I don't know," Mairi said. "I could see that he was as soon as they announced him, but Father sent me away. Whatever it was, I expect Jardine got short shrift."

With a sudden mischievous glint, Fiona said, "Think you that Robert Maxwell will take supper with us this evening?"

Mairi rolled her eyes. "He has already departed, Fee, likely for Applegarth. Sithee, it has begun to rain, and he would never make Dumfries before dark."

Inside Spedlins Tower, the Jardine stronghold at Applegarth, Rob changed to warm, dry clothing and found his younger host awaiting him in the great hall.

"Come in and take a whisky to warm you," Will said. As he poured from jug to mug, he shot Rob a look from under his eyebrows. "Did Dunwythie submit?"

"Nay, but I did not expect it," Rob said, gratefully accepting the whisky and taking a sip as he moved to stand by the fire. The ride back in increasingly heavy rain had chilled him to the bone. But the fire and the whisky warmed him.

Will's father, known generally as Old Jardine, entered soon afterward. As he shook Rob's hand, the old man said, "I'd wager ye got nowt from Dunwythie."

"You'd be right, sir," Rob replied evenly.

His host grinned. "Ye'll get nowt from me, either, for all that we be friends."

"I know that," Rob said. He knew, too, that although the Jardines were currently Maxwell allies, they were apt to change shirts with any passing breeze. Regarding taxes, at least, Old Jardine was at one with the men of Annandale.

Pacifically, the old man said, "I've nae particular quarrel wi' Dunwythie at present. Sithee, he's a peaceable chap most days."

"Peace is good, sir," Rob said. "We would be wise to encourage more of it. The last thing we want is for war to erupt hereabouts."

"'Tis true," Jardine said. "With Dunwythie's connections to the Lord o' Galloway and Douglas o' Thornhill, anyone who stirs trouble in Annandale risks bringing the whole lot o' them down on us. I've nae wish to stir up any Douglas."

"No one has such a wish," Rob said. Trailinghail lay in Galloway, and he knew that men had good reason for calling its lord "Archie the Grim."

"Aye, well, the Jardines have strong connections, too," Will said.

"We Maxwells amongst them," Rob said amiably. "But you cannot want to quarrel with the Dunwythies. Sakes, you'd make friends with at least one of them."

"Which o' them would that be, lad?" Old Jardine said, shooting his son a narrow-eyed look.

Will shrugged. "Just a wench, Da. Nae one of import, although I'll admit she'd be a tasty morsel. Ye'll be leaving us come morning, Rob, won't ye?"

Rob agreed that he would and took the opportunity to change the subject to one less likely to stir debate. He was glad to bid them both goodnight right after supper, although he was not looking forward to returning to Dumfries.

He had gathered the information Alex wanted about Annandale landholders. But he knew the sheriff had hoped—even expected—that he would somehow manage to persuade Dunwythie and the others to submit to his authority.

Rob still doubted that anything short of an army could accomplish that goal. The Maxwells could certainly raise one if necessary. But so could others, including Archie the Grim. And Archie would surely side with his kinsman.

Heaven alone knew what the result of such a clash as that might be.

Chapter 3

Waking the following morning from a dream in which she had been riding from Annan House to Dunwythie Mains in the company of Robert Maxwell, rather than with her parents and Fiona, Mairi eyed with a sense of unreality the sun streaming through the window of the bedchamber she shared with Fiona.

The rain had stopped.

Her sister still slept, so Mairi crept out of bed without disturbing her while silently scolding herself for allowing Robert Maxwell to invade her dreams.

As she poured water from the ewer on the washstand into the basin to wash her face and hands, she continued to wonder at such a foolish dream. He was not even the sort of man she had hoped one day to meet, let alone to marry.

Someone, doubtless the same maidservant who had come in quietly, and as quietly had opened the shutters and filled the ewer with fresh water, had set out clothing for Mairi and Fiona to wear that day. The pink-and-green embroidered gray kirtle she had put out for Mairi laced up the back. So, after slipping on her soft cambric shift and tying its white silk ribbons at her cleavage, Mairi opened the door and peeked around it to the landing.

No one was there. But hearing footsteps above, she waited. And presently the plump, rosy lass who served them came into view round the turn.

"Flory, I need help lacing my kirtle," Mairi said quietly.

"Aye, m'lady, I were just a-coming. Be the lady Fiona up yet?"

"Nay, but I doubt we will wake her."

"That lassie does sleep as if she were deaf," Flory said, straightening her cap. "Will I brush your hair first, m'lady?"

"Nay, I'll dress first. The air is gey chilly in here."

While she concentrated on dressing and not waking Fiona, who would sleep soundly for only so long, Mairi did not think of Maxwell. But as she made her way downstairs to the hall to break her fast, she wondered if he might still be angry.

That he had been fuming just before he'd taken leave of them would have been plain to the meanest intelligence. She was sorry for that, although her father had been the one to anger him. Even Dunwythie had admitted that a sheriff generally did command a whole shire. Still, the Maxwells were overstepping tradition. That, too, was clear.

Never in Annandale's history had its nobles paid their share of the Crown's demands to anyone save their own steward or seneschal to deliver to the King. That the sheriff hoped to change that tradition was one thing. That he had the right or the power to do so without Annandale's consent was another question.

Still, she could wish that Robert Maxwell had come into her life in some other way—and as some person other than a Maxwell.

Chuckling at her own whimsy, she thrust all thought of him from her mind at the hall landing and stepped onto the dais with a smile for her father and another for her stepmother. The latter had come down earlier than usual.

"I trust you slept well, madam," Mairi said.

"Och, aye, as well as I ever do these days, I expect," Phaeline said.

Dunwythie was halfway through his breakfast, his attention clearly on other matters. But after Mairi had taken a manchet from the basket and allowed a gillie to serve her ale from the flagon, and a small fried trout doubtless caught fresh from the river that morning, she said to her father, "Sir, do you think the Sheriff of Dumfries can just force his authority on Annandale?"

Giving her a fond look, Dunwythie said, "Ye women! I tell ye, ye needna fret about such things."

"Mayhap we need not, sir," Mairi said. "But one dislikes seeing anyone leave here in anger, as Robert Maxwell did yestereve. And he did say the sheriff has power to seize our estates. *Can* he, sir?"

"Nay, nay, lass. Dinna be thinking such things. It willna happen. I mean to make it plain that I'll have nae bowing down to the Maxwells. They just want to exert such power to raise more gelt for their own purpose. I ken fine what it be, too—rebuilding Caerlaverock!" With a look that included his lady wife, he added, "We'll be saying no more about this now, d'ye hear?"

Mairi willingly complied with what amounted to an order. She nearly always preferred peace to its absence.

Although her father shared the same peaceful nature, like many men accustomed to command, he was apt to lose his temper when anyone who owed him duty defied him.

Despite her intent to banish thoughts and memories of Robert Maxwell, they continued to plague her, stirring oddly conflicting emotions as they did. She would recall his arrogance one moment, how clear his eyes were the next. Uneasily recalling his anger, she remembered the look he had given her as he'd turned to go.

There had been no anger in *that* look.

Calling her wits to order at last, she thrust him out of her head and focused instead on diverting Fiona from thoughts of Will Jardine and on fixing her own thoughts on what her father could teach her about the Dunwythie estates.

Leaving Spedlins Tower as the sun peeked over the eastern hills, Rob and his men enjoyed a peaceful ride back to Dumfries, fifteen miles to the southwest.

Mist rising from the river Annan and the still rain-damp landscape clung to shrubbery and trees in shredded skirts, but by the time the sun had climbed above the hilltops, the mist had disappeared.

Rob and his men forded the Annan a few miles south of Applegarth. Staying north of the springtime morass of water meadows and bogs surrounding Lochmaben Castle, they met the Dumfries road a few miles to the west.

Two hours later, they reached the royal burgh of Dumfries and followed its High Street to the tall stone edifice known as Alan's Tower.

Overlooking the river Nith, the tower was ancient. It had

belonged to Alan, last Lord of Galloway until Archie assumed that title 140 years later. Rob's branch of Maxwells having owned the Tower for some time before that, it had long served as the residence and court of the hereditary Sheriff of Dumfries.

Dismounting in the yard, Rob tossed his reins to a minion, then paused to exchange a few words with the itinerant knacker, Parland Dow, who had his cottage rent-free from the Maxwells as payment for his many services to them.

Touching his cap, he said to Rob, "Good to see ye, sir. I be a-heading into Annandale from here but I mean to be in Kirkcudbright again nae more than a sennight from now, ten days at most."

"I should be back at Trailinghail by then easily," Rob said. "Fin Walters will have work for you there in any event."

Bidding the knacker a safe journey, Rob strode inside. He was not looking forward to his interview with his brother, but he rarely put things off merely because they would be unpleasant.

Even so, when the elderly porter informed him that Alexander Maxwell wanted to see him at once, Rob felt his stomach clench just as it had so often in his youth under similar circumstances. The reaction was brief but annoying.

"The master be in his wee chamber off the hall, Master Robert . . . sir, I should say," the old man added with a smile. "Mind how ye go now."

"You sound just as you did when I was twelve and Alex was in rare kippage, Edgar," Rob said, clapping him on a shoulder. "I'm gey old now for skelping."

"Aye, sir, and too big, I'm thinking. And much too skilled wi' a sword, come to that," the porter added dryly.

"I just meant ye should avoid the solar. Herself and Lady Maxwell be a-talking in there."

That information drew a smile from Rob. The servants referred to only one person as "Herself," and that was his maternal grandmother, Arabella, Lady Kelso. "I'll go in to them after I see my brother," he said.

"Herself will be that glad to clap eyes on ye, aye. As for the master . . ." He spread his hands eloquently and left it at that.

Rob nodded and thanked him, although he had needed no further warning about the state of his brother's temper. If anything was likely to exacerbate it, it was the presence of Lady Kelso with her ever-sharp tongue.

Outspoken as she was, she was Rob's favorite kinswoman. When he left the porter, the knowledge that she was home acted on him as it always had when he was younger, too. It made him smile, knowing what she would say to him if she knew that Alex was in a temper and wanted to see him at once:

"Then you probably deserve the rough side of his tongue. And if you dare to lose your temper when he's lost his, my lad, you'll deserve every lick you get."

As he crossed the great hall, where servants were setting up trestles for the midday meal, he drew a breath to ease his returning tension and resolved to keep *his* temper whatever Alex said to him.

Since Alex could not yet know what the Annandale report was, Lady Kelso or Alex's lady wife, Cassandra, had likely stirred his temper before Rob's return. Not that it mattered what or who had stirred it. Rob would have to deal with it.

He had faced many such occasions in the past, and his

own temper was ever uncertain. Although he had rarely dared to give his anger free rein with Alex, it had happened more than once. Worse than that was the fact that he had rarely bothered to restrain it with others then unless someone like Lady Kelso forced him to do so.

Keeping his temper in Alex's presence to avoid the additional consequences of losing it had been about all he could manage in those days.

Alex was a good man at heart, but he was also a man who knew his duty, and he'd believed strongly that he had a duty to raise Rob properly. Their mother had died when Rob was four, and their father had followed her three years later, leaving Alex as Rob's guardian when the former was barely one-and-twenty years old.

He had reached the door to the chamber Alex used as an office. With a single rap on the door to announce himself, Rob entered.

Alex sat in a two-elbow chair behind the long table on which he dealt with the castle accounts and business of the Sheriff of Dumfries. He was in his fortieth year and his dark hair showed gray at the temples with a salty scattering of gray and white throughout. He had put on weight over the past few years and would have jowls and a second chin before many more had passed.

He looked up and frowned at Rob's entrance. His blue eyes were a few shades darker than Rob's, his complexion paler.

"You're back," he said.

"I expect you knew I was, since Edgar said you wanted to see me at once," Rob said, shutting the door. There being no other chair or stool in the small room, he stood facing the table, trying to read his brother's expression. Although

Alex was clearly annoyed, Rob could not tell if he was annoyed with him or something else.

Alex said, "I did not expect you back so soon. Did the undertaking prosper?"

"No more than either of us expected it would."

"Damnation, Rob, Dunwythie is one man, whilst you had the authority of the Sheriff of Dumfries to insist that he comply with our demands. Meeting him face to face, as you did, you ought to have persuaded him easily."

"He paid my demand no more attention than he paid the warrant you sent him last spring or the second one you sent just before winter set in hard."

"He pretends I have no authority to issue my warrants, which is absurd," Alex said. "The man claims to hold to ancient ways of the stewartry. But such ways have no place in proper government today."

"The only dale in Dumfriesshire that agrees with that is Nithsdale, and it has long been a sheriffdom," Rob reminded him. "The others pay their taxes through a steward or directly to the King."

"Aye, but I mean to exert my full authority as sheriff over all Dumfriesshire. So any area that continues to resist me will quickly learn its error. I expected *you* to teach Dunwythie that lesson straightaway if he continued to defy me."

"How?" Rob demanded. "You did not want me to take an army with me."

"I'd have had you do whatever was necessary," Alex replied icily.

"That is not an answer to my question," Rob said, meeting his gaze. "We have enjoyed peace in the Borders long enough for men to grow crops again, after decades of cross-border strife. Now you suggest the Maxwells should stir conflict with our own Scottish neighbors? Do you *want* war with Annandale?"

"Don't act the dafty," Alex said irritably. "'Tis ever your way, Rob, to make outrageous comments rather than deal as you should with the matter at hand. You needed only to show our strength. I told all those lairds, in the formal writ I sent out last spring, that they had no lawful choice but to submit. Letting Dunwythie so easily defy my authority is just further proof of my own error in having entrusted you with such an important task. I had hoped the responsibility of managing Trailinghail had improved you. But I fear you are still the same scapegrace you always were. Or perhaps, having inherited land in Galloway, you no longer think of yourself as a Maxwell of Dumfries."

Gritting his teeth to keep from uttering the angry words that leaped to his tongue, Rob wondered if his brother would ever stop flinging perceived errors of the past in his teeth. Aware that Alex often read him more accurately than he could read Alex, Rob said, "Mayhap you have forgotten how fast the men of Annandale can assemble *their* army. Having an English garrison in their midst at Lochmaben has given them much practice in acting swiftly."

"And so they might have reacted had *I* led an army into Annandale," Alex retorted. "Did I not explain that *that* is why you were to take only your men with you, and none of mine? My writ of authority should have been enough to show Dunwythie that *you* meant business without an armed host. Were I to lead even my normal tail of twenty men into Annandale, it could stir the natives to a clash. Nevertheless, if they force me to summon an army of Maxwells to my banner, be sure that I will take enough with me to end *all* the impudence in Annandale."

Rob said, "I cannot imagine, nor could I from the outset, how you expected me to persuade a man of Dunwythie's stamp to submit to your authority with only a half dozen men. Nor have you yet told me how. As it was, Old Jardine warned that I should not take any of *his* men along other than Will, lest *I* stir conflict."

"Mayhap you should have ignored him and used your own judgment."

"He is our ally, Alex, and he knows the dale. He pointed out that Dunwythie would not allow so many enemies inside his wall and that they would be useless outside it, and might even ignite trouble with others in the dale. He made good sense, so I took only my own men. At least, his lordship heard me out."

"Aye, sure, and then dismissed all that you said to him," Alex said.

"Surely, you are aware that he looks upon Maxwells as lesser creatures who, in the past, have twice sided with the English. He flatly denies that he owes you either his submission or his fealty."

"Dunwythie is said to be a man of peace," Alex said, as if he were explaining something simple to a child. "You had only to explain to him that the law supports my authority, that his grace the King supports it—and explain my right of seizure."

"You've just said that your warrant explained all that," Rob said.

"Perhaps the man cannot read."

With Dunwythie's image still strong in his mind, Rob smiled.

"Do you find humor in my words?" Alex demanded, frowning.

"Dunwythie is an educated man," Rob said. "He knows his worth, and he wields great influence. Even Old Jardine respects him. In troth, from all I could learn about him, his influence extends far beyond Annandale. I'm telling you, if you threaten him, most of the other barons of Dumfriesshire will rise to his defense. And do not forget that the Douglases are kinsmen to his wife."

"Do you dare to try teaching *me* about kinships, my lad? You would do better to have carried out my orders. Instead, you return with nothing accomplished and excuses on your tongue."

"By God, Alex," Rob said, bristling. "I am no longer twelve years old, nor am I dependent on you or subject to your constant authority. You are my brother and a man to whom I owe familial duty, but I am *not* your lackey. Nor do I have to stand here and listen to this like a misbehaving—"

"Och, aye, I forgot," Alex interjected, his tone scathing. "*Now* you are a great landowner, the Laird of Trailinghail. And as that fine estate lies across the river Nith, *now* you count such small things as loyalty to your clan and loyalty to Nithsdale, to Dumfries, and to *me* as nowt."

"If that is what you believe, we've *nowt* to discuss," Rob snapped.

"Aye, sure, lose your temper. It is ever the same with you. The minute someone calls you to account for your actions, or their lack—"

"No more," Rob said curtly.

"Nay, then, although I'd hoped you had learned to use that stubborn head of yours to prove yourself a worthy member of our great clan. But you are still the hot-tempered, impatient . . . Damnation, Rob, I've no doubt now that you angered Dunwythie as much as you are angering me now. If you *were* still a lad—"

"Aye, ye'd skelp me blue. But you'd soon find yourself at a standstill, trying anything so daft now," Rob said. "If you need someone to treat again with Dunwythie, you will doubtless find a more competent man quite easily."

"Fiend seize you, Rob. I'd hoped . . ." He sighed. "God kens I'd hoped you had grown out of these ways of yours. But I should have known you had not."

"Good-bye, Alex," Rob said. "I'll not impose further on your hospitality."

"Och, aye, run back to Trailinghail," Alex said with acid dripping from his tongue. "'Tis ever your way. I'm told your people there think highly of you. One can only pray that you do not disappoint them as you have me."

Rob turned and left, striding back across the hall toward the stairway so angrily that men moving toward tables stepped hastily out of his way.

"Sir! Master Rob! Hi, there, an ye please, sir!"

The high-pitched voice interrupted his streaming thoughts, and Rob turned, wrathfully meaning to tell any gillie insolent enough to shout the length of the hall at him how much in error such behavior was.

The black-haired, blue-eyed lad looked only nine or ten years old. He met Rob's scowl bravely.

"What the devil do you mean by shouting at me like that?" Rob demanded.

His pointed little chin thrusting boldly forward, the lad replied, "Herself did say I should shout the house down if I must to keep ye from leaving. That's why."

"Oh, she did, did she?"

"Aye, she did. *And* she said ye'd look as red as raw beef, too. So she kens ye well, Herself does. And she tellt me never to mind your temper."

"You mind your tongue. Is that all she said to tell me?"

"Aye! Well, no the bit about raw beef . . . no to *tell* ye that bit, any road. But she did say to stop ye, *and* to say ye're no to go afore she talks wi' ye."

Rob looked past the lad to the dais, where his sister-in-law, the lady Cassandra Maxwell, stood near the high table gazing myopically at him. Apparently realizing he had seen her, she smiled warily.

Movement in the open doorway behind her—which led to the ladies' solar—diverted Rob's eye as his grandmother, Lady Kelso, stepped into the opening.

She gestured imperiously.

"I see Herself now," he said to the lad. "You can go, but I do thank you."

"Aye, sir. Ye'd no want to put her in a temper. *Nae* one would," the lad said with the emphasis of unhappy experience. "But she's a fine old trout, Herself is."

"Old *trout*?"

"Aye, 'tis what me da called me own granddame sometimes. Means he liked her, he said. I like Herself gey fine, too, mostly."

His sense of humor tickled by the boy's earnest candor, Rob bent nearer and said confidingly, "So do I, lad, mostly. But don't let me hear you call her an old trout again unless you want to stir *my* temper to the point where you *will* mind it."

"Nay, I won't, then. But ye'd best get a move on ye, sir. She's looking a bit umbrageous already, t' my way o' thinking."

"So she is," Rob agreed, pressing a coin into the lad's willing hand before striding to the dais and across it with a nod of greeting to his sister-in-law.

His grandmother, tall and stately in lavender silk with a surcoat of figured purple damask and a lavender veil, stepped back into the solar.

Following her, Rob noted the presence of his youngest nephew, five-year-old Sawny Maxwell, playing alone with a toy in the east-facing window corner. The little boy, seeing him, leaped to his feet and ran to him, shrieking his delight.

Catching him at the waist, Rob tossed him high in the air and caught him, still shrieking.

A white, long-haired cat curled on the settle in the window embrasure had sat bolt upright at the first shriek, with a narrow-eyed scowl at the child. Now it vanished into darkness under the settle.

"Hush now, Sawny lad," Rob said as he raised the boy overhead again. "You've frightened our lady granddame's cat."

"Nay, Cheetie's no frightened," the boy said, grinning down at him. She hides 'cause she dinna want to nurse her kits anymore, Granddame said. Do it again!"

Rob obliged, catching the delighted boy with ease.

From behind him, his sister-in-law said, "Prithee, don't throw him so high, Robert. Think how horrid it would be if you dropped him."

"Uncle Rob willna drop me, Mam," Sawny said with a grimace of disappointment as Rob stood him on his feet. "He's gey strong."

"He's right, Cassia, I won't," Rob said, turning to her.

"You cannot be sure of that," the lady Cassandra said,

glancing back through the open doorway. "Moreover, Alexander does not like him to get overly excited."

"Alexander can—"

"Robbie," Lady Kelso said, mildly warning.

Obligingly biting back his opinion of Alex, Rob ruffled Sawny's dark curls. "Do you dine in the hall with the grown-ups today, lad?" he asked the boy.

Noting Cassandra's widening eyes, he was sure that had not been the plan.

But Lady Kelso said, "That is just what Cassia had decided, is it not, my dear?" Before Cassandra could deny it, had she dared, her ladyship added, "Why do you not take him out to the table and get him settled now, dearling. His father will be along soon, and I want a private word with Robert before we eat."

"Of course, my lady," Cassandra said. "Come, Sawny."

Eyes alight, the child hugged Rob and went with his lady mother.

"That was neatly done, madam," Rob said to Lady Kelso as the door shut behind the other two.

"It was hardly a masterstroke," she said. "Cassia is far too meek to gainsay me. She is a kind and pleasant companion, but I'd like to see more spirit. Such meekness in a wife is not good for Alexander, or indeed, for any Maxwell. Abject submissiveness in a wife encourages strong men to think they can rule the world."

"My wife, if ever I take one, had better not be *too* spirited," Rob said, remembering some fierce quarrels between his outspoken grandmother and the late Lord Kelso. He disliked such battles. Memory suddenly stirred of Lady Mairi Dunwythie's serene gray eyes.

The image evaporated when his grandmother said

sharply, "Just what happened between you and your brother this time, my dear?"

"Nowt," Rob said shortly. Meeting her disbelieving gaze, he said, "Nowt but what always happens. He sent me on a fool's mission, and I failed to accomplish it. Rather than hear over and over how I've disappointed him again, I am returning to Trailinghail, where much work still awaits me."

"Your grandfather did not leave Trailinghail to you so that you could bolt off there whenever you quarrel with Alex," she said austerely.

Taken aback, Rob said, "Is that what you think I do? He said the same."

Lady Kelso grimaced. "Alex behaves badly whenever he feels inadequate to a task, my dear. He grows chilly and carps to distance himself. You distance yourself in more physical ways. I did *not* mean to imply that you are cowardly, for you are nowt o' the sort, as your grandfather might have said."

"Thank you for *that* much, madam."

She said dryly, "You almost manage the high tone, my dear. But you've not had nearly enough practice to carry it off with me. Where was I?"

"I distance myself physically; Alex gets icy."

"My point is that, thanks to his being nearly fifteen years older than you are, you and he have never learned to talk to each other as brothers, let alone as friends. The fact is, Rob, that Alex had too much responsibility thrust upon him at too young an age. Had he been even as old as you are now when your father died—or had your grandfather and I lived nearby at the time, instead of in Stirling—he might have managed you more deftly."

"What's past is past and cannot be changed, Gran. But when he treats me as if I were still a bairn, as he did just now—"

"You're a grown man, aye, but the troubles between you are as much your fault as his," she said bluntly. "As much as he needs to learn that you are a strong and capable man, *you* need to try to understand his position. Moreover, you have a duty to aid him all you can. Instead of riding off in a pelter, you would do better to stay and talk it out with him."

"Nay, I'll not do that, for there is no talking to him now. He sent me to do the impossible because he wants what he wants and expects that if he cannot do it, someone else will do it for him—somehow. Mayhap someone else could. But, given the situation in Annandale, I doubt it."

With a wry smile, she said, "I believe you. I was born there, as you know. We left soon afterward, but I've heard much about the independent nature of the dale."

"Even so, he blames me entirely for the failure. And I have more important things to do than to stay and attempt more of the impossible."

"Very well, you do know your own mind best," Lady Kelso said. "But prithee, do not fling off in a temper. Bid Cassia a kind adieu if only because you do not want to make it difficult for her to receive you when you return, as you will. Also, I have some things I want to send with you to Trailinghail. So, go now and make your adieux whilst I collect them. I will meet you in the yard."

Wondering what she could be fetching that she could not order a minion to fetch for her, and why she would go out to the yard just as the household was about to sit down to its midday meal, Rob nevertheless knew better than to ask. Instead, he bowed and went to bid Cassandra and Sawny good-bye.

Alex stepped onto the dais as Rob was leaving them, and asked curtly if he meant to go without dining.

"Aye, for there will be no moon tonight and it may rain again," Rob replied. "Even if it does not, darkness will fall long before we reach the tower."

Alex nodded and turned away, his jaw tight.

"Safe journey, Uncle Rob!" wee Sawny called from his place by his mother.

Rob waved, noting as he did that although Alex glanced toward the boy, he did not call him to order.

Nor did he send him from the table.

Chapter 4 _____

Without further delay, Rob went out to find gillies saddling fresh horses for him and for the other men from Trailinghail. His lads were tying bundles to their saddles, provisions for the journey. So he waited patiently for his grandmother.

She appeared some minutes later with a basket in hand. The black-haired lad who had shouted Rob down in the hall accompanied her.

"This is Jake MacCullie's Gibby," she said, putting her free hand on the boy's scrawny shoulder. "Jake and his wife died of a fever last year. I have kept Gibby with me, but he needs a strong man to teach him how to go on. I had hoped to find someone suitable here. However, Alex has too many as it is, he says, so I bethought me of Fin Walters, at Trailinghail. He'd be just the man, I think."

Rob nodded. Walters was his steward, married to a good-hearted lass, and had no bairns of his own yet. "He'll take the lad in if *you* send him, and I've no objection. Do you think you would like to live by the sea in Galloway, lad?"

Gibby shrugged. "To me, one place be as good as another, Master Rob."

"Have you a pony?"

One of his men, overhearing, said, "We saddled one for him, laird. Herself did send word out to us to do that soon after we arrived."

Rob shot a look at his grandmother but said only, "What is in the basket?"

"Another one in need of a home," she said. "Cheetie had a litter of five, and Alex said that any I leave when next I go a-visiting will have to be drowned. So I thought you might have use for a good mouser at Trailinghail. It would be fitting, as Cheetie herself was born there. Gibby can look after him until you get home."

"Nay, then, me lady," the boy protested. "That wee terror bites and scratches, and I dinna hold wi' cats any road! Nor, they dinna like me any better."

Taking the basket from her, Rob lifted the lid just enough to see a small, fluffy orange-and-white kitten with enormous golden eyes that instantly narrowed in wrath. As quick as lightning, the kitten tried to shove its head through the opening.

"Whoa, laddie," Rob murmured, pushing it gently back inside and fixing the lid's reed loop over its ring with a peg to hold it there. "Very well, madam," he said. "I'll take your wildcat and your orphan, too. Have you other commands for me?"

"Nay, my dearling," Lady Kelso said with the quick, charming smile that Rob had inherited from her but rarely saw. "I think I have burdened you sufficiently to ensure an entertaining journey. I shall miss you, but I do mean to go a-visiting before returning here for Easter. Mayhap, before

I go to Glasgow, I shall visit you at Trailinghail. That was ever one of my favorite places to stay."

"You know you will always find a hearty welcome," Rob said.

"I do know that," she said, nodding. "I also know that unless you ride until midnight, you won't get home today. 'Tis all of five-and-thirty miles after all."

"Aye, well, we'll see," he said. "'Twould be but seven hours on a dry day. But we've already traveled more than fifteen miles today, and the forest tracks will be boggy from the rain. I'll not mind making camp, if need be, but if we have clear starlit skies, I'll want to push on home. In any event, we must go now," he added, extending his free hand to her.

"I don't want to shake your hand, Robbie-love," she said, stepping close and putting her arms around him.

Hugging her as hard as he could without dropping the basket, he kissed her cheek and said, "I do hope you will visit us soon, Gran."

"Just mind that you haven't let the place go to rack and ruin before I do," she said gruffly, stepping back. "You'll suffer the rough side of *my* tongue if you have."

Smiling, Rob watched as she walked stiff-backed away until she was inside the keep. Then, turning to his new young charge, he said, "Get you on your pony, lad. We've a long journey ahead, and I want to hear no more sauce from you."

"Nay, then, I ken that fine," Gibby said. "Just dinna make me mind that wee terror ye've got in yon basket. Then ye and me will get on fine."

"We'll get on better if you mind that cheeky tongue of yours," Rob said.

"Aye, sure," Gibby said, flinging himself onto the horse provided for him.

A quarter of an hour later, they crossed Devorgilla's Bridge into Galloway. Below the bridge, the river Nith roiled in spate, its water so high that it threatened to invade the lowermost of the cottages on the steep hillside below the town.

"See how high the river can rise," Rob said to his young companion, who had chosen without invitation, or command to do otherwise, to ride beside him. "Such dangerous spates as this are why we have Devorgilla's Bridge."

"Aye, sure," Gibby said. "But 'ware now, sir! That wee terror's a-trying to get out o' his basket."

Glancing at the basket he had tied to his saddle, Rob saw two small white paws poking out from under the lid, clearly seeking freedom for their owner.

Grinning, he reached back and pulled out the peg that held the lid in place. Flipping the reed loop off its ring with a fingertip, he opened the basket and deftly grabbed the kitten before it could fling itself out.

"Mind your fingers, laird," the boy warned. "He's gey fierce!"

"He won't bite me," Rob said confidently just as needle-sharp teeth buried themselves in the soft skin between his thumb and forefinger. Yelping, he freed himself, murmured soothingly to the kitten, and tucked it inside his leather jack. For the moment, astonishingly, it seemed content to stay there.

Noting Gibby's gap-toothed grin, he said, "Not one word from you now."

The grin widened, but the boy did not speak.

As they rode on in silence, Rob found his thoughts returning to Dumfries and Alex. Was his grandmother right? Was the tension between them as much his fault as Alex's, and his own duty to his clan greater than aught else?

Had he come to think of himself as a man of Galloway rather than a Maxwell of Dumfries? Or was he right to believe Alex was incapable of accepting the fact that his younger brother was no longer a child who merited constant, watchful attention and dutiful censure? Should he exert himself more to aid Alex in his plan to extend their clan's power over all of Dumfriesshire or simply stay away from Alex for his own peace of mind—and mayhap for Alex's, as well?

What if he did stay away?

What if Dunwythie's defiance then spread to the other lairds, and worse?

Rob was sure that, before long, Alex's response would be ruthless enough to cost lives—men of Annandale and Maxwells alike. Might there, he wondered, be a way that would not result in the deaths of so many more of the region's young men?

What might Dunwythie care about more than he cared about impeding any extension of the sheriffdom? He cared about peace, they said. And he took pride in his forebears. Dutifully, Rob tried to focus his mind on potential strategies.

His unruly thoughts drifted instead to the lady Mairi Dunwythie.

According to the Jardines, her ladyship was Dunwythie's heiress apparent. But the lass herself was Dunwythie's treasure. His lordship had to be well aware of his good fortune in having such a beautiful, serene, and sensible daughter.

Because, Rob wondered, how could the man *not* be?

～

Their journey continued without incident unless one counted persistent efforts of one small kitten to escape captivity.

They reached the outskirts of Kirkcudbright by torch-light after clouds had hidden the last of the stars. As they prepared to eat, the kitten made it plain that it, too, had urgent needs. But when Rob put it down, it dashed into the shrubbery.

Shouting for his men to circle the area and warning them that Lady Kelso would take a dim view of the kitten's loss, Rob waited grimly for its reappearance. When it shot out from under a bush and frantically clawed its way up his leg into his arms, he felt a wholly unexpected surge of pure delight.

A generous helping of minced beef assured him of its continued goodwill.

Loudly purring, the kitten slept beside him that night, woke him at dawn with a rough, wet lap across his nose, and after they had broken their fast, rode contentedly inside his leather jack the rest of the way home to Trailinghail.

～

"But *why* must we leave Dunwythie Hall?" Fiona demanded that same fine morning. "And why go now in such haste?"

"Hush, Fee," Mairi said. "Your mam feels unwell again."

"If that is so, it is even more reason *not* to be mounting our horses and hurrying back to Annan House. Forbye, I don't *want* to go home."

Sternly, clearly having overheard her, Phaeline said, "Your father made the decision because of threats that dreadful Maxwell person made. 'Tis clear we will be *much* safer at Annan House until the Maxwells come to their senses. So, unless you would incur my gravest displeasure, Fiona, you will obey without further protest."

"Aye, madam," Fiona said with a sigh.

Mairi knew that, although her father had decided to leave Dunwythie Hall, her stepmother had likely prompted that decision, for so it often was. Phaeline always preferred Annan House, because she thought the area there more civilized.

Mairi also knew that Fiona's imposed silence would end as soon as they were well on their way. Indeed, the Hall had scarcely disappeared behind them when the younger girl hissed as they rode side by side, "I'll wager *you* are no more eager to return home than I am."

"I ken fine why you do not want to go, Fee," Mairi said. "But you cannot think that I have the same reason."

Fiona hunched a shoulder. "No one ever cares what I want. But Father will heed neither of us at home, especially as he means to visit the other lairds and warn them about the Maxwells' newest threat. One wonders what we'll have to occupy us there, other than our usual duties and needlework. Aye, and Lent began yesterday and tomorrow is Sunday. So we'll be all morning in kirk and until Mam grows tired of the sacrifice, we'll have no meat to eat!"

Mairi said, "At least we know more about the estates now than we did before Father took us to the Hall. Also, our people will have planted the fields below Annan House during our absence. So we can learn even more about such things at home."

"You know I don't care a blink for such stuff. All I want is to meet eligible young men, Mairi. And you should want that, too, or you'll have no one to think about *except* Robert Maxwell. What will you do then, eh?"

Slowing her mount to lessen the risk that Phaeline or Dunwythie might hear them, Mairi said, "I don't deny that I found the man intriguing, Fee, but I cannot even tell you *why* I did. Perhaps it is only that he seems so strong and sure of himself when I so often feel rather helpless in the uncertainty of my future."

"Sakes, what makes you think he is strong or confident when he failed so miserably to persuade our father to agree with him?"

"The strength I felt came from within him," Mairi said. "I do not think he counts success or failure in one such an attempt. It seemed to me more as if he were doing his brother's bidding, never really expecting to prevail."

"But—"

"Have mercy," Mairi pleaded. "This is foolishness, because it cannot matter *what* I think he feels inside, or why or how I sense it. His arrogant posturing when he said his odious brother could seize our estates went beyond what I think of as civil behavior. It infuriated Father, too, although he did keep his temper."

"Aye, and Father likely infuriated Robert Maxwell, too. *That* is why it all disturbed you, Mairi. You *always* hate disagreement. I think that whenever you see conflict, you feel as if you ought to be able to smooth it over," Fiona added sapiently. "When you cannot, *you* feel guilty."

"Mercy, you make me sound as if I think of naught save myself," Mairi protested. She was afraid, though, that much of what her sister said was true. Disagreements did upset her. But surely they upset most people.

"I know you are not so selfish," Fiona said. "You just

sometimes seem to assume responsibility when you need not and, when things go amiss—even when they have naught to do with you—to take it as a personal failure."

"Anyone with common sense prefers peace," Mairi said. "The plain truth is that it frightened me witless when Father just dismissed the sheriff's threat to seize the estates if Father does not submit."

"But such a threat cannot be real," Fiona said flatly.

Mairi feared that it was, however. Her annoyance with Robert Maxwell persisted. However, just thinking about the handsome wretch brought memories of his charming smile, his musically vibrant deep voice, and the strangely sensual air of strength and power the dreadful man projected.

In facing him that first time in the field, she realized now that although she had dreaded crossing words with him, she had found it easier than expected to make her point. It felt almost as if she had drawn her strength then from his.

Silently scolding herself for such foolish thoughts, she had the happy notion to remind Fiona that they would enjoy Easter with Jenny and Sir Hugh at Thornhill. Thereafter, as they followed the river's course southward, they chatted desultorily.

⌒

Rob was glad to be home and glad, too, that the day was turning out to be a fine one and showed Trailinghail at its best.

The stone tower stood atop one of the sheer cliffs forming the west boundary of Kirkcudbright Bay less than a mile from where it opened into Solway Firth. The position provided panoramic views of the bay and the more turbulent Firth. On such clear days, one could see Kirkcud-bright's kirk spire and the towering keep of Castle Mains, ancient seat of the Lords of Galloway and guardian of the town and its harbor.

The rain had passed, and the few clouds scudding across the azure sky were white and puffy. The air was chilly and smelled strongly of the sea. Gulls cried overhead, and Rob's people hailed his return with sincere delight.

He had inherited the tower and its forested estate from his grandfather, Lord Kelso, at the age of one-and-twenty. Before then, Trailinghail being one of his lordship's distant and lesser estates, the place had received less attention than his larger holdings and had suffered accordingly.

Lord and Lady Kelso had spent most of their time at his primary seat near Glasgow or at their house in the royal burgh of Stirling, just as their eldest son, Rob's uncle and the present Lord Kelso, did now. Rob was sure that his in-heritance had come at her ladyship's instigation, if only be-cause his grandfather had shown unexpected forethought in also leaving sufficient funds to set the place in good trim.

As isolated as Trailinghail was, although he had visited his grandparents there as often as possible, Rob had never expected to live there permanently. However, he realized now, rather than chafe under Alex's thumb in Dumfries, he had taken to spending a little longer at Trailinghail each time he visited.

The people on the estate had made it plain from the out-set that they looked on him as a blessing. Their delight in his first arrival and in his declared intent to visit several times each year had spurred him to exert himself more than he might have otherwise. As a result, he had come to love the place as much as they did.

The job of putting things in order had taken up much of the past four years. His fields were in good trim now, the wall was sound. And if the tower had received less attention, it was comfortable enough to welcome his grandmother if she did choose to visit. Despite her suggestion that she would, Rob doubted he would see her before summer. The present Lord Kelso and his family would press her to visit them, and Trailinghail lay miles away from the road to Glasgow.

Rob knew that Lord Kelso adored his blunt-spoken mother despite the trouble they had living together for long periods, and would do all he could to keep her until her annual return to Dumfries for Easter. And, despite her ladyship's independent nature, she doted on her son's family and would miss them dreadfully if aught happened to prevent her visiting them.

Thoughts of that mutually doting relationship brought Mairi's image to mind, and Dunwythie's. The odd connection spurred a tickling jolt in Rob's train of thought as if his mind had jumped ahead of itself. Letting the wisp go, he returned his attention to Trailinghail and the new projects he wanted to begin there.

His steward, Fin Walters, a sensible man in his midthirties, welcomed Gibby's arrival. Walters had grown up in service to Rob's grandfather and had a respect for Lady Kelso that bordered on worship.

"If Herself commends ye to me care, lad, I'm sure ye'll be a great help," he said. "I've any number o' things ye can do."

Gibby, who had been eyeing him askance, straightened noticeably and said he could do aught that anyone asked of him. "Except for herding carnaptious wee cats," he added stoutly with a sidelong look at Rob.

Suppressing a smile, Rob said, "You will do whatever Fin Walters tells you to do or suffer unpleasant consequences."

"Aye, sure, I said so, didn't I?" Gibby said, his demeanor wide-eyed and earnest. "Just *not* cats."

Grunting, and avoiding Fin's twinkling eyes, Rob left them to get acquainted and went inside to stow his gear.

He soon realized he had acquired an orange-and-white shadow.

Amused by the kitten's curiosity and its antics as it explored his bedchamber, he otherwise ignored it. He was certain it would soon find its way to the kitchen. As soon as someone down there fed it, it would forget all about him.

He had stripped off his jack and his shirt, and was scrubbing himself at the washstand, when a now-familiar voice spoke from the open doorway.

"Fin Walters did say I should ask d'ye ha' aught ye'd like me to do for ye."

Reaching blindly for a towel, Rob blotted his face as he turned to face Gibby. "Have you annoyed *him* already, then?"

"Nay, I just tellt him I'd served Herself mostly inside and rode with her when she went out, and such. So *he* said I should tend to things in the tower for a time, till I learn me way about and get to know the men. I expect he wants them to ken more about me afore he gives me to one o' them to train," he added sagely. "He said ye dinna ha' a man to look after ye, though. So I might make m'self useful."

"I don't need much looking after," Rob said. Noting Gibby's disappointment, he added, "You can clear up those things I carried up here if you like. The shirts and my netherstocks will need laundering, so take them downstairs when you go. You may also brush my breeks and boots if you think you can. And put those other things away in the two kists you see against yon wall."

Gibby soon tidied the chamber. As he rose from stowing things in a kist set in the east-facing window's embrasure, he moved to look outside, standing on tiptoe.

"Coo," he said. "Ye can see forever from up here."

"Not quite as far as that," Rob said. "You can see even more from the next level, and more yet from the ramparts. The large chamber above this one has a window looking over the Firth as well as one like that one overlooking the bay."

"Then why d'ye no take the two-windowed one?"

"Too many stairs," Rob said with a grin. When the boy shook his head, he added, "This chamber was my grand-father's whenever he stayed here. But I'm thinking that when Herself comes to visit, she'll want to use the great chamber."

"Aye, she would," Gibby agreed. "I could help ye get it ready for her."

What had been only a wispy tickle of an idea earlier took form as he considered how comfortable the upper chamber could be. As her ladyship was unlikely to visit soon, that chamber might even serve another purpose or person first. He would have to consider the notion more thoroughly, to see if it had merit.

Dismissing Gibby to help set up in the hall for the mid-day meal, Rob said, "I want to think a bit before we dine, Gib. But we'll go upstairs afterward and take stock of what we might do there."

"I told you so," Fiona said with a grimace the following Thursday morning as she and Mairi aired bedclothes on the hillside below Annan House's gateway. "At least we're outside, but only because Mam wants to keep us busy whilst she rests."

"She is tired," Mairi said.

The grassy hill sloped away more or less on all sides of the house. They could see the river below and the strip of narrow but dense woodland edging it. Across the river lay western Annandale and hills separating it from Nithsdale.

The woodland edging the river continued south and then east above the breeze-rippled waters of Solway Firth, sparkling now in the sunlight. From the woods upward, freshly tilled fields covered most of the hillside.

"I vow, Mam *must* be pregnant again," Fiona said abruptly. "She behaves as if she were. In troth, she has been with child more than she has been with*out* child for most of my life. And to what purpose? She has miscarried so many that she does not even seem sad anymore when she loses one. But then, before a person can turn around, she declares she is pregnant again and Father hovers over her, fretting about her health, just as he has been doing of late."

"It is natural that he should concern himself," Mairi said fairly. Her thoughts shifted abruptly to Robert Maxwell, as had happened far too often of late. This time it was to wonder if *he* might fret over a pregnant wife as her father did.

But, in truth, Phaeline was the fretful one, always talking of how she felt, and Mairi had a notion that a wife of Robert Maxwell's might have no cause to do that.

It occurred to her only then that she did not *know* he was unwed. Unlike Will Jardine, who lived in Annandale and was Old Jardine's heir, and would therefore occasion much remark when he took a wife, Robert Maxwell was an outsider.

Mairi had assumed he was unwed from the way he had gazed at her when they met. But he was certainly old enough to have a wife and *many* children.

"Why do you frown?" Fiona asked, startling her from her reverie.

With a self-deprecating smile, Mairi said, "I just happened to realize that although we can be nearly sure that Will Jardine does not yet have a wife, it is a different matter with Robert Maxwell."

Fiona's eyebrows shot upward. "So you were thinking of *him* again, were you? How you can let your thoughts dwell on that man for even a minute when you believe he and his wretched brother want to seize our estates, I do not know."

"No one can control the way thoughts form, Fee. They just do. For that matter, we don't know that *Robert* Maxwell wants to seize the estates. I believe he was just warning Father that the sheriff has the power to do so."

"Aye, well, I won't deny that *I* think about Will Jardine because I want to," Fiona said. "Even if we did not know he is unmarried, one could never doubt that he is. He would surely not flirt as he does if he *were* married."

"Do you think he would not? Men often flirt who should not, I think, even married men. In troth, if you stop to consider, our father's friends often flirt with us, and nearly every one of them is married."

"Aye, but they ken fine that we do not believe they mean it," Fiona said as she moved to help Mairi shake out their featherbed.

"Nor *do* they mean it," Mairi said, wondering at the odd ways of men, even gentlemen and noblemen. "If a married woman flirted the way married men do, her husband would soon sort her out."

After they had vigorously shaken the featherbed to settle its contents more evenly, Fiona said with a sigh, "Life is most unfair to women, I think."

"Even *women* are sometimes unfair to women," Mairi said a little tartly. "I am sure that Phaeline believes I shall *never* find a husband."

"She has certainly hinted as much," Fiona said. "One wonders how she expects the situation to change when it is *her* determination to produce a son that prevents any eligible man from learning what your fortune may be."

"Well, for all that she has been the only mother I've known and has, I think, been a dutiful mother to me, I think she would prefer to see me married and gone."

"Mayhap she would, but she will not say so," Fiona said. "I suspect that one thing keeping her from insisting Father *find* you a husband is that it would force him to offer a large tocher. You'd have to have enough so that suitors would not mind so much if Mam does succeed at last in giving him a son."

"I don't have any suitors."

"So we *must* persuade her to arrange for us to meet eligible men. Mayhap she would let us hold a feast here after Easter," Fiona added with a thoughtful air.

"Fee, you might as well admit that you are just scheming to invite William Jardine here. You must not even dream of such a thing!"

"Well, if I am not to think of Will Jardine, then you must swear never to think of Robert Maxwell again," Fiona said. "In time, I do think I can persuade Father to engage more kindly with the Jardines and thus make friends of them. Even if he does, though, he will never agree to let you marry a Maxwell."

"But I don't *want* to marry him," Mairi said. "I've no thought of marrying anyone yet. Nor will I until I meet a man with whom I could bear to spend my life."

She meant what she said. Her thoughts might now and again—without effort—turn to Robert Maxwell. But although he might be handsome and display reassuring strength and undeniable charm, he was no less an enemy, and he had behaved arrogantly when they'd first met. So that, she told herself, was that.

Since leaving Dunwythie Mains, she had missed it more each day. During the sennight they had spent there, her father had behaved as if she and Fiona were important to him and useful. He had exerted himself to explain things, and to introduce them to his steward, his bailie, and others who might aid them—if it ever came to that.

He had also promised to introduce them to neighboring landowners in days to come. Instead, he was traveling hither and yon to talk to other men about the sheriff's threat, leaving his daughters at home with Phaeline.

Mairi felt as if, after a week of pretending to be an adult, she had returned to her childhood. Fiona was right, she decided. Their life at Annan House was boring. If she had an ounce of spirit, Mairi told herself sternly, she would not stand for it.

She would *do* something about it.

Chapter 5 _____

Rob stepped out of Trailinghail Tower into the yard late Friday morning to find the knacker Parland Dow dismounting from his horse.

As Rob went toward him, an orange-and-white ball of fluff pursued by one of his hounds shot across the yard and up his leg. The dog saw Rob and skidded abruptly to a halt, tail wagging, tongue lolling. Rob bent to pat its head.

The kitten, climbing to Rob's shoulder, looked down and hissed.

"Hush, cat," Rob said as he ruffled the dog's ears.

He had feared for the kitten's life at first but only until he saw that the fearless little beast was able—with the aid of only one or two roared commands from him—to inspire the same respect in his dogs that it had inspired in Gibby. The cat apparently viewed the dogs as playmates if not as rather large, amusing toys, so Rob had relaxed his vigilance.

The hound trotted after him as he went to greet the knacker.

"I did hear at Dumfries about the wee gift Herself gave ye," Dow said, nodding toward the kitten as they shook hands. "I see ye're still plagued wi' him."

"So I am, but welcome to Trailinghail," Rob said. "What news do you bring?"

"As to that, sir, ye mayn't like some of it."

"Tell me anyway."

"Aye, well, I heard rumors in Kirkcudbright that the sheriff does intend to seize lands from men of Annandale and other such places as refuse to bend to his will," Dow said. "Men fear such talk may lead to clan war."

"Aye, it might," Rob said. Realizing he'd sounded curt, he said cordially, "What further news have you?" Most information of value that reached Trailinghail came from such itinerant tradesmen, who collected and shared it as they traveled.

"I've summat and nowt," the knacker said with a twinkle. "Ye did say ye ha' work here for a thirsty man, did ye no?"

"I do, and a drink for you first, if you'll come inside," Rob said. When they had settled by the hall fire, he said, "You told me you were for Annandale, I think."

"Och, aye, and I'll be there again afore too long," Dow said. "Ye ken fine that I take work where I find it, so I ken Annandale as well as Nithsdale or Galloway. I did hear that ye'd visited Dunwythie Mains and other estates whilst *ye* was there."

"I did," Rob said. "What can you tell me about Lord Dunwythie?"

"A gey good man," Dow said. "Treats his people well, and he's a fair man, too, highly respected and peaceable. More so than most o' that Annandale lot, I'd say. Lord

Johnstone o' Johnstone, now he be a fierce one. And I'm thinking ye ken Old Jardine and *his* lot for yourself, sir."

"I do. What do you know of Dunwythie's family?" Rob inquired mildly as he leaned forward to add more whisky to Dow's goblet from the jug.

"His lordship's ancestors were in Annandale afore the Bruce, and—"

"I don't care about his ancestors," Rob said testily. "I want to know about his immediate family. He has at least two daughters, for I saw them."

"Aye, he does, and nary a son," the knacker said. "His lady be frequently wi' child, but . . ." He spread his hands.

"I saw Lady Dunwythie when I was at Dunwythie Mains," Rob said. "She does not look much older than her daughters."

"She do still be *young* enough to bear babes," Dow said, doubt visible in his slight frown. "But aside from her daughter—"

"Daughters," Rob reminded him gently.

"Aye, sure, I expect she does look upon both o' them as hers."

"Are they not?"

"Nay, only the younger one, the lady Fiona."

"I see. Then his elder daughter . . ."

"Men say the lady Mairi would be his lordship's declared heir but for his lady wife's insisting *she* will give him a son. Meantime, nae one can be sure the lass will succeed to aught save her own mam's portion. If ye were a-thinking—"

"Nay, nay," Rob said hastily, although his thoughts were definitely busy. At least Dow had confirmed what the Jardines had told him about the lass. He added, "You must know as well as I do what the reaction from my clan would be—aye, and that of the Dunwythies—were I fool enough to consider such a marriage."

"I ken that fine, aye. But she be a gey handsome lass, withal."

"She is that," Rob agreed. "I expect her father thinks most highly of her."

"He does, aye, he does," Dow said, nodding. "I'm told, despite his lady wife's belief that she'll ha' a son, he has been teaching the lady Mairi all she'll need know to manage the estates should the worst befall him."

"A wise man," Rob said. "But I expect he cares much for the lass. She is not only beautiful but also seemed well spoken and sensible—surely a daughter in whom a father would take pride and for whom he would risk much to protect."

"More than for her sister," Dow said, grinning. "Nobbut what the lady Fiona be a beauty, too. But that mettlesome lass would lead any man a dance. Pert, she be, and from what I ha' seen, she likes nowt more than stirring mischief. Has a mind of her own, that lass does. The lady Mairi be the dependable one. I've nae doubt that, left to himself, his lordship would name her his heiress and call it good."

"One cannot doubt that he protects them both vigilantly," Rob said.

"Aye, sure. He's a practical man, is Dunwythie. I did hear that he has returned to Annan House—leastways, the family is there. I've nae doots ye frightened them back there yourself, did ye threaten to seize their estates."

"'Twas not *my* threat, just a warning of the sheriff's power."

"Aye, sure, that would be it."

Having no desire to discuss that matter, Rob said, "Annan House lies near the mouth of the river Annan, does it not? And therefore near the Firth?"

"It does," Dow agreed. "It sits atop Annan Hill, south of Annan town."

Seeds of the daring idea that had half formed in Rob's mind earlier began to take root, nourished by details that could help them grow into a feasible plan.

When they had finished their whisky, he told Dow to talk to his chief herd about butchering two lambs and an older ram past its prime. "When you've attended to them, seek out Fin Walters," Rob said. "He will have other tasks for you that require more skill than most of our lads have shown. I'd take it kindly if you could impart some of your knowledge to a few of them," he added.

"Ye'd ha' me train them that would do me out o' good labor, would ye?"

"Other than Fin and my stablemaster, the men here are sadly untaught in aught but horses and weaponry," Rob explained. "Also, I want to provide the tower's upper chamber for my grandmother's use when she visits, as she has threatened to do soon. She left a number of her things here, but I warrant she would prefer to see that chamber refurbished. If you come across aught in your travels that you think might suit or amuse her, prithee get word of it to me. And if you hear aught else about a clan war threatening, send word of that to me as well."

Dow agreed, and after he had gone about his business, Rob stared into the hall fire for a long time. He decided his grandmother and Alex were right in saying that he owed his greatest duty to his clan. But Alex had been wrong to declare him incapable of persuading Dunwythie to submit.

Rob was nearly certain now that with a little exploration and careful development of his idea, he just might succeed.

Normally, when he saw a problem, he attacked it, trusting his instincts to guide him aright. He thought of himself as a man of action rather than a schemer or plotter. Trying to manipulate people, as Alex did, never sat well with him.

Arguing, making his point, that was all fair and good. He could listen, too, and he could accept ideas that he recognized were better than his own. But it had gone right against the grain with him to think he must persuade a proud man like Dunwythie to submit to Alex's command and control.

Rob smiled grimly at that last thought, realizing that what might really have disturbed him about that was that *he* did not like submitting to Alex.

But he did believe in duty, and regardless of what Alex had said, he was loyal to their clan and he did understand that loyalty carried obligation as well.

It had become undeniably clear to Mairi that her life at Annan House was not going to change a whit, despite the many things her father had taught her before and during their recent visit to Dunwythie Mains. She was still trying to imagine how to alter that situation when Phaeline summoned her to her solar Monday afternoon.

Phaeline reclined against cushions on a settle by the small cheerful fire, her feet on a cushioned, embroidered stool. Her face was paler than usual, but she looked every inch the fashionable noblewoman that she was.

Her white silk veil draped perfectly at her shoulders and revealed just the right amount of the beaded caul covering her hair and her ears but for the tiny bit of lobe beneath which her pearl eardrops dangled. Matching pearls encircled her still smooth throat and dipped low enough for the long end to slide into her deep cleavage as she straightened a little at Mairi's approach.

Stopping in front of the footstool, Mairi made a brief curtsy and said, "What may I do for you, madam?"

Phaeline looked at her for a long moment without speaking. But Mairi was accustomed to such moments and waited. At last, Phaeline said, "Fiona tells me you are finding less of interest to do here after your visit to Dunwythie Mains."

Mentally condemning her sister for a telltale, and a false one if she had not said that she, too, was frustrated, Mairi said only, "In troth, madam, I had only begun to grow acquainted with the things my lord father was teaching us. I do think I might benefit by watching them finish preparing and planting the fields here."

"My dearling, you are a fool even to think of such things. No man looks for a wife who can properly plant barley. He looks for one who can give him sons, a woman who is decorative and kind to others. More, he wants an obedient, loving wife who will also be a good mother to his sons. As for learning more about fields, it is naught but fact that no woman can manage estates as well as a man can."

"My cousin Jenny knows as much as any man does about such things, madam," Mairi said. "I do not believe that your brother, Sir Hugh, thinks Jenny a poor wife for him."

"Mercy, you do say the oddest things, Mairi! I never said

our Jenny makes Hugh a bad wife. But her father raised her to manage his estates. Moreover, as her rank matches Hugh's and he is satisfied that she knows what she is doing, he is willing to let her make her own decisions."

"But, don't you see, madam? I would have such knowledge, too, and in the unfortunate event that—"

"Pish tush, Mairi, do not be pretending to *me* that you would look upon my failure to give your father a son as an unfortunate event! You would be twice the fool I sometimes think you are if you did *not* covet the estates for yourself. However, your father has faith that we will have a son. He teaches you only because Hugh reminded him that he could die at any time from a fall or other mishap, and that you should understand what your responsibilities would be. I have no doubt, though, that your father expects Hugh to guide you if such a tragic event should occur."

"Indeed, madam, I have no wish for aught to happen to my father, or to you. I would gladly welcome a brother, for that matter."

"I am glad to hear that, because if you have not already guessed as much, I will own that I am with child now. I have hitherto told only your father, because he cossets me enough without the entire household feeling obliged to do so."

Although Mairi was sure the rest of the household had recognized Phaeline's behavior and suspected its cause as quickly as she and Fiona had, she did not say so. She said, "I will do all I can to help you, madam. I do think that learning new things is good for anyone, though. And since Father has begun to teach me—"

"Bless me, Mairi, but you put me out," Phaeline said. "I know well how it is with you. Since you were small, if you got your teeth into an idea, naught would do but that you must carry it out. Very well, then, if you are restless and want to learn about management, manage your sister. Where is she? I do not believe I have laid eyes on her since we broke our fast this morning."

"I don't know, madam. I thought she was going to sit with you. I have been in the kitchen, assessing what we have of barley water, ale, and other such items."

"Well, find your sister. But here, take my keys," she added. "You may take over more of *my* duties, and welcome. But mind you do naught without consulting me first. Meantime, I would count it a boon if you can contrive to keep your sister out of mischief. And do, my dearling, at least *try* to think of ways to make yourself more pleasing to a suitable husband, or I do truly fear you may never attract one."

Mairi's sense of the ridiculous stirred, nearly drawing a smile at this echo of her own words to Fiona only days before. However, she accepted the keys, curtsied again, and went obediently to find her sister.

A long search of the house proving fruitless, she walked to the gate and asked the guard there if the lady Fiona had perchance left the premises.

"Aye, m'lady," he said. "She did take one o' the maid-servants with her, so I thought there could be nowt amiss in her taking a short walk to the river."

"Is that where she went?"

"I think so, aye," the young man said. "She started out that way, any road."

Thanking him, and seeing no need to take a maidservant or anyone else with her in this time of peace, Mairi set out across the hilltop toward the Firth-side slope, where a path wound down around the tree-protected field there, to the riverbank.

As she began the downhill trek, however, she heard Fiona calling her name, and turning toward the sound, saw her sister and Flory, the maidservant who waited on them both, hurrying across the hill and waving as they came.

Thinking it was fortunate for her sister that she had shouted when she had, saving her a hike down and back again, and at the same time feeling bereft of the freedom that a lovely brisk walk would provide, Mairi went to meet them.

"Where did you go?" she asked when she was sure Fiona would hear.

"Oh, just here and there, wandering where the fancy took us," Fiona said glibly. "In troth, Mairi, I was feeling so pent up inside the wall that I just wanted to be outside, if only to watch the tide go out. Do you not feel the same these days?"

"Aye, I do, Fee, but I'll thank you not to be telling your mother how *I* feel," Mairi said bluntly. "'Twas *you* who complained as we were leaving the Hall that we would have naught but our usual duties and pastimes to occupy us here and *you* who complained again after we returned."

"But you agreed with me! You know you did."

"'Tis true, I did. I've been feeling as if I'd returned to my childhood. I expected our father to provide me some duties relating to managing the house and the fields here. Instead, I do only the usual things. However, your mother did just give me her keys to the pantry and buttery," she added with a smile.

"You are welcome to them and to any duties Father might provide, but do not think I shall be sharing them, because I won't," Fiona said. "Heaven knows when he will return in any event. He left only a few days ago on this trip and said he means to stop at Dunwythie Mains after visiting lairds at the north end of the dale."

"He is concerned about conflict erupting here," Mairi said. "It has occurred to me, in fact, that we do not know what one does at Annan House to prepare against trouble. I mean to ask Jopson, and I think he will tell me. Do not you?"

"Sakes, I don't care what you ask or what he says. What do you expect you will have to do with it, even if he tells you? Do you imagine the men here will take orders from a woman? In troth, I think Mam must be right about leaving *all* such things to men. I think it would be very hard to take charge of a large estate."

"Hard, aye," Mairi said. "But if one knows what to do and tells other people what they *must* do, they will do it. Our people are accustomed to taking orders, Fee, and to trusting us Dunwythies to know what we are doing. If they believe the person issuing the order has the right to do so, they will obey."

"Aye, sure, but only if they think you are right," Fiona said sardonically.

"I mean to ask Jopson, anyway," Mairi said. "He may refuse to tell me, but I hope he will not."

~

Accordingly, the following morning, directly after Mairi had broken her fast, she sought out her father's steward, finding him in the forecourt, where he was talking with Gerrard, the captain of the Annan House guard.

"Good morning, Jopson, and to you, too, Gerrard," Mairi said as the two men made their bows to her. "I know that his lordship has been concerned about possible trouble arising hereabouts. He must have spoken to you about it."

"Ye need ha' nae worries about such, me lady," Jopson said with an air of bluff reassurance, exchanging a quick glance with the guard captain. "'Tis nowt to concern ye or Lady Dunwythie."

"I am confident that you two have all in hand to protect us," Mairi said, undaunted. "As you may know, though, his lordship has been teaching me things I may need to know in the event that he should suffer an untimely death."

"I did hear that, aye," Jopson said. "We ken fine how it would be then, me lady. But that sad event has no happened yet."

"And, God willing, it will not for many years. However, I want to learn all I can, because the more I know, the wiser I will be if it *should* happen."

"Aye, aye, but all in good time, me lady."

Drawing herself up, Mairi said quietly, "I want to know just how we will protect Annan House and our people here, Jopson, if trouble should break out."

"Aye, sure," the steward said hastily. "But 'tis nowt. Ye'd just tell me to see to everything, and I would speak to Gerrard here. He would set it all in train."

The captain of the guard, younger and larger than the steward, nodded and said earnestly, "To be sure, m'lady. We ken fine what to do. I'd double the guard and set men to watch on nearby hills where we ha' signal fires set and ready to light at the first sign o' trouble."

"Already set?" she said, surprised. "I know that people here use fires to signal English attacks when they occur.

But I did not think that anyone built such fires unless attack was imminent. As we have been at peace for so long . . ."

"Bless ye, no, mistress," the captain said when she paused, elevating her in status with that form of address. "We ha' fires ready always and keep them covered as best we can, in winter and spring especially. We could light such a fire here, and the warning would spread up the dale quicker than a man could ride his fastest horse. See you, me lady, time be gey important. So we try always to keep ready."

Jopson added, "We'd likewise ha' warning afore any such attack, aye, and plenty o' time to prepare against it."

"'Tis true," Gerrard agreed. "Annan House be well placed to see what comes. And there be signal fires ready to light the length and breadth o' Annandale. Yonder ridge o' hills to the west, as separates us from Nithsdale, would come alight wi' flames did threat come from Dumfries and yon carnaptious sheriff."

"We take good care o' the wall, too, m'lady," Jopson said. "And we'd ha' reinforcements from the town and from neighboring estates gey quick. Ye ladies would all be as safe as wee mice in a mill, I promise ye."

"Thank you," Mairi said. "Now, if you would just answer a few questions I have about the plantings here, Jopson, I would be grateful."

To his credit, the steward expressed his willingness so sincerely that she almost believed him. And he answered her questions with admirable patience.

When she had run out of things to ask, she went in search of Fiona and found her sitting with Phaeline in the solar. Each of them had a tambour frame before her and was setting stitches in what were to be new cushion covers.

"Prithee, sit with us, Mairi," Fiona said when they had exchanged greetings. "Mam says I must keep to this stitchery until we dine. Do you not have stitching that you could do?"

"I do," Mairi said. But just saying the words struck a chord of rebellion. The last thing she wanted to do was to sit with her tambour frame, stitching and talking of nothing. The day before, she had so nearly enjoyed a walk outside the wall, and she ached for such freedom now.

Managing a rueful smile, she added, "I will do as you wish after we dine, Fee. But I do have some tasks I must see to first. I just wondered where you had gone. As you are busy, I'll leave you for now and attend to my duties."

Before it could occur to either Fiona or Phaeline to ask what duties she had that were so demanding, Mairi fled upstairs.

In the chamber she shared with Fiona, she donned a pair of stout boots and a cloak to protect her from the chill that still lingered in the air even on the sunniest days, and tucked her hair up into a cap under her veil. Then, slipping an empty cloth pouch under the metal-linked girdle she wore around her hips over a faded old kirtle, she hurried back downstairs. Taking a manchet from the basket of a gillie hurrying to set the high table, she grabbed a hunk of cheese from another gillie's platter.

Stowing the food in her pouch as she hastily crossed the hall—lest Phaeline or Fiona emerge unexpectedly from the solar—she hurried downstairs and out into the courtyard. Only then did she realize that her stepmother would surely insist that she ought, for propriety's sake, to take a maidservant along.

"Faugh," she muttered, using her father's favorite expletive. "I'd wager Jenny does not take a maidservant when she visits *her* fields. No more shall I."

At the gate, if the guard looked surprised to see her, alone or otherwise, he made no objection when she told him to open up. And no one else tried to stop her.

Outside the gate, feeling a heady sense of release, she inhaled deeply of the crisp, salty air. A chilly wind blew, so she set off briskly down the hill toward the nearest field, noting as she did that the relatively calm waters of the Firth indicated that the incoming tide had ended its fierce morning surge and begun to turn. Tides always rushed into the Firth with roiling enthusiasm and ebbed more lethargically.

Two small boats were passing on the river below, clearly making for Annan harbor. Approaching the mouth of the river was another, larger craft, mayhap a small galley, perhaps bringing someone from the western part of the dale, or farther west, to do business in the harbor or in town.

The new crop already looked like rows of short grass, for barley grew fast. Men had been hoeing weeds and loosening dirt to discourage their rapid return.

Mairi went only a little farther before she realized somewhat to her dismay that the men were preparing to go up for their midday meal.

Having sought only to escape, she had given no thought to what excuse she might offer, should anyone ask why she had left the house. She knew she had little reason now to stay outside the gate and none that would satisfy her stepmother.

And Phaeline would certainly demand to know where she had gone.

The sensible thing to do, which she would have insisted

they do had Fiona been with her, was to go back and dine with her stepmother and sister in the hall.

Fiona had been right about one thing. There would be no meat.

Recalling the bread and cheese in the pouch under her cloak, Mairi smiled, reminded herself that she had resolved to find ways to ease the tedium, and walked on down toward the woods between the fields and the river. Phaeline would scold, but Mairi had decided to enjoy her brief freedom come what might.

She and Fiona had often walked along the riverbank together in springtime, and the weather had been fine for days. So, were it not for Phaeline's concern for their safety outside the walls, they would have walked there nearly every day.

Instead, except for airing their bedding on the grassy hillside, and the day before when Fiona had rebelled enough to sneak out with their maid, Phaeline had kept them cooped up inside the gateway if not inside the house.

When Lord Dunwythie got back, he would likely say the threat no longer existed, or at least had eased, and they would enjoy more freedom.

Meantime, Mairi meant to enjoy her stolen hour.

She would walk no farther than the edge of the woods, though. From the top of the wall, the guardsmen would still see her there. And as long as she remained within sight of the guards, she was sure she would be safe.

Accordingly, she strolled to the edge of the woods and along their perimeter for a time before turning back. Then, reluctant to return yet to the house, she sought a warm, sunny place to enjoy her bread and cheese.

The workmen had paid no heed to her, and she soon

saw the last one vanish over the brow of the hill. A sunny boulder ahead beckoned to her, and as she approached it, she heard a muffled shout of, "Weigh 'nuff!"

Pausing, she realized the river had quieted, telling her the tide was indeed on the turn. The lapping, wind-churned water, even muted as it was by the woodland, was not silent, though. She heard sounds of wood against wood and knew that a boat, doubtless the wee galley, had entered the river.

But "weigh enough"? Was that not the command to stop rowing?

Curious, and trusting the woods to conceal her, she stepped into them and followed what appeared to be a deer trail heading toward the water's edge.

Planted as a break against strong winds from the Firth, the densely growing trees and the shrubbery beneath them were well leafed. Mairi picked her way carefully, glad that her cloak was dark green and thus unlikely to draw anyone's attention as she moved through the trees.

She soon found a place where, by leaning and ducking slightly, she could see between two stout trunks to the water, which reached about fifteen feet higher on the slope now than it did at low tide. Moving closer to the two trees, taking good care to move slowly and quietly enough to avoid drawing notice, she crept up behind the one with the wider trunk and peeked around it.

A small eight-oared galley had beached on the strip of muddy hillside that showed below the high-water mark in all but spring tides. She heard a man shout, "Tether us to yon scrub, lads, or the first good wave'll sweep us off betimes!"

Tempted to tell them they were beaching on private land and ought to row upriver to Annan harbor, she decided against it. But, knowing she must go back and warn the guards about such visitors, she wondered if she could get a clearer view of them first. She had not seen any identifying banner or counted the men.

As she eased carefully back and away from the tree, she abruptly came face to face with Robert Maxwell.

He looked as stunned as she was, but he recovered more swiftly. Quick as light, he caught her up in his arms and carried her through the woods to the galley.

The next thing she knew she was aboard it, wrapped in her own cloak, with a horrid cloth tied tight across her mouth, furious, outraged, and helpless.

The other men, although wide-eyed, lifted not one finger to aid her.

Her captor cast a musty blanket of some sort over her, and minutes later, the men had launched the boat and were rowing hard for Solway Firth.

Chapter 6 _____

I'm sorry for this, lass," Rob muttered to his captive as he straightened the blanket that covered her and shouted for his crew to launch the galley and get them away as fast as possible.

The tide was already on the turn, so their timing had been well-nigh perfect. They had traveled most of the way on the swift incoming tide from the Irish Sea, gaining another boost from a brisk southwest wind. Conditions had been ideal for traveling east but risky, too. Such speed—as much as eight to ten miles per hour on a flooding tide into the ever-narrowing Firth—could also prove treacherous.

At Kirkcudbright Bay, tides were nearly normal, each cycle taking a little over six hours. But the farther into the Firth the flood tides pushed, the swifter they moved. From low to high tide at Annan could take just under four hours on a spring tide, while its ebb could take as long as nine and a half hours.

Traveling outward on the ebb was always slower and would be more so with wind from the southwest, but almost any wind could prove useful in sparing his oarsmen and would aid them when time came to enter Kirkcudbright Bay.

He had meant only to learn the lay of the land at Annan House. First he had intended just to see how well guarded the place was from a river approach. He would then have anchored in Annan harbor and explored more from there.

Depending on what he learned, he would either have returned to Galloway to reconsider his plans or stayed in the area until opportunity arose—or he had created one—to put his plan into action. Instead, the lass had stepped into his path, and he had seized the moment—and her ladyship as well.

He waited only until they were out of sight from Annan House, before stooping to free her. The big square sail was up, blowing full above them as he loosened her gag. Removing it, he expected a flood of reproaches, even tears.

But after an initial, unmistakable flash of fury, she remained stonily silent.

Deciding she must be too terrified to speak, he began to untie the rope he had wrapped around her over her cloak.

Quietly, he said, "You've nowt to fear, my lady. I mean you no harm."

She said nothing, merely shifting to let him deal with the rope more easily.

When he had finished, he said gently, "Take my hand, lass. I'll steady you whilst you stand. Then you may take a seat on that wee bench by the stem locker."

She let him help her stand but warily, and again he could sense her anger. Being a man who vented his anger whenever it stirred, Rob looked on her continued silence as proof that he had terrified her. That would not do.

"By my troth, Lady Mairi, *no* one will harm you," he said. "Your predicament is a matter of politics only—of necessity, in fact—to avoid much bloodshed."

"Indeed, sir?" she said tartly. "One hesitates to question such noble intent, but does your helmsman *mean* to smash us all on those rocks straight ahead?"

"Nay, they are but tacking against the wind," he said, relieved to learn that it was not him she feared. "Often, to move forward," he added pointedly, "one *must* take what seems a strange course. As you will see, though, we are about to turn."

Mairi had realized as much as soon as she had spoken, because one of the crew moved then to reset the angle at which the big sail caught the wind. The helmsman shifted the steerboard then, to take a course very near the wind and no longer heading toward shore.

Maxwell, apparently realizing that she did not want to talk to him, slipped off his heavy leather jack and rolled it up. "Here, lass," he said. "Put this behind you so you don't bruise yourself against the wood."

Accepting it with a nod and exerting herself not to reveal that she found the leather disturbingly warm from his body, she adjusted it to cushion herself. Then she turned so she could watch the water and the shoreline that they followed west.

He had clearly thought she feared him, but she did not. Perhaps she ought to, she mused. But for now, she was grateful to feel only anger.

She had occasionally been out in a small boat during

neap tides, when the rise and fall of the water level was minimal. Also, she and Fiona had ridden ponies across the open, muddy sands east of the Annan during low tide, when all twenty miles of the Firth from its head almost to the outflow of the river Nith looked more like a boggy desert—with two narrow rivers through it—than a vital waterway. The Firth was thus deceptive, and one dared never underestimate its dangers.

Only neap tides came in and went out courteously.

She had heard tales of raiding parties into England mis-timing a ride across the sands and hearing what seemed a distant roar. Men had looked toward it only to see the in-coming tide nearly upon them in a six-foot wall of water.

The nearby coast sloped gently to the water as it did near Annan House. The rhythmically undulating water of the turning tide was brown and silt-ridden.

Comfortably warm in her heavy cloak, lulled by the sounds of the wind in the sail and an occasional rhythmic thumping of oars, she drowsed.

When she opened her eyes, the sun was halfway to the western horizon and Caerlaverock Castle was coming into view, with the mouth of the river Nith beyond it. Apparently they had to head right into the wind now to follow the coast.

The sail was down, and the oarsmen were rowing hard.

She recognized the great ruin of Caerlaverock easily, because the previous year she and Fiona had traveled with their father and Phaeline to Threave, the Lord of Gallo-way's great stronghold on an islet in the river Dee. Gal-loway lay much farther west, making her wonder just how far the little galley would take her.

She stole a glance at her captor, who stood amidships,

eyeing the sky and casting glances coastward, mayhap judging the depth of the ebbing tide.

He truly was a fine figure of a man, she thought, for an unprincipled villain.

Wondering if he was daft or just much more dangerous than he had seemed at Dunwythie Mains, she wondered, too, what he would do with her.

His apparent comparison of her abduction to the way his helmsman steered his boat had made little sense, as little as his suggestion that by abducting her—capturing her, he had said—he could save untold numbers of lives.

Such a claim was absurd. It was also infuriating.

How outraged she had been when he had scooped her up so effortlessly, ignoring her struggles and useless cries, and carried her to his boat. She was still furious, come to that. But she had concealed her fury just as she had whenever such strong emotion had stirred for almost as long as she could remember.

Venting her emotions had rarely won anything but punishment and censure for unladylike behavior. So she had learned to control her outbursts.

By heaven's grace, she would continue to keep her temper until she could better judge her situation and the man who had stolen her. By then, she hoped she could devise an argument that would persuade him to take her home.

Whatever else he might do, she would not, under any circumstance, let him provoke her into losing control of herself.

Rob sensed her anger again. It radiated from her in waves even when she did not look at him. But he began to wonder if her continued silence might be due only to the presence of his men. He hoped that was all it was and that she would express herself more easily when they reached Trailinghail.

It had occurred to him only after he had captured her that he had terrified her. At the time, he had merely seized his opportunity without sparing a thought for her feelings. Hardly an excuse, but he had done it and could not undo it now.

Having become certain after talking with Parland Dow that disaster must result if Dunwythie's recalcitrance spurred Alex to invade Annandale, Rob had decided to see to the matter himself, not only to prove that he *could* influence Dunwythie but also, and more important, to avoid an outright clan war that could affect any number of clans both great and small.

Believing that Alex would pursue no violent course during the holy season of Lent, Rob had set himself to work out the details of his plan with care.

Alex clearly believed that Dunwythie's stubbornness was ill-willed, that he was simply defying the sheriff's rightful authority. But Dunwythie just as clearly believed that *he* was adhering to legal, time-honored tradition.

Lady Kelso had reinforced much of what Alex had said to Rob, primarily with regard to one's duty to one's clan but also regarding his habit of retreating to Trailinghail whenever Alex infuriated him.

Rob had never thought of his visits that way. He had loved the tower since first visiting his grandparents there. That it had provided a summertime escape from Alex's stern guardianship was true, so he could see how Alex might perceive those visits as he did. However, Rob had given no thought to living there permanently.

His tenants' delight over the improvements he had made did make it clear that *they* hoped he might make his home there. He would certainly not mind staying longer than usual. And with a hostage to look after, he would have good reason.

Other details had brought form to his plan. The unusual frequency with which thoughts of the lady Mairi had leaped to mind had led the way.

She'd had a strong impact on him from the moment he'd met her. Having no sisters and little memory of his parents, he had no idea how most men felt about their daughters. But he knew how *he* would feel about one such as she was. Surely, *her* father, having known the lass from birth, would value her even more. Would Dunwythie not therefore do whatever he must to ensure her safe return?

Sakes, Rob told himself, looking at her, any man would!

Aware that his brother's patience with Dunwythie, never long, had neared its end, Rob had decided he would have to settle the matter before Easter.

Having nearly six weeks until then, he had not meant to act so precipitously.

Impulse had occasionally led to his undoing in the past, and he had promised himself each time that he'd take greater care in future. But it was useless to make that vow now. The deed was done, and the tide was ebbing.

By now, the water was so low in the upper Firth that even if he'd wanted to take her back, they would run aground long before reaching Annan. But he did *not* want to take her back, for a multitude of reasons having naught to do with the tides.

Chief among them was that if he could get Dunwythie to submit, Clan Maxwell would gain considerable power, increase their wealth, and everyone would avoid war. Also, surely, the administration of the dales would be fairer for everyone under one sheriff, and local government would run smoothly.

There were risks, though, not least of which was the Lord of Galloway. The best course with Archie, Rob had decided, was to see that Dunwythie submitted and brought the other lairds into line quickly and without raising a dust.

As to Dunwythie, Rob's objective was to persuade the man without drawing suspicion to himself. But he had not yet decided just how to approach Dunwythie when the time came.

In the meantime, he meant to make the lass as comfortable as anyone could.

These thoughts, mostly reassuring, poured through his mind for some time between issuing orders to his crew, covertly studying his captive, and taking his helmsman's place for a few miles now and again to let the man stretch— until he realized he was just trying to assuage his feelings of guilt for taking her.

Aside from the flashes of anger he had detected, she had not even protested her capture. At present, she watched a pair of otters playing and seemed content, so he did not disturb her.

The men took to their oars and rowed whenever an especially strong current challenged their course or the fickle wind briefly shifted to a new quarter. Between bouts of rowing, they rested. But when they entered the widest part of the Firth, where wind and tide grew more turbulent, Rob set them all to rowing steadily.

Noting that the lass had put up her hood and huddled against the stem locker to avoid the wind, he went down the narrow center walkway toward her.

Her gaze met his, and he detected serenity in her eyes again.

When he was near enough, she said, "Prithee, sir, take me home."

~

Mairi saw a blizzard of oystercatchers flash through the air behind Maxwell as he stood there, apparently frozen in place by her polite request.

Then, with a hand to the gunwale, he shifted to lean his well-muscled backside against it. His booted feet were near those of the first-bench oarsmen. Holding her gaze, he gently shook his head and said, "You know I cannot do that."

"Why not?"

"Lass, the tide is nearly four hours into its ebb, and the sea here is roiling like water in a fiery cauldron. Surely, you know how the upper part of the Firth must look by now. Not only will it be dark in two hours but this boat would not get two miles beyond the river Nith before grounding in mud. Sakes, it would be sooner than that, because this wind would be of little aid against the power of an ebbing tide. As it is, we'll have an exciting ride into the bay."

"Which bay? Where are we going?"

"Kirkcudbright Bay," he said.

Noting puzzlement in his expression, she knew that her

steadily quiet, reasonable tone was surprising him. Clearly, he had expected temperament and tantrums, behavior of which Fiona was certainly capable but which Mairi avoided.

The mental image of her sister, flouncing about, declaring her privileged life to be *beyond* unfair—as she frequently did—nearly made Mairi smile.

He reacted to that near smile, too, with a slight one of his own.

Good, Mairi thought. If she behaved reasonably, he would do likewise. Then doubt stirred upon hearing an echo in her mind of Fiona declaring that if people would only treat others kindly, the others would react with equal kindness.

She knew less about this man in front of her than she knew about the Jardines of Applegarth. But after all she had heard about that fractious family, she knew she would be unable to persuade herself that quiet reason would win any argument with them.

Deciding that she would do better to accord Robert Maxwell the benefit of the doubt until he proved himself *un*reasonable, she said, "How much farther is it, then? I have been to Kirkcudbright only once before."

"When?"

"Last year," she said. Lest she sound as curt as he had, she added, "For the Lord of Galloway's anniversary celebration of the King's coronation."

A wry smile curved his lips, forcibly reminding her of what an unexpectedly strong effect the man's slightest smile could have on her.

Then he said, "Doubtless you seek to remind me that

your mother is kin to Archie the Grim and that he is gey powerful. But I do not fear Archie."

"I simply answered your question," she said tartly. "I am sure we do not go near Threave today. So where *do* we go, and how much longer will it take?"

"Not long, as you will soon see," he said. "Are you warm enough?"

That he would dare to pretend he was concerned about her comfort while he was forcing her to go God knew where with him made her lip want to curl. In fact, she thought it must have curled, for he looked surprised and then, oddly, rather hurt.

Compassion stirred, but anger raced at its heels, aimed inward for allowing herself for even one foolish moment to feel sorry for the odious creature.

She turned abruptly forward without another word, to watch the rolling waves. His presence loomed above her for a full, if silent, minute longer. Then he moved away until oars, wind, and sea were all she could see or hear.

The next time she looked for him, she did so because the sun had dropped so low that one had to look straight into it to watch the sea ahead. He was with the helmsman again, shouting for the oarsmen to weigh enough. The oars came out of the water for a short time then, fifteen minutes or so, she thought.

No sooner did they begin rowing again, though, than she sensed a change in rhythm, both in the wooden thumps of the oars and in the movement of the boat.

The landscape had changed, too. The gentle slopes of Annandale and Nithsdale had grown to higher hills and a much more rugged coastline. Ahead of her, she saw sheer cliffs that she remembered from the year before.

They were nearing Kirkcudbright Bay.

Soon, the bay opened to their right in a deep, cliff-lined vee. The water became turbulent as the sea from the Firth met water ebbing from the bay. Huge rollers sent spray high into the air, and the galley seemed suddenly tiny.

Their approach the year before had been nearer the turn of the tide than this, and their ship had been twice as big. For the first time, Mairi felt fear that they might capsize. Even in its midst, she realized that she had felt none before, only her anger.

The man was a thoroughgoing villain, but he did not scare her.

Nor did she think he would let the boat sink beneath them. Something in the very way he stood shouted confidence. So did the way his men heeded his every word and responded instantly and ably to his calm commands.

Her anxiety eased.

As oarsmen and helmsman battled the waves, she watched Robert Maxwell. She expected to hear him order the galley straight into the confluence of clashing currents, to steady it as one steadied small boats in similar circumstances.

But he did not. Instead, his men seemed to taunt the waves, daring them to strike broadside and try to overturn them. His commands came swiftly, and she saw how skillfully the men synchronized their strokes with the rollers to cut a shallow angle across the tumultuous waters wherever they crashed together.

Clearly, they were not making for Kirkcudbright, which lay at the head of the bay. The galley continued through the clashing waves until she saw that they aimed toward a point near the Firth end of the high, sheer western cliffs.

Those cliffs looked higher than the ones on the east side. The long, mostly sheer cliff face was rugged, its base forbidding. A multitude of sharp rocky outcroppings and toothlike formations poked out of the water there.

A tall stone tower stood on the cliff ahead. Below it, she saw an opening in the wall. As they drew nearer—too near—she looked at Maxwell in alarm.

His eyes were narrowed, his attention fixed. He murmured commands to the helmsman. The men still rowed hard, and the galley rocked over roller upon roller.

The air seemed colder, for the cliff wall hid the sun, putting them in shadow. The wind still blew, making the sail crackle, and gulls screamed overhead.

The hole in the cliff grew larger the nearer they drew, revealing itself as a deep cavern. Suddenly, the nearby water was calmer. Huge boulders formed a wide channel right to the opening.

The big sail came flapping down, startling her. Its mast followed as men laid it down the galley's centerboard. Water eddied around them but calmed more near the opening. Even so, she could feel it heaving under them.

Then Maxwell roared, "Hold water!" and Mairi held her breath as the galley swept through the opening to an almost glassy surface within. Despite the water's appearance and the thrusting of all oars into it, the galley pitched forward.

Astonishingly, a stone wharf with timber facing became visible against the cave wall to the left of the entrance. Three men stood on it, waiting.

The portside oars lifted, and men aboard threw lines to those on the wharf, who quickly hauled them in and made them fast.

"Come along, my lady."

She had been watching the men on the wharf and had not seen Maxwell move from the stern. But he stood right behind her with a hand extended.

Standing, she found her legs uncertain. The seemingly calm water was surging up and down just as the sea outside did. Much as she would have liked to disdain his help, she dared not. She let him grip her hand.

He steadied her as she stood. Then, without comment, he lifted her to the wharf, following agilely and so swiftly that she had taken but a step on the slippery surface and was still skidding when he caught her.

Again without comment, he scooped her into his arms. He was a full head taller than she was, and much larger. Nevertheless, she protested.

"I am perfectly able to walk. That is, I *will* be able to when I stop feeling as if I'm still rolling with the tide."

"Whisst now, we are not going to fratch," he said. "The stairs are as slippery as this wharf. I don't want you to risk injury."

"As if your carrying me could be safer," she said scornfully. "I am no lightweight, and if those steps are so slippery—"

"Whisst," he said again, already mounting the steep stone stairway.

Deciding she should not distract him, she obeyed. But above the cavern, what little light there was vanished, leaving them in pitch darkness. She could tell that the stairs spiraled and had narrowed until he seemed barely to fit with her as a burden.

She discerned a pale glow above that soon revealed itself as an open doorway. As they passed through it to a small, candlelit chamber, Mairi smelled onions and tallow, as if it were a storage cellar.

He carried her through it and along a narrow corridor, then up more stairs to one end of what was clearly a kitchen. Its fire roared, and she saw bustling people. But no one spoke to them as he crossed to another stairway, wider than the first.

That no one looked at them or spoke made her feel as if she were invisible.

From the next landing, she saw a large empty hall and another fire. On the next after that, two doors faced the landing. The next floor's arrangement looked the same. He paused there and set her gently on her feet.

Opening one of the doors, he gestured for her to precede him. As she entered a large room containing a moss-green-curtained bed and a sitting area fine enough for a lady's solar, he spoke at last: "Welcome to Trailinghail. This is your chamber."

"What do you mean, *my* chamber?" she demanded, whirling so quickly to face him that her skirts nearly knocked over a cushioned, three-legged stool.

As the stool thumped back into place, he replied evenly, "This is where you will stay whilst you are here."

"Just how long do you mean to *keep* me here? And for what purpose?"

With maddening calm he said, "You will stay as long as necessary, and my purpose need not concern you. As you see, this room is a fine one. Its windows face both the Firth and the bay, so you will enjoy some grand views. In good weather, one can see the kirk spire in Kirkcudbright, six miles from here."

"I don't *want* to see Kirkcudbright," she said, her voice

sounding shrill in her own ears. Her hands clenched into fists. "I want to leave at once."

"That cannot be. And 'tis best that you know from the outset that escape from this tower is impossible."

"Even if I could get out of this horrid tower, I doubt I could walk all the way home from here," she said, clipping her words and struggling to regain control. The truth was that if she could get out, she would. And if she did, she *would* get home.

However, experience with her father and stepmother had long since shown her that argument and tantrums only irritated people. Since the man in front of her was clearly as daft as any man could be, he was not one she wanted to irritate.

Looking around the chamber, although admittedly larger and more luxurious than she had at Annan House or Dunwythie Hall, and boasting two narrow window embrasures, she saw only a prison. That he dared to think he could so casually make her his prisoner, for any reason, was enough to make her think fondly of murder.

In the hope of regaining control of herself, she untied her cloak and cast it onto a nearby settle. Carefully avoiding the stool her skirts had disturbed, she moved to the nearer of the two windows, unshuttered now to admit a chilly breeze from the bay. A stout shutter was fastened back against the inside wall to her left.

Peering out over the deep, breast-high sill, Mairi tried to focus on the view, truly splendid in the last golden rays of the setting sun. Or so it seemed until she leaned forward far enough to look down and saw that the tower stood so near the cliff edge that she could see all the way to the water below.

"H-how far down is that?" she asked, wincing at the catch in her voice.

"One hundred fifty feet at low water," he said.

She swallowed hard but continued looking out, hoping to conceal her horror.

"If you fall, I'd advise doing so at high water," he said into the silence.

"Sakes, if I fell I'd die no matter how high the water was," she retorted.

"Aye, but with so many sharp rocks sticking up as they do, the result would be tidier than if you flung yourself out at low water. You will soon begin to see one particularly interesting formation. It is called the Misty Brig."

Turning to face him, she said with what, under the circumstances, she thought was admirable if caustic calm, "If you are *trying* to be cruel, it does *not* suit you." Moving nearer, looking right into his eyes, she added, "You should be thoroughly ashamed of what you have done today."

Looking annoyed instead, he said, "Do you not like this chamber?"

"I am sure it is pleasant," she said. "But it is no less a prison for that."

"Aye, well, you might have a look at the clothing in yon kists," he said. "I've provided everything I thought you might need—fine gowns and such. But some things may be a trifle out of date or of an unsuitable size. If you require aught else, you need only tell me. We tried to make this chamber as comfortable as possible, because I do want you to be comfortable. So if you are not—"

Her remaining control slipping, she exclaimed, "Comfortable! You want me to be *comfortable*? How could I be? By my troth, what manner of devil are you that you can even utter such a statement? You have stolen me from my home, brought me to this place! You say I must stay upon your whim or till you've had enough of me, but I should be *comfortable*? What then? Do you *ever* mean to take me home?"

"Aye, sure, I do," he retorted. "Sakes, I said I won't harm you, and I meant it. I also meant it when I said I want you to be comfortable. Surely—"

He got no further before she snatched up the nearest thing to hand, which happened to be the three-legged stool, and flung it at him as hard as she could.

Noting with satisfaction that she hit him a glancing blow with it but almost as much shocked by *her* act as by anything he had done, Mairi clapped fingers to her lips, eyed him warily, and stepped hastily back toward the window.

Chapter 7 _____

Rob had been feeling frustrated and angry, although he was not entirely sure why, but now he did not know whether to laugh or to shake her. He was glad to learn that she had spirit, though, and could express it. He had wanted to know what would make her display her temper, if anything would. And now he knew.

A temperamental lass was always more interesting than an insipid one, and Dunwythie, like most men, would surely care much more about a daughter with strong feelings than he would about a passive, entirely submissive one.

Rob had seen for himself at Dunwythie Mains that the lady Mairi could be self-possessed, and she was undeniably beautiful even now after a long day on the water. He admired both qualities.

But there was something else as well. It was the undefinable trait that had led him to believe that her father—in truth, that any sensible man—would do whatever he must to protect her, and to recover her if he were so unfortunate as to lose her.

He could not have named that special trait, but he knew instinctively that when she flung the stool at him, she had given evidence of it. He was glad, though, that no one else had seen, and that he did not have to explain his instincts to anyone.

Had her seemingly calm acceptance of the situation not muted his usual self-protective instincts, he'd have caught the damned stool easily.

He *had* managed to fling up a hand and deflect it slightly, thus saving himself a harder knock on the head. But he had missed catching the thing. One leg struck his head and another his shoulder before the stool clattered to the floor behind him.

Ignoring it, he said, "I *don't* advise you to do that again."

"Faith, sir, I have never done such a thing before in all my life," she said in a higher-pitched tone than usual. "By my troth, I do not know what to say to you. An apology seems too small. Forbye, I don't think I *am* sorry. I . . . I am too angry!"

"Then I shall leave you to recover your temper," he said. "My people will have supper ready in an hour or so. When they do, I will bring yours to you."

Ignoring her open-mouthed astonishment and stepping over the stool as he turned, he left the room and shut the heavy door behind him.

On the landing, he paused to lock the door, snapping the two iron hooks—one high on the frame, one low—into the iron rings he'd screwed into the door.

Stunned by Maxwell's abrupt departure, Mairi stared at the closed door for a long moment before she heard metallic noises on the other side, followed by rapid footsteps fading down the stairs to silence.

Her suddenly unpredictable temper stirring again, she crossed the room in swift, angry strides and lifted the latch. The door refused to budge.

The villain had locked her in!

Shutting her eyes and drawing a breath, she warned herself that losing one's temper brought no good, and wondered at herself for losing hers with him.

Even Fiona was no longer able to stir her to such fury. And she had long ago learned to take Phaeline in stride, accepting her authority and reacting with submissive calm even to her complaining and her scolds.

Turning from the door, Mairi picked up the stool and carried it back to where she had found it. Then, realizing that light was fast fading in the chamber, she decided it would be only sensible to take stock of its contents.

Her first and most urgent need was a night jar, and she found one near the curtained bed. Feeling better after she had relieved herself, she moved to the kists he had indicated and opened the first.

The fabrics inside were wonderful, silks and satins, soft cambric shifts and woolen scarves and gloves, even stockings, shoes, and slippers. Removing the stout hide boots she had put on to walk to the river, she soon found that the footwear was all a little larger than she normally wore, but not uncomfortably so.

Finding a hairbrush and comb, she took off her veil and the net she wore under it. Then, before unbraiding her plaits, she went to the washstand and poured water from the ewer to wash her face and hands. Next, collecting her cloak from the settle, she found a hook for it on the wall by the door.

Her first impulse had been to disdain the use of anything *he* had provided. But as she picked up the brush to deal with her untidy hair, she recalled that she had on her least favorite kirtle. She had chosen it on purpose for her walk to the river.

Now, she looked ruefully down at its rumpled, faded blue skirt.

The villain was bringing supper to her. She would be alone with him again, because although he plainly had servants—she had seen a number of them in the kitchen— he just as plainly did not mean to provide anyone for her.

"Faith," she muttered. "He cannot give me a woman even to help me dress. What self-respecting woman would agree to help him keep me captive?"

She often conferred with herself so. In a situation that promised long periods of undesired solitude, however, it brought home to her just how alone she was and how far from home.

At the thought, unexpected tears welled in her eyes. When one spilled down her cheek, she dashed it away. She would not let anything the man did upset her so easily. She would find a way instead to defeat him.

"I must."

Believing he would expect further defiance, she imagined Fiona in her place and knew that her sister would try to scream the tower down. She would surely defy Robert Maxwell at every turn until she had exhausted herself.

In fairness to Fiona, her tactics often worked. But they did not suit Mairi.

She wondered if coaxing would persuade Maxwell to free her but decided he was unlikely to succumb to such a strategy. She also doubted that she could bring herself to coax him. She certainly would not flutter her eyelashes at him the way Fiona fluttered hers at their father whenever she was being outrageous.

Mairi's thoughts continued along these lines as she sorted through the items in the two large kists. But no plan presented itself. Resigning herself for at least the one night to putting up with things as they were, she shook out a fresh cambric shift, a green woolen underskirt, and a tunic of deliciously soft rose-pink velvet.

Stripping off the clothes she had worn all day, still damp from their hours on the water, she noted again the cold breeze wafting more intensively now through the open window. Unwilling to shut out what little light remained by closing the shutter, she dressed quickly and slipped her feet into a pair of matching rose-silk slippers with ribbon ties. The tunic fit well enough, but the skirt was much too long.

Having seen a small covered basket with scissors, needles, and threads for mending in one of the kists, she might have hemmed it but decided to do so later and take care in the meantime not to trip. Only as she clasped her own silver-linked girdle over the gown and adjusted its position at her hips did she realize that she still had the keys to the Annan House pantry and buttery attached to it.

Biting her lip at the mental image that arose of Phaeline's likely reaction to their loss, Mairi decided her stepmother would curse her absence more sincerely than she might have before that discovery.

However, finding the keys reminded her that the only thing in the kists that might occupy her for a time had been the mending basket. She wondered how she would keep from going mad with boredom if her captor kept her locked up for long.

Time crept then until she feared she might go mad before she got supper.

She stared out the window until the cliffs opposite hers vanished into dusky gray shadows. Hoping that there might be a moon visible through the other, still shuttered window, she went to it and felt for its latch hooks, muttering to herself when she discovered they were of heavy steel and fit tightly into steel eyes.

She got the lower hook out, whereupon the shutter seemed to tremble with relief as great as her own. The higher hook fit tighter, and she had to stand on the three-legged stool to get purchase. By putting the heel of her hand under the hook and shoving upward with all her strength, she felt it move at last. Her hand hurt, so she stopped to rub away the indentation the metal had pressed into it before she tried again, giving the hook a sharp upward jab.

The hook flew up, and the shutter flew open, bringing a gale in with it and striking her shoulder hard enough to knock her off balance. Jumping awkwardly back off the stool, she stepped on the hem of her too-long skirt and sat down hard just as the door opened from the landing.

Wind gusted through the room from the newly opened window, blowing the bed hangings as it dashed wildly about and through the other window.

"What the devil do you think you are doing?" Maxwell demanded.

She glowered at him from the floor. He stood there in the doorway and appeared to be holding a tray. She smelled warm mutton, so at least he ignored Lent. "I wanted more light and thought there might be a moon," she said. "One can hardly see in here. Why did you not at least bring a candle?"

"I did," he said. "Your windstorm blew it out as I opened the door."

"Oh." She moved to stand up and trod on her hem again but managed, awkwardly, to get to her feet.

Meantime, he set the tray on the floor and hurried to slam and latch the shutter, evicting the gale. "Don't open this one without first closing the other," he said. "The wind nearly always blows from the west or southwest here, so the window overlooking the bay gets only a breeze. This one can bring in a tempest."

"You said only that it provided a fine view," she reminded him.

"So I did, but 'tis wiser to wait for a calm day to enjoy it. Wait until we have a storm, though. This wind is nowt to what you'll see—aye, and hear—then."

"I don't like storms, so I trust I'll be long gone by then," she said, lifting her skirts so she would not trip. The smell of roast mutton was making her mouth water.

"Did you hurt yourself when you fell?" he asked as he finished hooking the shutter back into place.

"Just my pride because you came in," she said. "I'm sorry you saw that, but thank you for bringing supper. Have you candles here—or flint, come to that?"

"I have both, aye. But let me get that tray up off— Here you!" he exclaimed, leaping with unexpected speed toward the still open doorway.

Mairi saw a flash of movement as a small shadow dashed through the doorway and no doubt on down the stairs.

"Mercy, was that a rat?"

"Nay, just a small feline thief," he said as he shut the door. "I think it may have snagged some of our food."

"*Our* food?"

"I want to share your meal if you've no objection." He moved to set the tray on the settle before he turned and added, "If my presence will spoil it for you, you have only to say so and I'll leave you in peace."

"Prithee, do not suggest peace to me just now," she begged. "I have been yearning for a task to occupy my hands and keep my mind from dwelling on my situation. In troth, I am more likely to die of boredom than to object to sharing a meal. Otherwise, I'd point out the extreme impropriety of your even being in my bedchamber. At this point, though, it seems priggish to quibble over such a thing."

"Your virtue is in no danger from me, my lady," he said with earnestness she had not heard from him before. "I promise you I will not harm you any more than I have already done by abducting you."

"Good sakes, you stole my reputation with that act alone," she snapped. "So do *not* tell me again that you will not harm me. I am grateful to know that I need not fear rape. But others will *never* believe that you didn't . . . That is, once my abduction becomes known . . ." She spread her hands, letting him fill in the rest for himself.

"Calm your fidgets, lass," he said. "When you inherit your father's wealth, if not long before then, you will have offers aplenty."

The breath caught in her throat, and she stared at him in horror as, with a scratch of flint and a glow of tinder, the candle he held caught flame.

Hearing Lady Mairi's quick intake of breath, Rob looked up to see horror on her beautiful, candlelit face. "What is it?" he asked. "What have I said?"

"They mean to kill him, don't they?" she said.

"Kill who?"

"Whom," she said, but as though her thoughts were elsewhere. "My father, of course. I can hardly say you did not warn us that there would be trouble, but—"

"Don't be a fool," he snapped. "And *don't* correct my grammar."

Her blush visible even in the candle's glow, she grimaced and said, "I fear I responded as automatically as I would have with my sister." Then, without actually apologizing for correcting him, she said, "Why is it foolish to believe that? You say I will inherit his wealth. And you did warn him that the sheriff would seize—"

Impatiently, he said as he picked up a gate-leg table near the wall, "I said the sheriff has the power to seize your estates, not that he would do so immediately."

"Prithee, do stop interrupting me."

"Was that not what you were going to say?"

"It was, aye, but—"

"Then I need not listen to the whole before replying." He set the small table down in front of the settle and began to put up its leaves.

"You cannot possibly know what I was about to say just *then*! But you interrupted me again. In any event—"

"It was rude. Aye, I ken that fine. And for the rudeness I will apologize. But I do know what you were going to say both times."

"What, then?"

"The same thing, that interrupting you was unmannerly.

So, now that we have that sorted out," he went on without waiting for her to reply, "shall we eat our supper—what that wee villain has left us of it?"

"It didn't look large enough to be a cat," she said. "How old is it?"

"Just weaned, if I understood my grandmother . . . or no, it was my nephew, or mayhap it was Gibby who told me its mother had stopped feeding her kits."

"Who is Gibby?"

"A lad of nine or ten who is another acquisition from my grandmother," he said as he moved the tray from the settle to the table.

"Does your grandmother live here, then?"

"Nay, she lives much of the year with my brother and his family, and the rest with her son in Glasgow. Trailinghail was part of her tocher when she married my grandfather, Lord Kelso. He left it to me when he died about four years ago."

"Was it not still hers if it was part of her portion?"

"Nay, lass, the lands usually become the husband's to dispose unless the wife bears a title in her own right, as you will one day."

"My future is not as certain as you make it sound," she said with a sigh.

"I know, aye, but from what I hear, 'tis likely," he said, lighting a second and third candle from the first and placing them all on the table. He liked to see what he was eating when he could. "Sit down, lass, here on the settle."

She hesitated, and he knew without her saying so that she did not want to sit beside him. "I'll draw up yon stool for myself," he said.

Catching her lower lip between her teeth and shooting him a rueful look, she said, "You do see what is in my mind. But I do *not* think I should apologize for it."

"Nay, you owe me no apologies. The boot is on the other foot."

"Sakes, I hope you don't mean to pretend that you are sorry for abducting me," she said scornfully. "I shan't believe a word of it if you do."

"What I did was necessary," he said. "That is not to deny, however, that I regret having to take such a course."

"Now *you* are quibbling."

"Aye, perhaps," he admitted, thinking as he moved the stool to the table that the way her eyes sparkled in the candlelight and reflected the flames made her look magical, the way a child might imagine a good witch or a fairy queen to look.

"Why do you stare at me like that? Have I got something on my face?"

He chuckled. "Nay, I was just admiring the way your eyes shoot sparks even when your voice sounds as soothing as water trickling over stones."

"Very pretty speech for a villainous rogue, sir," she said. "Do not think you will charm me again so easily."

"Are you saying that I have charmed you before?"

Ignoring that gambit without hesitation, she said, "What you did today was shameful, and I have yet to hear any good reason for it. Nor do you answer my questions. Are you going to serve me some of that mutton?"

He proceeded to do so, placing three generous slices on a wooden trencher for her, along with a cold chicken leg. As he set the plate of raspberry tarts where she could help herself, he was glad to see her take her eating knife from its narrow sheath on her girdle, and to see that the knife was the common lady's implement.

He would not have wanted to trust her with his dirk and had no doubt that he would anger her again if he suggested she eat with her fingers.

"Do you want some barley water?" he asked, hefting the jug.

"I do, aye," she said.

"What question have I failed to answer?" he asked as he filled both goblets.

"For one thing, you have not yet explained why you abducted me, although I have asked you more than once."

"I did it in the hope of avoiding clan war and the considerable number of deaths that would result from one," he said.

"You did say 'twas to avoid much bloodshed. That sounded ridiculous."

"You called it 'noble intent,' " he said.

"I expect I did not mean that," she said.

"It is not noble, but it *is* practical," he said. "I thought long before I decided it might work. You know that my brother sent me to Dunwythie Mains to persuade your father to submit to his authority. Sithee, he kens fine that if your father submits, others will emulate him just as they do now in his refusal."

Her mouth opened but shut again firmly. She reached for her goblet.

"What?" he asked.

"'Tis naught we need discuss now," she said. "By 'submitting,' you mean, do you not, that the sheriff wants my father to agree to let him collect all the gelt that Annandale owes to the Crown, rather than continuing in our usual way?"

"That, aye, and some other things," he said. "It is all rather complicated."

"I think it is simple," she said in much the same casual tone as his. "Your brother wants to acquire more power and thinks to do so at my father's expense. That brings me to the second question you have not answered."

"What is it?"

"You've not actually said that your brother does *not* mean to kill my father."

Words leaped to his tongue to deny it forcefully. But the intent way she watched him made him leave the words unspoken. He thought, then said frankly, "I cannot swear to what is in another man's mind, especially my brother's. I know only that he is angry because your father and the others refuse to bow to his authority. I will say, though, that he'd be a damned fool to kill Dunwythie."

"Why?" she asked as she finally took a sip of her barley water.

"Because to do so *would* start a war between the Maxwells and the Annandale clans. And it is not Alex's place as Sheriff of Dumfries to start clan wars. Nor is it his place as a chieftain of Clan Maxwell to do such a daft thing."

"Might there be any other powerful Maxwell who would wish to do so?"

"Nay, for that could only mean our chief, Maxwell of Caerlaverock. He prefers court life in Stirling or a peaceful existence at his house near Glasgow to greater exertion. I'd wager he expects Alex to *keep* the peace, not to break it."

Niggling doubt stirred even as he said it. Maxwell of Caerlaverock still called himself so despite years since the castle's ruin and his lack of success in stirring anyone else to aid in rebuilding it. He might rejoice at Alex's determination to control all of Dumfriesshire—especially if Alex did not ask for his assistance and presented him afterward with the "chief's share" of the income.

"You do not look as if you believe your own words, Robert Maxwell," Mairi said, eyeing him narrowly.

"You might find it more convenient to call me Rob," he suggested.

"You do make a good argument against assassinating my father," she said, clearly ignoring his suggestion. "However, I do not believe that your brother has considered that argument, or he would not be threatening to seize our lands. He did issue such a threat, did he not? It was not of your own devising?"

"Nay, it was not," he said. "But Alex believes simply knowing that he *can* seize them will bring your father and the others into line."

"Then he does not know them," she said tartly, pushing her trencher away. "Heed me well, sir. I can see that you hope to persuade my father by holding me prisoner until he submits to the Maxwell demands. But such tactics will persuade him of naught but Maxwell perfidy, and perfidy he will fight to his last breath."

"Nay, lass, you underrate your worth to him. Sakes, you *must* be more important to him than this defiance of proper authority."

"How easily you claim proper authority," she said, her anger clear again. "Maxwell authority *must* be proper, must it not? Dunwythie authority, which I'd remind you has held sway in Annandale for centuries, is as naught to you!"

"You would be wise to refrain from taking such a discourteous tone with me," he said, his own temper threatening to ignite. Not that he was angry with her. She just seemed to have a knack for arousing his more volatile emotions.

When she stood, it took every effort for him to remain as he was.

Her chin jutted. Her icy expression challenged him.

"Sit down, lass. You have not finished your supper."

"I have, aye," she said. "As have you. I am tired after today's adventures and do not want to debate further with you now. We are unlikely to agree, so I would bid you goodnight. Faith, though, if you can sleep after all you have done, you are a greater villain than you have yet shown yourself to be."

"By the Rood, woman, you will not talk so to me!" he exclaimed, coming to his feet so quickly that he rocked the table. Hastily catching and righting it before its contents could crash to the floor, he looked up to see that although her expression was no less chilly and she had hooded her eyes, they had not quite shut.

Before they did, he detected the glimmer of a twinkle.

Her lips pressed harder together.

Although he had come to his feet with a strong urge to shake her and tell her exactly what he thought of such impertinence, and though he still wanted to catch hold of her, he knew his reason was an entirely different one now.

Staring at her lips, waiting for them to soften, he felt himself stir, and he stirred again when her lips parted slightly.

Collecting his wits and naming himself every inch the villain she had called him, he said in a more controlled voice, "I'll not burden you further tonight with my presence, my lady. I will bring food to break your fast in the morning, though. Mayhap we can talk more then. For now, I *will* bid you goodnight."

"I shall need someone to help me dress," she said, her own words carefully measured. "Also, I *must* have some task or other to pass the hours."

"I'll help with whatever you need," he said, wondering what tasks existed that might keep her amused for more than an hour. He could always find something to do, but women's interests were none of his. Still, he'd have to think of something.

He realized she had said something while he was pondering what to provide for her. But her words had flowed past without penetrating. "What did you say?"

"Faith, you are standing right there! How could you not hear me?"

"I was thinking."

"By heaven, can you not think and listen at the same time? I said that while you must certainly find tasks I can do, I don't *want* you to help me dress. Surely, there must be a maidservant or someone's wife who could aid me."

He thought of Fin Walters's wife, Dora, a most capable woman and loyal. But she was less likely than most of his people to turn a blind eye to holding a lass against her will. He could trust his men to keep silent. But, although he had brought her in through the sea entrance, word of her presence at Trailinghail would spread.

He would need an explanation to give out. And none would survive long if she refused to agree to support it. But then he would be asking her to lie, and he would not do that even if he thought she might agree.

"Well?" she said, tapping her foot.

Her impatience made it easy for him to sound stern again. "We have said enough tonight. If you still wish it, we can discuss this more tomorrow."

"By heaven, we will talk of it now!"

"Nay, we will not!"

"I say we will!" She reached for the trencher, still laden with uneaten food.

"Do *not* touch that unless you want to start something that *I* will finish."

She froze with her hand hovering uncertainly above the trencher and glared at him. Then, with a sigh, she lowered her hand and looked rueful.

"I do not suppose you will believe me when I tell you that I had never thrown anything at anyone before meeting you."

"You are right," he said curtly. "I *don't* believe it."

With that, he turned toward the door, opened it, and took a long step out.

The little cat, poised to dart in, ruined the dignity of his grand exit when he had to stoop with startled swiftness to scoop it up before it could shoot past him.

Shutting the door with a snap, he lifted the first hook into place just as something crashed against the other side of the door and then to the floor.

Grinning, he set the kitten on his shoulder and went downstairs to his bedchamber. But his improved state of mind was short-lived.

He had long prided himself on his ability to plan his actions. But in this event, he had clearly failed to consider a number of things. Not least of them was what he should do if he came to like his captive and to feel as if abducting her might have been the greatest mistake he had ever made.

The lass was right about one thing. He would not sleep well.

*Chapter 8*_____

Mairi stared at the mess of cold, fatty mutton slices, bread, and raspberries on the floor, wondering what demon had possessed her to heave the trencher at him.

From the moment the devilish man had brought her into his tower, she had behaved in a manner most unlike her usual self.

She was not, by nature, an impulsive woman.

Staring at the mess, she sighed, wishing she were one who could just leave it all where it was. But she was not.

It had been such a futile act, too.

"I'd have done better to have flung it in his face," she muttered, then smiled at the thought. To her astonishment, she found herself wondering what he would have done if she *had* flung it when the temptation had first struck her.

Dangerous musing, she decided. To taunt or challenge a man so much larger and stronger than she was would clearly indicate that she had lost her senses. In some ways she thought she had. What else could explain this recurring desire of hers to throw things at someone most people would believe she ought to fear?

The plain fact was that although Robert Maxwell did not terrify her, he could easily enrage her. Rage certainly explained throwing the stool. His outrageous hope that she might find her prison "comfortable" had deserved such a response.

However, heaving the trencher at him had been no more than a simple, perhaps even childish, impulse born of frustration and unexpected opportunity.

He had been leaving the room. She could not.

Thanks to his so-provocative declaration of disbelief in the *fact* that she had never thrown anything before, her hand was still touching the trencher when he suddenly bent over as he passed through the doorway. Such a tempting presentation of his backside just then had made throwing the trencher at it simply irresistible.

Only by the worst luck had he pulled the door shut just when he had. She wondered as she took the towel from the washstand just *why* he had bent over.

There being no way to ask him before morning, she set about clearing up the mess she had made. The food on the floor was only part of the problem, since he had gone away without taking the other things he had brought on the tray. They were still on the table, including the pitcher and the goblets of barley water.

Deciding to leave them on the table since she had no idea what else to do with them short of hurling them into the sea from her window, she went to close the still open shutter in case it rained during the night.

At the window, however, she saw that she need not worry about rain. The wind had dropped, and the sky was a blanket of stars. The window was wide enough for her to put her head and shoulders out, so she did. If she had to remain a prisoner, at least parts of her could pretend for a time that she was free.

Smiling again at the odd routes her thoughts had been taking, she breathed deeply of the cold night air, savored the starlight for a while, then straightened and went to prepare for bed. Although she missed having a maidservant to aid her, she enjoyed being able to think in silence as she took off the tunic and underskirt.

A candlestand stood near the head of the curtained bed. So, after blowing out two of the candles he had lit, she placed the third carefully on the stand and opened the bed curtain. Soft warmth engulfed her.

The bed was larger than what she was accustomed to, and much more luxurious. Pressing down on it, she realized that it boasted more than one featherbed and a thick quilt. One quilt was all she ever used as a cover at home except in deepest winter when a second, wool coverlet customarily came into use.

The pillows were many and plump, and she soon found explanation of the warmth, in the stone wall at the back of the bed. Clearly, the wall was the same as the fireplace walls in the hall and kitchen, and their warmth spread upward.

She was glad she did not have to close the curtain to keep warm. She was prisoner enough without shutting herself in. The shutter stayed open, too. The only visitor that might enter would be a moth or an eagle. Neither would worry her.

Stretching out atop plush softness and against down-soft pillows, with linen sheet and quilt drawn to her chin, she suddenly felt emotionally drained. Taking herself firmly in hand, she decided that she had to consider carefully all that she had learned about her captor and try to think of how she could protect herself.

The next thing she knew, sounds at her door heralded a visitor.

Startled awake, eyes open wide, she saw morning sunlight spilling through the unshuttered window in a golden path across the floor. It revealed a few shiny spots from mutton fat that she had missed in cleaning up the night before.

The door opened, and a flash of orange and white briefly diverted her attention before she saw that her nemesis had returned.

～

Rob paused in the doorway when he saw that the table still contained the remnants of their supper. He had forgotten all about them and had simply ordered another tray of food to take up to her ladyship after he had broken his fast.

As he had clearly startled her, he apologized, adding, "I thought you would be up long since, lass. Also, I fear I never spared our leavings a thought last night. Too accustomed to having others clean up after me, I expect. But I ought to have sent someone up or taken away the remains myself."

She was looking beyond him.

He frowned, thinking she meant to offer him only silence again.

Then she looked at him, and her eyes twinkled. She showed not the least embarrassment to be still abed or for him to see her there.

"Apparently, you did bring a helper along to clear the

mess away," she said. "But I fear it may make itself sick if it eats too much."

Glancing over his shoulder to see the kitten on the table, he muttered an oath and hurried over, setting the tray on the settle as he had before.

The kitten, wolfing food as fast as it could, shot him a quick upward look without moving its head and then ignored him to concentrate on its breakfast.

When he grabbed it, it hissed at him and tried to wriggle back to the food.

Carrying the squirming, angry little creature to the bed, he handed it to her, saying, "Here, hold on to him until I can get those things cleared away. Then the two of us will leave you to dress and break your fast."

She took the kitten without a blink.

As Rob turned away, he said, "Take care, the wee devil bites."

"Nay, then, you malign him," she said in a cooing voice, clearly for the cat's benefit. "You're a princely fellow, aren't you," she went on. "And so soft. I don't believe you've ever bitten *any*one who did not deserve it. What's his name?"

"I call him 'cat.' Gibby calls him 'the wee terror.' And he does bite, so do not trust that innocent look."

A rhythmic rumbling sound reached his ears just then and he turned toward the bed to see that she had leaned back against the pillows with the little cat snuggled on her chest. It had its paws tucked under its chin and was gazing at her adoringly, purring loudly as she gently stroked its head with two slim fingers.

She smiled at Rob then so warmly that he felt something inside him melt.

Quietly, she said, "May he stay with me?"

"If he will, aye," Rob said, turning back to his task with a sudden wish that they had met under other circumstances and that she was not Dunwythie's daughter.

Calling himself a fool again, he swept the things from the night before onto the first tray and carried it to the landing. Then, wiping off the table as well as he could with a towel she had clearly used to clean up the food she had thrown at him, he carried the towel to the landing and dropped it atop the things on the tray.

Returning, he set the new tray of food on the table. "I brought bread and ale, barley porridge, some milk, and two apples," he said. "I don't know what you usually eat for breakfast, but if you will tell me, I'll see to providing it for you."

"You are too kind, sir," she said.

He gave her a look. "Just be glad you cleaned up what you threw at me last night, or you would learn that I am not kind at all. Not that you did much better with your cleaning than I did with that table," he added. "I nearly slipped on a greasy spot when I came in."

"It would have served you right if you had," she cooed. "A good thump on the head might knock some sense into you."

She did not look at him as she spoke, and he grinned at the picture she made, murmuring impertinent things to him in the soft, gentle tone she used with the little cat, which was still purring contentedly. As well it might, tucked snugly between those tantalizing breasts as it was.

She was still looking at the kitten, still stroking it, and still ignoring Rob.

"Lass."

She looked up, eyebrows raised.

"It is not wise when you are in someone else's power to provoke him."

"Is it not?" She frowned. "I think it is more unwise to treat me as *you* have, Robert Maxwell. Just what do you mean to do with me? Am I simply to remain in this chamber until you have got whatever you expect to get by keeping me? How long do you expect *that* to take?"

"That must depend on your father," he said.

"Then it will be forever," she retorted. The kitten stirred, and she softened her tone to add, "Believe me, sir, my father is *not* a man who submits to threats. He is a peaceable man and a good one, but he can be as stubborn as anyone I know. A threat will just anger him and make him go contrary to whatever you demand."

"That must be a load of blethers," Rob said. "No man would risk injury to his firstborn child, certainly not to such a daughter as *you* are to him. You underrate yourself a-purpose, I think, to dissuade me."

"I would dissuade you if I could," she admitted. "Faith, but I'd strike you down flat if I could, for you have made me angrier in one day than anyone else has *ever* made me. I had thought myself unable to achieve such behavior as you have stirred me to, and with so little effort! Moreover, you ruined the first true freedom I've had since my family returned to Annan House from Dunwythie Mains."

"Are you not free to do as you please at Annan House?"

"Not since you Maxwells threatened to take our land. My stepmother worries that at any moment an army will engulf us. Naught will persuade her that we would get due warning first. Your having so easily snatched me away will only increase her concerns," she added bitterly.

"'Tis always painful to learn that those in authority over us are right in what they say, is it not?" he said with a reminiscent smile.

Instead of the quick retort he expected, she looked at him for a long moment. Then she said, "So, you have had similar experience, have you?"

"Aye, too much of it," he said. "To hear my brother—"

"Who is that lady, and why are ye in her chamber whilst she's still abed? I'm thinking Herself would no approve o' *that*."

Whirling on Gibby, who stood in the doorway, eyeing him with strong disapproval, Rob snapped, "Who the devil said you could come up here?"

"Nae one did," the boy retorted, still eyeing him askance. "I were a-looking for ye, and when ye were no in your chamber, I came out again and heard ye talking. So I came a-looking up here. Shall I take this tray below for ye?"

"Aye, do that," Rob said. "Then wait for me downstairs."

"But who is that lady?" Gib asked, swinging an arm around to point at her. "And— Coo, would ye look at that now? That wee terror's no a-biting her!"

In fact, the kitten, still purring, had stretched out with its head still resting between her breasts. It rolled onto its back then, fore and aft legs extending in a long stretch, and she stroked its furry white stomach. The damned cat seemed almost to be taunting Rob, saying, "Just look at me now, will you, chappie?"

"You must be Gibby," the lass said to the boy with a smile.

"Aye, and ye must be a witch," Gib said, clearly awe-struck. "Ye ken me name wi' nae one telling ye, and ye've cast a spell on that wee terror."

"I am not a witch," she said. "I know your name because the laird told me you call the kitten a wee terror. Sithee, he is no such thing if you treat him kindly."

"I dinna treat him at all," Gib said firmly. "I dinna hold wi' cats, 'specially cats which would rather than nowt eat me, like that one. Ye take care, me lady."

"And you take yourself off now with that tray, Gib," Rob told him.

"Ye didna tell me her name. I should ken how to call her, should I no?"

The lady Mairi looked at Rob, challenging him to lie.

"You need know only to address her as 'my lady,'" Rob told him sternly. "Also, you are not to talk *about* her to anyone else unless you want to explain your loose tongue to me when I learn that you've been gabbling, as I will."

Meeting that look, Gibby hesitated. Then he said, "What if Herself should ask when *she* comes? I dinna lie to Herself, and nor should ye lie to her neither."

"I don't," Rob said curtly. "Now, be off with you."

The boy offered no further argument but picked up the tray and clattered off down the stairway with it.

Rob stared at the empty doorway, lost in thought of what consequences might result now from the lad's having seen his prisoner.

"Who is Herself?"

"My grandmother," he said, turning slowly toward her.

"The one whose property this tower was?"

"Since you would have it so, aye, that one. She is properly Arabella Carlyle, Lady Kelso. My Maxwell grandmother died before I was born."

"*Is* she coming here?"

"I expect you mean the one who still lives," he said.

"Aye," she said, but she smiled, saying it. "Now we are even where proper grammar is concerned, sir. The lad did suggest she would be coming."

And would likely snatch him baldheaded, Rob mused, the minute she learned he was holding a noblewoman captive at Trailinghail.

Suppressing that thought, he said, "She did suggest that she might visit. That was when she gave me the kitten to look after, and the laddie. She often says she will come, but she has not seen Trailinghail since I inherited the place. I warrant she fears I will have changed it too much for her to enjoy it."

"Have you?"

"Nay, I have tried to do what I think she will like," he said. "I had happy visits here as a boy. It provided a welcome escape for me now and now."

"Did you need an escape?"

He shrugged. "I expect most lads do from time to time."

"I would have liked a place to escape to," she said with a sigh.

To which, without thinking, he said, "Aye, well, now you have one."

⁓

Mairi stared at him, finding it hard to believe he would think his abducting her to Trailinghail, as he called the place, could be anything like his having visited his grandparents there as a boy.

Meeting her gaze, he looked rueful again. "I ken fine that it is not the same thing, lass, and I did mean what I said last night about making you comfortable here. I see, too, that I cannot keep you locked up until your father acts. But the last thing I want is for a great scandal to spread through the dales. I thought bringing you here would prevent that, as isolated as the place is. My people are discreet enough, but the more who know about you, the greater the risk grows. I hope your father submits quickly when he learns that he must."

"He will not act soon," she said. "He has gone to the north end of the dale and did not expect to be back at Annan House for at least a sennight."

"When did he leave?"

"A few days ago."

"How many days, lass? Do not pretend you cannot count them."

"Three, then, as of yesterday, so four now. But he is often away longer than he expects to be on such journeys."

"I'll wait," he said. "The risk of spreading gossip from here remains small, I think. In any event, I am in no great hurry."

"Faith, I thought 'twas a matter of life and death," she said.

"It will be, aye," he said. "But I'm thinking Alex will do nowt till after Easter. He won't want to offend religious folks by starting a war during Lent."

"But I must be home *before* Easter!" she exclaimed. "We are to visit my cousin Jenny and Sir Hugh Douglas at Thornhill for the holy day and go to kirk with them on Easter Sunday."

"Then we must see that this is all over by then," he said.

"But are you sure your brother will wait? Is *he* so religious?"

He shrugged. "No more than most Borderers, I expect, but Alex does care about what others think. And, to many people, Lent is most holy—no time for violence. Sakes, we are all religious when it is expedient or when we fear we are about to die," he added. "Nearly all Borderers go to kirk to celebrate Christ's birth and rising. All say the grace before meat. Some even have their own chaplains."

Mairi's father had a chaplain who said the grace. And Annan town had a kirk where her family went most Sundays. But like the Borderers he described, Lord Dunwythie paid heed to little beyond his own domain. The Pope in Rome and his grace the King in Stirling were not close enough at hand to trouble him.

Remembering the kirk spire she had seen from the boat some distance along the cliffs north of the tower, and closer to the town of Kirkcudbright, Mairi wondered if he would take her there if she pretended to be pious. But the more she talked with him, the clearer it became that he believed he was doing what he must. If so, he would be most unlikely to let her sway him from his course.

"Do you truly care about my comfort?" she asked him, still stroking the kitten's soft, furry belly and enjoying its loud purr. Its eyes were slitted, its breathing slow and even, its trust in her clear.

"I have said that I care," he said. "I expect, however, that you just hope to persuade me to let you do something I won't want you to do."

"I *cannot* stay in this chamber without going mad, sir. Prithee, believe that. I think that my behavior last night was no more than a reaction to losing what little freedom I had. You professed to disbelieve me, but I swear to you, I had never flung anything at anyone, not even a pillow, before I hurled that stool at you."

His eyes gleamed—with humor, she hoped, although she could not be sure.

As the thought formed, she felt vulnerable and much

too exposed to him. Until that moment, she had felt nothing but flashes of anger. He might have been her brother, had she had one, for all the discomfiture she had felt in his presence.

The gleam in his eye vanished as swiftly as it had come, and he said matter-of-factly, "What is it, lass? What would you have me do for you?"

Still strongly aware that she wore only her borrowed shift and that the quilt had slipped to reveal the upper halves of her breasts—but aware, too, that her sudden tension had affected the kitten—she drew a breath and tried to relax again.

He took a step toward her, increasing the sensation tenfold.

Whatever words she had meant to say stuck to her tongue. Her body tingled its awareness of him.

"Go away," she said. "I want to dress and break my fast."

"But I want to know—"

"*Go!*"

Stopping still, he cocked his head, studying her.

The little cat leaped to its feet on her chest. When he took another step toward her, its eyes slitted again and its back went up. But it did not hiss or spit.

"You may leave my protector," she said, her amusement easing her tension.

"I will, aye," he said, and left without another word.

She heard the solid metal clinks that announced the locking of her door, and grimaced at the sound. Although she felt relief at his departure, she looked forward to his return—*after* she had dressed.

∽

Rob was not sure what had just happened. He frequently experienced odd feelings when he was with Mairi, similar to what he sometimes felt on the water with lightning in the air. These sensations, now that he gave them thought, had other traits in common with elemental wonders.

When he was with her they ebbed and flowed like the tides. They would strike when he least expected them. And when one was upon him, the slightest change in her expression could warm him or send warning tension through him.

He had noticed the phenomenon first at Dunwythie Mains in the way she had filled his senses to the exclusion of nearly everything else around them at the time. So strongly had her very presence struck him that he had known in an instant what an astonishing effect she must have on other men.

He still had no doubt that Dunwythie would react as he'd predicted as soon as his lordship learned of her disappearance.

Watching her stroke the kitten, bewitching the wee devil, he had felt bewitched himself. He could scarcely take his eyes from her slender, stroking fingers. He could feel her touch, and at one point, he had experienced a distinct twinge of jealousy toward the damned cat.

Her smile had the power to bewitch, too. Sakes, between watching her with the cat and listening to her cooing voice, he had nearly forgotten she was his captive. Then, when she had so wistfully said she would have liked to escape to some refuge as he had escaped to Trailinghail, he had replied like a right dafty.

Then she declared again that although she had hurled a stool at him the previous night, she had never done such a thing before. As he realized that he believed her, the strange connection had strengthened so much that he could not look away from her. It felt as if some magical power had possessed them both.

The kitten had diverted him by putting a forepaw on the billowing softness of one bare breast that peeked above the quilt. When she had snapped at Rob to go and the kitten had leaped up, ready to defend her, he had not known what to say.

He was glad now to leave the little brute with her. Only the clanking of the iron hooks as he pulled the door shut reminded him to lock it.

Not that he could keep her locked up indefinitely. To have imagined doing so while he'd formed his plans was one thing, reality quite another.

He had known that much when she had asked the evening before how he expected her to occupy her time.

His imagination presented him with an image of himself in her place. What the devil would *he* do to keep from going mad? At least she could hem the skirt that had tripped her, and other clothes in the kists. But what then?

Recalling the fright her fall had given him, he told himself she was lucky he had not picked her up and shaken her. Attending to the shutter had kept him from losing his temper, but he hoped she would attend quickly to shortening those skirts. He had known his grandmother was taller. He had not realized by how much.

Still, he could not imagine himself sewing, let alone doing so for hours on end. Even for a woman, it must be a most tedious occupation.

He decided he would give her time to dress and break her fast. Then he would return and discuss the problem with her. She was astonishingly easy to talk to, and clearly found it easy enough to talk to him—even to throw things at him.

Whatever the cause of the latter tendency, though, she would have to give it up before it became a habit. No man would find such behavior amusing for long.

He entered the great hall just as Gibby threw a stick across the chamber for one of the dogs to fetch. As the retriever dashed after it, skidding on thresh near the fireplace and nearly sending a pile of it into the flames, Rob said, "Gib, come here."

Gibby approached, eyeing him warily. "D'ye want I should do summat for ye, laird?" he asked.

"I do," Rob said. "I want you to take that beast outside if you are going to throw sticks for it. And if you see Fin Walters, you may tell him I want to see him when he has a few moments to talk. I'm going to the stable."

"Aye, sure, I'll find him." Grinning and shouting for the dog to bring the stick, he dashed with it to the stairway and down.

Rob followed at his normal pace, letting his thoughts drift as they would until he decided what he would do.

His steward found him in the stable, discussing a suggestion from the tacksman that they order new harness straps from the currier in Kirkcudbright.

"'Tis a good notion," Rob said, nodding. "Talk it over with Walters, and unless he objects . . . Ah, here you are now, Fin. The lad here says we need some new tack, so decide how much and order it. But I want a word with you first."

Walters nodded at the beaming tacksman as Rob added, "We'll go outside." When they were beyond earshot of anyone else, he said, "Sakes, don't look as if I'm going to bite you. I ken fine that you knew about the tack. However, I do have a problem, and I think you're the man to aid me. First, how is our Gibby getting on?"

"He's a good lad, laird. Me Dora fair dotes on him, so I have to take a stern tone now and now, with one or the other. But he suits us well, that lad does."

"Good. I'd hate to be asking you for aught else if you were cursing me for handing that fountain of impudence to you."

"Sakes, sir, if he's been impudent—"

"Nay, just honest and saying what he thinks, so do nowt to change it. I can manage the lad with nobbut a look or a word."

"I'll warrant ye can, laird," the steward said with a twinkle.

"Now, who is being impudent?" Rob demanded. But when Walters just smiled, he said bluntly, "The problem is, I need a woman, Fin."

Eyebrows arcing upward, the steward said, "Sure, and ye dinna need help from me to find ye a willing one, laird."

"Not for me, for the lass I brought here yestereve."

Walters nodded. "I willna say I were no curious about that, sir, for I were. And I still am, come to that. What sort o' woman had ye in mind?"

"A good, well-mannered lass, someone like your wife's sister, Annie."

"Ye'd want Annie to be staying here? Nights, too?"

"Aye, but only whilst the lass stays with us," Rob said, choosing his words.

"I'll tell ye plain then, sir, that I dinna like the sound o' that. Nor will Dory. Annie's a good, obedient lass, but she's nobbut fifteen. I'd no want her serving a—"

"Nay, nay," Rob interjected hastily, realizing that his own choice of words had stirred Walters to think as he did. "Her ladyship is no bed wench of mine."

"Her *ladyship*! Beggin' your pardon, laird, but what *ha'* ye been up to?"

"Only what was necessary, and by my troth, I have not used her as you must think. But she has requested a maid-servant to see to her needs. Would Annie agree to that? Being your kinswoman would protect her whilst she's here, I should think."

"Aye, sure, and she'd do it, too, for she's been a-hoping ye'd wed soon and need a few maidser— But I be talking above me place, laird. Ye havena said ye'll be staying on here at Trailinghail. And if the lady will be here only a short time . . ."

"Only as long as necessary," Rob said. "But as I cannot say how long that is, I'd prefer that her presence not become a matter of local gossip."

"Our people ken fine to keep still tongues in their heads, and have done since the old laird and Herself was here, sir," Walters said. "Nowt has changed since, but we canna speak for villagers in Senwick and such places."

"I know," Rob said. "Also, the knacker Parland Dow will be along soon. He is a fine source of news from far and wide, but when he arrives, take good care that we do not hand him her ladyship's presence as fodder for his tittle-tattle."

Chapter 9

Mairi dressed quickly while the kitten, curled on one of the bed pillows, tracked her every move with its bright golden eyes.

"You look very comfortable," she said to it.

Its ears twitched encouragingly, but Mairi said no more, lacing herself into her own old blue kirtle, which she had draped over the kists the night before to air.

Thanks to sea air through the open window, the kirtle felt dampish. But it was no more so than clothes often felt at Annan House when one put them on.

Unbraiding her plaits, she brushed them out, then braided them into one long, thick plait over her shoulder before moving to the table to break her fast.

The porridge was warm, and she poured a little milk on it. When she sat on the settle to eat, the kitten jumped up beside her, looking hopeful.

"You should not beg for food," Mairi told it.

Unpersuaded, it continued to sit and stare at her.

Forcing herself to ignore it, she finished her porridge

and spread bramble jam on a bit of bread, deciding to save the apples for later.

As she moved to get up the kitten mewed softly, still hopeful.

"Very well, I expect you are hungry, too," she said. But she placed the nearly empty wooden porridge bowl on the floor.

The kitten, approving the arrangement, lapped happily for a time. Then, abruptly, it lifted its head and looked intently at the door.

Mairi heard hurrying footsteps on the stairs. Metal scraped against metal, the door opened, and Maxwell appeared at the threshold.

"Get your cloak," he said without preamble. "I'll take you to the ramparts for a splendid view. Then I want to talk."

Delighted—as she would have been with anyone who offered to take her out of the chamber—she got up to go with him. Remembering the uneven stone steps, she said, "I should put on my boots first. The shoes in yon kist are a bit large for me and lack soles thick enough for those stairs."

He nodded, and as she sat to put on her boots, she saw his gaze drift to the still lapping kitten. "I hope you did not let that beast eat *all* your porridge," he said.

"And what if I had?" she retorted with one slipper in hand, the other still on. "Are you now going to command my every move and decision?"

Rob understood from her choice of words that she had not given the kitten her porridge, but he could not help responding to her challenge. "I command all here," he said. "If I decide to command you, lass, be sure that I will."

"And do you hope to undo me by addressing me so improperly?"

"Sakes, lass—" He grinned then and shook his head. "Lady Mairi, the plain fact is that I do not spend much time with women I must address formally. So it is by habit that I call you so and not by any wish to demean you."

"Surely, you do not call your grandmother 'lass,' or your good-sisters," she said as she leaned against the bed to pull on one hide boot.

"Nay, I call my only good-sister 'Cassia' and my grandmother 'madam' or 'Gran.' " He smiled again at the thought of her ladyship's likely response to a less formal address. "If I may, I'll call you Mairi, but I hope you will forgive me when I forget, as I am sure I will. If I lose my temper—"

"Aye, sure, *that* would excuse all, would it not?"

Spreading his feet, he folded his arms across his chest and looked sternly at her. "Do you provoke me a-purpose, my lady?"

Looking rueful, she bit her lower lip, then attended to tying a boot before she met his gaze to say, "I think a demon possesses me at times, with you. I seem to say whatever comes into my head, and *that*—like hurling objects at people—is *not* my usual behavior."

"I used to think the same thing about myself at times," he said.

"That you were possessed?"

He chuckled. "Aye, perhaps. When my temper was up, I'd too often say whatever impertinence jumped to my tongue, as much as daring my brother to do whatever he would in response."

"Your *brother* would punish you?"

"Aye," he said more soberly, remembering. "Sithee, back-chatting Alex was always a mistake, because he was much older and bigger. But I'd do it anyway."

"Did you also dare to flout your parents' authority so?" she asked without looking up as she tied the second boot.

"They both died before I was seven, but I did try it on my grandparents the first time I visited them. That was a mistake. Are you ready now?" he asked, reaching to take her cloak from the hook by the door.

"Aye," she said. Turning to let him drape the cloak over her shoulders, she added, "How great a mistake was it, with your grandparents?"

"Great enough that my grandfather skelped me blue and my grandmother vowed to do worse if she ever heard me speak so insolently again to anyone."

"Mercy, what could she have done that was worse?"

He chuckled. "I never had the courage to find out."

She laughed then, and he felt an unexpected sense of accomplishment in having provoked her laughter. Her beautiful eyes were alight with it. As she threw back her head, the delicate skin of her slender throat seemed to invite a kiss.

Turning abruptly from that dangerous thought, he put a hand gently to her shoulder and urged her out of the room, nearly stepping into the wooden box of dirt he had set down there before opening the door.

"Oh, what a good notion!" she exclaimed when she saw the box. "I feared he might use the floor or even the bed. I meant to ask you what we should do."

"I hope he'll use the box," he said. "Cook set one out in the kitchen, and I think the wee devil has used it. But we can leave this door open for him now. I'll just set one of the kists by it to hold it open against the draft from yon window."

He did so, noting that the kitten had leaped onto the bed and looked as if it meant to stay there.

"That way," Rob said then, gesturing up the stairway.

Catching up her skirts—her own skirts, he noticed—she hurried ahead of him to the top, where she waited by the door to let him open it.

He held it for her to step out onto the flat roof of the tower. The parapet surrounding it was low enough that the wind off the Firth caught her skirts and blew them tight against her body, outlining its curves.

Rob shut his eyes to ease the effect the sight stirred in him, and wished he could relieve his body's less controllable reactions as simply.

The wind felt bracing and Mairi could, with relative ease, control her skirts' inclination to fly up around her. But she was glad she had decided to arrange her hair in a single plait and had not bothered to wear her veil. Silk cloth whipping at one's cheeks could be most annoying.

The view from Trailinghail's ramparts was spectacular enough to delight anyone's soul, she thought. Although she had seen that one side of her chamber overlooked the bay and another the Firth, she was glad to have a clearer idea of the tower's position and layout.

From the uppermost floor of Annan House, she could often see the English coast. She could not see it now. To the south lay only open sea.

Looking north, she saw the kirk steeple she had seen

from the galley and the whole coastline of the bay. She also saw the towers of Castle Mains near Kirkcudbright and the kirk spire in the town, northeast of the castle.

A man-at-arms stood at the southeast corner of the ramparts. When he turned to look at them, Maxwell gave him a wave, then drew Mairi to the southwest corner. The wind still blew from that direction. She loved facing into it. It felt good, and she no longer had the morning sun in her eyes.

Looking down over the south parapet to a small inlet, she saw that the tide was still flowing in, crashing against immense boulders and shooting spray high.

Strongly aware of the man beside her, she remembered why he had said he was taking her outside. "What did you want to talk about?" she asked.

He was quiet long enough to make her wonder if he feared that what he wanted to say would make her angry again, or upset her in some other way.

Then, with a look of rueful amusement, he said, "The truth is that, although I do have a wee surprise for you, I knew you were chafing to get out of that room. My brother often accuses me of failing to consider details when I make plans, and I fear that this time, that is just what I did. I thought only of how your father would react, and of providing for your physical comfort. It did not cross my mind to wonder how you might occupy yourself as a prisoner here."

"In other words," she said, "*my* feelings did not concern you."

He met her gaze more easily than she had thought he would. "I did not know you then . . . my lady, and I did not expect to abduct you when I did. I cannot claim to know you much better now, but I do owe you truth when we talk. Your feelings did not affect my plan then. Now they do."

"Why?"

"Because I cannot keep your presence here a secret," he said bluntly. "Nor will I ask you to lie about why you are here when you talk to my people."

"I have talked only to Gibby."

"Aye, but you should have female company—someone to look after you. So I've arranged for my steward's good-sister to attend you. However, there is a rub."

"Mercy, I should think there would be more than one," Mairi said.

"My steward, Fin Walters, dislikes the idea that she might stay overnight and would be going about her tasks in a tower filled with men. He will be at ease with the notion only if she comes in just by day, or sleeps with you at night."

"But you assured me that *I* am safe in this tower full of men."

"I did, aye, and 'tis true. It would be true for Annie, as well, especially with her good-brother as my steward. No man here would harm either of you. But Walters fears that tongues may wag in Annie's case, and I agree they may."

"Will they not wag about me, too?"

"None so much," he said. "Everyone for miles knows Annie, so if she were to begin spending nights in the tower, people would talk. They don't know you, so although word may begin to spread of an unknown female staying here, as long as no one knows exactly who you are, your reputation will be safe. 'Tis why I mean to call you Mairi when others are about and would like you to call me Rob."

"Gibby knows he is to call me 'my lady,'" Mairi reminded him.

"As will others know that they should," he agreed.

"Annie will know you as Lady Mairi, so others will know that, too. But Annie will be discreet. 'Tis the Dunwythie name that would undo us, so I want to keep that quiet."

"I thought you *wanted* my father to know I am your captive."

"Nay, only that he is more likely to get you back if he behaves sensibly. I'd be unwise to tell you just what I mean to do. But I will keep you safe. In fact, the greatest danger to your safety arises if he *does* learn you are here and tries to bring an army into Galloway to fetch you."

"If you are thinking that Archie Douglas would try to stop him—"

"Nay, lass, I ken as fine as you do that Archie would join him. But the sheriff will do all he can to keep a Dunwythie army out of Nithsdale, let alone allow it to cross into Galloway and raise Archie's ire. Sithee, in that event, the clan war I hope to avoid would start in Dumfries. We'd learn of it only after many had died."

Mairi knew the Maxwells might not have things all their own way if that clash did occur. Her good-brother, Sir Hugh Douglas, lived in Nithsdale, and he felt no loyalty to the Maxwells. Before marrying her cousin Jenny, Hugh had served Archie Douglas. The Lord of Galloway was as much his kinsman as his sister Phaeline's.

Mairi did not share these thoughts with her companion. Instead, she said, "I don't want anyone to die, sir. But neither do I believe my father will submit . . . for any reason. I wish I could make you understand that."

He gave her shoulder a pat as he said, "You don't know your own power, my lady. But I do. All will be well in good time, I promise. Now, about Annie."

"I'll welcome her help and her companionship," Mairi admitted, accepting the change of subject. "Most of the gowns in those kists fasten up the back, and there is not nearly enough thread in the wee sewing basket to hem them all."

"I'll get more then," he said.

"But about your Annie," she went on. "I must say I'd prefer not to share that chamber day and night with a stranger, however kind or helpful she may be."

"That must be as you wish," he said. "If you change your mind, you need only tell me. Shall we walk now and drink in this splendid view? I promise you, the weather is rarely so kind this time of year. We should enjoy it."

She agreed, and she did enjoy the grand panorama before them. From the eastern parapet, she could see across the bay. The incoming tide made the cliffs look lower than they had looked the day before.

"How high does the water come?" she asked him.

"The difference between high and low tide most of the time is about eighteen feet here," he said. "During spring tides, it can be as much as twenty-six."

"Then you cannot use that sea entrance at high tide," she said.

"Nay, nor keep a boat inside the cavern, come to that. I beach my boats below Senwick village when the tide is out. The spire of Senwick's kirk is the near one you see from here. The water there often gets too rough for safety, though, so I generally keep the boats in Senwick Bay, farther north, where they can anchor more securely to ride with the tides. If the weather gets too bad, my lads move them to Kirkcudbright harbor, near Castle Mains. That would be the two towers—"

"I know that castle," she said. "We stayed there overnight last year before we went on to Threave."

"Aye, sure, you would, for you'd likely have arrived in the evening if you traveled with the morning ebb as we did."

She supposed they had traveled with the tide, although she had not thought about it at the time. Drawing her cloak more tightly around her, she leaned on the parapet to gaze at the opposite shore and the softly undulating hills beyond its cliffs.

"Beautiful, is it not?" he said. "Or are you getting too cold up here?"

"Nay, but you must have other things you must do."

"I do have duties," he admitted. "Moreover, I told Fin Walters to send Annie along up as soon as she could come, so I expect we should go back downstairs."

Nodding, Mairi followed him to the door and through to the stairway. Holding her skirts, and glad she had worn boots and not the shoes that were too big, she quickly made her way down to the landing outside her door.

The door stood open, as they had left it, and from the landing, she saw Gibby inside. He was staring toward the window overlooking the bay, but he turned with a wide-eyed look and hastily put a finger to his lips.

Wondering what was amiss, she went quietly in. Breath and feet stopped dead at the sight of the kitten on the windowsill—at the outer edge, looking down.

~

Rob saw the lass stop and tense, and the lad beyond her looking scared.

Crossing the threshold, he saw the kitten.

Gibby's presence and the stool beneath the window told their own tale.

"I didna ken he'd jump up there, I swear!" Gib said wretchedly. "I'd no want the tiggie wee terror to kill hisself, even an he does bite ye as quick as look at ye."

"Of course, you did not mean any harm to him," Mairi said quietly.

"I'll get him, lass," Rob said, taking another step.

"Nay, sir, stay where you are," she said in the same quiet tone. "He will heed me, I think. Won't you, my wee cushie-doo?"

The kitten glanced at her, then looked back and dipped a paw over the edge.

Rob's stomach clenched, but Mairi remained calm.

As she murmured and cooed to the kitten, she stepped quietly nearer until it turned toward her. Its hind legs remained so perilously near the outer edge that Rob felt his innards churn and saw that the lad had lost his remaining color.

Mairi hesitated briefly, then continued toward the window. "Such a bonnie laddie," she cooed. "Such a dearling towdy-mowdy. Come now, come to Mairi."

The kitten chirped, stepped closer to her, and she gently scooped it off the sill.

Rob did not know he had been holding his breath until he let it out.

"What did you call him before, Gibby?" Mairi asked the lad.

"D'ye mean when I said he were a wee terror? I didna mean nowt—"

"Nay, the other word you used . . . tiggie? Might that

be a good name for him, since he does not seem to have one?"

"Aye, well, 'tis nobbut much the same as t'other," Gibby said, turning pink. "Sithee, 'tis what Herself calls me when she thinks I ha' been a mite fashious."

"Oh," she said.

"It means cross-like, and carnaptious, like what that wee biter is," Gibby said, nodding. "In troth, Tiggie would be a *good* name for him."

"Oh, but I don't—"

"Sakes," the lad retorted, "it be gey better than calling him 'cushie-doo' or 'towdy-mowdy'!"

Rob chuckled. "The lad's right," he said to her. "People don't call someone cat-witted to denote a sweet temper or, come to think on it, sharp wits."

She held the kitten up to look into its small face. "Tiggie?"

It patted her cheek with a white forepaw.

Smiling, she said, "Prithee, Gibby, move that stool away from the window. We don't want our wee Tiggie Whiskers to make use of it again."

"I put it there so I could look out," the lad said. "But then I saw that the place could use a tidying up. I didna think it were bad to leave it there a spell."

"What were you doing here, Gib?" Rob asked him.

"I come to tell ye Annie were here, laird. In the hall wi' Fin Walters," Gibby said. "She didna ken should she come up here or wait for ye, so I came to ask ye."

"Then you may go down and bring her to us, Gib," Rob said. "I'm sure her good-brother will entrust her to your care."

"Aye, sure," Gibby said. "I'll see to it then."

He ran off, full of importance, and Rob said with a smile, "I wanted another word with you before Annie comes. She's a kind lass, and competent, but do not think you must put up with her if you do not get on well together."

"I'm sure we will get on fine," she said. "But I hope you don't think having a female companion will reconcile me to staying in this room all the time."

"Nay, I do see that you'll want time outside, lass. I had thought mayhap you would like to see some of the countryside of Borgue, which is what folks call this district. We can ride along the cliffs tomorrow morning if the weather stays fine."

She agreed that she would enjoy such a ride, but he received the distinct impression that she would have agreed to ride to the gates of hell if it would have taken her out of the tower for a while.

~

Mairi was delighted and relieved. That she would be able to leave the tower even for an hour or so was a heady thought, especially as he had admitted that his original intent had been to keep her locked in her room until her father submitted. That, she thought, would most likely have meant until she died of old age.

Annie's arrival with Gibby added to her relief. Younger than Mairi had expected, she was a cheerful lass with carroty hair parted in the middle and ruthlessly contained in two sleek plaits coiled behind her ears. She had an infectious grin, her blue eyes sparkled, and she seemed to bring more sunshine into the room with her.

Gibby strutted as if he had produced Annie by some feat

of legerdemain. "She can sleep wi' ye or no, as ye please, Fin Walters did say. Did he no, Annie?"

"Aye, he did that," Annie said. "Fin be like an old hen, m'lady. That be right, to call you so, I hope. Gibby did say I ought."

Mairi nodded, saying, "I am pleased to meet you, Annie. I have two kists yonder with clothing the laird provided, but nearly all of it is too long. I found a mending basket with needles, some threads, and a pair of thimbles—oh, and a wee pair of scissors fit only for cutting thread. I hope you are handy with a needle."

"Aye, m'lady, I can do plain mending and white stitching, sheets and smocks and such, and simple embroidery."

"I'd liefer sleep alone," Mairi told her at once. "But if you live far—"

"Nay, mistress, nobbut a step, and me da doesna feel the same as Fin does about me staying in the tower. Fin says he can look after me, but me da and me mam would rather I be home afore dark—unless the laird bids me stay wi' ye."

Mairi assured her that the laird would issue no such order and then introduced her to Tiggie. They settled quickly to work, enjoying the kitten's antics as it displayed intense interest in the mending basket, and their threads.

Gibby left but returned an hour later with their midday meal, explaining that the laird and Fin Walters thought it would be best if the women ate privately.

The next morning, the laird kept his word, appearing shortly after Mairi had broken her fast. She had found a gown suitable for riding the afternoon before, and Annie had helped her shorten it, so she was eager to be off.

A gillie waited in the yard with their horses and a third for himself.

Hearing the barmkin gate shut behind them made Mairi smile, and the ride was all her host had promised and more. The gillie kept his distance, the sun shone, the wind had dropped to a whisper, and the air was crisp without being icy.

Spring seemed to have settled in to stay.

They rode toward the Firth, and westward along its coast. Waves crashed below, and she was glad the trail lay a safe distance from the cliff edge.

Maxwell could tell a good story. Although Mairi knew that Archie the Grim had imposed peace on Galloway after many others had tried and failed to tame the place, she had not realized what a feat it was until Rob—as she had begun to think of him, albeit without yet saying the name— described the wild, aggressive, lawless Celtic tribes that Archie had successfully tamed.

"I *do* understand their resistance to the Scottish laws imposed on them when their ways had served so well for centuries," she said at one point with a smile.

He chuckled, but to her relief, he did not take the remark as an invitation to discuss her father's views or the sheriff's.

After their ride, however, hemming skirts and gowns with Annie that afternoon seemed especially tedious, although they had only a few more yet to do.

The laird had provided her with nearly any article of clothing a woman might need. But when Mairi learned they had belonged to Lady Kelso, she was shocked.

She said so at once, only to have Annie, who had told her, inform her that the furniture in the chamber had also belonged to Lady Kelso or to her husband.

"I expect the laird did inherit everything here when he

inherited the land," Annie said comfortably. "So it can make nae difference an ye make use o' them."

Mairi felt as if she were stealing her ladyship's clothes, and said as much indignantly to Rob the next morning as they rode into Borgue forest with a gillie trailing well behind them again.

"How did you dare give her things to me?" Mairi demanded.

He shrugged. "If you knew how many garments the woman has, you would not let it fidget you," he said. "She travels with a string of sumpters, carrying not just piles of her clothing but her own sheets and favorite furnishings, as if she fears that her host may lack some item she *thinks* she cannot do without."

"Even so—"

"You may believe me when I tell you she will not recall what she left here, lass. Nor will she care. You clearly do not follow fashions as carefully as she does or you would know that all of those items are at least four or five years out of date. You *must* have noticed that they have scarcely been worn."

"My stepmother would notice such things, I expect," Mairi said. "I care less about the look of a gown than how it feels. I am forever putting a foot wrong with fashions and must depend on Phaeline to guide me. My sister Fiona would wear sackcloth, though, if she knew it was what fashionable women were wearing."

"Do you like the clothes you found here?"

"I do, aye. The fabrics are lovely. One wants to hold the velvets against one's skin. And I stroke them so often that I think Tiggie grows jealous."

"Sakes, he should be grateful that you let him spend so much time with you! Are you sure he is not a nuisance?"

"Nay, of course he is not," she said. "Even Gibby is coming to like him. He has twice called Tiggie a braw laddie since he jumped to that windowsill."

He fell silent, and Mairi glanced at him, noting a slight frown. Had she not known better, she might have thought he was a trifle jealous of the kitten. But such a thought was absurd. Grown men did not envy cats.

Clouds had gathered in the west, so Rob decided to cut their ride short, declaring that he had much to do that he would not get done if it rained.

They rode home without speaking again, but the silence was comfortable. Indeed, Mairi could not remember anyone she had known with whom she could converse as easily and comfortably as she did with Robert Maxwell.

The next morning, they rode along the bay cliffs toward Senwick, but they did not go into the village. Nor did they visit Borgue village, a couple of miles west, but Mairi did not care where they went. She enjoyed their rides.

On the other hand, she was just as much the laird's prisoner as when she had arrived. His people treated her with respect, but all knew she was not to leave until he said so. And all, including Annie, seemed to see naught amiss in his keeping her.

When she told Annie that she was there against her will, Annie said simply, "Och, well, I ha' nae doots the laird has good reason, m'lady. By the bye, me mam sent a bag o' quilt pieces wi' me today. She ha' be feeling low, and as them pieces be meant to become a quilt for your bed, she thought we might like to stitch them together when we've finished your hemming."

Mairi agreed with a sigh, deciding she must be growing reconciled to her captivity and to the extraordinary loyalty that Rob's people showed him as well.

Occasionally he gave her a look she could not decipher but that touched every part of her in unfamiliar but extraordinary ways. Whenever it happened, he would say something to break the spell and take an abrupt departure soon afterward.

On the following Monday, as he was lifting her down from her horse after their ride, he said with a laugh, "You should always wear pink, lass. I vow, though, you already fill my mind so that—" He broke off, his gaze still locked with hers, and the twinkle in his eyes faded. Then, abruptly saying he had things to do, he escorted her silently up to her door and strode off to look for Fin Walters.

Entering her chamber alone, Mairi found it empty and recalled that she had given Annie leave to help her mother at home that morning.

Annie soon arrived, though, with Mairi's midday meal and news that the laird had a visitor. "'Tis the knacker, Parland Dow," she added. "Fin sent me up straightaway, and he says I'm no to talk to the man. D'ye ken the knacker, m'lady?"

"Aye, sure," Mairi said, her thoughts suddenly racing. "He goes everywhere, for he has many skills and helps the landowners, doing their butchering and such."

She was surprised that Dow roamed as far as Trailinghail but decided that if he served the Maxwells in Dumfries and could find work in Kirkcudbright, it was not strange at all. Moreover, if he was going back to Annan House, he could tell her father where she was, and warn Dunwythie not to begin a clan war to fetch her.

Chapter 10 _____

As it had been only ten days since he had seen the knacker, Rob wondered if Dow had been back to Annandale yet or was stopping back by to tell him of something he'd seen that Lady Kelso might like, before returning to Dumfries. Receiving him in the hall, and seeing him big with news, Rob felt his hopes rise.

"I am gey glad to see you again," he said, shaking the knacker's hand. "Fin Walters assures me we have more work for you if you're looking for some."

"Aye, sir, Fin did tell me ye'd ha' more lambs for slaughter when I were here afore," Dow replied. "But I'll own I didna think I'd return so quick. See you, I went to Castle Moss in Annandale after I'd finished at Kirkcudbright. And there I heard such news o' Dunwythie that I could scarce credit it."

"Indeed?" Rob said, lifting an eyebrow.

"I did, aye, and as I kent fine that ye'd had business wi' his lordship none so long ago, and I never want to bring ye news that might prove wrong a day later, I betook m'self to Annan House as fast as I could go."

"What news was this?"

"'Tis a dreadful thing. His daughter the lady Mairi has vanished and nae one kens what became o' her. His lordship be beside himself."

"Aye, he must be," Rob said sincerely.

"See you, he'd gone north in the dale. So he didna learn o' the lass's disappearance till three days after the event."

"How long ago was this then?"

Counting on his fingers, Dow said, "I make it about a sennight that she's been gone, laird. I came straight here when I heard, it being gey strange that we'd talked o' the lass such a short time afore. Her da asked did I ken aught o' her, but I couldna help him, for I'd heard nowt but that she had vanished. That were nae help to the man, but I said if I learned aught I'd tell him straightaway."

"I'm sure you will," Rob said, hoping he could trust his people as much as he thought he could. "Did you learn more, then, during your trip back here?"

"Aye, sure, but nowt o' the lady Mairi," Dow said.

"We are about to dine, as you see. You can tell me all you think I'd enjoy hearing whilst we take our meal together."

Accepting the invitation, Dow regaled him with information, mostly gossip, much of which was amusing. Then he said, "Bless me if I didna forget, though! Ye'd be friendly wi' young Will Jardine, aye? Old Jardine o' Applegarth's son?"

"I am," Rob said, wondering what mischief Will had got into now.

Dow chuckled. "Seems he has set his heart on the lady Fiona, Will has."

"Fiona Dunwythie?"

"Aye, the same. At least, that be what folks be a-saying, 'cause his lordship caught him sniffing round her young ladyship near Annan House. After ringing a rare peal over the lad, his lordship ordered him to stay off his land entirely."

"I don't blame him," Rob said. "I'd not want a daughter of mine to catch Will's eye, either."

They continued chatting until they had finished their meal. Then Rob turned the knacker over to Fin Walters, knowing Fin had a list of tasks for him.

Knowing, too, that Fin was unlikely to say aught to the knacker save what was necessary to set him to his duties, Rob returned to his chamber to think.

Little thought was necessary, however, to persuade him that Dunwythie was in just the frame of mind he had been expecting, and that Will Jardine's mischief had likely put the poor man in an even better mood to do as Rob wanted.

He might even offer to talk to Will, say that he'd heard of the lad's mischief with the lady Fiona and knew that such an alliance would be unwelcome. Sakes, but Old Jardine would have the hide off Will if he learned he was sniffing after a lass with few prospects. Jardine wanted his heir to gain a wife with a healthy tocher.

If he rode to Applegarth, he'd be away at least two and a half days. As the moon was nearly full, a spring tide was due, so he could get to Annan in less than four hours. He was unlikely to get home on the same day again, though, even if he talked only with Dunwythie.

He had about decided that he could not leave at all until Parland Dow had gone when he remembered that Dow would sleep at Fin's cottage. With luck, he could count on

Fin Walters to handle Dow so the knacker never knew his host had left Trailinghail. In fact, if all went as Rob hoped, no one would know he was gone save Fin Walters and his boatmen.

Then he realized that Mairi would have to know of his absence, because she would miss him and likely set Annie to asking others where he was. That meant Annie should know, too. He'd warn Fin to talk to her.

~

With a sigh, Mairi set aside the piecework she had been stitching and wondered what hour it was. The afternoon had passed slowly, and the overcast sky threatened rain. A glance at Annie told her the other young woman was also thinking of something other than her stitching.

"Is aught amiss?" Mairi asked her.

Annie's head jerked up as if her mind had been miles away. "Och, it be only that me mam were sick this morning. But she's a strong woman, so I warrant she's herself again by now." She smiled. "'Tis just she's rarely ever sick. Says she has nae time to be ailing, what wi' me and me brothers to look after, and me da."

"If she is still sick tomorrow, you should stay with her," Mairi said. "Gibby can attend to my simple needs for a day, or even two if necessary. The laird also sees to my comfort."

"Aye, 'tis true, that is," Annie said with a smile. "He's a kind man, is the laird. Still, it isna right ye should be here without another woman, m'lady. Me mam says, by rights, he should be hiring maidservants, now he's got a kinswoman wi' him here. 'Tisna right, she says, that ye keep to your room as much as ye do."

Tempted to remind Annie that she was not a kinswoman, Mairi held her tongue. If Rob's people had decided that she was respectable, now was hardly the time to quibble about it. As it was, Annie and every other person who depended on him at Trailinghail believed he could do no wrong.

So Mairi said with a slight shrug, "I do not mind solitude, Annie. In troth, at home I am busy from the time I get up in the morning until I go to bed at night. This makes for a nice change, although it can grow tedious sometimes."

Sakes, she thought, much as she liked Annie, being in the chamber always grew tedious, with her or without her.

The truth was she could talk freely only with the laird himself. Even trying to persuade anyone else there to aid her would be foolhardy. Knowing how his people felt about Rob, how could she trust a promise any one of them made to her?

"Well," Annie said, "I do thank ye, m'lady. If me mam still be ailing, I'll likely bide wi' her the morning at least, as I did today. Then, if she be better in the day, I'll come to ye. Otherwise, I'll come to you Thursday. I ha' nae doots the laird will ride wi' ye again in the morning, any road."

"I expect so," Mairi said, although with Parland Dow there she doubted it.

Annie left earlier than usual that afternoon at Mairi's urging. When the maidservant apologized, Mairi said, "I see naught amiss in a daughter seeing to her mother's wellbeing, Annie. It is right for you to do that."

Even so, the next hour crept so slowly that when the door opened and Rob stood at the threshold, eyeing her speculatively, she cast aside her work and rose to her feet with relief.

"I let Annie go early," she said. "And I stupidly neglected to remind her to have someone bring up my supper."

"I'll have Gib bring it or I'll bring it up myself," he said, crossing the threshold and leaving the door open as he moved nearer. "I just came to tell you that I'll be away tomorrow and mayhap a day or two after that."

Disappointment stirred, then dismay. "May I ask where you are going?"

"You may," he said with a smile. "The knacker Parland Dow arrived today."

"Annie told me, aye," she said. "He visits us, too. Had he news of Annan?"

"He did. I think your ordeal here may be nearing its end, lass."

Seeing no point in fighting a position from which she had been unable to move him since the beginning of her captivity, Mairi felt only despair.

When she did not reply, he said, "Come now, I expected the news that you will soon go home again to cheer you, lass."

"You ken fine that I do *not* believe that is going to happen," she said more fiercely than she had intended. But having begun, she went on, "I know my father well, sir. And do *not* call me 'lass'!"

He touched her cheek, and his touch stirred the usual warmth through her, despite her annoyance. It did not alter her certainty that Dunwythie would act as he always did when challenged, however.

Gently, Rob said, "You may know him, Mairi, but I know a few things, too. And when a father has such a daughter as you, believe me when I say that if he loses her, he will swim the sea or move a mountain to bring her home again. My only regret in this is that I enjoy your company. That is one more detail I did not anticipate. By my troth, though, I will miss you when you go home."

Trying to swallow the ache that crept into her throat at his words, she could not reply. To care about one's captor was the act of a fool, and she was no fool.

Every woman knew that most men behaved differently with women than they did with men. In her time at Trailinghail, thanks to Gib and Annie, she had heard more than one tale of the laird's short temper, his proven skill with a sword, and his occasional ruthlessness.

That she had seen little of such traits meant nothing. His certainty that Dunwythie would do as he had predicted was bound to increase the fury Rob would surely feel when he learned the truth. Then what would he do?

Would he return chastened, ready to take her home simply because, having failed in his undertaking, returning her would be the right thing to do?

Her inner self sneered at the thought while she fought to retain a calm expression. It was far more likely that he, like so many other men with volatile tempers, would vent his on the person nearest at hand. She did not fear him, but the fact was that no one else was going to help her. She would have to help herself.

He was looking at her now much too shrewdly.

"When will you leave?" she asked, only too aware that he often read her expression even when she was sure she had it under control.

"If that sky sheds its cloudy blanket soon, as it looks like it may, I mean to leave whilst the early tide is stemming up," he said, still eyeing her narrowly. "If all goes well and nowt delays me, mayhap I will return tomorrow night on the ebb."

A flickering frown as he added the last part made her say, "Do you anticipate a delay?" Then, more sharply, "Surely, he will give you your answer quickly. I shouldn't think it would take him five minutes to refuse you, although it may take much longer for him to tell you what he thinks of your *reprehensible* demands."

"Less of that, if you please," he said curtly. "I believe I know more than you do about men, just as I am sure that you know more about how women think than I do. As to what might delay me, I was just wondering if I should tell you."

"Good sakes, why should you not?"

"Because the news may distress you," he said just as bluntly. "However, as you will soon be home again and able to add your mite to any discussions that may ensue there, I expect I should tell you. Sithee, Parland Dow also told me of a row between your father and Will Jardine."

"At Annan House?"

"Aye, sure. Dow said he went to Annan House, so one must suppose the land your father ordered Will to keep off was the Annan property. I expect his lordship meant every Dunwythie estate, though, come to that."

"I expect he did." She turned away, dying to ask more but reluctant to say anything to him that might disparage Fiona or make him think the worse of her.

"Dow said his lordship caught Will with your sister," Rob said.

Whirling back to face him, she said, "What can you mean by *that*?"

"Easy, lass," he said, resting his hands on her shoulders.

"Sakes, do you not listen? Not only do you persist in calling me so, but now you address me as if I were a nervous mare," she snapped. Hearing the echo of her own words, she pressed her lips firmly together and glowered at his broad chest.

"Then don't always assume that I mean the worst," he retorted. "I meant only that I may be able to help. I could speak to Old Jardine. *He* won't want mischief between Will and your sister any more than your father does."

Biting her lower lip, Mairi shut her eyes, wondering at her own angry outburst and knowing that it was directed as much at Fiona as at anyone else.

It was not the first time in their acquaintance that Rob had wanted to give her a shake or a kiss, or wished he had the right to do both.

Firmly gripping her chin, he tipped her face up, making her look at him. "Mairi," he said evenly, "I did *not* mean what you thought I meant."

"Release me."

He held her chin, and her gaze. With an audible edge to his voice, he said, "What Dow said, exactly, is that your father told him he had caught Will sniffing around the lady Fiona and ordered him to stay off his land. Does that answer you?"

She started to nod but found she could not free her chin. Licking her lips, she said, "Aye, sir, it does. *Now* will you release me? You are bruising my chin."

Stifling a curse, he relaxed his hold and gave her chin a rub with a forefinger, as if he could erase the bruise before it surfaced. "I'm sorry, lass," he said.

"I angered you. Again."

"Nay, you only irked me, and it is not wrong to speak up. I should fetch your supper before we fratch more, though. I'll bring mine up, too, if I may."

Her eyebrows arched upward in an exaggerated way. "*Now* you ask my permission? Good sakes, sir, how is this?"

He chuckled. "Put away your stitching, you unnatural termagant, and wash your face and hands whilst I'm gone. I'll bring a game board, too, and chess pieces."

"'Twould doubtless be wiser for us both to get to bed early," she said. "I believe the tide will be stemming up about two hours after midnight."

"So, you heed the tides," he said. "You are right."

"Aye, well, when one has little to occupy one's time, one does become aware of changes in one's surroundings. Mark you, I would not recognize the sounds of rising or falling tides from anywhere but this chamber. However, from here, I can now tell you without looking how high the water has risen or fallen."

Chuckling at her air of wisdom, he left her and hurried down to tell a gillie to put their supper on a tray, while he hurried to his bedchamber to wash and don a clean shirt and doublet. As he tied the cord lacing of the latter, he realized he was far too eager to sup with her. Annie, he recalled, would not be there.

Going more slowly down the stairs than he had come up them, he took the tray from the gillie who waited with it at the hall landing. Then, seeing Gibby put a jug on a nearby trestle table, he said, "Gib, leave that and come with me."

~

As soon as Rob had gone, Mairi bustled about, thrusting the quilt pieces she had been stitching together into their basket, then tidying herself and her chamber.

To the voice in the back of her head that wondered why she should care, she retorted that she did not want anyone mistaking her for a disorderly woman.

She had pulled the little table into place and drawn the stool up to it when footsteps sounded on the stairs. Sitting quickly on the settle, she strove to look as if she had been relaxing there quietly, if not demurely, since he had gone.

The door opened, and he stepped across the threshold, carrying a laden tray. Pausing, he frowned at the open window. "That breeze seems to have freshened since I left," he said.

"Aye, perhaps," she agreed. "Mayhap more rain is coming."

Only then did she see Gibby following him. The boy looked at her curiously, even warily, and Mairi realized she must be frowning, too. She smiled at him and said, "I see that the laird brought you along to protect him from my temper, Gib. He stirred it earlier, so mayhap now he thinks he needs protection."

The boy's expression relaxed. "I ha' me doots about that, m'lady, but if ye look too fierce at him, I'll step betwixt ye. Where be the wee terror a-hiding?"

"Why, I don't know," she said. "He may be sleeping behind the bed curtain, or he may have slipped out whilst the door was open."

"Look for him later, lad," Rob said. "Come sup with us now."

"Cor, sir, I *ate* me supper. As I'm here, I should serve ye, I expect."

"Nay, I'll do that," Rob said. "You take a chicken leg then from the tray, and find your wee terror. He'll be hungry if you are not."

"I can always eat a chicken leg," the boy said, grinning. "But I'll share it wi' him an he behaves himself."

His hunt for the kitten soon took him onto the stairway.

Mairi said, "If you brought him with you to ensure propriety, sir—"

"Nay, just to remind me of my promise to you," he said. "I'll not deny you tempt me, my lady, but I will keep my word. That the lad could reappear at any moment should be sufficient."

She smiled, sure she was safe with him. He had made her feel so from the start. That she attracted him was no bad thing. That he attracted her as well was unfortunate, because she must not let him keep her captive if she could escape. It went right against nature to let him use her so, or to lead him to think she did not mind. Moreover, if she could escape, it would be a good lesson to him.

That she even found it necessary to have such a discussion with herself was unsettling, but she liked the man. She could not say she had liked him from the start, because she had not. Attraction and liking, after all, were different things. But in the time that she had spent at Trailinghail, despite being his captive, she had come to like him. She could not say, however, that she understood him.

Even now, he was eyeing her with what looked annoyingly like amusement.

Keeping her tone light, even disinterested, as if she merely made conversation, she said, "Does the knacker stay long?"

He paused with a bite-size chunk of mutton on his knife, halfway to his mouth, and said just as casually, "Oh, a few more days, I think. He'll take his meals with Fin Walters and his wife at their cottage, though, as he usually does unless I invite him to eat with me. I doubt he'll even be aware that I've gone."

It was all she could do not to gnash her teeth, especially when his eyes glinted and his mouth twitched as if he were now struggling not to smile or even chuckle. Turning the subject to the weather, rather deftly she thought, she asked if he thought it *was* likely to rain again before his return.

He said it well might, and they continued to chat until she found herself thinking again how comfortable she felt even when he disconcerted her as he just had by seeming to know her thoughts. She could so easily say what she wanted without considering how he might react. If he fired up, she could fire right back at him and naught would come of it except a better understanding.

After he bade her goodnight, though, her thoughts shifted back to his upcoming departure, its likely result, and her own need to act.

Gibby returned with the kitten in his arms not long after Rob had gone.

Smiling, Mairi said, "I see the two of you have declared a truce."

"Och, aye," the lad said. "The wee beast likes to play wi' string, and I were a-twitching one for him by the hall fire.

But Fin Walters said I should bring him up now, so ye could go to bed. He said ye like to ha' him with ye in the night."

She thanked the boy, bade him goodnight, and began to prepare for bed.

As she did, her thoughts returned to her dilemma. Totting up details such as Parland Dow's presence, Trailinghail's nearness to Kirkcudbright and Castle Mains, and her knowledge of the tides, she concluded that if she were careful, and lucky, she might just succeed in escaping while Rob was on his fool's errand if only . . .

On the thought, she stepped to the chamber door and touched the latch. Hesitating long enough to send a prayer aloft, she lifted it.

Gibby had not locked the door.

~

Rob made a mental list of things he needed to do before his departure, then sought out Fin Walters to tell him to look after things in his absence.

"Don't share this information with anyone," he added. "Especially Dow."

"Aye, sir," the steward said, nodding. "I'm mum."

Rob then told his oarsmen to slip out of the tower without drawing attention. "Prepare the galley now," he told his helmsman, Jake Elliot. "I'll meet you at the beach as the tide begins to turn unless a storm blows up. If we row out of the bay then, we'll be ready to sail toward Annan on the spring tide."

The helmsman nodded. "A good notion, sir. We'll find ourselves against the outflow from the Firth for a time, but 'tis better than fighting a spring tide out o' the bay. If ye truly want to go quiet, though, we could leave from the beach and pick ye up in the cavern afore the tide gets too low. Then none would ken that ye'd gone."

Agreeing to that plan, with full confidence that Jake could get the men to the boat without drawing attention, Rob retired to his chamber to prepare for bed.

As he did, an enticing image of Mairi as she had looked at supper captivated his thoughts. The candlelight had turned her smooth skin golden and her hair to silver-gilt. She had not worn a veil or caul that evening but had worn her thick plaits simply, coiled at her nape.

A few tendrils had escaped, and a long one had persisted in tickling her cheek. Again and again, she tucked it behind her right ear with a fingertip. It would stay for a time only to escape as soon as she gestured or nodded her head.

More than once he had nearly reached to tuck it back but restrained himself. He found it harder each day to remember that she was a captive and not a friend.

He knew now that abducting her had been a much graver mistake than he had realized, because no sensible woman would ever forgive such an act or the man who had committed it. At the time he had thought only of his goal, and Alex's, and his belief that he had hit upon the way to achieve it.

The best thing he could do for her now, and for himself, was to persuade her father to submit quickly, so he could take her home again. He could not hope that Mairi would ever forget what he had done, but perhaps, in time . . .

Rob's thoughts went no further, because he was sure that his lifetime—however long it might be—would not be long enough for him to win forgiveness, let alone to win her heart. He was a fool even to be contemplating such things.

He would do better to get on with the business at hand.

Accordingly, he retired, giving himself a mental order to wake before low tide. Then he slept deeply until his appointed time.

Awakening in a chamber filled with moonlight, and hearing the rhythmic sounds of the waves below his window, he got up, dressed quickly, and stole downstairs, past the hall where many slept but all was quiet and into the kitchen where embers in the fireplace cast orange-gold light on the hearthstones.

Taking a lantern from a shelf there, he lit a twig from the embers and used it to light the lantern. Then he went down one more level to the storage cellar.

A small room opened off the cellar, where they kept buttery stores—jugs of whisky, ale, and claret. At one corner a tall door led into the tunnel. He unbarred it, leaned the two heavy bars against the wall, and opened the door. Coming back on the long ebb, they would be unable to use the cave, so he did not bother to pull the latch chain through before he shut the door and rapidly descended to the wharf.

The galley awaited him there with several of the lads holding it against the swell. The water was already lower than he liked, so he doused the lantern, jumped in, and they were off. They emerged from the cavern without incident, and headed toward the mouth of the bay. By the light of the full moon, he could see that beaches below the northern end of the eastern cliffs were already showing.

A full moon or a new one produced spring tides, rising higher and falling lower than normal. Leaving before the tide reached low water meant a shorter, easier departure from the bay and opportunity for him to use the cavern.

Waiting outside the bay for the tide to turn would add

time to their journey, but it would spare the oarsmen, because once it did turn it would be swift enough to carry them to Annan by dawn.

Spring tides were the most dangerous ones to ride up the Firth, because they ran so swiftly, and the initial inflow up the narrowing vee of the Firth could create a wall of water as high as eight feet. His men were all experienced, though, and they knew the Firth well. Even so, they would have to take more than usual care.

"Did you have trouble entering the cavern, Jake?" he asked his helmsman as they waited, rocking with the waves, for the tide to be right.

"Nay, laird, rode in as sweet and smooth as honey, we did."

"Aye, we did," a familiar voice said cheerfully, drawing his attention for the first time to the small shadow between two of his oarsmen. "I thought sure we'd crash on the rocks, laird, but we did nae such thing."

"What the devil are you doing here, Gib?" Rob demanded.

"Herself did say I ought to learn all I could whilst I were wi' ye, so I thought I ought to learn about the rowing."

"He said ye'd given him permission, laird," the helmsman said grimly.

Rob shook his head, but said only, "We'll see what Fin says to you about telling lies, my lad. I doubt you bothered to ask *him* if you could come along."

"It come on me after I heard ye talking," Gib said. "I didna like to trouble Fin, so I betook me out the window and followed some o' your men to the boat. We be rocking a good bit just a-sitting here, like. Will we be off and away soon?"

"I hope you enjoy yourself when we do, because if you get sick, I'll likely throw you overboard," Rob said sternly. "Sakes, but it would serve you right if I took you straight back now and woke Fin up to hand you over to him. I cannot do that, so I'll leave you to explain your absence to him yourself when we get back."

"Aye, sure," Gib said, undaunted. "It'll be grand, though, meantime."

Rob turned away to hide a grin, then glanced back at the tower, where doubtless the lass lay peacefully sleeping.

Mairi, dressed and wearing her cloak, waited at the window until she saw the galley row in toward the cave below the tower and depart soon afterward toward the mouth of the bay. In the moonlight, she saw Rob clearly, standing in the stern near the helmsman as he had before. She had no idea what time it was, only that it was late, the moon was high in a cloudy sky, and the tide had not yet begun to turn.

She made her bed, picked up a bundle of the few necessities she would need and, taking a candle to light her way, hurried downstairs. Tiptoeing past the hall landing, then on down and across the kitchen, she hurried down to the lowest level.

Chapter 11 _____

Easily finding her way to the room with the cave entrance, Mairi took a last peek outside the storage chamber to be sure no one had followed her. As she turned back, her candlelight revealed two heavy bars leaning against the wall between tall sets of shelves. Relieved that Rob had not arranged with someone to replace the bars after he left, she examined the long iron door handle, seeking its latch.

At first, she saw none and, with a sinking feeling, wondered if there was a secret to opening the door. Perhaps, the laird did not want anyone, inadvertently or otherwise, leaving such a door open to an enemy. Still, there had to be a latch. She saw a heavy bolt at the bottom, but it was open. Even so, the door would not budge.

Holding her candle higher, she spied the iron latch at once—a strong-looking one—attached near the top of the door, much higher than ordinary latches and well above her natural eye level. A chain at the free end of it ran through a ring near the center of the door. But the chain was long enough for her to reach on tiptoe.

Spilling a small pool of wax from her candle onto the floor far enough back to be out of the way of her skirts and still cast candlelight on the door, she set the taper in the wax and held it so until it would stand alone. Then she moved back to the door and pulled the chain. The latch lifted, but the door still resisted her tug. So she let go of the chain to use both hands.

The latch dropped right back into its iron notch.

She would have to hold the chain with one hand and pull harder with the other at least until the door opened enough to let the latch clear its notch.

The process was awkward, because the thick timber door was heavy and fit snugly. But she managed it at last. Turning to retrieve her candle, she moved into the colder air at the threshold of the spiral stairway with a sense of accomplishment.

Lifting her skirts with her free hand, she stepped carefully down to the first step and reached back to adjust the door so that no one looking into or entering the storage area would see at once that the door was ajar. Such a likelihood at that hour was small but not impossible. And she did not know how much longer it would be until low water would give her access to the shingle beach.

As she neared the end of the spiral portion of the stairs, she felt her skirts stir in an icy draft that slipped under them and swirled up around her feet and legs.

Her candle blew out, and she heard distant moaning.

With a shiver and a few second thoughts, she decided against going back to find another candle and peered into the blackness ahead. As her eyes adjusted, a pale glow from below penetrated far enough up the stairway for her to discern its narrow stone steps. Putting one hand to the slimy wall and realizing she had forgotten her gloves, she reminded herself that the stairs would be slippery, too, and continued carefully down them, seeking the light.

Her intent was to take advantage of the low water to follow the shore outside the cave until she came to a path leading up to the clifftops. There had to be such a path below Senwick, where Rob beached the galley. How much any guard might see of her from the ramparts she did not know. She had not been able to see the shore below when she had stood up there. But the water then had been high.

Even in the light of the full moon, she thought she could keep the watchman from seeing her if she hugged the cliff face as she made her way along the shore.

She ought likewise to be able to conceal herself on the way up the path. And, once she was atop the cliffs, she would be able to see where she was going without having to concern herself with any vagaries of the shoreline.

She and Rob had ridden the track north along the clifftop, and Annie had told her that at Senwick, it met the track heading west to Borgue village. It went the six miles straight on to Kirkcudbright as well. Mairi's intent was to follow the cliffs to the head of the bay and make her way from there to Castle Mains, where she would surely find someone willing to help her get home to Annan House.

The light improved, and as she emerged from the enclosed spiral stair to the steep open stairs against the cave wall, she saw moonlight pouring through the tall arch of the cave opening below to her left. The long stone wharf stretched along the wall toward it, and the shiny dampness of the cave floor gleamed below.

She could feel a stronger, more direct breeze through the opening, and the moaning she had heard was louder.

It was, she decided, as if a wind god outside were blowing over and across the bay, sending his breath humming past the opening and creating the odd sensation of wind dancing over the cave walls and drifting up the stairs, as if to see where they led.

Then, as if her wind god had inhaled, the fickle current of air drifted down again, giving her cheeks an icy caress as it passed her on its way back outside. She was smiling at her own whimsy when she heard a distant dull thud above.

Tensing so much that she was sure her stomach must be curling up inside her, she listened for any other suggestion of imminent discovery. Hearing only the sighing wind and the rhythmic soft lapping of waves outside, she relaxed. Doubtless the noise had been no more than a strange echo of the restless water.

Continuing down the open stone steps with even greater care than in the stairwell, Mairi reached the wharf and walked to the end nearest the opening. Only when she looked for a way down to the cave floor did she see clearly that what she had taken for a damp sheen there was a sheet of dark, calm water clear enough to reveal the rocks below. Although the tide had to be nearly out and no water was entering the cave other than occasional droplets of spray, the shallow area between the base of the wharf and the cave opening was water-filled.

Refusing to let the sight daunt her, she examined the wall from the end of the wharf to the archway. With care, she thought she could find enough hand- and footholds to get outside. Although she saw only water from where she was, she assured herself that the area nearest the cave must, at low water, be sand or shingle. Not until she reached the opening and looked out did she see that that was not the case.

Beyond lay only surging and retreating water. She had seen from her window that at low tide, a beach ran from below Senwick to the head of the bay, leaving only the river Dee's channel as water. But Senwick lay a mile or more north of her.

Looking up, she saw that the cliff face jutted sharply outward, making it clear that she could not climb it even if she were foolish enough to try such a feat.

As for inching northward along the face of the cliff until she could reach the beach at Senwick, she could never manage that safely in her long skirts and cloak.

"Damnation," she muttered, borrowing a favorite epithet of Rob's.

No wonder the man did not bother to post guards at the door to the cavern. She ought to have known from that alone that no one could simply walk in—or out.

The only remote possibility for escape seemed to be a challenging swim. But she was not a strong enough swimmer to attempt it. In any event, that she would have to remove most if not all of her clothing would deter her. At home, with her people at hand and her life at stake, she might have risked it. But the thought that one of Rob's men might find her naked on the shore and take her back to the tower was enough to put the idea of trying such a stunt right out of her head.

"I would rather die," she said with a sigh, certain that she spoke the truth.

Making her way carefully back to the wharf, she decided she would have been wiser to have learned more about the bay's shoreline before attempting such an escape. Hoping the shore outside the cave might prove more accessible if the next cycle brought the water even lower, she made her way back upstairs to the top of the dark spiral tunnel and pushed against the timber door. It did not budge.

She knew then that the thud she had heard had been the draft pulling it shut.

In the darkness, feeling up and down its rough-timber length, she could find no latch or latch chain, no way at all to open it from outside.

When she pounded on it, she hurt her hands and her fists made only soft thuds. No one inside would hear her, even if someone were there.

She had trapped herself in the cave, the tide would soon turn, what light there was in the cave would be gone, and she had no idea how high the water would rise.

Something touched her skirt, making her jump and cry out in alarm.

Her unexpected companion replied with a plaintive "Mew."

~

The journey to the river Annan was swift and, Rob thought, uneventful.

That Gibby did not share that view had been plain the moment one of the first huge incoming rollers had caught the galley and heaved it forward. While the men rowed hard and skillfully to keep from capsizing, the boy watched it all, wide-eyed, as if he thought the great froth-topped rollers were demons chasing them.

Watching his alarm change to grinning delight, Rob remembered his own first such experience. He had been terrified they would overturn and sure he was not a strong enough swimmer to make it through such rollers to shore. It had taken him just a short time, too, to realize he loved the sense of pitting himself against the waves.

Gib clearly had the makings of an oarsman, even helmsman or captain. But Rob would have to keep an eye on him. Even outstanding oarsmen—and his were the best—had capsized boats while running a spring tide into the Firth.

Despite their speed, by the time they entered the river Annan, the tide there had already begun its turn. The sun had not yet risen above the eastern hills.

Rob motioned for quiet and the lads did what they could to muffle the sounds of their oars as they rowed past Dunwythie's land and onward.

"Take it a little farther," he murmured to Jake Elliot as they passed the harbor. "It is too early yet to request entry to Annan House, so look for a place to set me ashore on the riverbank. I'll walk back to town from there with one of the lads, and we'll hire a pair of horses."

"I'll go wi' ye," Gib offered.

"Nay, you will stay here and behave yourself," Rob said sternly, signing to one of the oarsmen to accompany him.

How unfortunate it was that humans were such superstitious creatures, Mairi thought grimly. She sat on the top step, wedged into one corner, hugging the warm sleeping kitten to her chest and wishing her wool cloak were thicker. She wished, too, that she had never decided to escape or known about the wretched cavern.

"Such foolish wishes, Tiggie," she murmured to her

softly snoring companion. "But, oh, how I wish I knew more about this awful place!"

She had no idea how much time had passed since she had trapped herself, or even if morning had come yet, because the incoming tide had raised the water level high enough to plunge her into pitch darkness.

Meantime, she was cold despite the kitten's warmth, and had been fighting a primordial fear of the dark. Until the noises of the water had stopped altogether, every thunderous roar, sudden slosh, thump, or mutter had made her shiver as if ghosts, demons, and boggarts roared or gibbered at her from secret lairs in the impenetrable blackness. But now, she was sure the water was still rising, stealing quietly up the stairs toward her, and she had no idea how high it would get.

Wondering next if spiders could tolerate the damp chill of the place, she decided sternly that she should turn her thoughts to pleasanter things. However, imagining herself atop Annan Hill, looking out at Solway Firth, reminded her only of how wild the Firth could grow in a storm.

She disliked storms—especially thunderstorms, unless the lightning and noise were distant. But it *had* been overcast the day before, and she had seen clouds when she looked out at the moon. If the wee galley got caught in a big storm . . .

Tearing her thoughts from the weather, she considered what she would like to do to Rob Maxwell to pay him back for bringing her so far from home.

But thoughts of Rob abruptly took a different tack. She could see him in her mind's eye more clearly than she had seen the stormy Firth, although his image was just as stormy. She had no doubt he would be furious to learn what she had done.

But she would endure his wrath, would even look forward to deflecting it, if only he would return quickly.

However, Rob was nowhere near Trailinghail, and she did not know when he would come. Also, she had given Annie leave to stay home and had left her own door open and the bed tidily made, hoping anyone who found her gone would think Rob had taken her with him. "And I have no doubt now that they will think just that," she muttered. Her sleeping companion made no comment.

The plain fact was that Rob had left in the middle of the night, so no one was likely to inform anyone that she had *not* gone with him. It was even likely that no one would think to ask. Had she not seen for herself that Rob's people did not express curiosity about much of anything their laird did?

Unless someone just happened to open the unbarred door, it was unlikely that anyone would find her. Those who knew he had taken her into the tower through the cave entrance were most likely the men with him. If Annie did come, she or Gib might look for her. But neither would look in the cave.

Mairi wondered again how high the water had crept. Even if it did not rise high enough to drown her or suck her down the stairs—and if she did not die from lack of air— how long could she survive if no one found her? Hours or days?

Please, God, she prayed, bring Rob home swiftly!

After an adequate breakfast at a harbor inn, Rob and his man rode to Annan House. Admitted to the yard, Rob left his companion with their horses and asked the captain of Dunwythie's guard to inform his lordship that he wanted to speak to him.

After keeping him waiting nearly an hour in a small room off the entry where Rob suspected tradesmen waited to talk to his lordship's steward, Dunwythie received him in the hall, greeting him politely but without enthusiasm.

Matching his lordship's civility while fighting his own impatience, Rob forced concern into his voice as he said, "Forgive me if I intrude, my lord. I heard the disconcerting news in my travels that one of your daughters is missing. I have come to offer you any help I can give in finding her."

"Have ye now?" Dunwythie said, with a sour look. "And why would I welcome aid from a Maxwell? If English ruffians took her, God kens ye Maxwells were once their allies. If 'twas Jardine mischief, ye'd be their ally even now!"

"Good sakes, sir, I had the honor to meet both of your daughters at Dunwythie Mains. I ken fine that you must be gey fond of them, so I should think you would gladly accept any aid in finding Lady Mairi, no matter who took her."

"So I would from most men," Dunwythie agreed. "Ye'll have to forgive me, though, if I wonder why any Maxwell would make such an offer."

"'Tis easy enough to explain," Rob said. "As you know, the sheriff has any number of men at his command who could aid in your search for the lady Mairi—and access to places your own influence cannot reach. Sakes, I could gain his aid swiftly on your behalf if you would but accept my offer to do so, to track down Jardines *or* English raiders.

But you cannot expect him to pay for all the men and supplies such a search would require, to help a nobleman who refuses to contribute his share of the shire's expenses."

"Is that how ye Maxwells define the added sum your sheriff demands for collecting Annandale's taxes? 'Tis nobbut our fair share of the shire expenses, ye say? It is nobbut *extortion*. But he will *not* succeed."

"Will he not, my lord?"

"Nay, for all the lairds of Annandale I've talked to have agreed we must go on as we have done. We have never required the sheriff's aid, nor will I seek it now. I'll find my daughter by myself, Robert Maxwell. So, hie yourself back to Dumfries or wherever you've come from."

"My lord, by my troth, you would do better to hear me out," Rob said, fighting back his rising temper.

"You've nowt to say that I want to hear. When you see your thieving brother, tell him you had no better luck than he did in persuading me or any other Annandale laird to hand over our gelt to the Maxwells of Nithsdale."

"But I *can* help you find her!"

"Nay, then, ye cannot! Now, go. I dinna want ye finding my Mairi any more than I wanted your gallous friend Will Jardine sniffing round her sister. Ye'll have heard of that event, too, I shouldn't wonder, belike from the same devious source."

Any thought Rob had had of ending Will's thirst for the lady Fiona vanished.

But as he commanded himself yet again to ignore his host's understandable ire and keep to his own purpose, Dunwythie abruptly left the room, shouting for his porter to show the unwelcome visitor out.

The next time Mairi awoke it was to pale light, a thunder of waves below, a lower rumble near at hand, and a soft paw patting her chin. She was stiff, damp, cold, and sore. But at least she could be nearly sure now that she would not drown.

"Cold comfort," she murmured to the purring kitten. "I'll wager you're hungry and thirsty, just as I am. And you probably also wish you had eaten more supper than you did, and drunk more water. In troth, I crave a drink much more than I want food. All that water down below and none for drinking."

The kitten made a chirping sound but otherwise went on purring.

Wondering if the tide might be lower than it had been before, Mairi set the kitten on its feet, picked up her skirts, and made her way down the stairs again.

She saw as soon as she emerged from the spiral part of the stairway that the sea was still making its presence much felt. The wharf rose only inches above the water, with occasional surges washing over it. The gray light entering the cavern indicated either that the sun had dipped behind the western cliffs already or that the sky had grown overcast again. She sighed. It did not matter much which one it was.

With no reason to go down to the wharf, had it even been safe, she scooped up the kitten, which had followed her, and carried it dejectedly back upstairs.

Rob saw as he and his oarsman rode back into Annan town that it might already be too late to return on the ebbing tide. It would likely leave them aground before they reached the river Nith. With the tides at their extreme as they were, the receding sea would leave only sand and mud for twenty miles.

He would, he decided, discuss the problem with Jake Elliot.

Although Rob cursed Dunwythie for his obstinacy, he soon realized the man's reaction had surprised him less than he had thought such behavior would. His thoughts shifted next to Mairi in half-grudging, half-admiring acknowledgment that she had been right about her father. She would have good reason to gloat, if gloating were in her nature.

She would not gloat, though. Indeed, he had a feeling that whatever she had said about her father, and no matter how deeply she had believed he would refuse to submit, she would be deeply disappointed to learn that she was right.

They were still some distance from the galley when he realized that, as he had been thinking of her, a prickling unease had begun to creep through him.

Dismissing it, he told himself it was no more than his irritation with himself colliding with his fury at Dunwythie's utter failure to protect his precious daughter.

But with his next breath, he said to his companion, "Walk faster, lad."

Waking from a doze in pitch blackness and abject terror, Mairi heard the sound of lapping water so near that she knew the sea was creeping closer. She was in what she had decided was the more comfortable of the two corners near the door.

The kitten had been in her lap but was not there now.

She had no idea how long she had slept. But surely, she thought, this was the same incoming tide she had heard crashing about below her for a long hour or two before falling asleep. The same thunderous noises that had accompanied its surging in would surely have awakened her in its ebb.

Wanting to know the worst, she shifted position enough to feel carefully for the step below the one on which she sat.

Finding it cold but still dry, or as dry as it ever was, she bent sharply forward to feel below it and nearly lost her balance. But the next step was dry, too. Below it, the next was damp. Moving one foot to it, she leaned forward again, expecting to find the sea with her fingertips but finding only the damp, shivering kitten.

As she began to straighten with it trembling in her hands, it squirmed and dug claws into her bodice, trying to climb higher.

Water surged then, soaking Mairi's feet and the hem of her gown. Snatching her skirts up, she scrambled blindly up the steps and reached her corner, gasping.

Forcing herself to concentrate on calming Tiggie, whose claws still hooked tight in her bodice, she wondered if the sea just might swallow them after all.

The sun dipped below the horizon as the galley passed Southerness Point a mile west of the river Nith's outflow.

Although Jake Elliot had expressed skepticism about Rob's decision to sail with what remained of the ebb tide, they had made it far enough, barely, to clear the sands. They took shelter as the tide turned by beaching the galley in an inlet northeast of the point, where they waited out the hours of turbulent inflow.

They had rested and eaten their supper. But they still had nearly five hours before they would enter Kirkcud-bright Bay.

The weather had begun to concern Rob. The wind was blowing straight toward them from the open sea, forcing them to furl their sail and row hard to keep a westward heading. Jake suggested once that they make for shore, but his laird's curt reply made it clear that a second such suggestion would be unwise.

Rob would brook no delay now that he could avoid. In the west, clouds that had provided a spectacular sunset billowed black, and he already had seen a few flashes of lightning. But the storm remained distant, and the moon had come up.

Unless the storm fell upon them with unexpected swiftness and ferocity, he would stay on the water. The wind had blown icily from the north earlier, had shifted often, and would shift again as the storm came nearer.

He was aching to reach Trailinghail.

In truth, though, he knew it was not Trailinghail he ached to see but Mairi. He felt himself stir just thinking about her, and wondered what demon possessed Dunwythie that he had not instantly agreed to anything that would bring her home.

But he knew that that thought was no more complete than the one before it had been, because while he condemned Dunwythie for rejecting the chance to reclaim her, he had to admit lurking admiration for the man's loyalty to his own people and to the stewartry of Annandale.

"Laird?" Gibby's tone was both wary and determined. "Jake Elliot says them clouds yonder be a great storm a-brewing."

"We'll be home before it reaches us," Rob said reassuringly.

"Good then," Gib said, and returned to his place.

Rob hoped his prediction was right. He wished the contrary wind would shift round behind them and drive them to Trailinghail as fast as the early tide had carried them from it. The irritating sense of unease was still with him and growing stronger. He could not shake the feeling now that it had to do with Mairi.

During the next hours, the fickle wind shifted several more times in front of the oncoming storm, more than once threatening to blow them to the English coast before its strength began at last to wane.

The ebbing tide, however slow, and the dropping wind made it easier to maintain a steady pace and stay closer to the coast as they neared Kirkcudbright Bay. From time to time, the bright moon still peeked through the gathering clouds.

As the galley entered the bay, Rob saw that the water was much too low for them to use the sea entrance. The moon vanished as he ordered his men to row for the beach below Senwick. But he could still make out the cliffs and the kirk tower lantern.

The stormy black clouds had lowered and were leaking rain in huge drops that spattered on the wood deck of the galley and on the oarsmen. Although the wind had picked up again, blowing hard from the west, the cliffs on the western side of the bay blunted much of its force.

Rob kept the sail up until the last minute, when two lads brought it down smartly in flapping protest as he shouted for the oarsmen to raise their blades. Jake Elliot disconnected the steerboard, and the galley glided neatly onto the beach.

Pulling their oars inboard, the men leaped out and hauled the boat high onto the beach, burying its anchors under sand and rock to keep it in place at least until they could attend to it properly.

"Look after the boat and the men, Jake," Rob shouted. "Gib, you stay with Jake. I'm going on ahead."

Dashing up the steep path, he ignored the increasingly noisy, driving rain as his thoughts rushed ahead to Trailinghail and Mairi.

Soaked and bedraggled by the time he reached the tower, he ran nearly to the gate before men atop the wall recognized him and shouted for others inside to open it. The wary expressions of the two men who did told him something was amiss.

"What is it?" he demanded. "Damnation, talk to me! What has happened?"

"Nowt, laird," the elder of the two said hastily. "Leastways, we hope 'tis nowt. Just only that ye be in a gey grand hurry for a man wha' ha' left the lady Mairi behind ye to look after herself in this pelter o' rain."

Stabbing fear replaced his unease. "What the devil do you mean?"

"She doesna be in her chamber, laird, and them inside were a-thinking she must be wi' ye. Did ye no take her wi' ye when ye left?"

"I did not," he said. "I left her safely here. Where is Annie?"

"Sakes, laird, she be safe in her own bed, a-sleeping."

"Have someone fetch her, *now*."

He wasted no time asking how Mairi could have escaped the tower, let alone got outside the wall. He would deal with those questions when he was sure she had succeeded in either endeavor. Curtly, he said, "How long has she been gone, and are you certain she did *not* leave by this gate?"

The spokesman said, "Nay, sir, she didna go by us. They did come and ask did we see her, but nae one here did. Nor did anyone pass through this gate till ye came. In troth, though, we dinna ken when she went missing. Annie's mam be sick, and the lady Mairi gave Annie leave yestereve to stay home wi' her. But, sithee, wee Gib has disappeared, too. Mayhap he kens what became o' her ladyship."

When the second guard nodded, Rob said, "Gib *was* with me. He and the others are close behind me. So stand by to open the gate when they get here."

Without another word, he hurried inside.

Chapter 12 _____

Rob tried to think. Where would she go? *How* could she go? What dangers might she face? Was she daft enough to think she could escape from Trailinghail?

If he roused everyone in the castle at such an hour and began questioning them, he would create the very stir he had worked to avoid and would learn no more than that they all thought she had gone with him.

When he looked into her room—as if she might magically have reappeared there—he saw from its extreme tidiness why Fin Walters or others who had looked in had assumed that she was with him. Especially as Annie had apparently not come that day. Had Mairi purposely told her to stay with her mother?

Only as he was about to return to the gate to question the guards again did he recall bringing her in through the cave entrance.

Chills swept through him at the thought. If she had remembered how to find the cave door and managed to get outside the cavern, could she have been mad enough to try to swim or otherwise try to reach Kirkcudbright?

On that thought, he lit another lantern in the kitchen and hurried down to the storage chamber, finding it as he had left it. Or so he thought until he noticed the pool of wax on the floor. Realizing that she must have put it there herself to hold a candle so she could use both hands to open the door, he noted with a new surge of fear that the latch chain still hung inside.

Did she not know to put a latchstring through its hole before shutting a door?

Sakes, as small as she was, had she even seen the hole?

Unlatching the door, he ripped it open and caught her as she slumped across the threshold. Lifting her into his arms, he failed to see the kitten until it hissed indignantly at him, jumped to the floor, and darted out of the chamber.

She felt icy cold, and her head fell back limply against his shoulder.

Quickly shifting her weight in his arms to hold her closer, he saw her eyelids flutter, and breathed more easily.

"You're back," she murmured with a soft sigh as he kicked the door shut and strode with her into the main part of the cellar, leaving his lantern behind.

"Aye, I'm back," he growled, heading for the stairway.

"Put me down," she said before he got to the steps. Her voice sounded hoarse, and her teeth were chattering, although they had not been before. "It will be safer for us b-both, going up the stairs, and I'll w-warm quicker, I think, if I m-move."

He doubted she would warm quickly. But as wet as he was himself from the rain, he did not argue. Setting her on her feet, he gestured toward the stairway.

She took a step but lost her balance, stumbling and nearly falling.

Rob quickly slipped an arm around her to support her.

She clutched him, swaying. "My legs went to sleep," she said. "Curse them!"

Holding her close again, he could feel her shivering, or himself trembling. In the dim glow from the lantern back in the storage cell he could not tell which it was.

"I'll d-do now," she said after what seemed to be both too long and too short a silence. She let go of him and stood a moment uncertainly, as if she were testing her balance, before she said, "Thank you."

But when she took another wobbly step only to sway, he picked her up again. "You'll do as I bid you," he said sternly. "It will be gey easier for me to carry you than to catch you when you fall on those steep stairs."

He went carefully until he could see that the door at the top remained open. Light from the kitchen spilled down the steps, showing the way clearly and telling him the cooks were there, stirring up the fire and the bake ovens.

He went quickly past the kitchen to the great hall, knowing that the kitchen servants would need its fire. They'd be preparing food for his supper and that of his returning men. The baker would also begin baking his bread for the morning.

But the hall fire would be blazing now, too.

Skirting men who slept on pallets in the hall, he carried Mairi to a wooden settle by the fire. As he set her on it, he could hear her teeth still chattering, and he saw that her lips were blue.

His still smoldering temper ignited. "What the devil were you thinking?" he demanded, managing only with effort to keep his voice low. "By heaven, lass, you deserve . . . Sakes, I don't know what you deserve for doing such a daft thing!"

Her voice still raspy, she said wearily, "Are you consigning me to the devil or to heaven, sir? You should make up your mind. I did not know that door would shut. It was so heavy, I thought it would stay put. But a demon draft drew it shut."

A nearly overwhelming urge to tell her exactly what he thought of reckless women who took daft notions into their foolish heads brought the words right to the tip of his tongue. But before he could utter even one, her eyes shut.

"Find Annie," he shouted when Gib looked anxiously into the hall from the stairwell. "Go, lad, run! Tell someone to bring blankets to me here and dry clothing for her ladyship. Then fetch me some bricks to warm by the fire."

The lad hesitated. "Be the lady Mairi a-dyin' then, laird?"

"Go!" Rob roared.

Gibby fled.

Annie came running minutes later with a screen that Gibby, following her, helped her set up. Thus Mairi had privacy and warmth. With Gibby guarding the screen, Annie shooed Rob outside it, saying, "Get ye hence now, laird. Her ladyship will be more comfortable a-changing down here without ye hovering over her."

"She does not deserve comfort," Rob muttered. But he obeyed Annie, pacing back and forth outside the screen until she announced that Mairi wore dry clothing.

"Her hair do still be damp, laird," Annie said. "I'll just go and fetch her comb and brush if I may." She eyed him speculatively before she added, "Nae doots, she'll talk more sensibly after she has some supper."

"If you are daring to suggest that I am not to talk to her until then, you are wasting your breath," Rob said.

"Aye, well, ye'll no be taking her ladyship to task here in the hall afore all these rough men," Annie said stoutly. "I ken ye better nor that, laird."

"Do you?" He glowered at her. "Tend to your other duties now, Annie. I'll look after her ladyship."

"Aye, sir," Annie said. With a sympathetic look for Mairi, and her own dignity perfectly intact, Annie left the hall, sweeping young Gib before her.

Rob shifted his gaze back to Mairi and saw that she was watching him. As had happened far too often with the lass, he could not quite read her expression. But her lips twitched as if she might dare any moment to smile.

~

Rob still looked so angry that Mairi was tempted to thank the Fates that he had not found her until she must have looked as if she were teetering on death's doorstep. The cave's chilly dampness had penetrated bone-deep, making her fear for a time that she would never get warm again even if someone did find her.

But despite Rob's own wet clothing, her body had begun to take warmth from his much larger one as he had carried her up the stairs. Now that her feet were dry and she wore fur-lined slippers, a warm silk shift, and a woolen kirtle in place of her damp clothing and boots, she felt warm enough that she would have liked to take off the thick shawl Annie had wrapped around her.

Common sense warned her, however, to remain at least a bit feeble looking until after Rob had had his supper. She had learned long since that a well-fed man was less likely than a hungry one to erupt in fury.

The stern, speculative expression that had made him look as if he were trying to decide how best to punish her had changed to a worried look that for some inexplicable reason made her lips twitch as if they wanted to smile.

However, his deepening frown banished that sensation.

She said, "You must be tired after such a long journey, sir. Surely, you also want to change to dry clothing before we sup."

"Aye, I do," he agreed. He looked around the hall, which was beginning to fill with more hungry men than just the soggy-looking ones who had traveled with him. "When Annie comes back, I will," he added.

She let herself smile then. "I ken fine that you are angry with me, and I deserve that you should be," she said. "But before you say all that you want to say, I must tell you that I have never been so happy to see anyone as I was to see you when you opened that wretched, contrary door."

He grimaced, and she knew he was struggling again to keep his temper. But then Annie returned with a hairbrush in hand, as if he had never told her to tend to other duties. Instead of objecting, he visibly relaxed when he saw her.

Even so, he shifted his gaze back to Mairi and said in a calm tone more alarming than she had thought such a tone could be, "You and I will talk later."

Annie bobbed a curtsy and said, "Shall I see to her hair afore ye sup, sir?"

"Aye, and stay with her until I return."

Mairi watched him stride away. It was a pleasure to

watch the man move. His damp leather breeks hugged his thighs and buttocks so that if one watched only those parts, one could imagine him as a rather magnificent beast of the forest—a very strong beast, capable of making one feel warm and cosseted even when it snarled.

Annie cleared her throat loudly.

Startled, Mairi felt heat flood her cheeks as she met her gaze. Sure that she must have missed something Annie had said, she said, "Did you speak to me?"

Eyes atwinkle, Annie replied, "Will ye be wanting me to sit beside ye to do me brushing, m'lady? Or will ye turn so I can get to them tangles more easily?"

"Fetch that stool yonder," Mairi said, gesturing toward one standing near the wall on the opposite side of the fireplace. "I should sit nearer the fire so my hair can dry as you brush it, but I shall grow too hot if I do not take off this shawl."

"Aye, m'lady, your cheeks look gey hot now," Annie said with a grin.

~

Men still slept, but those who did not were sitting at their own tables when Rob returned. Mairi and Annie sat at one end of the high table, the latter looking uncertain to be there. She eyed him warily as he strode to the dais to take his place.

After speaking the grace before meat, he sat down and riveted his attention to his food. Nevertheless, he could hear every movement Mairi made, every breath and swallow. Her silence seemed contagious, too, because the usual bustle and chatter died away. It was, he thought, as if every man there were watching her and wondering about him and what he meant to do.

Word had clearly spread that she had done something to displease him, and they all knew their laird well enough to be sure he meant to learn just how she had done it and who had helped her. They were doubtless also certain that those who had helped would suffer for it, as she would.

Annie ate quietly, but she, too, kept glancing at him.

Gib came in with the kitten draped over a shoulder and a mutton chop in the other hand. Ignoring the adults, he went to the settle and sat down to share his chop.

Only Mairi seemed content in the silence. She looked toward him once, and he had to fight to keep from looking away like a lad caught staring at something he ought not to see. He forced himself to meet her gaze only to feel a strange shifting inside, a physical sensation that nearly brought tears to his eyes.

Had the sea taken her, he knew he would never have forgiven himself. Focusing firmly on the men in the lower hall, he noted with some satisfaction that as they caught his eye on them, they swiftly returned to their quiet conversations.

When he had finished, he stood. "We will go upstairs now," he said to Mairi. "We have much to discuss. Annie, Fin will collect Gib and see that you get home."

Mairi drew a long, steadying breath and exhaled it slowly before she stood to follow him from the hall. At the stairs, when he gestured curtly for her to precede him, she did so without comment.

She was grateful for his silence, chilly though it was.

At least, *she* was no longer cold. Her hair was dry and loosely plaited beneath a simple white veil. Her thirst was gone, and her stomach no longer grumbled emptily as it had for hours before he had found her. She knew his anger was due to her actions, and she had known from the moment she looked out of the cave and saw only water there that she would have to face him.

Even so, the nearer they drew to her chamber, the less certain she was of her ability to deal safely with him. She had seen him angry before but not like this.

At the landing, he leaned past her to open the door, pushing it wide and then putting a hand to her back to urge her inside. Annie had left candles alight, and their golden glow danced on the walls. When he followed Mairi in and shut the door, defensive words of protest stirred in her throat but she swallowed them unspoken.

She had not felt so vulnerable in his presence since the day he had captured her and brought her to Trailinghail.

"Now, by heaven, you will give me an explanation for this madness," he snapped as he turned from shutting the door to face her.

"I'll willingly explain," she said more abruptly than she had intended. "I *never* asked to come here, and I *don't* want to stay here. You are keeping me captive without any right or reason to do so, and I want to go home."

"Just how did you expect to get home from my cave?"

As he spat out the words, he loomed over her, much too close and much too large for her comfort. But Mairi stood her ground.

She had to tilt her head considerably to look up at him, but she refused to give him the satisfaction of seeing her step back. All the same, she realized that neither could she allow herself the satisfaction of spitting her answers at him.

"When you brought me here, I saw sand or shingle along shores to the north as we sailed into the bay," she said, fighting for calm. "From that window yonder, I can see a sandy shoreline across the bay. So I thought with such low water today, I could follow the beach on this side a good part of the way to Kirkcudbright."

Even by candlelight, she saw the color drain from his face. He was still angry even so, for he said grimly, "Then what? A lass, wandering alone—"

"I told you, I stayed at Castle Mains with my family last year on our way to Threave," she said.

"So, what if you did? Did you think you could claim hospitality there? I doubt that Archie is even in residence. He is more likely to be at Threave or riding round Galloway, making a show of his ability to keep all in order here."

"Even if he is away, some of his people must know that my lady stepmother is his cousin, sir. I am sure they would help me get home again."

"Then, thank God the sea stopped you," he snapped. "For of all the fool—"

When she grimaced, he caught her by the shoulders and gave her a hard shake, his eyes blazing as he stared into hers. "See here, my clever lass," he said furiously, "even had the tide lowered enough to leave sand or shingle near that cave, which only a few folks hereabouts have lived long enough to see happen, had you tried walking on it, you'd most likely have drowned. In *any* tide along any shore here, huge waves can strike hard and swiftly, carrying unwary folks away."

"But—"

"Parts of this western shore *are* sandy," he went on. "But much of the sand hereabouts is unstable, just as it is along much of the coast around the Firth. Such sand helps protect us, because it shifts easily and never gets completely dry. That deters English invasion by all but a handful of routes. Sithee, waves and the shifting sands have sucked even strong men under."

He paused as if he expected her to comment, but she said nothing.

"Even if you had somehow made it to a firmer beach, paths to the cliff tops are steep and high. And waterfalls spill from the cliffs on this side until fall. You'd have found it hard going even had you got that far."

Although she believed the route she had hoped to take was as dangerous as he said it was, she had experienced too much fear and self-rebuke in the tunnel to fear now what *might* have happened, since it had not.

So, instead of carefully heeding his words, she had fixed her attention on the man scolding her, on the strength of his hands gripping her shoulders and the tense anger in his voice. If he had seemed too close before, he seemed much more so now, sapping whatever energy she might have had left to defend herself.

He held her tightly, perhaps with more strength than he knew, but his hands were warm, too. He glowered down at her, still waiting for her to reply.

Supper had apparently not eased his temper at all, and she knew that when he was angry, he was unpredictable.

With a hope that she might defuse his anger with an apology, she said, "I did not know how dangerous it could be, sir. It *was* foolish of me, and wrong, to sneak into the cave. I was as foolish as you say I was, even stupid, to attempt such a thing. I expect that Cousin Archie would be even angrier than you are now had I reached him and told him what I'd done."

"If he cares a whit for you, he would be, but if you think you'd rather face my anger than his, you are dafter than I thought," he said. "Even if he didn't care about *you*, he *would* care what people would say, learning that a young kinswoman had walked six miles alone without heed for danger from the sea or from strangers on the way. You live near enough the Firth to know that rogue waves are a danger. How did you think you could avoid one of them with a sheer cliff at your back?"

"I *said* I was sorry," Mairi said, wishing as she saw his expression tighten that she had not spoken so curtly.

"Nay, you did not say that," he retorted. "You said you were stupid to think you could follow the shore. I doubt you are sorry that you tried to escape."

"It is all the same," she said. "Sithee, sir, I have *said* I ken fine that I acted heedlessly. I know, too, that you must have been angry and mayhap even frightened when you did not find me where you expected me to be on your return."

His grip tightened bruisingly.

"I *am* sorry if I gave you a scare," she said hastily. "But I—"

"Enough," he snapped, giving her another shake. "I want to hear no 'buts' from you, and no more of your apologies if that is how you make them. Any apology that includes a 'but' is no apology at all. It should be enough for you to know that if you ever do such a thing again, I will make Archie the Grim's anger seem as nowt to mine. Do you understand me?"

"Aye," she snapped, wanting to tear herself from his grip but forcing herself instead to meet his angry gaze, aware that neither sheer fury nor utter submission would restore peace between them yet. "I ken fine what you mean, Robert Maxwell, and I don't doubt that I deserve your . . . your . . . H-however, I . . ."

She could think of no more to say, either because she was exhausted or perhaps because he continued to hold her gaze until she felt an inexplicable urge to touch him, to bring him back from wherever his thoughts had taken him.

The tension between them had increased in a new way during those few seconds. Her breath had stopped and her lips felt dry.

Rob had gone from wanting to shake her to fearing that if he did not let go of her, he would break his resolve to keep his increasingly strong feelings for her under rein. It was bad enough that he had lost his temper again but even worse that she knew she had the power to frighten him. Still, he kept his hands on her.

Her face looked pinched and thinner. Small shadows touched the hollows at her temples and under her eyes. She was pale, and her eyes looked darker than usual, like shadowy pools.

Another wave of fury seized him. But seeing her wince, he realized he had exerted too much pressure where he gripped her. Angry now with himself, he released her and stepped back, saying—he hoped in a well-controlled voice, "Your shoulders will be bruised, I fear. I didn't think."

"Aye, well, if that is all you mean to do to me, I . . ." She hesitated and he saw her swallow hard, as if the reality of what might have happened—or still could happen—were just sinking in. Then, in a rush, she added, "I'd have suffered worse if I'd fallen down those steps, and much worse than that if the sea had taken me."

"Aye, you would," he said, putting a hand to her shoulder again, gently.

"I won't make such a nuisance of myself again," she said.

"Sakes, but you must ken gey fine that ever since I clapped eyes on you, you have made a nuisance of yourself," he retorted, expressing his raw feelings for once without a thought for how the words might sound to her.

She gave him a speaking look but was kind enough not to remind him that he, not she, was the one whose actions had put them where they were. Instead of stirring his temper again, it led him to explain further. "I fear that, from the outset, you have unsettled my ability to think sensibly," he said. "You make what I have done more difficult than I, or anyone, could ever have expected it to be."

"I have done naught," she said, rallying. "Had you stopped to think *at all* before you snatched me from my home, you might have recalled that I am far from tractable . . ." With a wry smile, she added, "I did inherit a certain stubbornness, sir, from my father. You will note that I have not asked you what he said, for I *know* what he said. But mayhap you would like to tell me how your visit progressed."

"It did *not* progress," he said, gesturing for her to sit and feeling oddly pleased that she wanted to hear about it, though the result was hardly to his liking. "You were right," he said. "I do not know what ails the man that he would consign his daughter to stay in an unknown place with an unknown captor."

"Art so sure he believes my captor is entirely unknown?" she asked.

He frowned. "He cannot know you are here. I said nowt to make him leap to such a thought. Indeed, I hired horses in Annan town before visiting him."

"You had better hope he does *not* learn that I am here," she said. "What if he leaves his army at home and simply seeks help from Archie the Grim?"

"I have thought much about Archie," he said. "I've sworn to follow him in aught concerning Galloway. But he kens fine that I side with Maxwell in matters concerning Dumfries. That would include your father's dispute with Alex. In time, Archie will expect all in Galloway and Dumfriesshire to bend to *him*. Mayhap by then our various forms of government will all grow clearer. Meantime, I think he will leave Alex to settle disputes relating to Dumfries, as he should."

"But you forget my cousin Jenny's husband, Sir Hugh Douglas. If he should apply to Archie *with* my father, might they not all come here to talk to you?"

"Your father doesn't know you are here, either," he reminded her.

"He could guess," she said. "You introduced yourself as Trailinghail's laird."

"But I told him . . ." He realized that although he had told Dunwythie he had only *heard* of Mairi's abduction and wanted to help if he could, Dunwythie had doubted his sincerity. Rob wondered if he did suspect Maxell involvement and had hoped to disarm him by saying he would find Mairi himself.

She was still watching him, waiting, so he said, "Sakes, I cannot say what your father may suspect. He gave me no cause to think he blames any Maxwell for your disappearance. He suggested Englishmen or the Jardines may have taken you."

Shaking her head, she said, "He would not suspect the English, sir. Why *would* they? So that he might persuade Douglas to leave them in possession of Lochmaben? My father would laugh at such a notion. As for the Jardines, I cannot think why they'd want me, but you can blame your friend Will for drawing his suspicion."

"I told you, I don't know what motives he thinks anyone may have," he said. "He must have enemies other than the Sheriff of Dumfries, though, ready to seize on any situation that could aid them in achieving their own ends."

"Perhaps he does have such enemies," she said. "But he has not mentioned them to me. Moreover, he has a long reputation as a man of peace and would, I think, be slow to suspect that he is now at odds with more than one enemy."

Rob had no quick response, and he did not want to discuss any further the possibility that Archie might take even slight interest in a matter undertaken to aid the Sheriff of Dumfries. That would not only irk Archie *and* Alex but would create more trouble than anyone wanted. Having hoped only to avoid clan war and perhaps help simplify the administration of Dumfriesshire and aid his clan in the process, he had certainly made his own life far more complicated than he had expected.

He did not, however, wish any longer that he had never abducted her.

Mairi watched him, trying to gauge his mood, but when he grimaced and turned toward the open window without saying more, she could think of nothing to say, either. His posture seemed to suggest that his spirits were low.

In that moment, she could think only of the strong man who consistently showed concern for her, the warrior gentle enough to enjoy the antics of a kitten and so beloved by his own people that even when they did not approve of what he had done, they would defend him in the doing.

He was a man to whom she could talk as she could talk to no one else. She could express even her most basic feelings to him. After spending so many years having to conceal much of what she felt, such freedom was heady, especially as she had had to become his prisoner before she experienced it.

Although he was quick to criticize, quick to offer advice, and quick to condemn behavior he disliked, he was more self-contained, intelligent, thoughtful, and gentle than other men she had met. And somehow, she could draw strength from his whenever she needed it, without knowing how she did it.

Before she knew what she was doing, she was standing right behind him and had reached out a gentle hand to touch his elbow.

He turned, and a moment later she was in his arms.

Chapter 13 _____

Rob held Mairi close. He could feel her heart beating rapidly against him. Everything around them—the bed, the floor beneath them, the very chamber and the still rainy night outside—flashed fiery images in his mind's eye as they vanished on a wave of ecstasy that stirred his body as it had never stirred before. Everything in him, every masculine instinct, every nerve and sinew, ached to take her to his bed.

For one long delicious moment, he felt as if he were alone in the world with her, as if everything and everyone else had vanished and nothing mattered but the lass he held and his desire for her. He could do whatever he wanted to do. He was a king in his castle with the woman he wanted in his arms.

A soft breath escaped her, a tiny sigh of content. And with that trusting sigh came the understanding that he must let his moment go.

She put a slender hand to his cheek. He gripped it and

pressed the back of it to his lips, then turned it and pressed his lips to its warm, soft palm.

"Prithee, sir," Mairi whispered softly, trembling against him. "No more."

"Just this," he murmured. Taking her beautiful face between his hands, he bent his head, kissed her on the mouth, and felt her lips come alive beneath his.

He let her go. "Don't expect me to apologize," he said. "You are too damnably enticing for your own safety or mine, my lass."

She stared at him, her soft lips slightly parted, her body still pressed to his.

Furious scratching at the door startled them both, and Rob turned with near relief to admit the kitten. It strolled past him, tail high, and leaped to Mairi's bed without so much as a glance at him.

Turning to Mairi with a smile, he said, "Would you believe I was annoyed at first that young Tiggie so quickly showed the good taste to prefer your company to mine? But now, I swear, I envy the wee devil." It was the truth, and he was astonished to realize that he did not mind at all admitting it to her.

She continued to stare at him as if she did not quite know what to say to him. Then she, too, looked relieved. Quietly, she said, "You should go, sir. In troth, although I must have slept much today, I long to sleep again now. It seemed as if I was in that cave forever. Is it truly still the same day as when you left?"

"Nay, 'tis a new one. I left here early Tuesday morning and it has now turned to Wednesday. But get you to bed now. We will talk more after we sleep."

She nodded, and he left her. But he could not put her

out of his head so easily. He wanted her, and the likelihood was that he could never have her unless he broke his vow to her—and to himself—that he would resist her.

He slept late and broke his fast hastily, feeling a strong need to get outside and away from the tower.

He had dreamed of her. He was sure of it, and the dream had been pleasant, but he could remember none of the details. His thoughts remained full of her as he went through his usual duties and dealt with the business of Trailinghail.

Although he reminded himself several times that he had said they would talk, other things intervened, one after another, until he knew he was avoiding her.

The truth was that he could not trust himself anymore just to talk with her.

～

Mairi slept longer than usual, too. When she awoke to the sound of the kitten scratching in its box of dirt, she saw that the rain had stopped. And although the sky outside her open window was still cloudy, it showed large patches of blue as well.

Getting up, she donned a robe, slipped her feet into furlined slippers, and went to wash her face. The door opened quietly as she poured water from the ewer into the basin. Glancing toward it, she saw Annie peeping in.

"Och, good then, ye're up," Annie said. "I didna want to wake ye."

"How is your mother today?" Mairi asked.

"She's herself again, thank God," Annie said. "But I'd

ha' come anyway, m'lady." She paused. "Ye didna say much yestereve about what happened to ye."

"Nay, and I'd liefer not," Mairi said with a slight smile.

"Then ye won't," Annie replied. She moved to take a yellow kirtle from one of the kists, then selected a tunic to wear over it, while Mairi washed her face.

The rest of that day and the next three passed in much the same way. The weather remained uncertain, with clouds billowing up and either showering the landscape or moving on to shower elsewhere.

Mairi supposed the weather was what kept Rob from inviting her to ride. She doubted he was punishing her, and she missed his company. He brought up her supper Friday evening but excused himself with other duties the rest of the time.

When he did come up, he brought Gibby with him. Annie was still there, too, so they had no opportunity for private talk.

Saturday morning, as Mairi was wishing they could find such an occasion, she realized she did not know what she would say to him if they did.

She and Annie were making such swift progress with the piecework that Mairi began to believe her bed would soon have a new quilt. But she had grown bored enough to ask Rob when he visited briefly Saturday evening—while Annie was still with her—if they might not go riding the next morning.

"It will probably rain again," he said.

"We won't dissolve, sir."

He agreed, and the following morning he came to escort her to the yard, where three horses awaited them, with Gibby mounted on the third one.

Noting the absence of their usual gillie, Mairi shot Rob a look.

When he did not meet it, she hid a smile. She had recalled the stern exception Gib had taken to Rob's presence in her bedchamber when she had arrived, and the lad's near threat to tell "Herself." Clearly, Rob thought Gib stronger protection than a gillie. It was good, she thought, that Rob wanted to protect her even from himself.

He put her on her horse and saw her settled with reins in hand before he turned to the boy. "Art comfortable enough, lad?"

"Aye, sure," Gib muttered with a grimace.

"Do you not like to ride, Gibby?" Mairi asked.

To her surprise, he flushed bright red as he gave her a quick nod.

Rob's lips twitched a little wryly, and he said, "I expect he has not yet told you that he has seen the river Annan and Annan town, my lady."

"Sakes, sir, surely you did not take him on that journey!"

"I did not *choose* to take him. He told my helmsman I had given him permission to go. By the time I discovered him, we were in the bay, rowing for the Firth at the end of an ebb tide. The water was too low to get back to the cave. And to row back to Senwick's beach would have meant leaving him on it. Such rarely exposed parts of our beaches can be unsafe, as I think I warned you."

"So you did," she said, flashing Gib a sympathetic look as she added, "I hope you were not too harsh with him, sir."

"Not I," Rob said.

"The laird made me tell Fin Walters what I'd done,"

Gibby said. "And now he's a-making me ride this horse today. It ha' been some few days now, though. So I ha' nae doots it willna be so bad as it might ha' been."

"Aye, well, I need you to protect me from the *laird's* temper, Gib," Mairi told him. "He's none so pleased with me, either, I think."

Gibby looked ready to ask for details, but Rob intervened before he could.

"I did not invite you along today to listen to you chatter," he said. "You can follow behind us now. This track is too narrow for three abreast."

The boy fell back obediently, whereupon Mairi said quietly, "You were cruel to bring him, sir. Surely, our usual gillie would have been a better choice."

"I think you know I brought Gib because he'll keep his mouth shut about aught we say but will speak up if he disapproves of aught I do," he murmured back. "I do wish you would call me Rob when we can talk privately like this."

"Do you, sir?" she said with a smile.

He shook his head, and they rode for another hour before black clouds billowing in the west again persuaded him to insist that they return.

It occurred to Mairi only then that he might have had another reason to put off their ride for a few days. Casually, she said, "Is the knacker still here, sir? That shutter that blew open when I first arrived does not seem to fit properly now. It whistles whenever the wind blows hard."

"Dow left Thursday for Dumfries," Rob said. "But I'll have a look at that shutter for you later."

The wind had risen again by the time they reached the yard, and Mairi was glad to get back. They had conversed desultorily like friends. But the boy's presence seemed to cast a damper on their usual easy conversation.

She was sorry it had.

～

Rob, too, was aware that something had been missing in their ride. But he was not sorry he had taken Gib along. He had hoped that if he saw less of Mairi each day, the feelings that had nearly undone him after her adventure in the cavern would ease if not disappear altogether. Instead they had intensified.

No matter what he expected from her, no matter what he said to her, she had continually surprised him. Looking back, he marveled that she had never shown fear of him—wariness, but never fear. Moreover, she still seemed willing, despite that stolen kiss, to trust him not to harm her.

He knew that her trust had affected him deeply then, that without it, he might have pressed for more than a kiss, even in the face of her softly murmured protest.

He did not think of himself as an aggressive lover, nor had he ever taken an unwilling partner or one lacking experience. But experience told him that women often said no when they meant yes—especially when they protested softly.

Thinking about that, he admitted that some of his previous partners might have felt obliged to please him. But most Scotswomen, especially Borderers, were outspoken enough to express their true feelings. He knew, too, that lairds who took unfair advantage of their people were likely to lose their respect.

Mairi did not feel obliged to please him. Nor, despite

telling him she had generally sought peace at home, did she seek peace with him by keeping silent. She listened and did not judge him even when he made her angry. She could be sharp-tongued, even caustic at times. But she never assumed the worst of him. She would say what she thought—bluntly perhaps, but without carping or grousing.

He kept busy in the stable for some time after their return, going inside only as the servants were setting out supper. Fin Walters told him that Annie, having sent Gib down earlier to inquire about the laird's whereabouts, had come down herself to collect the tray with her supper and her ladyship's.

Rob nodded, deciding it was just as well. He invited Fin to take supper with him so they could discuss a project Rob wanted to begin when the weather cleared.

Their conversation continued over a fresh jug of whisky that Gib carried into the wee chamber behind the hall for them when they adjourned there as the men began to lay out pallets in the hall for the night. Fin then sent Gibby off to bed.

By the time they bade each other goodnight, Rob felt sleepy enough to doze where he stood. Making his way to his bedchamber, he did no more than wash his face, strip himself, and fall into bed, where he slept deeply until a bright flash of light and an explosion of thunder woke him.

Wind was screaming around the tower, sending icy fingers in through the unshuttered window that set the bed curtains swirling.

Mairi was also asleep when the thunder crashed. But she awoke with a start, sitting bolt upright and shaking. She had left the east-facing window unshuttered from the day of her arrival, feeling no need to shut it even when it rained.

Now, wind attacked the tower from all sides, roaring and howling as fiercely as ever she had heard it. Flashes of lightning, one after another, and deafening cracks of thunder punctuated the din, in a storm so turbulent that it shook the very walls.

She had long hated big storms, especially in the hilltop Annan House, but she trembled at the force of this one. Trailinghail's location high on the cliff, exposed to the strongest winds from the sea, magnified the storm's effects. Reminding herself that the tower had withstood many such storms, that there was naught to fear, she sympathized with Tiggie when, trembling, he squirmed under an arm, into her lap.

Despite her fear, she took a moment to soothe the kitten before getting up and grabbing her robe. Slipping it on, fighting to tie its sash with the wind madly blowing it awry, she turned toward the open window. As she did, she recalled her complaint to Rob that the other shutter whistled.

It did whistle whenever the wind blew past it just so. But she had mentioned it only to give herself reason for asking about the knacker. Doubtless it was whistling now, but she could not hear it over the uproar outside.

The wind raged from the east straight into her room. By the next lightning flash she saw that rain also poured in through the window.

Just as she saw it, she stepped in a puddle on the floor and slipped.

Struggling to keep her balance and avoiding most of the

incoming rain, she grabbed the shutter, unhooked it, and was fighting the wind to close it when a crash of thunder much louder than the others made her duck and clap her hands to her ears.

The shutter slammed and then crashed open again and against the wall, coming so near her head as she straightened that it brushed her hair. The wind had reached gale force when the door banged open and glowing light entered the room.

Glancing toward it as she reached again for the shutter, she saw Rob's unmistakable figure looming at the threshold with a covered lantern in one hand.

"Get away from that window!" he shouted at her over another flash and its accompanying explosion of thunder.

She stared at him, deafened and quaking, hoping he was real.

Stepping in and quickly shutting the door to stop the wind's headlong plunge down the stairway, Rob set the lantern on the settle and hurried to help Mairi.

He was barefoot and had pulled on only his breeks when he'd recalled her damaged shutter. As soon as he did, he had rushed upstairs to be sure she was safe.

She had not moved, and the wind was whipping her robe around her legs, baring them to her thighs unheeded. She just stared, so he said firmly, "Lass, get away from the window. That floor is wet, and the lightning is gey close and too dangerous. I've heard of it striking men who stood too near such high windows."

The wind still screamed and howled round the tower,

louder in her room than in his, making the unlatched shutter bang back and forth while lightning bolts and explosions of booming, cracking thunder hurled themselves about outside.

Wide-eyed, she had frozen there, unable or unwilling to move.

He pushed past her and grabbed the thick shutter, forcing it shut and snapping its two hooks snugly into their iron eyes.

Then he turned and took her firmly by the shoulders. "You're safe now," he said, pulling her closer. When she melted toward him, her arms opening, his hands slid from her shoulders to embrace her, and the rest of his body reacted instantly.

"You're trembling," he murmured against her hair. "Ah, lassie, don't be afraid. I'm here, and this tower has stood far worse. That shutter is sound, so the other must be the one that needs fixing. Sithee, I forgot till I heard that first great crash. But if you'll get back into bed, I'll see if I can fasten it better."

"There's naught amiss with it," she murmured against his bare chest, her arms tightening around his torso, her warm breath stirring new and wonderful sensations through his ever-willing body.

But he heard her words and understood them.

"You just wanted to know if there was still a chance you could get a message to the knacker," he muttered back sternly, hoping that if she looked up, his body blocked enough of the lantern light to keep her from seeing his smile.

Another crash sounded outside. The tower trembled in

the wind, and she clutched him tighter. "I'm sorry I lied," she said. "But don't leave me yet."

Her shivers were from fear of the storm, he decided, not from cold.

His cock stirred forcefully against his breeks, suggesting that the least he could do was divert her thoughts from the storm. Putting a hand to her chin, he tilted her face up, gazed searchingly at her, and when her lips parted, he kissed her.

Her lips moved at once beneath his as they had the first time, and she moaned low in her throat. Needing no further invitation, he slid his hands over the silk robe, damp now and apparently all that she wore. He pressed her closer, enjoying the sensation of her soft, silk-clad breasts against his bare skin.

Moving one hand to cup the back of her head, he thrust his tongue between her willing lips and began to explore the interior of her mouth. It was a moment before he realized that her soft hair was damp, too. Even so, he did not want to stop.

She was responding with a passion equal to his, and he felt sure he could stop before things went too far.

Before then, however . . . He moved his hand from her head down inside her robe to cup a warm silky breast. His thumb brushed over its nipple, drawing a soft moan. Her hands moved, too, caressing his sides and back until it was all he could do not to take her to the bed and ravish her.

"'Tis so cold in here; mayhap we should get under the covers," she murmured then, astonishing him and stirring his cock straight to attention.

"That is *not* a good notion, lass, believe me."

"But my feet are freezing. You *must* be cold, too. And my robe is damp."

And she wore nothing underneath it.

Another crack of thunder made her jump, although it sounded more distant, as if the storm were deciding to move on.

"Please," she whispered.

He picked her up and carried her to the bed, where the kitten sat, watching. As he laid her down beside it, the tower trembled in another fierce gust of the wind.

"I should go," he said.

"No! Please stay."

"Lass, if I stay, I cannot trust myself to keep my hands off you."

"I don't want you to," she said. "I want you to stay, and I want you to go on touching me. I have never felt such things, and I want to know what you will do."

"But—"

"Sithee, I doubt I shall *ever* marry. Even if I do, I may not be able to ask a husband the sorts of questions I know I can ask you. You will not tell me I do not *need* to know, as my father so often does. Even now, though he teaches me much about estates I may never own, he has told me naught about men and women."

"Has not your stepmother explained such things?"

"Nay, only that a woman must obey her husband in all he says to do."

"All?" His cockstand became painful.

"If you do not want to show me, mayhap you can just describe it for me."

He could scarcely breathe. His voice was hoarse as he

said, "My lady, it would be my pleasure to show you if you are *sure* that is what you want."

"I am, aye."

Picking up the kitten, he put it outside the door and turned back, assuring himself that he could end things before he risked getting her with child. But once he had his breeks off and had climbed into bed with her, his body wanted her as much as his mind did, if not more fiercely.

Mairi watched him stride to the door and put down the kitten, smiling when it spat at him. Rob made a powerful dark shape against the lantern glow. As he shut the door and went next to light candles from the lantern, his torso turned golden.

Her body tingled where he had touched her. Her mouth still seemed full of him, the taste of him, and her breasts . . . He had touched only one, had thumbed its tip for less time than it took now for a flame to leap to life on the candle. Yet, she could still feel his touch, could still feel the heat of the flame he had lit there.

It had spread to her very center, had warmed her all through. Was this what it felt like to be with any man, a husband? Something, some ill-wishing demon within her, whispered that it was not, that all men were different and one's experience with any two was likely to be different, too. Still, coupling was coupling, a physical act that all animals knew how to do—or should know.

Her thoughts stopped, and her body tensed again as he moved toward her.

"Did you say your robe is damp?" he said, setting the candle in its dish.

"Aye, a little."

"Then you should take it off and wrap yourself in your sheet. I'll just slip under the blanket then."

"Aye, sure," she said, beginning to slip off her robe.

⁓

Rob turned his back, aware that he still felt the effects of the two jugs of whisky he had drunk with Fin, and knowing he could not trust himself if he saw her naked. Not with candle glow turning her lovely, silky, curvaceous body golden all over. By rights, he had no business staying one more moment. But he hungered for her, and she wanted him to stay. Moreover, she feared the still tumultuous storm.

Sakes, it was the least he could do. Accordingly, he slipped under the coverlet as he was, feeling an absurd, cocky sense of having taken the place from the fierce little kitten. He chuckled at the absurdity of such a thought.

"What is funny?" she asked as thunder rolled again outside.

"I was just thinking that Tiggie must hate me right . . ." He paused, touched bare skin that was not his own. "I told you to cover yourself with the sheet."

"Did you? But I want you to hold me again, and it would get in the way."

It would, he agreed silently.

Deciding he had protested enough, he gathered her close, turning onto his left side so he could hold and stroke her—to warm her. But he scarcely made it past her nearest elbow before he captured her mouth again.

She responded as swiftly as she had before, stroking him wherever she could reach. When she caressed his chest, her fingers found a nipple, stopping his breath. Although it was not, by any means, the first time a woman had touched him there, Mairi's touch went deeper than he could remember anyone's going before.

He rarely made verbal sounds when having sex and usually heeded his partner's reactions only insofar as they would help get him to his goal.

With Mairi, determined as he was to stop things before he might get her with child, he savored every feeling she created in him and paid much heed to how she reacted. He wanted to know which things he did stirred her most.

When he took her right nipple between his lips, then between his teeth, she stopped stroking him and went still. He used his tongue then, laving her nipple, and delighted in the gasp he startled out of her.

When he stopped, she said quickly, "Go on, that feels wondrous good. Does it feel so to you when a woman does it?"

"If you'd like to find out, try it," he said.

"Sakes, have you never *had* a woman do it to you before?" she asked as she turned toward him and pushed him gently onto his back.

"That would be telling. Ouch!" She had nipped him with her teeth.

"You are too old not to know such things about yourself," she said as she stroked his chest and played with his nipples.

The more she did, the more he lost himself in his reactions, until he knew he could stand it no more and surged up again, pushing her back and taking control. He caressed her until she moaned and squirmed beneath him. Then his hand moved to the fork of her legs, and she moaned louder but squirmed less as he caressed her there. A lingering crack of thunder made her jump, and his fingers slid inside.

"I thought the storm had passed," he muttered, his fingers still busy below.

"Don't talk," she said.

A voice in his head said, "Easy, laddie, stop!"

Another murmured, "But I don't want to stop."

"Neither do I," she cried on a near wail as her body arched against his teasing fingers. "So, don't!"

Evidently the latter of the two voices in his head had been his own, not an imaginary one. But he wanted her then more than he had ever wanted anything.

Although his better nature argued against it, his baser one strongly suggested that he could deal with any problem that taking her might create in the future. He had, after all, come to care for her *much* more than he had ever thought he would.

When she moaned again, he knew she was as ready as any inexperienced woman could be, and his own body screamed its hunger for her. Without allowing his better self another word, he moved over her, murmuring soft nothings without hearing them through the roaring in his ears as his body responded with every fiber of its eagerness to join with hers.

She cried out once, giving him pause. But her breathing came rapidly, and she seemed as immersed in their passion as he was. When he reached his peak, his better self screamed warning, inspiring him to pull out at the last minute and spill his seed onto the sheet between her legs.

As he lay spent atop her, she squirmed. Realizing he was probably crushing her, he shifted to lie against the pillows and draw her in close to kiss her. Holding her as he did, with her head on his shoulder, he felt deep content.

"I just thought . . ." she murmured. Then, after a pause, she added, "Will you have got me with child, do you think?"

"'Tis unlikely," he said. "I pulled out to avoid it. But in troth, lass, I'm told that doing so is no perfect assurance that one has *not* begun a child."

"I see."

"I'd apologize," he said. "But once again, I'm not really sorry. I could blame the whisky I drank earlier with Fin. But the plain truth is that I wanted you."

"Aye," she said. "Me, too."

Chapter 14 _____

After brief reflection on the delights their coupling had provided, and on all he had just said, Mairi murmured, "Still, I expect we should not have done it."

"Mayhap we should not," Rob agreed. "But I could not seem to stop myself. Nor do I wish it undone. We must marry, of course. I'll see to arranging it at once."

"Nay, then, we cannot," Mairi said firmly, determined not to let him see that the idea did appeal to her. The fact that it strongly appealed astonished her. But she could imagine how others would feel about it—especially her father . . . and Phaeline.

"Lass, we must not fratch over this. 'Tis too important. What we've done—"

"What we have done, we did together," she said. "There can be no dispute over that. But we cannot marry, sir. I am still underage, and my father would never permit it. Nor could I disappoint him by marrying without his consent into a clan that he deems an enemy. He would view it as the basest of betrayals, I promise you. In troth, I believe it would kill him for any daughter of his to betray him so."

"But your own reputation," he protested. "You must consider that, Mairi lass. People will believe the worst of you if they learn what has happened here."

"People believe what they believe," she said. "Sakes, but my having been with you here for as long as I have ensures that those inclined to believe the worst will believe it now in any event. I would not have them say instead that you forced me to marry you. And they would! You must know that they would."

"We would deny it. By my troth, I would not force you even if I thought I could. Which," he added dryly, "I do *not*."

"Well, you could, of course, simply by overpowering me, for you are gey strong," she said. "But otherwise, you could not. Sithee, I have learned much about marriage law from my cousin Jenny, enough to know that no one can legally force a Scotswoman to marry if she does not want to. I know my rights regarding marriage settlements, my father's barony, and other such things, too."

"I'll remember that and take care not to cheat you."

"You would never cheat me," she said. "I do know that much about you. But it does not matter. There can be no marriage between us—now or ever."

"We'll see about that," he said. "I will *not* have people saying wicked things about you. So that is all there is to—"

"My family has grown accustomed to my lack of suitors," she interjected. "They already fear that I'll never wed, so I have only to let them go on thinking that. They will tell others so, and so sincerely that those others will believe it, too."

"Aye, they *will* believe it," he said grimly. "Because, whatever anyone may have thought was the reason *before* I abducted you, they will now believe that you remain unwed because I took advantage and then *refused* to marry you. We must marry, lass, if only so others can know of our feelings for each other and—"

"Enough, sir. You begin to make me believe you would marry me only out of pity or a hope that you might then avoid being called a rapist. Why should anyone believe aught but that you married me because you *had* taken advantage—mayhap in hope that you could thereby gain control of the Dunwythie estates?"

"You don't believe that."

"I don't. But many others would."

"Aye, perhaps, but what if I *have* given you a child?" he demanded.

"Then mayhap we'll talk again," she replied, refusing to let something that might or might not be the case sway her from seeing the certainties. "There may come a time when I *will* marry," she said. "But if I inherit the estates, my husband may not care about what happened here. Meantime, sir, I must think about my father and my own duty. To marry you and live at Trailinghail would be a further betrayal of him as long as I remain heiress to his estates and responsibilities."

～

Rob was silent.

He understood familial duty only too well. How the

devil could he insist that she ignore such duty when he had abducted her in its service?

The annoying voice that too frequently piped up from the back of his mind suggested then that duty was not all that had spurred him to that injudicious feat.

He hushed the voice. He was sure he would never have thought of abducting Mairi Dunwythie had his grandmother and Alex not both insisted in their own ways that he owed absolute duty to his clan and to his family, and had each not done so, so soon after he had laid eyes on her.

Although he could not deny that he had wanted her then, or that her beauty and her casual dismissal of him had stirred a primal urge to conquer her, duty had certainly spurred him to consider planning her abduction.

When she'd presented herself to him, so near the galley, during his exploratory visit to Annan House, his nemesis, impulse, had seized hold and forced his hand.

"You are smiling again," she said, visibly irked. "This is serious."

"Aye, lass, I ken fine that it is," he said. "I was just thinking back. Sithee, when I saw you in those woods, I acted without considering *any* consequences."

"But you must have considered them! You were only there to abduct me."

He realized that although he had thought much about that day and they had often mentioned the abduction, he had never told her exactly how it had happened.

"I just wanted to see if my plan was feasible," he explained. "I'd heard you had all returned to Annan House, but I was sure that your father must have the place well guarded, so I went to have a look."

"And ran right into me, because I had escaped the house

and walked down to the barley field," she said. "Sithee, I heard your boat, the oars thumping. And when I realized you had beached it on the riverbank, I moved closer to see."

"So here we are," he murmured, shifting up onto an elbow to kiss her again. "I must go now, truly," he added. "The men downstairs will be stirring soon, and I need at least an hour or two more sleep. But we will talk more of this, believe me."

Getting up, he pulled on his breeks and fastened them, then checked her shutters again. The wind had eased its ferocity, and the only thunder he had heard for some time came from well to the east, so he picked up the lantern, used the candle to light it, and blew out the candle. Then, bidding her sleep well, he opened the door.

Tiggie, stretched full length across the doorway, gave him a slant-eyed look, arched up to his feet, stretched again, and rolled to his back.

Rubbing his belly with a bare foot, Rob said, "Get you inside, laddie, if you mean to. I'm shutting this door."

When the little cat had obeyed, Rob left and went to his own bed.

~

In the darkness of the bedchamber, Mairi watched the door shut behind Rob and listened for a moment to the diminishing wind. Feeling Tiggie's slight weight on the bed just before he bumped his nose into her face, she greeted him and waited until he had settled on his favorite pillow before letting her thoughts return to Rob.

Her imagination replayed details of their coupling from

the moment he had entered the room until he had gone. She did not think much about their talk, because as far as she was concerned, the subject required no further discussion.

Even if her father were a man who would allow his heiress daughter to marry where she chose, she was not at all sure she wanted to marry Rob. He was and would always be a Maxwell, after all, and that fact alone would cause trouble with her family and perhaps with their Annandale neighbors as well.

Also, although Rob was a landowner and Trailinghail a beautiful place, unlike Sir Hugh Douglas, he was not a baron or even a knight. Moreover, his proposal, if one could call it so, had come so impulsively on the heels of their coupling, he could not have considered fully the fact that he would be marrying a woman who might become a baroness in her own right.

She was sure that the consequences of that would be worse for him, or indeed for any man who expected to control his family and all of its affairs.

Jenny had explained to her how it would be, and Dunwythie had confirmed it. Mairi's husband, unless he had a title of his own as Hugh did, would have naught but a styling. That meant that although people would properly address him as "my lord," the words would be no more than acknowledgment of his marriage to a baroness. She would remain Dunwythie of Dunwythie unless she agreed to relinquish the barony to him, something she would not do.

"Maxwell of Dunwythie" flew right in the face of all that her family believed in. Her son, if she had one, would become Dunwythie of Dunwythie, just as his ancestors had been, as her father was now, and as she would be if she succeeded him. She could not and would not consider any other course.

As she tried to imagine what Rob would say if she were to explain *that* to him, her imagination boggled. But if she did not tell him, then . . .

She did not wake until Annie came in with her breakfast and the news that the laird would be busy most of the day but would try to join them for supper.

"There be trees down and roofs gone all over, m'lady," Annie said. "So they'll be lucky if any man amongst them gets his dinner today. They be a-scurrying hither and yon. Gibby says even Fin Walters's cottage lost much of its thatch. But at least the rain has stopped, and the sun be a-playing 'all hide' wi' the clouds."

They tidied the chamber and stitched pieces of the quilt together for an hour before their midday meal, then worked on it afterward until Annie produced a dice cup and they threw dice together, competing for exorbitant if imaginary sums.

Annie had just suggested that she ought to go down and see how much longer it would be before supper when they heard footsteps on the stairs.

They stopped on the landing below.

"That will be the laird, m'lady. I ha' nae doots he has come up to change his clothes before supper. We'd best get ye tidied up gey quick."

Mairi decided to change her gown, so Annie shut the door, and they bustled about. Mairi was sitting on the stool while Annie finished plaiting her hair when Rob rapped at the door and asked if she was ready for her supper.

Barely waiting for her answer, he entered, leaving the door open behind him.

Annie got up quickly and bobbed a curtsy.

He gave her such a long look that Mairi expected him to send the maidservant away. Instead, he said, "Gib and one of the other lads will be bringing our supper up shortly. I just came ahead to see that all was—"

Breaking off, he turned toward the open door.

Mairi heard a female voice in the distance, a commanding one that echoed up the stairs. She also heard a male voice that sounded like Fin Walters, placating.

"Sakes, I must go!" Rob exclaimed. "Shut the door behind—"

"It is of no use to stand in my way, Fin Walters," the unfamiliar female voice declared loudly enough to be heard quite clearly. "I know where his chamber is. If he is not dressed yet, with supper awaiting him in the hall, he ought to be. But I have a few things to say to him before he eats that supper, so stand aside, my man!"

Rob stepped hastily out to the landing and pulled the door to with a snap.

Mairi turned to Annie. But Annie looked as mystified as Mairi felt.

~

Rob straightened his cap and tried to muffle his footsteps on the stairs. But it did him no good, because Gibby came bounding up the stairs ahead of her. Before Rob could hush him, he exclaimed, "Laird, she's here! Herself be here!"

"Hush!" Rob hissed just as his grandmother came around the bend in the stairs behind the lad.

"It is of no use to hush the lad, or scold him, either; I am coming up," Lady Kelso declared. "You will scarcely turn me from your door, after all."

"Madam, I would not, but it would have been good to have warning."

"I do not doubt *that*," she said, eyeing him shrewdly. "Where is she?"

He opened his mouth, words of denial leaping to his tongue. But he could not utter them, not to her. Instead, he said, "Why have you come?"

"Gib, go below and tell them I do *not* like my mutton overcooked. I shall expect my supper just as soon as my people have brought my things in. I expect you can spare a basin, a ewer, and a drop of water for me, Robbie lad."

"Aye, Gran, but you'd best come into my chamber to use them, I expect."

She nodded but said, "She *is* here then. Faith, lad, what were you thinking?"

Rob looked sternly at the fascinated Gibby. "Get hence," he said.

"I thought I should wait until ye take Herself into your chamber, lest—"

"Get!"

Gib slid hastily past Lady Kelso and fled down the stairs.

"So you, too, prefer this chamber," she said when he opened the door for her. "You can leave me to my own devices, if you like," she added, giving him a wry smile. "I warrant you would like to warn her that I am here. She should take her supper with us, I think. My Eliza will be up directly, though, so prithee, leave that door open so she can find me. It has been years since last we were here."

"Aye, but tell me first why you have come," he said, meeting her gaze.

With a slight grimace of distaste, she said, "I thought I ought to warn you that Dunwythie came to Dumfries and confronted Alex, demanding to know what the devil Alex had done with his daughter. Alex tried to order me out of the room, of course. But I am not so yielding as his Cassia is."

Too concerned to smile at her understatement, Rob said, "What happened?"

"His lordship, justifiably furious, said his daughter had vanished and your offer of aid had made it plain to him that the Maxwells had taken her. He demanded that Alex return her at once. He ripped up at Alex, too, told him that *his* despicable tactics would never persuade his lordship to let Alex extort gelt from Annandale."

"I see."

"I warrant you do," she said tartly. "What I should like to know, however, is just when you took leave of your senses!"

Ruefully, he said, "I think it must have happened the moment I laid eyes on her, Gran. If not then, it must certainly have been when I went to look over Annan House and ran bang into her at the riverbank."

Shaking her head, she said, "Mayhap, henceforward you will learn to control your impulses, though little good that would do you now. The plain fact is, my lad, that Alex is furious. He told Dunwythie that *no* Maxwell had done any such thing, but the confrontation ended badly. His lordship having had at least sense enough not to bring an army with him to Dumfries, nevertheless departed with threats to do that very thing, whereupon Alex informed me that *he* would soon teach you a lesson."

"So he leaped to the conclusion—"

"Don't cry out about *that* to me," she snapped. "You deserve to hear whatever he has to say to you, for you need a good down-setting. And, as I believe he is close upon my heels, it will come to you soon enough."

"He is on his way now?"

"Aye," she said. "I was nearly ready to depart for Glasgow, in any event. So I put my journey forward a day and hied myself here instead. I doubt that I fooled him any more than you have, however. He is far too likely to be acting in haste. You understand what this could mean, I expect."

"Clan war," Rob said curtly. "I never meant that to happen."

"Mind your tone," she said. Her expression was rueful, though, when she added, "I realized on the way here that you must have thought you were acting for Clan Maxwell. I ought to have recalled how headstrong you can be when you react to anger or resentment. I had second thoughts after I'd mentioned the clan, but I hoped . . . Never mind that now, though," she said briskly. "I want to meet her, so go and tell her that I am here. I trust you at least had the kindness to lock her in the great chamber and not in the smaller one upstairs."

"She is in the great chamber and has not been locked in since just a few days after her arrival," he said. "In fact, she has already tried to escape."

"Then she has more spirit than I'd expected. Go quickly now and fetch her. You may bring her to me here, and we shall go down and sup together."

"I'll have to bring Annie along as well, then," Rob said.

"Annie?"

"Fin Walters's good-sister," Rob said. "You'd know her as Dora's sister."

"Sakes, that bairn was no more than ten the last time I was here!"

"Then it is time and more that you came to us, madam."

"Get her before I hand ye a clout on the lug," she said sternly.

Remembering other times she had made his ears ring with a slap, Rob grinned but decided not to tempt her further.

Hurrying upstairs, he opened the door to Mairi's chamber without ceremony.

Annie was setting the stool at the table for their supper, and Mairi stood by the window, her figure outlined by the light there. She stood in profile, drawing his gaze briefly to her memorable firm, silky breasts before he looked her in the eye and said, "My grandmother is here. She wants to meet you."

Her mouth dropped open, which, he was sure, was how he had met the news himself. "Come along, lass. Annie, you will sup with us at the high table, but Lady Kelso wants to speak with Lady Mairi privately before you join us. So you can have a few minutes to tidy things here and lay out whatever her ladyship will need later, if you will."

"Aye, laird, just shout when ye want me," Annie said.

He nodded. Then, noting that Mairi had not moved, he said, "Now, lass. Gran has less patience than I have."

Smiling then, she moved toward him. He was glad to

see that she wore the pink velvet that became her so well, until he remembered whose dress it was.

Suppressing any alarm that stirred at the memory, he put a hand under her elbow and ushered her out the door, murmuring for her ears alone, "She can be a termagant. But if one does not show fear or defiance, she will remain civil."

"Am I to thank you for telling me that?" she asked with her eyebrows raised. "I own, you have put me in a quake, sir. Yet, how *any* Maxwell could feel aught but shame for what one of her own has—"

"Enough of that," he said sharply. "She was born a Bruce of Annandale, not a Maxwell. And what she feels is anger, not shame. But she will reveal neither to you. She came to help us both, lass. Of that you can be sure. Now, come."

⌒

Mairi drew a deep breath and was glad when he released her elbow and stepped ahead to precede her down the stairs as any gentleman would. He stood in such awe of his grandmother that she had half expected he might let her go first.

They rounded the turn before the next landing, and she was able to see beyond him enough to note that the door in the same position to the landing as hers stood ajar. He paused at the threshold there until she was beside him.

Drawing her inside then, he said respectfully, "Madam, I would present to you the lady Mairi Dunwythie of Annandale."

The woman who turned toward them from the window looked nearly as tall as Rob was. She was elegantly dressed in a pale green tunic over a skirt of soft brown camlet that swirled gently around her legs as she moved toward them.

Watching her, Mairi saw feminine versions of Rob's eyes and nose but a kinder expression. Her ladyship's lips were thinner, her chin more pointed. Unlike Phaeline, who insisted that fashion decreed a perfectly oval, hairless face, she had kept her natural eyebrows. That tended to endear her to Mairi from the outset.

Realizing that she was staring when she ought to be making her curtsy, Mairi hastily dipped low.

"Rise, my dear," Lady Kelso said. "I want to have a good look at you."

Her voice was pleasant, her tone cheerful, and Mairi willingly complied. "I am honored to meet your ladyship," she said. "The laird has spoken often of you."

"Has he? He did not say a word to me about you until I commanded him to, my dear. I hope he has at least apologized to you for his scurrilous behavior."

"Why, nay, madam, I do not believe he has," Mairi said, avoiding Rob's gaze. "But in troth, he has treated me most kindly from the start."

"He abducted you *kindly*?"

Feeling fire ignite in her cheeks, Mairi said hastily, "Not that part. But for the rest, he has been most considerate."

"He did learn some manners, then. But enough of this, for I am ravenous after my journey. I do want to say just one thing more to you, though. I could not be sure until I had met you, but . . ." She hesitated, glancing at Rob.

"Sakes, madam, do not let *my* presence dissuade you," he said. "I cannot think what else you might say to her ladyship, but it is unlike you to hesitate."

"It is not on her account that I do, Robbie," she said. "I

trust that you will heed what I say, however, and think carefully before you refuse."

"Go on," he said.

Turning back to Mairi, she said, "I am quite willing to tell the world you have been safely with me all this time, my dear. If I do, the most censorious critic will not guess that you and our Rob have been alone here at Trailinghail with no better protection for you than young Annie."

Mairi nearly protested that Rob had taken care to protect her reputation. But after the previous night's activity, she doubted she could say it with a straight face.

Before she could decide what to say, Rob said to his grandmother, "By my troth, madam! *How* can you make such an offer when you have been staying with Alex in Dumfries? Would you expect *him* to support your claim?"

"I have not the least intention of asking him to do so," she said. "I shall simply make the declaration the first time I hear anyone discuss Mairi's abduction. If I assure *that* person that you, having excellent cause for your actions, brought her to me— We must arrange a stronger tale to explain *why* you took her, of course."

"Gran—"

"*But* once we have plotted out what that must be, I shall simply make the statement. You need not fear Alex. He will not dare to contradict me, especially as to do so would incriminate you. Say what you like about him, dearling, Alex knows what is due to his family. Now, what do you say, my dear?" she asked Mairi.

The door snapped open and Gibby burst into the chamber. "Laird! The sheriff ha' come and he be looking black as thunder!"

"Run back down and tell him I'll be at his service

straightaway, lad," Rob ordered. "Wait, though! Does he lead a large company?"

"Aye, a score, mayhap two! But Fin Walters did tell him they couldna come in as the place be gey small for such a crowd. 'Twas Fin told me to come quick and tell ye that the sheriff be in the yard and in a right foul temper."

"Then do exactly as I bid you and speak to Fin, not to the sheriff unless he calls you to him. Tell Fin he did right and to keep them all out but for the sheriff's personal servants if he brought any. Hurry, Gib. I don't want the sheriff to come up here, so I shall be close behind you. Madam?"

"Aye, I'll go down to him," Lady Kelso said. "But keep the lass out of the way, Rob. It will not do for him to see her here. Faith," she added. "I forgot you put her in the great chamber and that I told Gib to send my woman to the small one. Mairi, lass, hie thee upstairs and tell my Eliza that she is to move my things swiftly into the great chamber. You and your Annie will take the smaller one tonight."

Mairi opened her mouth to explain that Annie did not stay nights, but Rob intervened, saying curtly, "Do as she says, lass, and hurry. Tell Annie she must expect to stay. The bed in the small chamber is the same size as the one in yours."

Knowing she could take up no more of his time, Mairi caught up her skirts and ran up the stairs, only to meet Annie coming down.

"We've had a change of plans," Mairi said, and explained.

Annie turned around at once, and Mairi followed her, wondering if even the indomitable Lady Kelso could keep the Sheriff of Dumfries at bay.

It occurred to her only then that she no longer wanted or needed rescuing.

～

Rob followed his grandmother downstairs, thinking it typical that she had no hesitation in bearding Alex in a fury. Then he realized that he had no hesitation, either. In fact, if he were truthful, he was looking forward to it.

Lady Kelso paused on the landing outside the hall. Then, straightening her shoulders and raising her chin, she entered the great hall with regal dignity.

Rob lengthened his stride to walk beside her.

Alex stood staring into the fireplace, where a fire roared. Gillies scurried to and fro, putting food on the lower tables. Others did likewise at the high table.

Alex looked up with a frown, directing it first at his grandmother but shifting it at once to his brother. "This is a fine thing," he snapped.

"I am surprised to see *you* again so soon, too," Lady Kelso said blandly.

"Do not hope to cozen me, madam. I ken fine why you came here."

"Welcome to Trailinghail," Rob said, extending his right hand.

Alex looked as if he would ignore it. However, Lady Kelso said tartly, albeit in a tone unlikely to carry beyond the three of them, "Alexander, recall where you are!"

Grimacing, Alex shook Rob's hand and said, "Where are you keeping her?"

"Who?" Rob asked, meeting his angry gaze with uncustomary ease. "I'm told you brought a large force with you, Alex. Has aught occurred to warrant that?"

"You must know it has. Dunwythie, may the devil fly off with him, accused *me* of abducting his daughter. Sakes, I don't even know the lass's name! But I have no doubt that *you* do. What is going on, Rob, and where the devil is she?"

"Not now, and *certainly* not here," Lady Kelso said crisply. "You ken fine that you cannot roar at him here just as everyone is about to take supper, Alexander. Not unless you want Maxwell affairs bruited over all of Galloway and Dumfries."

"It can be here or elsewhere, but we are going to talk! And I'll be damned if I'll sit down to *sup* with him before I have learned all I want to know."

Raising her chin, Lady Kelso said, "Do you mean to say, sir, that you would leave *me* alone here to take my supper on that dais by myself?"

Alex hesitated, but Rob said, "It must be as you choose, madam. However, the great chamber is prepared for your use, and I will have a lad take supper up on a tray for you and your woman if you will only agree to it."

Her eyebrows shot upward. For a moment, she looked into his eyes. But her expression did not otherwise alter before she said, "I see too much of Eliza as it is and would much prefer to enjoy the company of my grandsons. However, if Alex is bent on fratching, his company would be unpleasant. Just be generous, Rob. I'm famished." Turning toward the stairway, she paused to say, "Send up that imp Gibby with the tray, dear. He'll likely amuse me more than either of you would."

"Aye, madam," Rob said. He motioned one of the gillies

over and gave the orders, then said, "Come with me, Alex. I doubt you remember much about this place, but there is a chamber beyond this one that will serve our purpose."

"Only if it boasts a gallows, Robert. I'm ripe to hang you for this mischief. And by heaven, if it results in clan war, I'm likely to do that."

Although Rob knew he was exaggerating, he also knew that Alex was angry and even frightened that Dunwythie might persuade the other Annandale lairds that the Maxwells had taken his daughter. If they joined him, clan war *would* result.

He had to hear Alex out, to learn all he could about exactly what Dunwythie had said. He wanted to be sure that his lordship's threat had been sincere. If he meant war, then war there would be unless Rob could stop it before it began.

To do that, he knew he would have to choose between his loyalty to his clan and his vow to protect the woman he had wronged, a woman he was rapidly coming to realize meant more to him than his life did.

Chapter 15 _____

Mairi and Annie, with the help of her ladyship's Eliza, quickly shifted enough items to the small room so that if the sheriff came up, he would see naught to show that anyone save her ladyship had occupied the great chamber.

"What if he looks in *here*?" Annie asked Mairi as the two carried one kist of clothing into the smaller room and Eliza shifted the other aside to make room for it.

Much the same age as her mistress and nearly as stately, Eliza smiled and said. "He won't come in, lass. That *I* can promise ye. Master Alex kens fine that I'd no welcome him in *my* chamber. And for all he'll ken, this one be mine alone."

"I am sorry to be doing you out of a private chamber," Mairi said to her.

"Never fidget yourself, my lady. 'Tis me own mistress gave the command, and I ha' nae objection to aught that she asks o' me."

"There be somebody on the stairs," Annie hissed.

"I will go," Eliza said. "Shut the door behind me and dinna speak!"

Whisking out, she returned shortly afterward to assure them that it was only her ladyship, come to ask them to take supper with her in the great chamber.

Mairi's hair was curling in damp wisps around her face and on her neck. She washed quickly and let Annie pin her plaits up under the white veil before returning to the great chamber with Eliza and Annie, to face Lady Kelso.

Although she had been wishing she still had Rob to support her, she quickly realized she need not worry. Her ladyship was thinking only of her supper.

"I shall be grateful for your company, my dear. Eliza, prithee meet whoever is bringing our food. I asked Master Robert to send our Gibby up, but as Rob will not have entrusted our tray to the lad, he will also be sending a gillie. So take it from him. I'd liefer not remind the servants of her ladyship's presence here."

"They are all completely loyal to the laird, my lady," Mairi said, recalling how many had seen her take a late supper with Rob the night he returned from Annan House and found her in the cave.

"I know they are loyal," her ladyship said. "But 'tis gey easy for anyone to slip if a question is put the right way. 'Twill be safer an Eliza brings our food."

"What of Gibby?" Mairi asked her when Eliza had left the room with Annie at her heels. "He has been much in my company from the outset."

"Gibby would tell you that he does not talk to Alexander."

Mairi smiled. Although she doubted Gib would defy

the sheriff's order, the lad was resourceful enough to elude Maxwell if he thought it wise to do so.

In the small chamber beyond the hall, Rob faced his older brother, feeling confident for once and determined not to lose his temper.

"Damn you, tell me what you did with her!" Alex demanded again. "I'm telling you, Dunwythie has blood in his eye. He was brazen enough to inform me that he means to return with all Annandale behind him. He is certain that Maxwells took her. But I know only *one* Maxwell daft enough to do that."

"I see," Rob said. "Has anyone else suggested that I took her, Alex? Or do you just assume as much because Dunwythie suspects a Maxwell? I'd remind you," he added caustically, "that you, not I, inflamed his hatred of Clan Maxwell."

"I have done nowt but my duty," Alex growled. "And we do not talk about some *possible* role of mine in this but of what you have *done*, Rob. Once again, I expect, you let impulse rule what sense you have and acted without thinking. Good God, but the lass is yet unwed *and* his heiress. Did you expect him—?"

"I expect nowt of him," Rob said. "As for clan war, Alex, *you* planted its seed by threatening to raise the Maxwells against him to force his submission to your self-assumed authority. You told me you made that threat. By my troth, I acted to *prevent* bloodshed. Mayhap one reason the Annandale lairds refuse to submit is that they think you serve

Clan Maxwell as sheriff more than you would serve any of them."

"I can certainly call together all the Maxwells to aid me *against* Dunwythie. He may call up Annandale, but few will answer. They ken fine that Clan Maxwell is larger and stronger than they are."

"Stronger than Douglas?" Rob countered. "Recall that Archie intends to control all of southwest Scotland. He may decide that such an attack is reason enough to impose his will at once on Dumfriesshire. Have you considered that?"

"Aye, sure. 'Tis why we *must* settle this before he moves to take the shire. He will not dismiss its hereditary sheriff, though. When he does take over, we can still take our rightful share of the rents before he takes his and those of the Crown."

"You are ever quick to overreach," Rob said tersely. "If you were the leader you'd like to be, Alex, you might accomplish what you want. But you are not. You carp, complain, and criticize men who would serve you when they fail or when the result of their action is not exactly what you had imagined it would be."

"Now, you listen here—"

"Nay, then, *you* listen. You push others to do *your* work, Alex, even to issue unpopular or difficult orders so that you need not do so. If things go well, you take the credit. If not, you shift the blame. Believe me when I say you had better think again about *this* business, because if you have misjudged Archie, you will lose. And you will lose not only Annandale, I fear, but mayhap all of Dumfriesshire."

"Enough!" Alex roared. "You just want to turn the subject from your own ill-doing, but by the Rood, I won't allow it! I am already in control here, Rob. My lads will take over Trailinghail and search it top to bottom for that young woman. If she is here, I will take her. If not, you may be sure I will apologize for accusing you."

"You won't take this tower, Alex. It is impregnable, and your men are outside its wall, where they will remain. You may breach the barmkin, but the walls are eight feet thick. And if you try to breach them, you will have to do it whilst our lady grandmother is here, for she won't leave. Would you endanger her?"

"Again, you try to change the subject. I mean only to take Dunwythie's daughter to Dumfries with me and arrange her safe return to her family. If you think our lady grandmother will disapprove of *that*, you are mistaken. She knows I am head of our family, and *she* respects that position. Moreover, returning the lass will end any conflict before it begins."

"I doubt that," Rob said grimly. "Now that the notion of taking custody of her has occurred to you, I think *you* would try to use her yourself to force Dunwythie's submission. Even if you did not—"

"Damnation, Rob, I am not such a fool. Can you look me in the eye and swear to me that you did *not* abduct that young woman?"

"Nay, why should I, when I *did*," Rob said, beginning to capture the glimmerings of a plan that might let him outwit Alex.

"So you *do* have her!" Alex exclaimed, his voice rising again. "But you know perfectly well that you denied having any part in her abduction."

"You never did listen well," Rob said. "You should strive to do so. I simply pointed out how quick you were to *believe* I had taken her. And for no better reason than that Dunwythie had accused the Maxwells. If you recall, *you* are the one who told me to do whatever was required to force his submission. You raised a din when I failed to persuade him, saying I should have done aught that was necessary. So I thought about how I might force him, and I made a list of what must be important to him. Sithee, I had met his daughters. Both are beautiful young women, and at present, Mairi is his heiress, although his wife may yet give him a son before he dies."

"Fetch the lass to me at once," Alex said sternly.

"I won't even tell you where she is. Nor will I let you search my tower."

"*I* should think not," Lady Kelso said, entering the chamber on her words and thus making Rob, at least, aware that she must have inched the door ajar to overhear them. "Why would you want to do such an obtrusive thing, Alexander?"

"He is holding Dunwythie's daughter hostage here," Alex said. "I mean to return her to his lordship, who may even now be on his way back to Dumfries."

"Then you should hie yourself home, my lad," she said. "If Dumfries is in danger of attack, it is your sworn duty to protect the town, is it not?"

"I mean to search Trailinghail first."

"My faith, you impudent man, do you dare to think *I* would be standing here as I am if that young woman were *here*?"

"With respect, madam, I doubt you would know aught about it."

"Respect?" Her mobile eyebrows shot up. "*Respect* is what you call it when you threaten to send your rough men to paw through *my* belongings in search of heaven knows what evidence of her presence! Prithee, have the goodness to recall that I know everyone here at Trailinghail. If Robert were holding a woman hostage here, do you think not *one* of them would have sent word to Dumfries to inform me of such an outrageous ill-doing?"

Rob felt his own eyebrows drifting upward and took firm control of them. He could not be sure of controlling his voice, however, so he kept silent.

Alex was staring at their grandmother, his suspicion as clear as Rob's own.

But Alex lacked the courage to challenge her.

He drew a long breath and let it out before he said, "In troth, madam, I do not know what to believe. But I will say this. I mean to keep watch on this tower from now until Dunwythie gets his daughter back. Meantime, my men will search anyone who leaves, male or female. However, if you choose to depart, madam, you may."

"Faith, sir, as if anyone here would dare try to stop me!"

"Be that as it may, my rules will apply to you and to your Eliza no less than they apply to everyone else. Having no more to say, I will bid you both goodnight."

With that, he strode angrily from the room.

"Dear me," Lady Kelso said. She might have said more, but Rob put a finger to his lips and moved silently to the door. Easing the latch up with one hand, he jerked the door open with the other to see Alex facing him, mouth agape.

"Ah, good, you hadn't gone far," Rob said mildly. "I just wanted to tell you that you are welcome to sleep here as you had planned. Gibby told your servants to put your things in the room opposite mine. I am sure they will have seen to your comfort, but Gib did tell them that they must sleep in the hall. The tower is not large enough to provide chambers for our visitors' servants."

"Thank you, but I don't want a guard at my door looking to prevent my creeping about the place in search of *your* guest," Alex said stiffly. "I shall sleep outside with my men. But we are not leaving, Rob, if that is what you had hoped."

"Well, it is," Rob answered frankly. "But I knew it was too much to expect."

Alex did leave then, still in a huff, and Rob listened by the open doorway until his footsteps faded in the distance.

Then he went back into the room, shut the door, and faced his grandmother.

"You shock me, madam," he said, grinning.

"Do I? I vow, I did not shock myself at all. Indeed, I barely told a falsehood. *Would* you have placed a guard at his door?"

"Two stout fellows at least, aye. I fear that he does mean to camp outside the gate, though. That could make things difficult for a time."

"Laying siege to us, as it were?"

"Aye, although our people lie in no danger."

"Can you be sure of that, Rob?"

"I have commanded Alex's men more often than he has over these past few years," Rob said. "They trust me and would most likely balk at an order to harm anyone here should Alex be daft enough to issue one. They'll be a damned nuisance out there, but they'll behave. So will Alex, especially if you mean to stay here, Gran. I do hope you will."

"I will, my dear. 'Tis far more interesting than Dumfries

or Glasgow. In faith, I am very glad I came. If you need me to aid in the lady Mairi's protection, you need only say so. I quite like her."

"So do I, Gran."

She placed a hand on his shoulder and gave it a squeeze. "Then you must find a way out of this mess, Robbie. It is of your own making, as you know only too well. Moreover, if Dunwythie returned to Annandale meaning to raise the other defiant lairds to follow him, you have little time."

A rap at the door startled Rob so that he turned and jerked it open, expecting to see that Alex had somehow returned unheard.

Gibby stood there, his eyes wide. "Should I no ha' rapped the door, laird?"

"Come right in, Gibby," her ladyship said cordially. "What is it?"

"'Tis that knacker what were here afore, laird," Gib said. "He would talk wi' ye, he said, on a matter o' some import. He wouldna tell me what it was, though."

Lady Kelso said, "Knacker? Do you mean Parland Dow?" Turning to Rob, whose thoughts were racing, she added, "Sithee, he came with *me*, my dear. Said he preferred to travel with a larger party, but I did think it strange that he was off away from Dumfries so soon. I vow he'd not been in town but a day or two. Then, when we drew near, he stopped at Fin Walters's cottage. Said he always sleeps there."

"And so he does. Fetch him in, Gib, and fetch a jug of whisky, too," Rob added. To her ladyship, as the boy ran off, he said gently, "He may provide the answer to a problem I need to solve."

"You mean Dow, of course," she said. "You cannot mean Gibby."

"Aye. For one thing, Dow collects gossip. For another, he carries messages."

"I begin to see that I must leave at once, lest I cast a damper," she said, moving to bestow a kiss on his cheek. "I'll bid you goodnight, my dearling, and prithee sleep well when you do. I am confident that you will soon sort this all out."

She was more confident than Rob was.

Not long after she left, Gib ushered Dow in. Rob saw by the man's expectant expression that he had something to say. "Pour the whisky for us, Gibby," Rob said. "This will help us *both* sleep well tonight," he said to the knacker with a smile.

Shooing Gibby away when he had filled two mugs, and making sure *he* had gone, Rob shut the door again and said, "What brings you back to us so soon?"

"Well may ye ask," Dow said, setting down his mug and wiping his lips with a sleeve. "It were seeing his lordship in Dumfries—Dunwythie, that be—and learning he believed the Maxwells had his daughter. I kent fine ye'd want to hear that. So, when her ladyship took her leave, I attached myself to her party. Imagine my surprise when she said she were bound not for Glasgow but for Trailinghail."

"I am gey glad to see you, and you were right to think I might have need of you. Sithee, I have ken of the lady Mairi since last we saw each other, and would return her to her father. But quietly, so as not to stir strife amongst the clans. 'Tis better, I think, that he have her safe before others learn she is no longer missing. However, I hear he means to return to Dumfries with an army. That must not be."

Dow nodded fervently. "'Twas why I came, for 'twould be a great disaster, sir, if Annandale attacked Maxwell— or Maxwell attacked Annandale, come to that. Sithee, the lairds say if they must pay an additional sum first to the sheriff and next, nae one doots, to Archie o' Gallo-way . . . well, where does it end? 'Tis nobbut a Maxwell scheme to steal gelt from Annandale, they say, and bad cess to Maxwell!"

Rob smiled. "I wonder, do they say the same of Archie the Grim?"

"Nay, they do not, and I'll tell you why, sir. The Lord o' Galloway ha' tamed that irascible place, they say. Sakes, but raiders from Galloway used to be near as fierce toward the dales as the English ha' been. With Douglas control-ling Galloway and the English resting quiet, men can plant crops again for the first time in decades. They be willing to pay Douglas an he asks them to. Some say he willna ask but will allow the present schemes to continue as they always have."

"You understand the situation, then, and one can hope you are right about Douglas," Rob said. "I want you to carry a message to Dunwythie for me. Tell him I have found his daughter. If he will send his army home and go back to Annan House, I will take her to him there straightaway. If he agrees to my request, you will hie yourself to Dumfries and tell the lads at Alan's Tower that you need a smoky fire set to signal me. We'll easily see the smoke from here."

"Sakes, sir, even if that be true and ye could winkle her away from wherever she be now, Dunwythie will think ye took her yourself. The man be beside himself wi' rage and he wields the power o' the pit and gallows. Ye'd be risking your life to offer him such, let alone to take his daughter right to his door!"

"I have met the man," Rob said. "He is well known to be generally a man of peace. So, I must hope he will agree that having his daughter back and keeping the peace are worth more than starting a great clan war to avenge her abduction."

"But what if he does *not* agree? How will I let ye ken that?"

"You need not, because his refusal will make no difference to what happens next. The sheriff will wait here, as he has planned to do. And when Dunwythie reaches Dumfries, he will learn that the Maxwells are here in force."

"I expect he'd assume she were here, too, then," Dow said, nodding.

"Aye, so sithee now, if Dunwythie said he'd lead his army from Annandale as soon as he could raise it, I make that a matter of three days, four at most. If you leave for Dumfries at dawn, you should be there in good time to meet him."

"Aye, easily." Dow nodded again and drank the rest of his whisky

"If he is not there yet when you arrive, you must ride to meet him," Rob said, "Then, *you* must build a fire near where you meet and where we can see its smoke from here—some hilltop or other. I doubt you will set any forest afire if you do."

"Nay, it be still too damp for such. Forbye, I'm thinking a fire wherever I'd light one would smoke like the devil, as wet as most wood is by now."

"Good, then go. If the sheriff's men ask questions when you leave, tell them I'd told you I had more work here for you if you found extra time. You just stopped on your way to some other place to see how much work there might be."

"Aye, sure, they willna trouble me," Dow said, making his bow to leave.

Rob said, "I owe you for this, Parland Dow. I shan't forget it."

"Sakes, sir, I may be helping ye to your death. Ye willna thank me for that."

Holding the door open, Rob smiled and bade him goodnight.

Dow's parting words echoed in his mind, but Mairi's safety had come to mean more than anything else. If Dunwythie's army met Alex's at Trailinghail, the clash might erupt so violently, and other clans join in so quickly, that her father might not even learn that she *was* there until it was too late.

Clearly, then, the only way to be sure of protecting her now was for Rob to see her safely back to Annan House himself—in effect, to give her up entirely.

If her father decided to hang him for it, so be it. He did not think the man would, but he had been dead wrong about him before.

It was a risk he was willing to take, for Mairi.

~

Mairi was fidgeting. With her ears attuned to sounds that might mean someone coming upstairs rather than to what anyone in the great chamber was saying, she had for some time contributed little to the conversation.

It did not occur to her that Lady Kelso might also be

listening for Rob's step until she heard Eliza speak loudly to her mistress, as if repeating something.

Looking then toward her ladyship, Mairi saw a twinkle in her eyes.

Lady Kelso said, "Hush, Eliza, I ken fine that you think it is time for bed, but I am not at the brink of my grave yet. I mean to stay up and talk to the laird."

"Aye, sure, my lady. But be ye sure he'll be coming up here?"

"Quite sure, but he had not yet had his supper when last I saw him."

Mairi concealed a grimace. Her ladyship, having invited them to sup with her, had barely taken a bite when she had recalled an important message she had meant to give Rob. With no more than that sharp exclamation, she had hurried away. And that had been that until minutes before, when she had returned.

The remains of her supper were cold, but she did not seem to mind. A truly redoubtable woman, Mairi thought, much as she would like to be one day herself.

She wondered if she ever would be. Her cousin Jenny was sure of her role and was already redoubtable enough to hold her own with Hugh, because Jenny had run her estates for some time under her father's guidance before her father died.

Mairi had run nothing yet and might never do so.

"But I could," she told herself. "I know I could. In troth, I believe I know enough now to ask the right questions, at least. And I'd know whom to ask. I just wish I had nerve enough to ask her ladyship what they said below."

That thought occurred to her while she was still looking

at Lady Kelso, and Lady Kelso stared back at her. One dark eyebrow arched. It was query enough.

"I was wondering, madam," Mairi said. "Your message to the laird must have been gey long. I should not ask about it, I know," she added hastily.

"Nay, then, child, why not? If one does not ask questions, one learns little. I had no message for him, as doubtless you guessed. 'Twas nobbut my cursed curiosity getting the better of me, as my dear husband was wont to say."

"But I am curious, too," Mairi said.

"I ken that fine," her ladyship said cordially. "But we must both be patient until Rob comes to us. What I heard is not for me to repeat. But he will tell us all about it, and more, I'm thinking. Parland Dow wanted to see him when I left."

"The knacker is back? So soon?"

"Aye, and I think Rob was glad to hear it. But tell me more about your family, my dear. I should know Annan House and Dunwythie Mains, I expect, since my Bruce forebears all lived in Annandale. But my lot left when I was small."

Eliza clicked her tongue. But Mairi willingly complied with her ladyship's wishes until at last they heard Rob's quick footsteps on the stairway.

~

Rob was still munching sliced mutton and bread with butter when he entered what had become his grandmother's chamber to find the four women seated on settle and stools, chatting amiably.

Mairi was looking toward the door when he opened it, so he knew she had been listening for his step.

"All is well," he said. "I expect the sheriff and his men will camp outside the gate until he grows tired of it. But we are safe enough in here." Looking at Mairi again, he said, "I want to talk to you privately."

"By my faith, Robert Maxwell," Lady Kelso said. "You cannot be private with her. You have done her enough harm already."

"Nevertheless, madam, she has already tried to escape. And, with the sheriff at the gate, I want to be sure she has better sense than to view him as a rescuer."

"You need not fear that, sir," Mairi said. "I would not trust the sheriff or his men to treat me kindly. Nor would I trust them to ask my father to fetch me, or him to trust them if they did. To be a prize of war is not a role I yearn to play."

He nodded, believing she did understand. But he still wanted to talk with her. "If you will take my advice then, my lady, you would ready yourself now for bed and sleep," he said. "Fin Walters is below, waiting to take Annie to her cottage as he usually does. As loyal as my people are, I cannot doubt that Alex will soon know you are here in the tower. He won't get in, but I'd liefer keep to our usual routine."

"But I thought Annie was to stay with her," Lady Kelso said. "I assure you, I mean to keep Eliza with me."

"Both chambers have strong bolts on them," Rob said. "Mairi can throw hers and be as safe as she would be with any number of Annies. And Annie's mother wants her home. So go along now, my lady, if you want her to aid you."

To his relief, Mairi got up at once and nodded for Annie to go with her.

Satisfied, he sat down to chat with his grandmother, managing to deflect with glib replies her questions about what he planned to do. He wanted to discuss his thoughts and his half-formed plan first with Mairi.

When he thought she had had sufficient time to prepare for bed, he bade Lady Kelso goodnight and went across the landing to rap lightly on Mairi's door.

Annie answered.

"Ready to go?" he asked her.

"Aye, laird," she said with a smile.

Leaning closer, he said, "Bid your mistress keep her eyes open yet a while."

Nodding, she said, "I'll just fetch my cloak." She pushed the door to and opened it a moment later wearing her hooded cloak.

After turning her over to Fin, Rob went quietly back upstairs. Easing the latch on Mairi's door up gently, he pushed the door open.

She stood just a few feet away, looking expectant.

Shutting the door, he opened his arms, and she walked into them.

After kissing her thoroughly, he set her away from him and said, "We must talk. But Gran will have my head off me if she hears us, so we must not fratch."

"Are we likely to fratch?" she asked.

"I don't know," he admitted. "I'm going to take you home."

Mairi's breath caught in her throat. She had yearned for that moment from the day he had captured her. But had anyone asked about her feelings just then, she could not have described them.

One thing she knew was that she did not want to think she might never see Rob again. At the same time, nothing good could come of wanting him. Nor did she dare let him see how much she wanted him, lest he decide not to take her home.

Calling upon years of experience to keep her voice under control despite her feelings, she said evenly, "I cannot think why we should fratch about that, sir. We both knew the time would come when you would have to let me go back."

"Aye, lass, and now is that time. Although you must not speak of this to anyone, even Annie, I will tell you what I mean to do. Parland Dow is taking a message from me to your father. He'll tell him I've learned of your whereabouts, and if he will take his army back to Annandale, I'll return you safely to him."

She swallowed hard. "I expect you mean to take me back yourself, sir. But you would be wiser to entrust me to your helmsman and crew."

"Nay, I took you from your home, lass. I will take you back. Not another word now," he added, putting a finger to her lips. "We'd only fratch."

Moving his hands to her waist, she said, "Hold me." When he complied, she leaned into him, savoring his warmth and his strength. She imagined him sweeping her off to a place even farther away, where no one could ever find them.

She thought then of her father and wondered if his fury

was because of her abduction and his concern for her safety, or if it had erupted over his apparent belief that the sheriff had got the better of him in their continuing dispute.

She wanted to believe Dunwythie cared deeply about her. But experience told her that Phaeline was the only female for whom he ever spared much thought.

Not that she begrudged the attention he paid Phaeline, for she did not. Her own life had been comfortable enough. But never, until Rob had come into it, had she known anyone to whom she could speak her thoughts as she thought them. She would miss him for that but also for many other reasons.

She hugged him tighter and tilted her face up, hoping he would kiss her again.

He did not hesitate, and she sighed with pleasure as his warm lips captured hers. Hers parted at once, and she savored the taste of him, noting a difference from the night before, which she ascribed to the whisky he had drunk with Fin Walters.

"Prithee, take me to bed, just one more time," she said.

"I should not," he said, his voice no more than a rough mutter.

She did not speak. She just held him and nuzzled her head into the hollow of his shoulder. Letting her hands wander as they would, she felt the hard muscles under his doublet and remembered how his skin had felt next to hers.

He tensed, and just when she thought he might have heard something, he caught her up in his arms and carried her to the bed.

Then, without a word, he turned back toward the door.

Bolting the door, and telling himself that he was more fool than ever but refusing to sacrifice the last night they might have, Rob returned to the bed, undressed her, then stripped off his own clothes and climbed into bed with her.

His head was clearer that night, though, despite the whisky he'd had. So, although he pleasured her and took pleasure for himself, he took more care. If he had not given her a child the previous night, he would not do so now.

He also took care not to visit her again and, two days later, greeted the shout from the ramparts that smoke was billowing in the east with as much relief as regret.

Chapter 16

Running up to see for himself, Rob saw at once that the angle was wrong for the smoke to be rising in Dumfries. It rose from hills farther away, to the southeast.

Either Parland Dow had met Dunwythie before he reached Dumfries, or someone else had lit a signal fire.

The thick smoke persuaded Rob that Dow was responsible. Having already warned his oarsmen and Jake to be ready, he went downstairs and shouted for Gib.

"Go and tell Jake Elliot that I'll want to take the morning tide *just as I did before*," Rob said with emphasis. "Mind now, Gib, not a word to anyone else."

"I be a-going, too, then," Gib said. "Like before."

Refusal was on Rob's lips when he realized that the boy might be safer with him. He could trust Lady Kelso to protect him inside the wall, and mayhap Gib would stay inside. But the lad had much initiative and more curiosity, which could be a dangerous combination in one so young.

Rob did not trust Alex. He was sure that if Alex thought

Gib knew something and decided to get it out of him, he would find a way.

In any event, Gib might be useful on the trip in other ways, too, Rob thought. Mairi would enjoy the lad's company, for one.

"Very well," he said. "You may go. But you will come back here after you give my message to Jake, and you will keep near me today."

Finding the four women together in the great chamber, he sent Annie and Eliza away so he could speak privately with his grandmother and Mairi.

"Dow met with Dunwythie, and his lordship has agreed to return to Annan," he told them. "So I hope to leave well before dawn tomorrow."

"Are you sure all is well?" Lady Kelso demanded. "How can you know?"

"I'm as sure as I can be without waiting for Dow to return," he said. "If I'm wrong, and he is on his way, then I can still get Mairi safely away to Annan House."

Seeing her nod, he added, "Your task, Gran, will be to see that Alex does not suspect anyone has left the tower other than folks going about their usual duties or going to their cottages. I want him to suspect that the signal fire means Dunwythie is on his way to Dumfries. Alex will then stay right here as he has planned to do."

"I won't stand for a clan war on this doorstep," Lady Kelso said tartly. "So see that you manage your end of the business well, my lad."

"Aye, madam," he said. "If all goes as it should, we will leave before the early incoming tide stems up and I'll be back with the evening ebb."

"But how will you get Mairi out of the tower?" she asked. "Surely not . . ."

"She knows all about the cavern," he said, with a quick smile for Mairi. "'Tis how I brought her in. More important is the fact that Alex does *not* know about it, for I have never told him, and I'm sure that Grandfather did not, either."

"What do you want me to do?" Mairi asked.

"Prepare to leave, lass," he said. "Take what you like of the things you have worn here, or nowt if you prefer to forget them all. I will scratch at your door when it is time to go. But tell Annie no more than you must. She should behave as if you were still here, so tell her she must come at her usual time, collect the usual trays, and go home at her usual time. If Alex demands entrance to the tower, Gran," he added, "do as you think best, but do not let him upstairs on any excuse."

"Aye, I can manage him," she said. "I vow, though, I will miss *you*, Mairi."

Rob did not want to think about missing Mairi. Giving her one more, hasty smile, he took leave of them and went to have another word with Gib.

The rest of the day and evening crawled by. But, at last, it was time to go.

⁓

Mairi was ready, wearing her cloak, and listening for Rob. She barely heard the first scratch before she pulled the door open. He carried a lantern, so when he reached for the small bundle she had prepared, she refused to let him take it.

"I can carry it easily," she said. "'Tis only one gown,

two shifts, and one tunic, so it is not at all heavy or cumbersome."

Gibby waited at the turn of the stairs. When she expressed her surprise to see him there, he hefted two small baskets.

"Food," he said sleepily. "Herself did order some for ye."

They hurried down to the storage chamber, where Rob opened the cavern door, pushed the latch chain through its hole to the outer side, and closed it when they were on the stairs. Only then did Mairi realize that Gib was going with them.

The galley was waiting at the wharf, so they were off and, before long, riding the flood tide up the Firth. Along the way, Gib opened one basket of food and provided Mairi and Rob with bread and cheese to break their fast. They arrived at Annan House soon after dawn, so they had no need of his second basket.

"Faith, I cannot believe it," Mairi said quietly as they made their way the short distance up the river Annan to where the galley had beached before. "It all looks just the same."

"Sakes," Gib said. "'Tis the same place. Did ye *expect* it to look different?"

"I suppose I did," she said.

"Come now," Rob said to her as men jumped to drag the boat higher on the shore. "We'll walk up together. You lot wait here for me," he told his crew. "If I'm not back within the hour, go into Annan harbor and wait there."

"I'll just come along wi' ye now," Gib said.

"Aye, Gib, you should," Mairi said hastily when Rob

hesitated. "If aught goes amiss, you can run back and warn Jake Elliot."

"Nay, he should not," Rob said. "You wait until I know it is safe to come up, Gib. Until then, though, you stay here and look after that basket of food. I'll take your bundle now, lass," he added, reaching for it. "No need for you to carry it up the hill."

She handed it to him, and they took the path she had taken the day he abducted her. To her astonishment, as they crested the hill, she saw that the gates stood open.

Inside the yard, many horses neighed and stamped the cobbles.

"Mercy, are they just now returning?" Mairi asked. "I'd have expected them to get home yestereve."

"Aye, they would have," Rob said. "That looks as if they are leaving again."

As they entered the courtyard, she saw Jopson rushing toward her.

"My lady, 'tis a gey great blessing to see ye home again! But there has been grave mischief a-brewing here, and the laird be in a rare kippage."

"This is our steward," she said to Rob. "Good sakes, Jopson! What is amiss?"

"'Tis the lady Fiona, m'lady. She ran off wi' that Jardine. And the laird . . . I'm telling ye, I dinna like the look o' him, withal. The man be ripe for murder!"

The ground seemed to shift beneath her. Horses blurred, voices buzzed.

〜

Rob put a hand swiftly under Mairi's elbow when he saw her sway, wishing fervently that he dared put his arm right around her and hold her close.

She straightened, blinking and biting her lip, visibly taking herself in hand. "Where is my father?" she asked. "Does he know yet that I am home?"

"Nay, m'lady," the steward said. "Seeing just one man and a woman walking up the hill, the men on the wall wouldna ha' thought it were trouble a-coming. Not wi' the gate open and all o' us men here well armed. Forbye, what fools would ye be to walk into an army did ye mean mischief? This army will soon grow, too," he added grimly. "His lordship does expect to gather dunamany more as he rides up the dale to fetch her ladyship home."

"I should go with him," Rob murmured for Mairi's ears alone.

"Sakes, no, sir," she said sharply, apparently not caring who heard her. "You should *leave* is what you should do. If he is enraged over this latest start of Fiona's— Faith, though, I could slap her senseless. And what I'd like to do to your good friend Will Jardine . . . Well, it would get me hanged, I expect."

"Will Jardine is no friend of mine, for all that he may once have looked so," Rob said. "Jardines have often ridden with Maxwells, so we count them amongst our allies. But rarely does anyone count them as friends. It was but a—"

Dunwythie was striding across the yard toward them, his face choleric.

"Och, and so ye *did* bring the lass home again, did ye, Maxwell?" he snapped. "Had I but time to deal wi' ye now, and could do the right thing, I'd hang ye sure. But I'm no a man to go back on my word, whatever others may do.

And I did tell Parland Dow I'd leave ye go in peace. So I will. But he said I ought to thank ye for putting my Mairi's safety afore aught else. And that I will *not* do. To my mind, there be nae difference betwixt ye and yon thieving Will Jardine!"

His lordship's face was nearly purple. His entire torso shook with his rage.

"My lord, pray calm yourself," Rob urged. "I swear to you, I condemn what Will Jardine has done and would help set it right. By my troth, sir, if you will allow me, I would ride with you and lend my strong sword arm to your cause."

"Nay, then! But ye *will* get yourself hence from here as fast as ye can go! I have nae need of such help as yours. Nor would I be fool enough to trust that ye'd aid me against a Jardine."

"Father, prithee," Mairi said.

"Nae more talk," he said. "I must go. But before I do, lass, ye should ken this much. I turned that Flory girl off for aiding your sister, so dinna be taking her back again! And, to protect ye, lest I fail to end Will Jardine's mischief—aye, and Will Jardine, too—I altered my will to leave this house and its estates nae longer to Fiona but to ye as my heiress unless the babe my lady wife carries proves to be male."

"But, sir—"

"Nay, Mairi," he added fiercely. "By the *Rood* ye must promise me, lass, that if aught should happen to me, ye will *not* sign over this house or any of its lands to Fiona as long as she is with any man o' that villainous tribe!"

"I do promise, my lord," Mairi said solemnly. "But you should not ride as you are, sir! In troth, you do not look well. Art so sure our Fiona left willingly?"

"Aye, because the daft lass met with that scoundrel du-namany times these past weeks—sakes, even afore ye left us," he retorted as if, Rob thought, his lordship blamed Mairi for her sister's mischief.

He nearly spoke up to defend her, realized he would only make things worse, and kept silent. It made no difference, because Dunwythie rounded next on him.

"*You!*" he exclaimed, pointing a shaking finger. "This be all on your head, yours and your thieving brother's heads both! Trying to turn all here upside down to your own ben-efit, and from nowt but greed. Greed for power, greed for *gelt*! 'Tis all that matters to Maxwells and their sort! May God curse them all from now through eternity. And Jar-dines! May *they* be twice cursed beyond Maxwells as—"

He was screaming the curses. But as the stream of words broke, he looked at Mairi with his mouth still open.

She reached toward him, clearly meaning to soothe him.

Rob moved to stop her, fearing he knew not what from his lordship in response, yet something.

But the man only gaped at her glassy-eyed for a too-long moment before he crumpled to the ground.

Rob heard Mairi cry out as he dropped to one knee be-side Dunwythie.

His lordship's eyes were fixed, still staring. His breath-ing had stopped. When shaking him drew no response, Rob felt for his lordship's neck where a man's pulse usually beat strongly. Finding no movement there, he looked to the steward and said, "He is gone. If you will look after him, I will take the lady Mairi—"

"Nay!" she cried, falling to her knees beside her father

and bending over him. Urgently, she shook him as Rob had, but with tears streaming down her cheeks.

"With respect, sir," the steward said quietly to Rob, "I would send a man for the lady Phaeline. We must tell her in any event, and I ha' nae doots she will attend to the lady Mairi, too. So, mayhap it would be wiser did ye go now, whilst ye still can. There be some here as would ha' your eyes, sithee—wi' respect, sir."

"Send for the lady Phaeline by all means," Rob said. "But I will stay here unless the lady Mairi herself bids me go."

The steward looked long at him.

Only when Rob saw the man's expression shift from stern determination to acceptance did he turn back to Mairi. "Come, my lady," he said gently. "You can do nowt for him now. He is at peace."

She stayed where she was as if she had not heard him. Then, abruptly crossing herself, she drew a breath, let it out, and stood to face him. With astonishing calm, she said, "I thank you for bringing me home in time to see him before he died, sir. But I do agree that you must return to your men now."

A high-pitched scream from the entryway drew everyone's attention to a plump woman in the fashionable garb of a noblewoman, whom Rob had no difficulty recognizing as Phaeline, Lady Dunwythie. Catching up her skirts, she flew down the steps and across the yard as men and horses scrambled to make way for her.

"What have you *done* to him?" she shrieked to no one in particular. Then, fixing her gaze on Mairi, she shrieked again and flew at her, claws outstretched.

The steward jumped out of her path, whereupon Rob

stepped swiftly into it. Catching her by her arms, he said sternly, "Hold now, my lady."

When he grabbed her, she stiffened and her shrieks ceased. His command to her therefore dropped into the sudden silence like stones into a pool, spreading ripples of visible unease through the men watching them.

"How dare you lay your hands on me!" she demanded shrilly.

"Madam, prithee recall your condition," Mairi said as Rob released her ladyship. "You do not want to endanger the bairn you carry."

The older woman looked briefly bewildered, then irritated. "Thank you for your advice, Mairi," she said with caustic hauteur. "Doubtless, our Fiona learned her pretty behavior from you. I do not doubt that you schemed to distress your father and now have killed him by returning as you have. I hope you are happy."

Rob saw the lass stiffen, but she did not reply in kind.

Instead, coolly, she said, "We are both distressed, madam, but distress will not bring him back. We must send at once to inform Fiona of what has happened, although I fear for her state of mind when she hears of this. She will likely blame herself as quickly as you blame me."

Turning to the steward, Mairi said, "I shall depend on you, Jopson, to send a reliable lad who will not just blurt the news to her ladyship. But first, tell Gerrard he must command our men to stand down. We'll send no army to Applegarth today."

"But, my lady—"

"If my father was sure that the lady Fiona *chose* to elope with Will Jardine, then until we learn otherwise, I say she shall have her way."

Lady Dunwythie said fiercely, "And who are *you*, pray, to be giving orders here?" she demanded. "Orders about *my* daughter!"

Still outwardly calm, Mairi said, "Until your bairn arrives and proves himself male, madam, I remain heiress apparent to my father's estates. His will, unless he altered that part as well as the part about Fiona's inheriting Annan House, does proclaim that I am to take charge in just such an event as this. Jopson, did his lordship say aught to you about changing that portion?"

"Nay, my lady," the steward replied. "And he would ha' told me. So his will do be as ye say. I'll give your orders straightaway." He turned away to do so.

Mairi turned next to Rob.

Hastily, before she could speak, he said, "This event does alter things, my lady. I would be of service to you if I may, in any manner that you deem useful."

"I thank you, sir, for your kindness," she said, meeting his gaze with deep sorrow in her own that he knew was for her father and not for him.

He also knew what she would say, so again he spoke first, saying, "I will carry the message for your lady sister to Jardine Mains and bring her back to you, my lady. I can also deal swiftly with Will Jardine, and as your lord father desired."

"Nay," she said, her voice warm enough in that single word to melt his heart, although the word she spoke was the wrong one. "Will Jardine did not act by himself or . . . or kill anyone. Nor did aught that *you* did, or I," she added. "My father was a man of peace. He loathed conflict and would nearly always seek peace at any price. He is gone now, and we cannot change that. But we will have peace in

Annandale if I can manage it. To that end, sir, you *can* help me if only you will."

He knew she meant that he should dissuade Alex from his sworn course of taking Annandale under his power. The knowledge entered his mind with a thud.

Nevertheless, he said, "I will do all I can, my lady, but—"

"No buts, sir," she interjected with a wan smile. "I want your promise. And promises, like apologies, should never marry with a 'but.'"

He was sure his expression matched hers as he nodded in agreement, but he could not speak, because his throat was full. He wanted so much to take her in his arms that he could not trust himself to touch her.

Nodding again more abruptly, he made his bow and left the yard.

He was not yet halfway down the hill when he saw the defiant Gibby coming up with a basket in hand.

Remembering what it contained, Rob smiled.

⁓

Mairi watched Rob walk away until he had passed through the gateway and disappeared below the grassy crest of the hill, wishing he would turn and look back but feeling relieved when he did not.

She watched men gently lift her father onto a thick blanket and carry him into the house, where maidservants and women from the cottages would prepare him for burial. Beside her, Phaeline burst into gusty, sobbing wails.

Mairi felt then as if the past weeks had been only a dream.

Drawing a breath and letting it out slowly, she turned to cope with Phaeline.

Phaeline's woman, Sadie, came running toward them, her skirts caught up high, and seeing her, Mairi felt a rush of gratitude.

Warmly, she said, "I'm gey glad to see *you*, Sadie!"

With a wry smile and a glance at the still sobbing Phaeline, Sadie said, "I'll warrant ye are, me lady. 'Tis relieved we be to ha' ye back again, and gey sorrowful for his lordship's death. What would ye ha' me do first?"

"See to her ladyship," Mairi said.

"Aye, sure. And will I tell the housekeeper to send for the women then?"

Agreeing, Mairi saw how deftly she dealt with Phaeline, and was calling down more blessings on Sadie when a youthful voice behind her said, "Beg pardon, me lady, but the laird did say I should come to ye, that ye might ha' need o' me."

Turning, she beheld Gibby, his wide, gap-toothed smile on full display.

"Gib! Surely the boat has not gone without you!"

"Nay, the laird did say I should bring ye a wee gift. But ye're no to open the basket even a crack till ye've gone inside. So if ye be too busy yet here, I'll wait."

"But will the boat wait?"

"Aye, sure, till I go and wave it off. Unless the tide do run afore then."

Mairi hesitated. "But surely, you do not *want* to stay here, Gib. You like it gey fine at Trailinghail with the laird and Fin Walters."

"Aye, sure, and I'll go back soon enough. The laird did say that mayhap ye could take me into Nithsdale when ye go to Thornhill for Easter. Sithee, Herself will be back in Dumfries by then, and the laird did say that, one way or t'other, she'd help me find how to get back to Trailinghail. Meantime, he said I could learn much here. Sithee, I be a grand chap for learning."

"So you are," Mairi agreed, but her thoughts had shifted to Thornhill and Easter. Giving herself a shake and returning her gaze to the hopeful child, she said, "Go then, if you are sure, and wave the boat off so they do not miss the tide, whilst I finish sorting things out here. Then we will go inside and see what you have in that basket. Unless you want to spare yourself the burden and leave it with me now."

"Nay, I dinna mind carrying it. And ye might peek."

As he strode back to the gateway, Mairi realized she was smiling.

Before he returned, she concluded that although Jopson's quiet acceptance of her authority had assuaged any doubt she might have had about assuming control, he could easily do all that needed doing outside without her. And the housekeeper and her women would see to Dunwythie's laying out.

That left Mairi with little to do but go in to face Phaeline—and a household bursting with curiosity about her long absence, and all it might have entailed.

It was enough, she thought, to make anyone want to turn tail and run.

How she wished Fiona were there, if only to have someone with whom she could talk without minding each word. Realizing she would have their bedchamber to herself stirred new sadness, and tears that she had not expected to shed.

Dashing them away, she hurried to the great hall, where

she found the housekeeper in a bustle to arrange his lordship's laying out.

Agreeing with all that the woman suggested and assuring her that she perfectly understood her desire to supervise it all, Mairi dismissed her with relief and turned toward the stairway.

"Lady Mairi, d'ye want to see what be in me basket now?"

Turning to find Gibby right behind her, holding up the basket, Mairi lifted the lid to see Tiggie curled up inside.

"Good sakes," she said, "I never suspected *this*! Indeed, I thought *you* were the present, with the basket just containing your clothes and more food."

"Aye, sure, I am *part* o' the gift," Gib said. "Nae doots, ye *need* me to look after that wee scruff. As to clothes, I'll do well enough wi' these."

"You would look after Tiggie for me? I thought you 'dinna ha' nowt to do wi' the wee terror,'" she said, teasing him with his own words.

Gibby shrugged. "We get on good now. Any road, the laird did say I couldna come in the boat without I agreed to look after the lad and keep him quiet."

Mairi lifted the kitten out. By the look of it, it was still more than half asleep. When she set it on the floor, it took a tentative step, swayed, and shook itself.

"Why, what's amiss with him?" she asked.

Gib shrugged. "Whisky, I expect."

"Whisky!"

"Aye, sure, the laird himself did say not long since that whisky gives a man good sleep. So I gave a thimbleful to the lad there, and as ye see, it worked a charm."

Mairi bit her lip, reminding herself that her father lay

dead in the house and that kittens almost certainly ought not to drink whisky, but it was no use. Try as she might to stifle the laughter bubbling in her throat, it pealed out and filled the hall.

"Sakes, but he liked it fine," Gib muttered.

Rob's journey back to Trailinghail passed without incident and without wind. Thus it also passed in a fog of boredom with naught to divert him from thoughts that remained at Annan House with Mairi. He was sure she would miss her sister, Fiona, as much as, or even more than, she would miss his lordship.

But he remembered his gentle mother's death, as well as his stern father's, and he knew that losing any parent was dreadfully hard.

He also knew, however, that his continued presence would have done more harm than good. It would certainly have caused tension with her stepmother and also much gossip and many accusations.

Moreover, he did not doubt for a minute that when she considered the matter at length, she would blame him at least a little for Fiona's elopement.

Not only had he taken Will to Dunwythie Mains the day they had all met but *he* had abducted Mairi while Will was working his devilry with Fiona. If only to spare Mairi more pain, Rob knew he was doing the right thing by going home.

The decision did not make the long, dull trip easier to bear.

They did reach the mouth of the bay shortly before dusk.

But, having used up the entire ebb tide to get there, they arrived at low water.

Holding off, far enough out to avoid being seen, they waited for the incoming tide to rise so Rob could use the sea entrance to get back inside the tower.

By the time he did, the sun had been down for several hours and darkness was fully upon them. If Alex's men were watching the sea, Rob decided, they had probably watched the sun go down and gone about their business.

Bidding his men goodnight, he reminded them to return to the tower by ones and twos in the morning so as not to draw undue attention. Then, taking the stairs, he let himself in with the latch chain, pulled it back inside, replaced the bars, took a jug of whisky from the shelf, and went to the kitchen to get supper.

Feeling more his usual self after he'd eaten, and knowing his grandmother would be in the great chamber, he went up to tell her he was back.

"Mercy me," she said when Eliza let him in. "You did explain about the tides, but I did not think you could truly make so long a journey in so short a time."

"It did not seem short to me, coming back," he said.

"Aye, well, you got her home safely," she said.

He told her what had happened. Then, after she exclaimed her dismay at Dunwythie's death and he had answered all the questions he could, he asked if Alex was still outside the gate.

"Aye, sure, and stubborn enough to stay until Christmas, I'm thinking."

"Nay, then, he will not," Rob said. "I mean to have him inside tomorrow to tell him he must parley with Lord Johnstone or one of the other Annandale lairds if he persists with this foolish scheme of his."

"So it is foolish now, is it?"

"Aye, and always was," he told her. "When one hears only one side of an argument, that side seems right. But in this case, the other side's reasons make more sense. To my mind, Gran, when a thing is working, one ought not to meddle with it. The system in Annandale *has* worked well for a century and more, so there can be no need for us Maxwells to assert power there, or any good to come from it."

"I don't disagree with that, Rob, but what about Archie Douglas?"

"Douglas is another matter," he said. "If he asserts power, it is because he needs many men to assure the safety of the Borders, and all ken that fine. So they think it no great thing if he should ask for more gelt or goods to supply his army. The Douglases have long proven their ability to protect us from the English. We Maxwells lack that repute, thanks mostly to other, long dead Maxwells."

"So you mean to challenge Alex on the matter, do you?"

"If necessary, I will, for I promised Mairi I would. At present, I mean to let him know only that she is no longer here, so he can go home and take his men with him before they lay waste all the land around Trailinghail."

Chapter 17———————————

Accordingly, the next morning, Rob sent a lad to invite the sheriff in to break his fast with Trailinghail's laird. Not much to Rob's surprise, Lady Kelso and Eliza entered the hall shortly after Alex did.

Having brought two of his own men along, Alex said as he approached the dais, "I trust you do not mind my escort and will welcome them at high table."

Rob nodded, knowing that Alex would be more civil with them there and more discreet. However, it was too much to hope that the two henchmen, whom Rob knew well, did not know most of what was going on.

Signing to the gillies to begin serving, Rob shook hands with Alex and nodded to the other two.

Alex said, "I brought them in the hope that your invitation this morning means you have come to your senses, lad, and will let me take custody of her ladyship. She will doubtless want to bring along a maidservant, as well."

"I have spared you the necessity of assuming that burden," Rob said. "The lady in question is safely at home.

Moreover, your dispute with Dunwythie is at an end, Alex. His lordship is dead."

"Are you daft enough to think I'd believe that? My lads have kept careful watch, as you must ken fine. *No* female save that Annie lass has left this tower since I came here. Moreover, I would surely have had word of such a death if you have."

"I swear to you by all I hold dear or holy that she is not here, Alex. If you do not believe me, then search until you content yourself that I speak the truth."

Alex frowned at him, then shifted his gaze to Lady Kelso. "Madam, do you also swear that the lady is not here?"

"I do, Alexander. Moreover, you should think shame to yourself that you accuse your brother of lying when he gives his oath. Likewise, if he says Thomas Dunwythie is dead, the man is stone cold and likely in his grave by now."

"But how . . . how can you know all this? And how could she have been here two days ago and gone now, when we have searched all who left here?"

"Because you did not see all who left, of course, including me," Rob answered. "Do not ask me to share the secrets of Trailinghail with you, however, even without your henchmen. Before you came here and threatened to lay siege to my tower, mayhap I would have shared them, Alex, and gladly. But no longer."

"But Dunwythie was headed to Dumfries! How *can* you know he's dead?"

"Because I saw him die and declared him so, myself."

Alex was quiet, and Rob did not like the pensive look on his face.

Then Alex said, "Who will inherit?" And Rob knew he had been right to suspect he was already scheming again.

With a shrug, Rob said, "As Lady Dunwythie is with child, we cannot know the answer to that yet. However, you may be sure the Douglases will take interest, too. My advice to you now is to let be."

"Aye, likely you've the right of it . . . for now," Alex said.

"Certainly until after Easter," her ladyship said. "You would be most unwise, my dear Alex, to flex your power before the holy season has ended, lest you hear the priest at St. Michael's denounce you before the congregation on Easter morn."

Alex smiled at her and said, "You ken fine that I would never defile the holy season, madam."

Hopeful that he had fulfilled his promise to Mairi, Rob watched with relief as the sheriff's party departed later that morning. When he went back inside after seeing them off, Lady Kelso awaited him in the empty great hall.

Without bothering to exchange pleasantries, she said, "You do know that he covets the Dunwythie estates, do you not, Rob? One could see it in his eyes the first time he mentioned his right to seize the property. Your brother has developed a voracious taste for power, I fear."

"I agree with you," he admitted.

"At first, it showed only in the pride he took, governing Dumfries," she said. "But with the chief of your clan always away in Glasgow or Stirling, Alex has had a free hand to do as he likes without hindrance. Such freedom from restraint is not good for any man. And Easter, my dear, is just a fortnight from tomorrow."

"You believe he'll take those estates if he can." When

she nodded, he said, "Well, so do I. But I won't allow it, Gran. I don't know yet how I'll stop him. I'm loath to seek aid from Archie Douglas, because I don't want to humiliate Alex or other Maxwells. But I'll not let them harm Mairi or take her land."

"Ah, well, he'll do nowt until he learns who inherits," she said.

At Annan House, Mairi was finding life hard without Fiona. Never before had she realized how much of a buffer her sister provided against her stepmother.

Without Fiona, she endured entirely too much of Phaeline.

Although Phaeline did not carp or correct her as she often had before, she refused to take Mairi's authority seriously, insisting that anyone who could so mindlessly let a man abduct her from Annan House while she carried the keys to its pantry and buttery could hardly claim to be a good manager.

"'Tis of no use to say you brought those keys back," she added when Mairi reminded her of that fact. "We had to break in, so we have a new lock."

Phaeline also wondered aloud two or three times a day how Mairi would ever find a husband with such a scandal to discredit her.

And Phaeline took strong exception to Tiggie.

"Cats do have their place," she said austerely the following Friday morning as the two women and Sadie sat together in the solar.

Phaeline was embroidering at her tambour frame. Sadie

sat just behind her on a stool, sorting threads for her. And Mairi had set aside her own work to pick up and stroke the now-purring Tiggie, who was otherwise determined to "help" Sadie.

Although no one encouraged further comment on the subject of cats, Phaeline went on to say, "Suppose I should trip over him and fall?" She touched her belly. "What then for the bairn I carry? Surely, that cat could live quite happily outside where it can chase mice and other vermin and make itself useful."

"Tiggie amuses me, madam," Mairi said quietly. "He is either in motion, in mischief, or so sound asleep that one can pick him up without waking him. And he purrs whenever I touch him. Surely, you do not begrudge me amusement or comfort, or deny the need for such yourself. We both grieve, after all."

"Aye, we do," Phaeline said with a sigh. "I miss having a man about more than I can tell you. One simply needs someone about the place to see that all is done properly. Females do *not* convey the same strong air of authority."

"Sakes, has someone dared to be rude to you?" Mairi demanded.

"Nay, nay, 'tis just that when your father was here . . ." She sighed again.

"He did seek always to make you most comfortable, madam, 'tis true. He was a good man. I will try to keep Tiggie out of your way, if that will please you. But, prithee, do not ask to have him put outside, for I will not allow that. He must come and go as he pleases, because that pleases me."

"You take too much authority on yourself, dearling.

Prithee, do not grow too accustomed to it, lest you suffer jealousy of your wee brother when he comes."

Mairi saw Sadie's lips tighten. The maidservant got up abruptly from her stool and set upon it the cloth of threads she had been sorting.

"Forgive me, madam," she said to Phaeline. "I must visit the garderobe."

"Bless us, I hope that lass is not ailing," Phaeline said as Sadie crossed the room. "If I should take sickness from her . . ."

Mairi, noting that Sadie was still within hearing, said nothing.

Phaeline also expressed surprise that Mairi had allowed "that Robert Maxwell" to saddle her with one of his minions, "possibly his own offspring if we but knew the truth." Mairi had said nothing to that, either, preferring peace to war.

Gib preferred to be outside, and she did not blame him. Jopson liked the lad and willingly put him to work, telling Mairi after a day that the wee chap was gey reliable and quick of mind, which she knew was high praise from the steward.

She soon saw that she had fallen into her old ways of yielding rather than expressing her feelings, all in the name of keeping peace, much as her father had done. The knowledge annoyed her. It also made clear the difference between the present and how she had felt at Trailinghail, where she had spoken as she thought.

In truth, she had liked herself better when she was with Rob.

On Monday, three days before their planned departure to spend Easter with Jenny and Sir Hugh at Thornhill, when Mairi and Phaeline sat down for supper with Sadie in attendance, Phaeline said after a deep sigh, "I fear we cannot go to Thornhill, after all, my dear. Such a long way! And *then* to Dumfries for Easter service. 'Tis *such* a disappointment! But I have been feeling so weak of late . . ."

She paused, clearly expecting sympathy and agreement.

Anger leaped in Mairi, and as it did, she knew it was not only because she would miss seeing Jenny and Sir Hugh but also because she hoped to see Rob. Guilt steadied her. She said, "Jenny and Hugh will be even more disappointed, madam."

She said nothing else and remained civil through the rest of the meal.

When they left the dais and reached the stairway, however, Mairi excused herself, meaning to go down and walk off her anger outside.

As she turned away from Phaeline, who went on up the stairs, Sadie said, "Forgive me, mistress. May I have a word?"

Believing that Sadie spoke to her own mistress, Mairi did not turn until the maidservant touched her elbow and said, "If it please your ladyship?"

"Forgive me, Sadie. I thought you spoke to the lady Phaeline. *She* is your mistress, after all."

"Nay, then, she is not, and I dinna call her so," Sadie said. "I call her madam, same as ye do. And *ye* be the mistress here, m'lady."

"Nay, by my troth, not yet," Mairi said. "Sithee, if the lady Phae—"

"Nay, mistress," Sadie interjected, adding swiftly, "I dinna mean to be pert, but madam just *says* she be wi' child. Her courses came as usual three days ago."

Mairi gaped at Sadie then, as fury threatened to undo her.

~

At Trailinghail, Lady Kelso was preparing to return to Dumfries to celebrate Easter Sunday in her favorite kirk, that of St. Michael's near the great bridge.

Alex had insisted that Rob join them in Dumfries, and Rob had agreed so quickly that he knew—after the way he and Alex had parted—that he must have astonished his brother. Rob was to escort her ladyship, with two score of his own men, since her ladyship's sense of her worth demanded that she travel in style.

Also, Alex had taken back with him the escort her ladyship had provided for herself under the pretense of going to Glasgow.

Rob had no idea whether Sir Hugh Douglas would bring his family to celebrate Easter at St. Michael's. But it was the finest kirk in Nithsdale, so nearly everyone who lived near enough did celebrate there. At all events, he could hope.

~

Mairi waited until Tuesday morning to confront Phaeline. Having warned Sadie in the meantime to make herself scarce, and finding Phaeline in the solar alone, Mairi did not equivocate.

"I have learned that you are *not* with child, madam, and have not recently been so. Nay, do not speak," she added when Phaeline bristled in apparent indignation. "I have much to say, and I am not interested in hearing spurious denials."

"That you *dare* to speak so to me—"

"'Tis most unlike me, to be sure, but to have worked such a deception on my father is inexcusable, and I shall not excuse it," Mairi said as caustically as she had ever spoken to Rob Maxwell. Thought of him encouraged her to go right on:

"Good sakes, madam, I do not know whether to be sorry or grateful that Father did not learn of your wicked deception," she said. "But what is done is done. Now, however, as there can be no doubt of who is rightful owner here, you *will* listen to me. You are entitled to live in this house, and so you shall. But I am going to Thornhill for Easter. You may go with me or not, as you will."

Phaeline eyed her angrily, but Mairi looked right back, just as angry.

"Sadie will be very sorry to have betrayed me so," Phaeline said with a sigh.

⁓

They left for Thornhill just after dawn Thursday morning.

Mairi had not visited there before, and her first view of the house was a fine one, for it stood on rising ground above the river Nith. She felt at home the moment she entered and saw her cousin Jenny, Baroness Easdale, rushing to meet her.

Jenny's golden-brown hair, parted in the middle, showed beneath her caul in two soft, narrow wings. She wore a plain but most becoming moss-green kirtle with a girdle of square silver links, elegantly engraved, around her hips. She greeted them all, laughing with delight and hugging Mairi hard.

"I was so sorry to learn of Uncle's death," Jenny said then, turning a more solemn face to Phaeline. "You must miss him sorely, madam, all of you."

They had not yet told her about Fiona but did so as soon as the ladies were settled together in Jenny's pleasant solar where a cheerful fire burned on the hearth. They had sent Sadie—now happily serving Mairi, Phaeline's new maid-servant, and Jenny's Peg upstairs to deal with baggage and prepare their bedchambers.

So the three of them could talk freely.

"Eloped!" Jenny exclaimed when they told her. "How dreadful! And with Will Jardine of all men! Sakes, I well recall what Uncle thought of *that* family."

"Aye," Phaeline said. "He was furious beyond measure with our Fiona. But the unfortunate truth is that Mairi, too, bears some of the blame for his tragic death."

"Surely not, madam," Jenny said. "One cannot doubt that Fiona's running off with Will infuriated him. But Mairi had naught to do with that."

Phaeline grimaced, saying, "Her disappearance did affect him, my dear. He was outraged that she had been so long with an unmarried man—and a *Maxwell* at that. Sithee, he believed Maxwell and Jardine acted in concert.

'Twas a disgrace! His fury at having *two* such scandals looming over us was what sent him off."

Frowning, Jenny turned to Mairi. "We did know that someone had abducted you, because Hugh helped search for you. But we heard naught of a conspiracy."

Calmly, Mairi said, "It is untrue that Robert Maxwell and Will Jardine were in league together, Jenny. I will tell you all about it, I expect. But not just now."

With another glance at Phaeline, Jenny nodded and smiled. "I am willing to wait, for I want to show you the house and our wee son. Hugh will be in soon to take supper with us, so shall we see the house now? Or would you prefer to rest for a while, madam," she added. "Hugh told me you are with child again."

Phaeline hesitated, so Mairi said, "That is no longer so, I'm afraid."

"Then I am sorry for that, too, madam—a double tragedy," Jenny said. To Mairi, she said, "So you are now a baroness in your own right, too, are you?"

"Aye, but I feel like the same old Mairi," she said.

Jenny chuckled. "I did, too, when my father died. But one swiftly comes into one's responsibilities, as you will soon see if you have not already done so."

Phaeline accompanied them as they wandered over the house, and Sir Hugh—a tall gentleman, stern of face but with a twinkle in his eyes for his wife—joined them in the solar before suppertime. Therefore, it was not until Mairi retired to the chamber allotted to her use that Jenny joined her for a comfortable talk.

"Tell me," Jenny said without ceremony. "Was Phaeline faking it?"

"Being with child, do you mean?"

Jenny nodded.

"Good sakes, has she done it before?"

"I don't know for certain," Jenny said. "But my Peg did suspect as much and told me so not long before I married Hugh. Sithee, Peg used to help Sadie with laundering our things when we were all living at Annan House."

"Sadie told *me* because Phaeline used her supposed pregnancy to say she could not manage the journey here for Easter, after all. When I learned the truth, I told her I was coming with or without her but she could do as she pleased."

Jenny's merry chuckle rippled forth. "Good for you," she said. "I'll wager Sadie is happy about her change of situation, too. Phaeline has a sad tendency to slap her servants when they displease her, Peg said. But, now, tell me all about your abduction. Was it horrid? You seem little the worse for the experience."

Mairi told her more than she had told Phaeline, although she did not tell Jenny everything. Nevertheless, it was a relief to tell someone who did not display greater shock with each thing she did say. Even the fact that Rob had left Gibby and the kitten with her did not faze Jenny except to make her laugh again.

"Did you bring them both with you?" she asked.

"Nay, just the lad," Mairi said.

Despite Jenny's apparent acceptance of all that Mairi did tell her, knowing that less information had shocked Phaeline to the bone had already persuaded Mairi that the abduction had destroyed her reputation through-out Annandale—at least, as far as her stepmother was concerned.

"Pish tush," Jenny remarked when Mairi explained as

much to her. "She said the same to me after I ran away with the minstrels. But I can tell you this, Mairi. When a woman bears a title in her own right, such events become just interesting facts about her life. Even a countess may draw dour looks, to be sure. But people forgive her much that would destroy an untitled woman, unfair as that may be. A husband will make a difference, too, when you wed. I promise you that."

"Aye, perhaps," Mairi said, striving to look disinterested. "But a baroness who takes her *maidservant* with her when she runs off with minstrels is a much different matter than a lady stolen from her home and kept prisoner by a laird she had met only once, and gey briefly."

"I expect it is different," Jenny said. She looked as if she might ask a more ticklish question next, but Mairi went right on to describe the sheriff's attempt to take custody of her, and the moment passed. Still, she was sure Jenny must wonder if Rob had taken advantage of her.

He had, of course, but only with her aid and consent. And he had proposed marriage directly afterward. But that detail was another she did not mean to share.

She still believed that while a husband could make a difference in her situation, no one would react well to the idea of any woman marrying her abductor.

Nor could she blame anyone for thinking badly of such a plan. It was clearly daft. So, she would put it right out of her head. She would certainly not tell Jenny that the notion had ever crossed her mind. Nor would she allow it to do so again.

In fact, it was possible that Rob did not even love her, and just as well.

After all, when she had asked him to leave, he had put

up little argument. And, in view of Fiona's elopement and their father's death, even the thought of trying to explain to Phaeline, or to anyone else, that Mairi *might* want to marry the man who had abducted her was beyond her ability just then to imagine.

Jenny asked next about Dunwythie. Learning that he was properly interred in the hillside cemetery at Annan House, she had only one question.

"Did you read his will?"

"Aye, straightaway. 'Twas just as he had told me, including leaving Annan House to me, although Phaeline retains her tocher right to live there until she dies."

"'Tis odd that Fiona did not show herself even for the burial, is it not?"

"I sent messengers twice," Mairi said. "First to tell her he had died and urge her to come home. I said Phaeline needed her, and I, too. Then I sent to remind her that we were all to come here for Easter. She did send a message that time, saying dearest Will thought they ought not to travel whilst she was so upset by her loss and that mayhap they would see me when next I visit Dunwythie Mains."

"Sakes, how *very* odd," Jenny said with a sigh. "I still miss my father. I felt close to him right to the minute he died. Still, I'm glad we Borderers do not make such a great fuss of death and burial as the English do, and some Scots."

Mairi agreed, but Dunwythie's death was still raw within her, and she missed Fiona. Although she had not felt as close to her father as Jenny had to hers, neither had she lived alone with Dunwythie as Jenny had with Easdale after *her* mother died. Easdale never wanted to remarry and, from the outset, had accepted Jenny as his heiress.

That would not have been Dunwythie's way, Phaeline or no Phaeline.

"Attending to burials quickly and without fuss was only sensible hereabouts when the next raid or invasion might occur before they were done," Mairi said. "Mayhap now that we've had peace for a time, things can begin to change."

"Perhaps," Jenny said. "But life is for the living, and one should get on with it."

Easter Sunday arrived in the royal burgh of Dumfries with sunshine blazing.

The sky was clear, grass green, and a large crowd gathered for the Mass in St. Michael's Kirk near the nine-arched bridge spanning the river Nith.

The kirk was a splendid structure. Its interior was solemn but well appointed to provide for all who attended services there.

The public area near the front was large and open for prayer stools or cushions. Private pews nearer the main entrance were grand enough and screened well so that royals and nobles could worship, safe from the stares of lesser folk.

Sir Hugh's party had seats in a private pew that the Douglases provided for any kinsmen who had business that might keep them in town over a Sunday.

Mairi lowered her eyes demurely as she and Phaeline followed Sir Hugh and Jenny inside. Gibby, Hugh's man Lucas Horne, and other servants had gone ahead to the open space in front to find places for the prayer stools they had brought.

Sir Hugh stopped at a pew, opened its gate, and gestured for Phaeline to enter. Mairi, just behind her, looked at Hugh to see if she should go next. As he nodded, abrupt movement beyond him diverted Mairi's attention, and she was suddenly looking into Rob's eyes.

He had paused to let others in his party precede him into the pew across from and a row ahead of theirs. She saw Lady Kelso just going in, head bowed.

"Go ahead, my lady," Hugh murmured to Mairi.

Startled, and realizing that her mouth had fallen open, she shut it, gave Hugh an apologetic smile, and hurried to take her place with Jenny and Hugh following.

From where Mairi sat, she could no longer see Rob over the privacy screen. But every time the congregation stood during the Mass, she could see him only too well. Each time, he glanced back at her, and she could not mistake the hunger she saw in his expression.

Wondering how many others might notice, she tried to fix her mind on the priest and the resurrection. But all she could see when she closed her eyes was another pair of eyes, clear pale-blue ones with long dark lashes. She had once thought them cold but knew now how much they could warm.

The service ended at last. Hugh waited for those in front to leave with their prayer stools before he opened the pew gate, stepped into the aisle, and made way for Jenny. As Mairi followed her and stepped past Hugh, she looked for Rob.

She found find him nearer than she had expected.

"Sir Hugh Douglas?" he said, extending a hand to Hugh.

"I am Robert Maxwell. If you will permit it, sir, I would beg a word with the lady Mairi."

Despite the low murmur of voices and footsteps of people leaving, Mairi could hear her own heart pounding in her chest as she looked next at Hugh.

To her astonishment, he said, "Well, lass? Art willing?"

"Aye, sir," she said. "To talk, at least."

Hugh nodded, and gestured for her to go ahead of him with Rob. They walked side by side, not talking, until they were outside.

"Come this way," he murmured then, turning toward an area out of the way of the main portion of the crowd that was heading back toward the center of town.

When they stopped, Mairi kept very still, wondering what he would do next.

She felt as if she could read his mind but wished he would say something to clarify *his* feelings if not her own.

Remembering the day he had abducted her, when she had been outraged and angry but never truly afraid . . .

He moved then and touched her hand, shooting a thrill through her that warmed her whole body.

⁓

Rob wanted to squeeze her hand but was afraid she would pull away if he did. Moreover, if they looked too intimately engaged, Hugh Douglas would likely intervene. He was watching them, and although his lovely wife watched, too, she was smiling. Hugh was not.

Rob heard Mairi murmur something and bent nearer. "What is it, lass?"

"What did you want to say to me?"

He would have been content with silence, just to be with her. But he had to speak, to be sure she understood. "I wanted you to know that I'm here," he said. "That is, that I will always come if you need me. You need only send for me."

"You are kind, sir."

"Nay, not kind, lass. Don't ever think me kind, for I am nowt o' the sort. Sithee, I feared I might never see you again. This is but a step to make it possible that I may. If I do not, it will be a grievous penance to me and a lesson."

"Prithee, sir, I do not think this is a good idea. I should go."

"Shall I tell you what I think? I think that if we had met at a different time, in a different way—especially a different way—you might have loved me. But because of what I did and all that has happened since, I spoiled what might have been. You think me arrogant and thoughtless, impulsive and—"

"I do not think you arrogant," she muttered. "Only that your behavior is sometimes so. Sakes, but you try to control all save your own impulses. Now you even try to tell me what I think and feel. But we cannot stand here any longer. People are watching. I must go."

"Not yet," he said, suppressing an urge to grab her, to make her stay. "Tell me first how bad it has been for you. Has your stepmother made you miserable? Does she continue to plague you with her certainty that the bairn she carries is a son? I own I was surprised to see that she would endanger the succession by—"

"Say no more, sir. She is no longer . . . that is, she never was. I am—" She broke off, blushing deeply.

"You are Dunwythie's heiress then," he said. "That is good, my lady, aye—Lady Dunwythie of that Ilk. Now, fewer people will dare to chide you."

"That is what Jenny said," Mairi confided. "But I *must* go."

Sir Hugh took a step toward them then, so Rob nodded, saying, "Aye, you must. But remember . . . if you need anything that I can provide . . ."

"I know. Thank you."

As she turned away, he remembered one thing more. "What of Gib?" he asked. "Did you bring him with you?"

"Aye, sir, he is here with the servants. But he has not said what he wants to do, and he is welcome to stay. He has impressed my steward, who admires his reliability. And Gib has made himself guardian-in-chief of the wee terror."

Rob chuckled, saw Sir Hugh striding toward them, and said, "Go now, my lady. Your own guardian approaches."

"I see him, but we return to Annan House in a few days' time and will pass near Dumfries," she said. "I will see that Gib gets to you then if he does decide to return, and if you are still here in the burgh."

Assuring her that he would be there, he watched as she walked gracefully away, wishing he had the words and time to tell her how she made him feel, that just looking at her put warmth in his heart, that she was all that he was not.

For months before he had come to know her, he had felt an emptiness inside him that was hard to define. In truth, though, he had not recognized the feeling until meeting her had made the difference, before that moment and after, so clear to him.

Although he had immersed himself in projects and

duties at Trailinghail, he had felt no true urge to live there full-time until he had been there with her.

Before then, he had itched for more, mayhap to ply his sword in service to the Lord of Galloway, to help Archie speed the remaining English from Scotland.

Still, he had not wanted anything enough to take the first step toward it.

He had therefore wandered from one objective to another, doing many things and nothing, chiefly tasks that Alex had demanded of him. He had nearly always felt angry about something, too—or about nothing in particular that he could name.

Then Fate had brought Mairi into his life.

He had talked with her, laughed with her, and fought with her. Even as she had fought back, even when she confided her own loneliness to him, she had shown that her heart was open to all and that she had soft words even for a harsh man.

She could light up a room by entering it. Sakes, but she lit up his mind whenever some seemingly disconnected thought brought her image into it.

He did not deserve her, and he could not have her. He was not even sure that he loved her, because he did not know how a man knew love when it came. But he did know that he wanted her in his life more than he had ever wanted anything else.

Chapter 18 _____

Later that day, during Easter dinner at Alan's Tower, Lady Kelso chose to make a commonplace of Rob's having met the lady Mairi in St. Michael's Kirk.

"Mairi looked to be in good spirits, I thought," she said.

"She seemed well enough, aye," Rob said, matching her matter-of-fact tone. "She and the dowager Lady Dunwythie are visiting Douglas of Thornhill. His lady wife, you will remember, is Baroness Easdale."

"Lord Dunwythie's wife should more properly be called simply *Lady* Dunwythie until the next heir marries, my dearling," Lady Kelso said. "You may believe me when I tell you that being always referred to as a dowager gets quickly on a woman's nerves. And Lady Dunwythie has not yet reached her fortieth year."

Realizing that she spoke from personal experience, Rob grinned at her but said, "Aged or not, Gran, she is no less a dowager, because Mairi *is* her father's heiress and thus is now Dunwythie of Dunwythie. Therefore, when people refer to *Lady* Dunwythie now, they will be referring to her."

"Bless me, so Dunwythie of that Ilk is now a woman," Alex Maxwell said thoughtfully. "'Tis a most thought-provoking situation, is it not?"

Meeting his gaze, Rob felt a distinct chill.

⁓

Mairi had rejoined the others after parting with Rob, and tried hard to pay heed to the general conversation as they rode back to Thornhill for their midday meal. She knew the others were burning to ask about her conversation with him.

But although Phaeline glanced at her several times as if she expected Mairi to initiate such a conversation, even she did not comment on their meeting.

Jenny did ask her about it when they reached Thornhill. Having put a heel through the hem of her dress, she asked Mairi to go with her to pin it up again.

"Peg is helping to set out Easter dinner," Jenny said. "Forbye, this way we can steal a few minutes alone, so you can tell me about what happened in kirk. If you do not want to talk about it, I will understand," she added as Mairi knelt to attend to the tear. "But Hugh told me who that man was that walked with you afterward. So you must know that I'm all agog to hear what he wanted with you."

"He is not as you must think he is," Mairi said. "He was kind to me, though he says I must not describe him so. He wanted to know if Gib is ready yet to return to Trailinghail. I told you about Lady Kelso, Robert's grandmother. She looked after Gib when his parents died. The sheriff had no place for the lad, she said, so she gave him to Robert."

"*Gave* him?"

"To train in some way or other," Mairi explained. "Gib will have to make his own way, after all, and Robert can do more for him than Lady Kelso can." She explained how Gib had ended up with her. "He said he likes to learn about places and people, but I think he is likely ready to return to Trailinghail. I'll arrange for one of the men to take him into Dumfries on our way back to Annan."

So sure was she that, two days later, when she told Gib of her arrangement, it came as a shock when he said, "But I'd liefer stay at Annan House, m'lady."

"Now, Gibby—"

"Sithee, we ha' been gone nigh onto a sennight now, and heaven kens what mischief that wee devil will ha' got himself into. I should go back to be sure all is well wi' the lad. Like as no, I'll ha' dunamany chances to get back to Trailinghail."

Rob was sure by the end of that week that Gib had returned to Annan with Mairi, and also sure that he knew his brother's mind as well as he knew his own.

Although Alex had said no more about the matter, he had clearly taken the news of Mairi's inheritance to mean that Dunwythie Mains, with only a woman to run the estate, was as good as his. In the intervening days, although Alex had gone about it quietly, Rob learned that he had begun gathering a large force of men.

The discovery frightened and infuriated him. But he

ignored his personal feelings and took care not to look at his grandmother when they sat down to supper Saturday evening. He believed that, much as Lady Kelso disliked the idea of Alex seizing Dunwythie Mains, she would accept his explanation that it was his duty as the sheriff and would do little, actively, to support Rob against him.

Accordingly, and with a strong if unusual sense of calm, Rob said, "I ken fine what you mean to do, Alex. But you have not thought this matter through."

"What matter do you think we are discussing, Rob?"

"Don't carp. 'Tis plain that you mean to take advantage of the situation as you perceive it to be. With only a woman to guard those estates, you imagine you can seize them, and you will begin with Dunwythie Mains."

"Seizing estates when their owners flout Crown law is no more than my official duty," Alex said, just as Rob had expected he would.

"But the same truths apply now that applied before with regard to seizing them," Rob said. "The new baroness is indeed a woman, but she is wise beyond her years. And the men who serve her are well trained and as competent as our own, if not more so. Do not forget that with the English occupying Lochmaben, the men of Annandale test their mettle more often than our Dumfries lads do. And *Lord* Dunwythie trained them."

"Faugh," Alex said. "Do not *you* forget that I am well experienced in the field. Moreover, you will be beside me with *your* sword this time, as you should be."

"Nay, then, I will not," Rob said. "Not to attack the young baroness or the innocent people who look after her estates. And certainly not whilst Archie the Grim roams about with heaven kens how many men, not to mention all the others he can quickly summon to his banner if he wants them."

"We've had no word of late that he is in Dumfriesshire," Alex said.

"But you ken fine that when he moves he moves swiftly," Rob countered. "Moreover, he is more popular in Annandale and with some folks here than you are, Alex. And with a kinsman at Thornhill to complain of your attack on Dunwythie, he might decide not only to protect Dunwythie Mains but also to punish you for your temerity in lately besieging Trailinghail, which I'd remind you lies in Galloway."

"He won't do any such thing, for that was not a true siege," Alex countered. "Archie will understand better than you do that I could not allow my own brother to flout my commands. I have *never* set myself against Douglas, nor would I."

"Sakes, man, you and your men rode across Douglas land to lay that siege you say was not one at Trailinghail," Rob said. "*All* the land betwixt Kirkcudbright and mine at Trailinghail belongs to Douglas."

"Mayhap it is, aye, but I have only to tell Archie that my purpose was to rescue the lady Mairi from you."

"Rescuing her *may* have been your intent," Rob said dulcetly, allowing himself a slight smile. "But if I were you, I'd think twice before mentioning *that* in support of your so-called right to seize the same lady's estates."

Reddening, Alex retorted angrily, "I will do my duty, come what may."

"Will you? Well, I cannot keep you from trying, but I *won't* ride with you."

"And if I command you to do so?"

Rob shook his head, saying, "I'll bid you farewell now, brother. I cannot wish you good fortune in your venture, but I do sincerely hope you come through such a mad scheme with your skin still intact."

"By God, you do not change," Alex snapped. "You would betray your own clan for the sake of a pretty face and figure. You should be ashamed to call yourself a Maxwell, Rob!"

"My only shame is that I allowed myself to be swayed by such arguments in the past," Rob said. "If being a Maxwell means attacking an innocent woman to take her rightful property merely to augment a kinsman's personal power, I think shame to the clan and to the man who instigates such an attack."

With that, and astonished by the ease with which he had held his temper, Rob strode out to the yard and shouted for his men and horses. An hour later, they were on the road, heading north from Dumfries by the river route to Thornhill.

⁓

Two days later, on the first day of May, Mairi was sitting in the ladies' solar at Annan House with a silent Phaeline when Jopson brought word that Parland Dow had arrived.

"Will I be tellin' him to be getting on wi' such tasks as his late lordship and me discussed, my lady, or will ye be having new ones for him?" the steward asked.

As Mairi paused to choose her reply, Phaeline said, "I should think that *you* must know much better than her ladyship does what orders to give Dow, Jopson."

Quietly, as if her stepmother had kept silent, Mairi

said, "Thank you for telling me, Jopson. Unless aught has changed since you and I talked after my lord father's death, tell Parland Dow what we decided and let him get on with it."

"Aye, mistress," the steward said. "He did beg a word wi' ye, though, if ye should find a convenient time to speak wi' him."

"I will go to him now," Mairi said. "I warrant he has brought news."

"Gossip, more like," Phaeline said. "The man is ever filled with it. But surely he can share what news he has gleaned with both of us this evening whilst we sup, Mairi. 'Tis what your father would have done."

That was her newest ploy, to try to get her way by declaring that whatever she wanted was what Dunwythie would have done. Mairi knew, though, that Phaeline was only aching to hear the news just as she was.

"My father would have issued his invitation personally, madam," she said. "And so must I. That way, we can all three be comfortable whilst we talk."

"'Tis a kind thought, dearling, but better to let Jopson do it," Phaeline said with the sweet tone and smile she used whenever she thought she had won.

Mairi did not comment, and ignored her stepmother's astonishment as she excused herself with an equally sweet smile to go with the steward.

"Does Parland Dow come to us from Dumfries, Jopson?" she asked quietly as they approached the stairway.

"I think he said he had come from Thornhill, m'lady."

"Thornhill? Thank the Fates you did not tell me *that* in front of her ladyship!"

"I knew better, mistress, for Dow did say I should tell

you in such a way that you would come to him alone. I could not mistake that."

"Sakes, I hope naught is amiss at Thornhill."

"Nay, for I did ask him straightaway if all was well with our lady Jenny."

Relieved, Mairi greeted Dow a few minutes later with a smile and a warm clasp of his hand. "I am glad to see you," she said.

"Ye mayn't be so when ye hear what I ha' to tell ye," he said with a grimace.

"Jopson assured me all is well at Thornhill. So what is it?"

"'Tis Sir Hugh sending me hotfoot to warn ye them blasted Maxwells be aiming to seize the estates at Dunwythie Mains in the name o' the Crown," he said.

"The sheriff did threaten to do such a thing, but I did not believe he would."

"Sir Hugh did say Sheriff Maxwell means to do so straightaway. See you, m'lady, the man doubts ye'll be strong enough to stop him."

"We'll see about that," Mairi said grimly. To the waiting Jopson, she said, "Send messengers north to Lord Johnstone and to anyone else who may be willing to help stop this outrage. Warn them to make haste to Dunwythie Mains."

"Should I send to warn the Jardines then, as well, mistress?"

Fiona's image leaped to mind, and she said, "Aye, tell them that we are on the way and will welcome their aid. We must not expect them to help, but I could not be easy of mind if I did not warn them that trouble is about to erupt so near them."

"Old Jardine be more apt to be a-siding wi' the Maxwells," Parland Dow said. "I ha' nae doots that fierce old man kens fine what be going on, and Will, too."

"They most likely do, aye," Mairi said. "But they may not, and the lady Fiona is with them at Spedlins Tower, so I *must* warn them. Jopson, tell Captain Gerrard about this and help him gather our men swiftly. I'll order food for us, change my clothing, and will be ready to ride as soon as the men are. Tell Gerrard they must dress as if they were raiding England, and to prepare themselves well for battle."

"Ye willna go yourself, m'lady!" the steward exclaimed. "Beg pardon, but . . . I mean to say, ye'd only be—"

"I ken fine that I am no warrior, Jopson. But I will not send our men into danger whilst I stay safely here. Dunwythie of Dunwythie will lead the way, as always. However," she added dryly, "assure them that her ladyship will pull aside before she can become a nuisance—most likely before we reach the chapel hill."

When he frowned, she added, "I should be safe enough riding that far with our men. The Maxwells, coming from Dumfries, will likely cross the Annan *north* of the Hall. With the recent heavy rains, the ford below Applegarth won't be safe."

"I think Sir Hugh expects ye to stay here at Annan House," Dow said warily.

Meeting her indignant look with a rueful grimace, he reached hastily into his leather jack and withdrew a narrow roll of vellum, adding as he held it out to her, "I did bring ye another message, as well, from Dumfries."

Taking it gently, she said, "Faith, who sent this?"

"I warrant it will bear a signature," Dow said, giving her a look.

"So it will," she agreed, noting that the red wax seal revealed only a small, narrow thumbprint. Stepping away from the two men, she broke the seal and unrolled the brief message:

My dearest,

Since Easter service, he has been most melan-choly and restless, so if you had doubts of him, you may dismiss them. Know that I shall do all I can to aid you if you seek what, in a more accepting world, you both so clearly would seek. He will not long allow himself to feel so haunted without seeking ac-tion. Know, too, that Archie the Grim is even now gathering an army for his latest purpose and will order that all men of Galloway follow him when he sets forth. —AK

Striving to suppress suddenly roiling emotions, and wondering if Lady Kelso could possibly have known when she wrote the message that her elder grandson meant to seize Dunwythie Mains and her other estates, Mairi rolled the message up again and said, "Tell our lads to hurry, but be sure they have all they will need, Jopson. We can still reach the Hall before sundown, I believe."

"Aye, mistress, easily. Moreover, I should think the Maxwells canna ha' set foot yet in Annandale, or we'd have had word of it."

She nodded, seeing no reason to mention that, just weeks before, several of the sheriff's men had come into Annan-dale without warning. If the sheriff headed a large force, as she expected he would, many would notice. In any case,

Jopson would send messengers out straightaway to warn as many as they could.

Without sparing another thought for the men's preparations, knowing that Jopson and Gerrard would see to them and that she could trust both men implicitly, she went in to order the food and tackle Phaeline.

Gibby was piling wood in a basket by the hall fire with one hand and dangling a string with the other for Tiggie, so she sent him to issue her orders for food. "Tell them to pack what the men will need and send it outside," she ordered.

"Aye, mistress, I'll see to it," the boy said as he ran toward the kitchen.

Next, she found her stepmother still in the solar. Relating the news Parland Dow had brought, Mairi said, "Hugh is on his way, madam, and I shall go with our men, of course. But we will leave enough men-at-arms here to keep you safe."

"Godamercy, *no* Maxwell has the right to seize our estates," Phaeline protested. "Doubtless the sheriff thinks he can do so only because you are a woman. So 'tis just as I warned you it would be. Faith, but I suspect he thinks it is his *duty* to take them, if only to run them properly. But we will just see what my cousin Archie thinks of such impudence."

"Doubtless Sir Hugh has already sent word to the Lord of Galloway," Mairi said. "However, I cannot dally here. I don't want to delay the men."

"Sakes, you will delay them simply by insisting on riding *with* them," Phaeline said. "What do you think *you* can do to aid them?"

"My father, for all his peaceful ways, never let his men

ride into danger without leading them. Nor shall I. I shan't wield a sword, but I *will* be nearby."

"Utter stupidity," Phaeline said with an unladylike snort. "But you will have your way, I expect."

"In this matter, I certainly will," Mairi said.

"Then it is no less than my bounden duty to go with you," Phaeline declared.

"Nay, then, you need not!" Mairi exclaimed in dismay.

"My dearling child, *no* unmarried female should be riding with an army of rough men, no matter where their loyalties may lie. Moreover, I *am* still your mother, so do *not* argue with me."

Mairi had no time to argue. Furthermore, she suspected that Phaeline was more concerned about Fiona than she had yet let anyone see. They had heard not a word from her, or about her, since their return from Thornhill.

Therefore, saying only that Phaeline would have to make haste, as they would not wait for her, Mairi hurried to her own room and summoned Sadie. Dressing quickly, she snatched up the bundle of clothing that Sadie packed hastily for her and rushed back to the yard to find all in train for their departure.

As Jopson strapped her bundle to her horse, he reported that he had sent word to every baron for twenty miles around that the Maxwells were coming.

"The lad I sent on to Lord Johnstone will learn if his lordship had already sent out word himself, mistress. If not, the lad will ask him to warn all north o' him," he added. "Ye'll ha' a good-sized Annandale army a-joining ours soon."

"Good," Mairi said. "The more help we can gather the better. By the bye, Jopson, the lady Phaeline will be riding with us." Anticipating his dismay, she added, "I hope you do not think I ought to have stopped her—"

"Nay, mistress, I think nowt o' the sort. In sooth, it be a load off me mind, that ye'll ha' her ladyship wi' ye, though it do take me aback that she be willing to go."

To Mairi's surprise, for she had expected her to keep them waiting just to prove she could, Phaeline hurried out a few minutes later. It occurred to Mairi only then that, as Applegarth lay south of Dunwythie Mains, Phaeline might be thinking that they could seek shelter there. If so, she would learn her error.

Mairi's place was with her own people at Dunwythie Mains.

Rob and Sir Hugh Douglas, between them, led a party of eighty-five men, but Rob was certain they would need more. As they crested the long ridge that divided Nithsdale from Annandale, he half expected to see Alex's army filling the landscape below them.

Aware of Hugh's gaze, he met it and saw a twinkle in the older man's eyes.

"What?" Rob demanded curtly.

"Here now, lad, don't be snapping at me," Hugh warned. But the twinkle deepened. "I cannot help it if I still feel amazed at receiving a warning from a Maxwell about a Maxwell attack on Annandale."

"Sakes, not all of Annandale, only the Dunwythie estates," Rob said.

"Even so," Hugh said. "Maxwells rarely turn against Maxwells."

"Nor have I," Rob said. "As I told you, I want only to protect the lady Mairi's estates by keeping Alex from seizing them. I don't want anyone killed."

"That may happen, though, if battle comes of this, as I believe it may."

"I could not allow the seizure, Hugh. You know Dunwythie attended to the Crown's business in Annandale just as seneschals of old did. That fact alone should satisfy everyone with a stake in the matter."

"So one would think."

"But Alex thirsts to expand his powers as Sheriff of Dumfries. He would see the Maxwells, under his guidance, control as much of southwest Scotland as he can lay hands on, your cousin Archie notwithstanding."

"He has sadly underestimated the Douglases then," Hugh said.

"I ken that fine. But Alex sees nowt save his own ambition, and so far, Archie has not found reason to thrust *his* power in Alex's face."

"So far, Archie has but dipped a toe in Nithsdale water to test its sheriff's intent," Hugh said. "If your brother were wiser, he'd see that."

"Archie is not *now* in Nithsdale," Rob pointed out.

"Art so sure of that?"

A chill tickled Rob's spine much like the one that had struck when he realized Alex meant to take Mairi's lands. He had no idea where Archie was.

"Has he returned to these parts, then?" he asked.

"Archie hears more than any other commander and moves faster. Those are facts that most men know about him, facts that your brother has clearly forgotten."

"But Alex keeps ears out, too," Rob protested. "Surely,

he would know if the Douglases had entered Nithsdale, and that's the most likely route to Annandale."

"Archie is like the wind—gone and then back again when one least expects it," Hugh said. "He has certainly visited Annandale, for he wants badly to get the English occupiers of Lochmaben out of this country."

"Aye, we must."

"Meantime, your brother is seizing what he thinks is a grand opportunity. Has he not wit enough to see how Archie will perceive a move against one of his own?"

Rob knew that Alex had discounted all risk, but he could see no reason to tell Hugh so. Alex was, after all, still Rob's brother. He said, "I'd hoped that you and I could stop him before it came to that."

In a gentle voice that did not fool Rob in the least, Hugh said, "Before you came to me at Thornhill, you must have guessed I would send to advise Archie of what was going forward. Did you not count on Douglas strength, in the end, to foil the sheriff's plan?"

"Aye, sure," Rob said. "But I counted on the threat alone to dissuade him. I thought Douglas was back in Galloway, at Threave, not anywhere near at hand."

"Aye, well, in future you should be minded of two facts about Archie. If you need him, he will come, and if you *don't* want him, he'll come all the faster."

Deciding to change the subject since it was far too late to change Archie, who might be needed, Rob said, "Do you trust Dow to warn them at Annan House without terrifying them or stirring the lady Mairi to ride straight to the Hall?"

"Mairi is always sensible," Hugh said in a tone that Rob thought he meant to be reassuring. "I told Dow to say the

message came from me, and not just because you asked me
to do so. I thought it wiser not to confuse her by telling her
you would be with me. She will trust me to deal with any
number of Maxwells."

As Rob had not told Hugh about his feelings for Mairi or
hers for him, Hugh's confidence did not reassure him at all.
He feared that Mairi might put herself in harm's way, hoping she could stop the sheriff—stop the Maxwells, in fact—
or intervene some other way, before anyone got hurt.

"She will think I ride with Alex," he said.

Hugh looked narrowly at him. "What if she does?"

Rob grimaced. "She will either hope I can keep him
from harming anyone else or will think I agree that we
Maxwells should control Annandale. Sithee, she has accused me more than once of trying to control *all*."

To his surprise, Hugh chuckled. "Women frequently
make such accusations," he said, "particularly when a man
issues an order he expects them to obey."

"You speak from experience, I expect."

"Aye, sure, I do—experience with another baroness in
her own right, come to that. Such women have little trouble
making decisions, so doubtless most of them take umbrage
when a man tells them what to do. I did therefore have the
sense not to issue anything resembling a command in that
message I sent with Dow."

A shiver shot up Rob's spine. "Mayhap you should have,"
he said. "I'm thinking we should ride faster, Hugh."

~

The fifteen-mile ride to Dunwythie Mains would take
Mairi's party at least five hours, because the men wanted

to spare their horses as much as they could. So, although she had wanted to ride faster, she contented herself with persuading Phaeline that only one stop was necessary to refresh themselves and partake of a light meal. However, their party increased its number shortly after they stopped, when Gibby arrived.

"I thought ye might need me," he explained when Gerrard snatched him off his pony and gave him a shake.

"I'll show ye who needs what," the captain of the guard said angrily. "Ye'll be riding straight back, me lad, and riding gey sore when I'm done wi' ye."

"Nay," Mairi said quietly, remembering her ride with Gibby and Rob at Trailinghail. "It may not be safe to send him back alone, Gerrard, and he will be no more trouble to you than I am. He can stay with the lady Phaeline and me."

"Aye, mistress, but I trust ye'll no deny me the pleasure o' teaching the lad a lesson in obedience when we get home."

Gibby gazed at Mairi with such soulful innocence that she almost felt guilty when she said, "Nay, Gerrard, I'll not stop you. He deserves skelping for this."

The boy grimaced but made no protest, and rode meekly in Mairi's wake when they were on their way again.

Although Rob and Hugh had picked up the pace, Rob's thoughts had raced ahead. No matter what notions came to him, the fact was that whatever course Mairi chose, he could do naught to alter it. He could only reassure himself that Alex would not harm her. He would value her instead as a weapon with which to control Rob.

The best thing Rob could do was to put her out of his mind, to stop feeling anything but the horse under him and the wind in his face. He could do no good by wasting energy on his rage with Alex or fear for Mairi. He must put all that aside.

To protect Mairi, he must stop thinking about her.

They did not know if Alex was in Annandale already or not. They had purposely stayed northeast of Dumfries until they were over the ridge and in north Annandale, to avoid word of their small force reaching the sheriff's ears. They rode now on the ancient Roman road that would pass within a mile of Dunwythie Hall.

Chapter 19 ————————

Mairi's party neared the south boundary of Jardine Mains an hour later.

Spedlins Tower lay near the river Annan just as the Hall did, not far from the Roman road they followed. Knowing that her party was large enough that word of their approach had likely reached the Jardines, Mairi said, "We must be cautious from this point so we do not unexpectedly meet Jardines or the sheriff and his men."

"We *must* stop long enough at the tower to pay our respects," Phaeline said. "Surely, they can *tell* us if there are Maxwells in the dale."

It was the first time she had spoken of the Jardines, but Mairi shook her head.

"I know you want to see Fiona," she said gently. "But not yet. The lad we sent ahead to them has not returned, so we don't know they got our warning. The fact is that they are likely in league with the sheriff. You know they are *not* our friends."

"Godamercy," Phaeline said. "Will Jardine is married to our Fiona. If you think *she* would allow—"

"Madam, prithee, hear your own words," Mairi replied. "Fiona is headstrong, to be sure. But I do not believe she willfully missed our father's burial or thought such a course to be 'wise.' Will is the one who decreed it so. If you think more carefully, I think you will agree that only if Will Jardine forced her obedience could he have kept her from us on such an occasion."

Phaeline grimaced and sighed. "You are right, of course. I have feared all along that he abducted Fiona as surely as Maxwell abducted you. Your father did not believe it, but if I had my way, both those men would hang for their crimes."

Mairi stared at her. "I had no idea you felt so strongly, madam. I knew, of course, that Fiona's elopement upset you dreadfully, as it did my father, but—"

"I do *not* believe she eloped," Phaeline repeated. "That man *took* her."

Mairi realized that since Fiona had not been daft enough to reveal her feelings for Will to her mother, Phaeline knew nothing about them. Unwilling to tell her when they did not know what lay ahead, she said, "I thought you blamed me as much as you blamed Rob . . . Robert Maxwell for my abduction."

"You are my daughter, too, Mairi, but I cannot fault you for believing I had few motherly feelings for you," Phaeline said with one of her sighs. "Until you vanished so abruptly and we had no idea what had become of you, I did not know that I *did* care. Recall how young I was when your father married me . . . a full year younger than you are now. If I showed stronger feelings for our ungrateful Fiona—"

"Prithee, madam, say no more on that head," Mairi interjected, touched by Phaeline's unexpectedly honest revelation. "Fiona is dear to all of us, and you *are* the only mother I have known. By my troth, I have never blamed you—"

"I know that," Phaeline said, cutting in as swiftly as Mairi had before. "You make me feel all the smaller, because you have never cast my bad behavior in my teeth. But I did behave badly, too often, I fear. Sithee, even your father did call me to account once or twice, although for him to do so was most unusual."

"He loved you, madam," Mairi said, knowing it was true.

"He did, aye, and I took advantage," Phaeline said. "I feel so ashamed now that I lied. Sithee, I thought no one would ever know. You were clever to confront Sadie, although I do think she ought to have warned me that you suspected I was not with child, and let *me* be the one to tell you. I'll not forgive her for that."

The words were at the tip of Mairi's tongue to admit that had Sadie *not* told her, she would not have suspected. Instead, she said, "But why *did* you lie?"

Phaeline grimaced. "I wish I could cite some noble reason. But the sad truth is just that your father treated me more kindly when he thought I was pregnant than when he knew I was not. Sithee, he wanted a son so badly, and I took advantage of that, too, I fear. I must be a wicked woman," she added with a sigh.

"Women often do what they think is necessary to protect themselves or their families or just to keep peace," Mairi said, remembering her own behavior before her discovery of more open, easier communication with Rob.

"Mayhap they do," Phaeline agreed. "But that does not excuse my behavior."

~

"The turning lies about a half mile yonder," Hugh said sometime later.

Rob nodded. He knew where they were from his last trip to Annandale. The Chapel Hill a mile northeast of the round tower keep made a good landmark.

"Do you think your man will find Archie?" he asked Hugh.

Hugh shrugged. "He will find him. But we won't wait for them."

"I'll send men on ahead to see what they can see," Rob said. "Alex will cross at the ford a mile this side of Dunwythie Hall, so we'll want to keep our eyes open."

The two lads he sent ahead returned to report all clear, so avoiding the track, he and Hugh led their men across the densely wooded slope toward the Hall.

As they neared the wide clearing around the wall that protected the tower keep, screaming men dropped from trees and sprang out of the dense shrubbery, swords and pikes at the ready.

~

Except for the horses' hoofbeats and a jingle of harness, most of Mairi's party had been silent for some time when Gib muttered urgently, "M'lady!"

Only then did the sounds he had heard reach Mairi's

own sharp ears. She raised a hand, unconsciously aping her father's signal to bring his men to a halt.

The nearer sounds ceased. The distant ones did not. Looking around, she realized that while she had been talking with Phaeline, they had reached their own land southwest of the Chapel Hill. They were less than a mile from the Hall.

Shifting her gaze to Gerrard, she saw from his narrow-eyed frown that he, too, had heard the distant sounds of clashing metal, faint shouts, and screams.

Meeting her gaze, he said, "There be a fight yonder, m'lady. The two o' ye and Gib should ride on east now, past yon hill, till ye reach Dryfe Water. Stay near the water, and dinna come back. I'll send lads to fetch ye when it's safe."

She did not argue but reined aside to let the men pass. As they did, she saw expressions ranging from wariness to outright grins and lust for battle.

"I'm thinking we would be safer at Spedlins Tower than Dryfe Water even if, or *especially* if Old Jardine is helping the Maxwells attack the Hall," Phaeline said.

"Nay, madam," Mairi countered. "Only think what Sir Hugh would say to us if we did that and the Jardines managed to take us hostage."

Phaeline grimaced, clearly remembering her stern brother's more unpleasant ways of making his views plain. "Very well," she said. "However, if our serving as hostages can be at all useful for those attacking Dunwythie Mains, it must be on your account, not mine. I doubt Hugh would submit to a Maxwell just to save me."

Mairi chuckled. "You underrate Sir Hugh's loyalty to his kinfolk, madam. Moreover, few men would esteem one of their fellows who did naught to protect his sister and his own beloved Jenny's favorite cousin from harm."

A smile touched Phaeline's lips, but it vanished at once. "You are right again, my dear. The truth is I do not want to ride two or three miles more to Dryfe Water, merely to wait there till called for. Heaven knows how long *that* would be."

"I agree," Mairi said. "I have meant all along to ride up Chapel Hill, to see what I can from the top. If you are willing, I still want to do that."

"Aye, that be a good notion, that," Gib said approvingly.

Phaeline nodded, clearly as curious as Mairi was. But what they saw when they reached the hilltop and skirted the stone chapel was carnage below.

"Gor bless us," Gib muttered.

~

Snatching his sword free of its belt across his back, Rob had dealt swiftly and savagely with his first assailant as Sir Hugh dealt with another. A half dozen of their men were afoot, knocked from their saddles by the attackers. But they all had their swords and dirks out and were fighting for their lives.

Others, still horsed, fought as fiercely, to the disadvantage of their opponents who, thanks to their places of ambush, were *all* afoot. So Rob shifted his attention to a second attacker, hoping none of his men would mistake any of Hugh's for the enemy or vice versa. Members of their party wore red cockades on their helms or caps, rather than clan colors. But a man might easily lose his badge in battle.

Recognizing one of Alex's men fighting one of his own lads as he dispatched his second opponent, Rob spurred his horse toward them, shouting, "Hold there, Jock MacGowan and Ian Rigg! Where is the sheriff, Jock?"

The two men flung up their swords at the sound of his voice and whirled to face him. Both looked shamefaced. The taller one met Rob's stern gaze and said defensively, "I didna hold wi' lying in wait for ye, Master Rob. But the sheriff did say that if ye came here, we was to arrest ye and all who rode wi' ye."

"Where is he?" Rob repeated grimly.

Jock gestured toward the keep. "Yonder, Master Rob, inside. He took a dozen men in wi' him, and he said he'd tell them at the gate he were expecting to speak wi' the lady Mairi, that doubtless summat had delayed her."

"So 'tis likely he surprised those inside, too, and has been asserting the authority of his office," Rob said. "Now, listen to me, Jock MacGowan. We have Maxwell men injured who need tending, so this must stop now. I warrant you do not recognize that man yonder," he added, gesturing toward Hugh. "He is Sir Hugh Douglas, cousin to Archie the Grim. The dowager Lady Douglas is likewise Archie's cousin and Sir Hugh's sister. Do you take my meaning?"

"Aye, sir, I'd ha' to be ten times a fool no to ken better than to stir Douglas tempers," Jock MacGowan said, his eyes widening. "Sakes, but we'll ha' the whole fearsome clan after us an we do that, I'm thinking."

"Not if we can end this now," Rob said.

Jock bit his lower lip, looking around. Bleeding bodies lay everywhere.

Rob kept his eyes on Jock, trying to ignore the dreadful sounds of clashing steel and injured men. When Jock met his gaze again, Rob said quietly, "Where is Abel the hornsman?"

Nodding decisively then, Jock gestured to someone beyond Rob on his right. As Rob turned, he heard the two-note Maxwell signal to cease fighting.

In almost the same moment, three sharp notes came from another horn. Looking swiftly toward Sir Hugh, Rob saw that Hugh's man, Lucas, held the horn. Hugh had lowered his sword. The rest of his men and Rob's were doing likewise.

Rob breathed a sigh of relief, although he knew the battle was far from over.

"You must have more men than these, Jock," he said. "Where are they?"

"A few be inside and a score o' them yonder," the man said. "Near the road, wi' Old Jardine's lot, a-waiting for them what may come from the south."

"From Annan House?"

"Aye."

Swearing, Rob shouted for Hugh.

~

The cessation of battle sounds raised Mairi's hopes until Phaeline, pointing to the road below, said, "Look! It must be a hundred men! They cannot be ours."

"I expect they are the sheriff's men," Mairi said. "I see no banner, but with all the talk that Archie the Grim means to take the dales, mayhap the sheriff hoped folks would think that his force, being so large, must be Douglases."

"Would they not wonder why they do not fly the Douglas banner?"

"Sakes, they'd be daft to wave the Douglases' banner when they dinna be Douglases," Gib said scornfully.

"Folks might wonder, but I wager most would keep clear," Mairi said dryly. "It might explain why we had no warning that the Maxwells were coming."

Phaeline nodded. "Gibby is right, too, though," she said. "If our Archie were to hear that men were falsely waving his banner or otherwise aping Douglases, he'd soon have their heads on pikes at Threave. Why has it grown so quiet below?"

"I heard horns, so it must be over," Mairi said. "But I mean to find out."

"You mustn't go down there!" Phaeline exclaimed. "I shan't let you!"

"Nay, m'lady," Gib said. "Ye must no go down. I can go and see *for* ye."

"I'm going," Mairi said. "This is my land, and they attacked my people. If those riders yonder did not join the fray, the sheriff's force must— Wait," she exclaimed, narrowing her eyes. "Is that large black horse not Gerrard's?"

"Aye, it is," Gibby said, his eyes wide. "Sakes, m'lady, they've got *our* men!"

"Then I *must* see what has happened at the Hall. But you stay here with the lady Phaeline, Gib." Giving neither time to argue, Mairi wrenched her horse toward the track downhill to the Hall. But before she reached it, half a dozen armed riders crested the hilltop from the south and quickly surrounded her.

They all wore helmets, but she recognized Will Jardine when he urged his mount up beside hers and grabbed her horse's bridle.

"Let go and get out of my way," she snapped. "You are on Dunwythie land!"

"Aye, sure, and don't I ken that fine?" Will said with a cheeky grin. "One day soon, though, it will all belong to me."

"Good sakes, Will Jardine, how do you think *that* can happen?"

"Aye, well, let me see now. Dunwythie be dead, and if *ye* be dead next, the land goes to my Fiona and hence to me," he said, ticking the statements off on his fingers.

"That is *not* going to happen," she said. "Even Sheriff Maxwell would not be party to such a theft, if only because he wants to seize my estates for Clan Maxwell."

Will chuckled. "Nay, then, for he sent word to me da that he were a-coming, sithee. And me da means to make the facts plain to him. He already has your lads, and he'll soon take anyone else who gets in his way."

"Where is Fiona?" Phaeline cried out to him.

"At home where a good wife belongs," he snapped.

"There are many others coming," Mairi said, striving for calm. "We sent men out to warn all the lairds in Annandale before we came here."

"Ye did, aye, and I warrant ye must be a-wondering what became o' them. Sithee, me da sent his lads out to collect yours, and others to relay the news that 'twas all a mistake and nobbut the sheriff and a few lads paying calls like before."

His men were listening and watching him with grins much like his own when Mairi saw Gib slide down the off-side of his pony and dive into nearby bushes. To give him time to get safely away, she kicked her horse, making it plunge and pull hard against the bridle Will held, nearly unseating the man.

He raised his whip menacingly. "Do that again, lass, and see what ye get!"

~

"Alex has more men with the Jardines' lot, lying in wait on the road just south of us for anyone coming from Annan House," Rob told Hugh. "Gather all these men here, ours as well as your own—"

Hugh's eyebrows rose. "Your *brother's* men?"

Rob looked at Jock and Ian Rigg. "My brother's men will do as I tell them," he said sternly. "Will they not, Jock MacGowan?"

"Aye, sir," Jock said, nodding hastily. Ian Rigg nodded, too.

"Very well, then," Hugh said. "What do you—?"

"Master Rob! Master Rob!"

Whirling, Rob saw Gibby dashing headlong toward him, heedless of armed men or injured ones. Brambles and twigs clung to his tattered clothes.

"Them Jardines ha' her ladyship!" he shouted. "*Both* o' their ladyships!"

Gasping, the lad stumbled, and Rob caught him, set him upright, and looked into his sweat-streaked face. "Where, lad?"

"Yonder . . . hill," Gib said, taking gusty breaths. "I ran all the way down!"

"How many men?" Rob asked him.

"Six on the hill, many at the bottom, but methinks lots o' *them* be Annan House men the Jardines caught. They got the lads that Captain Gerrard sent out to raise the other lairds, too. Lady Mairi were expecting many to join us, but them wicked Jardines— Sakes, laird, the one a-leading them . . . her ladyship did call him Will Jardine. He said her land will belong to him when *she* be dead like her da!"

"You've done well, lad," Rob said, squeezing Gib's shoulder as his own fury leaped within him. He was as angry with Mairi for putting herself at risk, and with Phaeline for letting her, as he was with the treacherous Jardines. Ruthlessly controlling his ire, he turned to the two Maxwell men beside him.

"Ian, look after the men seeing to our injured. Gibby here will help them when he gets his breath. Jock, are our own men on the gates yonder?"

"Aye, sir."

"Tell them they are to stay right where they are. Then get the rest ready to ride. But first, send Abel the Horn to me."

Hugh said, "My lads are ready, so what is our plan?"

"How many clan calls does your hornsman know?" Rob asked him.

Hugh grinned. "Any you need. Lucas Horne!" he shouted. "I want you!"

A dour-looking man with bushy dark eyebrows who had ridden directly behind them from Thornhill strode up to join them, "Aye, sir?" he said to Hugh.

"Maxwell here wants to know how many clans' horn calls you can blow."

Lucas raised his eyebrows in much the same way that Hugh had earlier. "Happen we be up to old mischief then, eh, Master Hugo?" Looking at Rob, he said, "Who d'ye want we should pretend t' be, sir?"

"Annandale clans, Johnstone, Kirkpatrick, whoever will impress the Jardines," Rob told him. Then, indicating Abel, he added, "This is my hornsman. Teach him one or two as we ride. Then I want the two of you to split off into the woods and make as much noise as you can when we get near the Jardines."

"Ye'll want Douglas, too," Lucas said. "But Sir Hugh has his own horn and can blow as good as most. Ye be lookin' to ha' armies in t' woods, I'm thinkin'."

"That's it," Hugh said, but he was frowning. "What if they run, Rob?"

"I want the Jardines to run."

"But they might take the women with them."

"Recall that Gib told us there are only six men with them on that hill," Rob said. "I doubt Will Jardine has the stomach to fratch with two resistant women if the rest of the Jardine men take off. And Mairi *will* resist. Recall, too, that Old Jardine has hostages to give *him* trouble. Mairi's captain and his men are unlikely to stand idle when they know reinforcements are on the way."

"I hope you're right," Hugh said.

"Me, too," Rob said. "Will Jardine better hope so, too. If I'm wrong, and I can get to him, he'll soon be a dead man."

⁓

Some time had passed since Mairi had stared back at Will until he lowered his whip. He had told her then that he did not want to hear another word from her, and she had kept silent, wondering what he would do next.

He had moved them farther east on the hill until they

could not see her men, Old Jardine's, or the road to the Hall.

Will was evidently waiting for a signal or for someone else to join them, because he had not told her or Phaeline to dismount. He had also sent two of his men to keep watch, one looking south along the road and the other north.

At last, he said to a third, "Go see if anyone be coming from the Hall yet."

As the fellow slid off his horse and tethered it, Mairi said curiously, "How did you stop my men? We heard no battle down there on the road."

"Nay, for me da be too clever for that," Will said. "Sithee, sound travels with such ease as might surprise ye hereabouts, up and down the dale. Me da didna want to warn anyone approaching the Hall that we were there."

"That *was* clever," she said. "What do you want us to do now?"

Phaeline said tersely, "*I* want to know how Fiona is."

"She's good is what she is," Will said. "Mayhap ye'll see her, mayhap no."

"I certainly will see her! You had no business—"

Her words broke in a sharp cry, as Will backhanded her across the mouth.

"Ye'll be silent unless ye want more o' the same," he said. Turning back to Mairi as casually as if he were just continuing their conversation, he said, "As to what ye'll do, ye'll first sign over yon Annan House to us, and then—"

Distant horns interrupted him, first one then another.

"Bless us!" Will exclaimed. "That be Douglas! And Kirkpatrick, aye!"

"Johnstone!" one of his men shouted.

"And Dunwythie," Mairi exclaimed, astonished when she recognized it.

Will's face paled. "They must ha' defeated the sheriff!" Turning, he shouted across the hill, "What be the old man a-doing?"

"Trying to leave!" the shout came back. "But them bastards he stopped be fighting our lads now. Do we ride to their aid?"

"Nay, we take these women to the tower, straightaway!"

"You won't!" Mairi said angrily, digging her heels into her horse and wrenching her reins hard to pull its head away from Will's grasp.

As he reached for it again, two horses came over the eastern brow of the hill. Both riders had swords drawn and Will, seeing them, lost interest in Mairi's horse. Grabbing his own reins with both hands, he whirled his horse southward and spurred it hard. His remaining two men followed.

As Mairi drew a breath and turned toward Phaeline, one of the approaching horsemen reached for her bridle as the other rode past her to take Phaeline's.

"Release our horses, damn you," Mairi said.

"With respect, m'lady, we dare not," the man said. "Ye must come wi' us lest there be more o' them villains hereabouts."

She recognized him then. "You serve Sir Hugh. Do you not know us?"

"Aye, m' lady, I ken ye both fine. But we were told to look after ye just now."

"Has Sir Hugh not taken command at the Hall?" Mairi asked. "I heard Dunwythie horns and others that must have been Douglas, I suppose. Why should Sir Hugh even have expected me or the lady Phaeline to be here?"

"*Hugh* did not expect that," a voice behind Mairi said grimly. "But *I* feared that you might do *just* such a daft thing. Then Gib told us that you were *both* here."

Mairi turned sharply to see Rob striding toward her, his expression as furious as she had ever seen it.

"What the devil were you thinking, coming here?" he demanded as he gestured away the horseman who had held her bridle.

"These are *my* people," Mairi said, her own temper soaring. "Would *you* stay safely in Dumfries if Trailinghail were threatened with attack?"

"Nay, I would not, but I am a swordsman, lass."

"Where is Gib? Is he safe?"

"Aye, he must have run like the wind for he had none left when he reached us. But he told us you were here. We'd feared Will might have taken you down to Old Jardine, but when I saw movement on the hillside, I sent these lads up around on horseback, left my own horse below, and crept up through the shrubbery."

"But there was a man on that side of the hill, keeping watch," she said.

"He won't trouble us further, or anyone else, come to that," Rob said.

She swallowed. "Will and the others rode off."

"So did Old Jardine, aye," he said. "I saw as much, for I came up the hill on that side before moving to see to yon watcher. Your own men fought bravely when they heard the horns, and most are safe. But you'll hear all about that later."

"We could not see anything after Will came. Where is your brother?"

"Still at the Hall," Rob said. "Hugh and I were about to join him inside when Gib found us. We still need to talk to him, so you must . . ." He paused, grimacing.

"Must what?" she asked bluntly. "Ride north to keep safe with Lord Johnstone? Or Kirkpatrick? Are they not both here?"

"Nay, the horns were ours. Did Jardine hurt you?"

Phaeline said urgently, "We must get Fiona away from those horrid people!"

"Not today," Rob said. "The Jardines will have entrenched themselves at Applegarth by now, madam. None of us wants more conflict if we can avoid it."

Mairi said, "If the fighting has stopped, we should leave this place. But I shall go nowhere except to my home, sir. You may come with me if you like."

From the abrupt way his eyes narrowed and his gaze bored into hers, she knew he had been rigidly containing his volatile temper.

She met that fierce gaze steadily, hoping Phaeline would have the sense to keep silent. Whether her stepmother recognized in Rob a man she could not charm or simply could think of nothing to say, she did hold her tongue.

Mairi let the silence lengthen but did not look away from Rob.

Then, softly, she said, "The Hall and its people are my responsibility, and the sun has gone down. If the sheriff and his men will not leave peacefully, then I will send again for lords Johnstone and Kirkpatrick. Together, surely we'll outnum—"

"Alex's men are with me," Rob said. "And Hugh sent

for Archie before we came. He will have told Old Jardine as much if he got a chance. In any event they will find out soon enough, and they have no allies here in the dale."

"Sakes, we don't want Archie here, either," Phaeline said, speaking for the first time. "He is more likely than anyone to want to take control of everything."

Mairi saw Rob's lips twitch then and allowed herself a smile. "Shall we go back to the Hall, sir? Together we should be able to persuade your brother that he has no good reason to stay there."

He hesitated for only a moment before saying, "I'll talk to . . . nay, then . . . *we'll* talk to Hugh and see—"

". . . and *explain* to him what *I* have decided to do," Mairi said firmly.

Rob drew a breath and suppressed a simmering urge to argue, recognizing it as simple proof of Mairi's accusation that he liked to control all around him.

She was watching him expectantly, braced for battle, and the lady Phaeline watched both of them. So he smiled and said, "Let's go find Hugh."

Mairi's smile flashed then, warming him and banishing the last shreds of his anger with her for scaring him half witless.

The two men who had ridden up the hill to help joined them, one leading a horse that Mairi explained was the one Gibby had ridden. Rob mounted it and on the way down to the road they collected his from the woods where he'd left it.

They found Hugh on the road with his men and their own, but no Jardines.

When Mairi asked Hugh what had become of them, he said, "Your man Gerrard here told me they hied themselves off when they heard our horns."

"Aye, m'lady," Gerrard said then. "We damaged them some, but our lot came through wi' nae more than a couple o' scratches."

Returning to the Hall together, they found more serious injuries there, and learned that three of their own men and several of Alex's had died.

As they dismounted, Gibby ran to Mairi. Nearly tearful with relief, he exclaimed, "Ye're safe, m'lady! Did the laird kill all them treacherous villains?"

"Nay," she said, ruffling his hair. "We let them go. The man who interfered with us on the hilltop is my sister's husband. Sithee, he fled when the laird and Sir Hugh came with their men, and for that we have *you* to thank."

"Aye, sure. But they must ha' been right cowards then. And so I thought them, too, when I seen that Will-one raise his whip to ye," Gib said with a grimace.

"What is this?" Rob demanded.

"Naught to concern anyone," she replied coolly. "He merely threatened me. We'll see to the burial of all the dead in the cemetery here, Hugh," she added.

"Thank you, my lads will see to it, aye," Hugh said solemnly. "We'll make camp in your woods, too, lass, if we may. I want to be away before dawn."

"Aye, sure," she said. "But I hope you will sup with us tonight, sir."

"I'm going to find Alex," Rob said to her when Hugh

had accepted her invitation. "Are you still going to come with me?"

"You know that I am," she said, giving him a look.

They saw Alex sooner than Rob had expected, because he strode out through the gate as they approached it. His demeanor suggested anger, but his expression was less decipherable. His mouth tightened when his gaze met Rob's.

However, instead of the angry remarks Rob expected to hear, Alex said, "I am glad to see you safe, my lady. I swear, it was never my intent to cause you harm."

"Indeed, sir?" Mairi said. "Then why did you send so many of your men to add to the Jardine army? 'Twas Jardines who tried to harm me."

"So my man told me, and I offer my deepest apology to you," Alex said. Then, meeting Rob's gaze at last, he said, "One of the lads on the gate told me you had come. I talked to Ian Rigg then and sent the others out to help with the injured."

"Sakes, Alex, you set them on us from the trees—on me!" Rob said. "And all to take a woman's property because you thought she was weak. As you have seen for yourself, she is nowt of the sort."

"I do see," Alex said, looking ruefully at Mairi.

She had not, Rob noted, accepted his brother's apology.

"Those who were killed died through sheer folly," he said. "I did not know the two who fell upon me, and Sir Hugh's men knew none of them. Once I saw Jock MacGowan and Ian Rigg, I was able to call our lads to order. You should have known they would respond to my orders as they always have."

"Oddly, I thought I was in command," Alex said on a bitter note.

"Aye, well, that is what happens when you entrust your duties so often to others," Rob said. "Your men outside accepted my command and that of Sir Hugh Douglas of Thornhill. And, by the bye, lest you think of stirring more trouble, you should know that he sent for Archie before we left Thornhill. So, before long, the Douglases are bound to descend on Annandale if not all Dumfriesshire."

"Tell him he let them vicious Jardines get their oozlie hands on my lady, aye, *and* her mam," Gibby said clearly from behind Rob. "*He'll* be sorry for that."

"What the devil!" Alex exclaimed. "Who dares to speak so insolently?"

"'Tis just me," Gib said, stepping forward, his bony shoulders squared. "But I'm thinking Herself will be gey wroth wi' ye, too, when I tell her them Jardines o' yours were a-going to kill our lady Mairi."

Chapter 20 _____

Mairi saw Rob's jaw tighten and dismay on the sheriff's face.

To them both, she said, "Will said that as my father was dead, killing me would make Fiona heiress to our estates. He said, too, sir," she added, looking at Sheriff Maxwell, "that you had sent word to Old Jardine of your coming. Will told us his father would make the facts plain to you, as he saw them. They captured the lads we sent ahead to warn the other lairds, too. Faith, but I fear for their lives."

Alexander Maxwell frowned heavily, and for the first time, she saw a true resemblance between him and Rob. The sheriff was a few inches shorter and heavier, but their frowns were just the same.

His voice gruff, he said to her, "That ought not to have happened, my lady. I certainly never imagined such a thing. I got word to them because they had aided us before and I thought they should know to expect trouble. And I sent men to meet them lest a much larger force from the south overcome them before they joined us."

Rob said, "We should get those lads of hers released, Alex."

"Aye, we must," the sheriff agreed.

"Oh, pray, sirs," Phaeline exclaimed. "You must rescue our Fiona, as well!"

Rob said, "Madam, pray try to understand that although the sheriff can demand the release of men seized whilst going about their lawful duties, as those messengers were, he cannot interfere between a man and his wife."

"Faugh," Phaeline said. "She is not his wife. He abducted her, Robert Maxwell, just as *you* abducted our Mairi."

Mairi saw Rob wince and wanted to defend him, but she kept silent. Although she would welcome rescue for Fiona, if the sheriff lacked the authority to interfere, it was more important that they do what they could for the gillies.

Sheriff Maxwell said quietly to Phaeline, "You have reason to be angry, madam, with both of us. But my brother is unfortunately right about the lady Fiona. If she is Will Jardine's wife, even if he has simply declared her so and she has not denied it, I can intervene only if *she* tells me she wants to leave him. Even then, he has the right to take the matter before a magistrate, who would hear them both."

Rob said, "It is too late to go tonight, I'm thinking."

"Aye, the days are getting longer, but darkness will fall in less than an hour," the sheriff replied. "I'd liefer not approach Applegarth after dark. In the morning they'll be able to see clearly who approaches. What is Sir Hugh doing?"

"His men will camp outside the wall tonight," Mairi said. "He means to take supper with us inside, though. You and your brother are welcome to join us."

"Thank you, my lady, but I trust you'll forgive us if we

camp with our men instead. I'm thinking you'll agree," he added, looking at Rob.

Rob nodded. "Aye, you're right, we should. I would like a private word with your ladyship, however, before we say goodnight."

She nodded and turned to Phaeline. "Will you excuse us, madam? I am sure you would rather go inside where you can be comfortable."

"I would, indeed," Phaeline said. "I will also see that they know to expect others for supper . . . if that meets with your approval, my dear."

Mairi smiled at the last bit but said, "Aye, sure, madam, do as you please." Realizing that Gibby had stood silently by, fascinated, through all that the sheriff had said, she added, "Go along with her, Gibby. Make yourself useful."

"Aye, sure," he said and followed Phaeline through the gateway.

Then, bidding farewell to the sheriff and allowing Rob to draw her well away from the men milling in the clearing, Mairi said, "Thank you for helping us today, sir. I'm sorry you won't sup with us, though. If you are still displeased with—"

"Nay, lass, nor do I want to fratch. I must go with Alex, because the men need to see us together tonight. Some of them will be wondering why he did not go with us earlier, and others will be thinking I usurped his power by ordering them to leave here and go with me. So, we must show ourselves as one, and do that as soon as possible. In any event, I want to encourage this mood in him. I don't doubt we'll be fratching again by midday tomorrow, if not sooner, but . . ."

He stopped then, gazing at her with such pain in his eyes

that she wanted to say something to make it go away. But she could think of nothing more intelligent than to ask him if that was all he had wanted to say to her.

"Nay," he said. "I wish things were different, Mairi. I wish I had not done the things that make it impossible for you to marry me, or even to trust me."

Reaching out to touch his arm, she said softly, "I do trust you, Rob, but—"

"No buts," he said, putting a hand over hers. His touch was gentle as he lifted it from his arm, and his voice was sorrowful as he said, "Like apologies and promises, sweetheart, trust must come unconditionally. That became impossible, I suppose, even before it all began. At times, I wish I had not been born a Maxwell. But I was, lass, and I will always be a Maxwell."

"But, truly—"

"I must go," he said. "We'll camp here until dawn. Then, if Hugh agrees to ride with us, we should finish at Applegarth well before noon. Even without Hugh's men, it won't take much longer. But I must take Gib back with me, or Gran will want to know why I did not, and Fin Walters as well. Ask one of your lads to see him to the Roman road, will you, so he can meet us on our way back to the ford."

"It is only a step to come here for him," she said.

"Aye, but I'd better not."

Dismally, she watched him walk away, fearing that he was going forever.

Inside, she found all in a bustle. Phaeline had set people to dusting and sweeping out rushes, and she was informing someone tartly that things had gone sadly awry since her departure just weeks before.

Leaving her to it when Gerrard approached, Mairi said, "Your men did well today, I'm told, whilst I nearly got the lady Phaeline and myself captured."

"I'll say nowt about that, my lady. I sent word to Johnstone, Kirkpatrick, and the others, so they'll keep a lookout. They didna light the signal fire here today, because they believed the sheriff when he said ye did expect him. By the time our lads knew aught were amiss, *his* men were on our wall and a-watching our gate."

She let him tell her what he thought of it all but listened with half an ear. Her attention at supper was no better. By the time she bade everyone goodnight and sought her bed, she was exhausted and sure she would fall asleep at once.

Hours later, she was still awake, but when she did sleep, she slept until sunlight poured into her room. Startled, remembering that she had said naught to Gibby about meeting the men on their way back, she got up hastily and dressed herself. Neither she nor Phaeline had brought maidservants with them, and none was at hand in the Hall unless women were in residence. She realized as she tied her boots that Phaeline might have attended to the lack, but by then she was dressed.

She also knew exactly what she was going to do.

First, she found Gerrard and asked him to send a gillie hotfoot to Lord Johnstone with a message. Next, she went to find Gibby.

"You're going to meet the laird and the other men on their way back from Applegarth, Gib," she said. "He expects you to return with him to Dumfries today."

"Aye, I thought he might," Gib said with a grin. "I think I'll go, too, wi' respect, m'lady."

"Do you? I thought you liked staying with me."

"Aye, I do, and ye might ha' need o' me again. But I like Trailinghail, too, and I'm thinking if I go to Dumfries wi' the laird, old Gerrard canna skelp me."

Mairi grinned, too, then. "I won't let him, Gib. You earned your way out of that skelping when you ran so fast for the laird. I want you to take a message to him for me when you meet him, and you must say it to him just as I do. Can you do that?"

"Aye, sure, I can!"

~⌒~

Rob accompanied Alex to talk to Old Jardine but left most of the talking to Alex. The fat old man was truculent but Alex spoke firmly. Rob had warned him that Old Jardine agreed with Dunwythie that the sheriff had no authority in Annandale, so he invoked his authority as a chieftain of Clan Maxwell instead.

"Moreover," Alex added when Jardine hesitated. "Sir Hugh Douglas is with us today, just outside with my men. Sithee, those Annan House lads you took are Douglas henchmen, sent with the lady Phaeline when she married Dunwythie. I doubt you want trouble with Douglas."

"Or us," Rob added when Old Jardine gave Alex a sour look.

"Nay, I want nae trouble wi' any o' ye," the old man growled.

"You should know then," Rob added quietly, "that Will threatened to kill the lady Mairi so that the lady Fiona might inherit her estates. We have been allies in the past, sir, but I'll tell you now to your face that if harm comes to her ladyship and I learn that Will had aught to do with it—"

"Aye, aye, I understand ye, and I believe ye. Nowt will happen to the lass. Now, then, take your men and get hence, the both o' ye."

"I have messages for the lady Fiona," Rob said.

"She's no here. Will took her riding afore ye got here. I expect I can pass them messages on to her for ye, though."

Stifling a sigh, Rob said to tell her ladyship that her mother and sister would like her to visit them at Dunwythie Mains.

"Aye, sure, that'd be likely, that would," Jardine said sarcastically.

"At least you can tell her mother you gave him the message," Alex said as they went out to the others and waited for the two Annan House men to join them.

When they did, the cavalcade wended its way north on the Roman road until Rob saw Gibby waiting beside it for them, alone.

Reining in by the boy, he said, "I thought one of the lads from Dunwythie Hall would bring you out here. Where's your bundle?"

"There by yonder rock, where I were a-sitting afore I heard ye coming, laird. But I brung ye a message ye're to hear first."

Rob frowned at him. "What is it?"

"Put your lug down here so I can tell ye without all these louts a-listening."

Rob dismounted and stood over the lad. "Is this close enough?"

"Aye, sure, if ye want all and sundry to hear."

Bending nearer, he said, "This better be good, Gib, or—"

"I'm to tell ye, if ye agree that trust be a thing as must be shared, one wi' another, ye should ha' a second look at yon barley field," the boy said carefully.

When Rob looked at him in astonishment, Gib exclaimed, "Sakes, dinna look at me like that, laird. It be a daft message, I'll agree, but it be what it be!"

~

What if he did not come?

The field was empty, the barley tall, and its heads full of grain, nearly ready for harvest. The woods were in full leaf, and yellow celandine bloomed below the trees. The sky was clear, and Mairi's heart was full. He would come.

But what if Gib forgot her message? He had repeated it correctly more than once, but he might have got nervous or mixed the words, or used his own.

Knowing that Rob wanted her, she told herself to be patient, but that did nothing to quell the tumult within her. Was she doing the right thing, or was she just reacting to loneliness or her dislike of living with Phaeline?

Was she—worst thought of all—seeking to replace the father she missed so much more than she had expected she would, with a husband?

And Fiona. What about Fiona?

The more Mairi thought about Fiona's missing their father's burial, the more she fretted. Fee did have a mind of her own, but such behavior was unlike her.

A horseman appeared at the edge of the woods, where she and Fiona had been when they had first seen him with Will.

With the sun almost straight overhead and glaring down, Mairi had to squint to see more than his shape. But she needed no more to recognize Rob. Stifling an impulse to run up the hill to him, reluctant to reveal the depth of her feelings until she could be sure she had been right to do what she had done, she stood at the bottom of the field and watched him ride nearer.

He might not react well to all she had to say to him, but she had thought half the night about it all before she had decided that her dilemma fell into the category of things she could not control. When that thought had struck her at last, she had relaxed and fallen into deep sleep. And as the memory of it touched her now, she relaxed again. Trust was trust, and that was that.

He dismounted a short distance away and dropped his reins to the ground.

The horse was young to trust so near the ripe barley. But Mairi did not care if it ate the whole field, because Rob was striding toward her, unmindful of the crop.

Without another thought for his reaction, she smiled and went to meet him.

"I knew you would come," she said, reaching both hands toward his.

He grabbed her wrists and pulled her close, letting go only to wrap his arms around her in a crushing hug. "I nearly didn't," he admitted. "But you are right to say that, unlike an apology or a promise, trust goes two ways. I've missed you so much, lass, more than I can say," he murmured close to her ear. "I'd have come to you wherever you were. Will the workers come back soon, or have we time to talk?"

"No one will come," she said. "Even Phaeline is safely inside the Hall."

"I sent Gib back to the Hall, too," he said, giving her a measuring look. "I'm hoping you didn't ask me here just to send a message to my grandmother."

"Nay, but did you see Fiona?"

"She and Will had gone riding, Jardine said. I don't think you will see her whilst you're here, though. Will and his father are doubtless angry to have been caught in their mischief. And there was nowt we could do, legally."

"I feared that would be the case, but Fiona wanted him and now she has him. Mayhap she is content so. But I did not invite you just to see you again or to talk of Fiona," she added conscientiously. "I wanted to tell you . . . that is, to ask you . . ." She hesitated. The words to express her feelings had escaped her. The phrases she had practiced in the night seemed stilted now, unnatural. He would think—

"Mairi, lass, say what you want to say," he said, holding her away and looking into her eyes. His gaze was steady, and his eyes held the twinkle that had so surprised her the first time she had seen it. When she still did not speak, he said gently, "If you summoned me here to tell me you never want to chance meeting me again without due warning, I'll—"

"You know that is not why," she said, trying to think and finding it impossible while he looked at her so.

"Then why? Come, lass. This is not like you, to be so reticent."

"Nay, I ken fine that it is not," she said, trying to smile. "I thought I would be able to tell you easily, because I can usually say what I like to you. But it is not so easy after all. Sithee, I want . . . that is, I have come to think . . . to realize . . ." Again she hesitated, grimacing until she saw that his eyes were dancing. "Sakes, sir," she said then with heat. "Do you *know* yet again what I want to say?"

"I hope I do," he said, his eyes still alight. "But I am not such a dafty as to put words in your mouth now, sweetheart. You must speak for yourself."

The endearment helped. She felt herself relax again and knew his demand that she speak her mind was only fair. Even so, every experience with her father and stepmother—aye, and with others, too . . .

"What I want to say seems improper," she explained. "Everyone has warned me that it is never a woman's place . . . that I must wait for the right man to say the words to me . . ." She looked up hopefully. But although the expression in his eyes had shifted from outright merriment to something gentler, he remained silent.

Mairi swallowed, looked at his chest for a moment as she drew a steadying breath and let it out. Then she looked up again and said, "I have come to believe that you would suit me well as a husband, sir. I know that others will disagree with me, may even think I have gone utterly mad. But so it is."

"Why?" he asked, his voice sounding deeper than usual and the single word oddly unsteady.

In that moment, she felt a lurching deep inside her, as if her heart had turned over. Sensing his sudden uncertainty, doubtless stirred by things she had said before, she wanted to put her arms around him, but she resisted. The two feelings coming together at that single word gave her the confidence to say, "I was feeling unusually weak, sir. When I asked you to come—"

"*Bade* me come," he said.

"Aye, if you like. I expect Gibby may have made it sound that way, because I told him he *had* to tell you just so. I knew I could trust you to come to me, but I did not want to tell Gib enough to put him in possession of my feelings. Indeed, I thought I must . . . Sithee, at least a portion of what I must say is a matter of great importance to me and may not seem so to you. Or," she added swiftly, "because it may seem to be a matter of much greater importance to you *not* to do as I ask."

"Enough, Mairi," he said. "Surely, you have learned by now not to try to couch the things you say to me in tactful ways. I cannot know *how* I will react, and neither can you until you tell me what you want of me."

"Very well," she said, holding his gaze. "I want to marry you, Rob Maxwell. I do trust you. The only 'but' in the matter is that I cannot do so if you will insist upon making Dunwythie a Maxwell holding."

"All I want," he said matter-of-factly, "is to make *Mairi* Dunwythie the beloved wife of Robert Maxwell."

"What if by doing so you had to agree that our eldest son, or whichever child of ours inherits my holdings, must do so as Dunwythie of Dunwythie?"

"Rather than as *Maxwell* of Dunwythie?"

"Aye," she said, eyeing him warily. "My father would never have understood my feelings for you, sir. And he would have been unlikely *ever* to agree to our union. I do love you with all my heart, but I could not betray him by allowing his title to become a Maxwell title. My cousin Jenny has retained hers. I can do no less for Dunwythie of Dunwythie."

He smiled. "You'll get no quarrel from me, sweetheart. What matters to you matters likewise to me. Alex will doubtless assure us that it is common in such cases for the chief or a chieftain of the clan into which a rightful baroness weds to claim her titles. But I can attend to Alex, and to any other Maxwell if necessary."

"My father explained that no one can simply claim Dunwythie, sir, whilst I retain it. But someone might try to seize it after my death, or force my minor son or daughter, if I have only daughters, to relinquish it. If I thought that any one of your clan might do that, I could not marry you."

"But you do *want* to marry me," he said.

She nodded solemnly and stared warily at his chest, unwilling to let him see just then how much his answer meant to her, as she said, "I do, aye."

"Look at me," he said. When she did, striving to keep her feelings from revealing themselves, he said, "Will you trust me to deal with that, Mairi—with my family, that is—and accept my word that I will protect your estates and title from such theft? Or will you insist that we sign all the pertinent documents first, before all the proper witnesses, and only then agree to be my wife?"

She looked straight into his eyes and said, "If you tell me you can keep Dunwythie from becoming a Maxwell property, I believe you will. You have always kept your word to me, Rob Maxwell, and I know you would not make such a claim unless you knew you could fulfill it."

He nodded, and she noted with satisfaction that his eyes were twinkling again.

～

In his exultation, Rob had all he could do not to snatch her up in his arms and whirl her about. But he knew that despite her trust, she remained vulnerable, and he wanted to do nothing that might make it harder for her to withstand

Phaeline's certain displeasure, which she would soon face. Mairi might believe that his joy stemmed from knowing that she loved him, but Phaeline would surely pour scorn on that belief and insist his joy came from knowing he would get her estates.

He knew what else Phaeline would say, because much of it would be the same as what Alex would say, and Lord Maxwell. None of them would believe as easily as Mairi apparently did that he could stand against a united Maxwell determination to seize the Dunwythie estates.

But he knew that he could. To Mairi, he said gently, "I am not such a fool, lass, as to believe I can stand alone against a Maxwell army. Nor could you stand alone against such a force, although in time the law would side with you. But Douglas will support your position, and I have already shown Hugh Douglas and Alex, too, that my services are yours to command, marriage or none. Moreover, Alex seems to have learned a few things."

"But the two of you are ever at odds, Rob. Art sure—?"

"He is still my brother, sweetheart. And he has come to see himself more clearly, I think. We talked more this morning, and he told me he understands why I took your side, and will not hold the incident against me."

"Doubtless your grandmother would like to have heard that."

He grinned, remembering. "Oh, thanks to Gibby's comment yesterday, she was there, lass. Not in person, sithee. But, in spirit, she certainly was."

Mairi laughed, and he pulled her close again, savoring the scent of herbs in her hair and the wondrous feeling of her slender, supple body against his again.

As his stirred in response, he eased her away again, saying, "How long must we wait to marry?"

She gave him a roguish look then. "That depends, sir, on just how much you will enjoy a wife who makes her own decisions and acts on them."

"How so?"

"Because when I decided to let things be, and realized that we do know each other and love each other, I took an action of which you may *not* approve."

"Did you, my love? Acting perhaps too hastily, in fact? I think you know well that if I disapprove of aught you do, I will certainly say so and make my own position plain. We will doubtless fratch like wildcats from time to time."

"We will, aye, but if you don't like what I did, you need only say so, and we will take another course. Sithee, Lord Johnstone is a man who keeps his own chaplain, and I have sent for him. He should be at the Hall by now."

"Mairi, my love, you will make a fine baroness."

"I forgot about banns, though," she said, looking dismayed. "Won't we have to wait till they're called? Three Sundays, is it not?"

"Not if that chaplain knows his business," Rob said. "We'll just tell him we'll declare ourselves married if he will not perform the ceremony. I warrant a few coins in his hand will procure us his aid in the matter."

"Then we can be married as soon as we get back."

At that moment he would have agreed to almost anything she wanted. But he knew he did need to make one thing clear to her from the outset.

"We can marry whenever you like," he said. "But although I can easily agree that you will remain Dunwythie of that Ilk and pass that name and title on to your rightful heir, I do expect one concession from you in return."

He expected wariness. Instead she smiled and said, "Tell me, my dearling."

The warm feeling inside him nearly undid his determination to settle the matter before they did anything else. Sternly suppressing the reaction, he said, "I cannot leave Trailinghail to my steward and bailiff year round. I ken fine that you will want to live in Annandale—"

"At the Hall," she interjected. "I must spend *some* time at Annan House, too, of course, but not nearly as much as you will want to spend at Trailinghail. We both have excellent stewards, so I'm thinking we can arrange to attend to our estates in turn, winters and a portion of each autumn at the Hall, a fortnight annually in—"

"We can discuss our schedule later," he said. "I was afraid you might never want to return to Trailinghail."

She shook her head. "My memories of the tower are happy ones, sir. I look forward to returning, especially to seeing Annie again. Indeed, I am eager to see Lady Kelso and her Eliza as soon as may be."

He chuckled. "She will want to see you again, too, lass. She told me from the start that she quite likes you."

Mairi smiled.

Holding her gaze, he put a hand to her cheek. "Art sure, sweetheart?"

"Aye, sir," she said, raising her face toward his.

He needed no further invitation to claim her lips, but neither did he allow his attention to linger there long before he suggested that they should get back.

"I left Hugh and Alex, and all their men waiting for me in the road," he said.

"Well, we should have witnesses, should we not?"

"Aye," he agreed, chuckling. "Alex will stand up for me, but you must ask your stepmother to be the other. I expect Hugh will want to give you away."

She nodded, but she looked so solemn that Rob wondered if she feared that Phaeline would refuse. Her stepmother was unlikely to support their marriage.

⁓

Mairi was indeed wondering what to do if Phaeline refused to stand up with her. But Phaeline agreed at once.

"I know better than to waste my breath when you have made up your mind," she said. "I have been thinking, too, that I should like to visit some of my kinsmen. But I could *not* leave you alone at Annan House or here at *this* place. I cannot say that I approve of your marrying this man, Mairi, but I will say no more about *that*."

Mairi realized then that her stepmother had found their living arrangement as much of a strain as she had.

"I expect you are very surprised at this, though," she said.

"Well, I knew something odd was in the offing when first that Gibby lad came in looking like he had a secret and then Johnstone's chaplain arrived. I see no reason for you to delay, my dearling, but you *must* tidy yourself first. That will give everyone time to see to supper. They all want to see you wed, of course."

Instead of taking herself immediately to her bedchamber, Mairi paused in the doorway to say, "Shall you be content to remain at Annan House by yourself?"

"I expect I have any number of female cousins who would leap at the chance to live with me," Phaeline said.

"My family has a house in Glasgow, too, so I will doubtless spend time there each year. But you must go now, dearling. I doubt your intended husband will be patient forever."

"You are right about that," Mairi said. "We can discuss everything more comfortably after the ceremony, at supper."

But the ceremony was brief. And, at supper, Phaeline showed little disposition to linger and Rob even less. The servants had scarcely taken away the meat platters before he made it clear that he was impatient to be alone with his bride.

His brother, who had helped himself generously to the whisky, raised a goblet to him and said, "Here's to a good future for the two of you, Rob. I'm thinking you'll enjoy being called 'my lord,' but how will ye like submitting to her ladyship's every wish and decree, eh?"

Mairi felt her breath stop in her throat, but Rob laughed and said, "Sakes, Alex, I thought you of all people would see that I have done the wisest thing a man can do. I've found a wife who will control all and leave me to do as I please."

Hugh hooted with laughter. When Alex joined him, Mairi relaxed.

Her husband stood and took her arm, and she went willingly with him to the stairs. He had exerted himself to be charming to Phaeline, who had reacted as most women seemed to react to him. So, Mairi teased him with tolerant amusement.

"She was as wax in your hands, sir," she said as they reached the landing near her chamber. "Faith, but I fear your skill with women will cause me—"

"Hush, lass," he said, bending swiftly to silence her with a kiss.

Releasing her a short time later to open her door, he

added quietly, "Fear nowt of such matters, sweetheart. Having won you, I am yours now and for all time . . . and, by the Rood, *you* are mine."

Inside, they wasted no time. Someone had thoughtfully left enough hot water for two, and the bed was freshly made. On the small hearth, a cheerful fire blazed, and the shutters were still ajar. A soft breeze stirred the bed curtains.

Going to the window to adjust the shutter, Mairi saw that darkness had fallen and the moon in its last quarter was rising.

Rob came up behind her and put an arm across her shoulders. "I have missed your conversation, sweetheart."

She hid a smile. "Do you want to *talk*, sir?"

"Nay, my bonnie vixen, I do not," he answered with a chuckle. "I have missed other things even more. This, for example," he added as he slipped a hand behind her neck, raised the silky hair there, and placed a warm kiss on her nape.

A thrill shot through her to her toes, and she turned to him eagerly, her fingers reaching for her bodice lacing.

His hand gently caught hers. "I want to do that," he said. "'Tis my right on this night of nights to see what I have won. Put your hands behind your back and leave your undressing to me."

With an involuntary gasp, she obeyed.

Dear Reader,

I hope you enjoyed *Seduced by a Rogue.* The bones of this story come from an unpublished sixteenth-century manuscript about a fourteenth-century incident in Galloway and Dumfriesshire. A sixteenth-century Lady Maxwell wrote it about her husband's Maxwell ancestors. So her version was a trifle biased.

It left out pertinent details such as what the exact conflict was between Alexander Maxwell and Lord Dunwythie that resulted in Alex's trying to take the Dunwythies' land. However, research and help from many folks here and in Scotland resulted in discovery of the odd differences in how the three dales composing Dumfriesshire were administered then. When I discovered that the office of Sheriff of Dumfries was hereditary and belonged to the Maxwells, the rest fell fairly logically into place. However, for the sake of this story, I took liberties with the timeline and some of the details.

The names of the following characters were real: Mairi, Robert, Alexander, Phaeline, Thomas Dunwythie (now Dinwiddie, Dunwoodie, etc.), and Fiona. Also, Archie the Grim and John, Lord Maxwell. The others are fictitious, and much about the main characters is the product of the author's imagination.

The Scottish office of sheriff in the fourteenth century was not only hereditary but included vast powers. However, to avoid complicating things, it is also one with which

I took great license. The actual hereditary sheriff then would have been John, Lord Maxwell of Caerlaverock. Hereditary sheriffs nearly always left everything to their sheriff-substitutes or sheriff-deputes (think deputy, today). We know Alexander Maxwell was not a lord but clearly wielded great power, so he was likely the sheriff-substitute for Lord Maxwell. To simplify things, I just let Alex *be* the sheriff.

Descriptions of problems regarding taxes and the administration of the dales are true, as well. Annandale was a stewartry, Nithsdale a sheriffdom, and Eskdale was a regality. That just meant the barons there paid their taxes directly to the King.

Those of you who have visited Galloway and seen its barren hills may wonder about the forestlands with which I endowed Borgue and much of the landscape west of Kirkcudbright. I refer you to the *Ordnance Gazetteer of Scotland*, p. 423: "In early times [the area] appears to have been covered with woods, and at a comparatively recent period it had several extensive forests."

Details of geography, towns, and dales come from many sources but primarily from *Ordnance Gazetteer of Scotland*, edited by Francis H. Groome (Scotland, 1892).

My primary sources for Douglas history include *A History of the House of Douglas,* Vol. I, by the Right Hon. Sir Herbert Maxwell (London, 1902), and *The Black Douglases* by Michael Brown (Scotland, 1998).

I must thank, first and yet again, the one and only Donald MacRae, who introduced me to this story by asking me if I'd be interested in a tale about a woman who nearly started a clan war. Little did he know it would result in three books. I hope he enjoys it and doesn't think I tampered too much with the facts.

If I explain that the real Robert Maxwell supposedly kept the real Mairi Dunwythie locked up in one room for two years without anyone else in the area ever suspecting she was there, you will perhaps understand why I changed a few details of Lady Maxwell's account.

The truly odd discovery was that the Maxwell-Dinwiddie (or Dunwythie) connection occurred twice, the second time in the sixteenth century with Lady Jane Dinwiddie marrying another Robert Maxwell. That time, however, the title did change to Maxwell-Dinwiddie—after Lady Jane's death.

As always, I'd like to thank my wonderful agents, Lucy Childs and Aaron Priest, my terrific editor Frances Jalet-Miller, master copyeditor Sean Devlin, Production Manager Anna Maria Piluso, Art Director Diane Luger, Senior Editor and Editorial Director Amy Pierpont, Vice President and Editor in Chief Beth de Guzman, and everyone else at Hachette Book Group's Grand Central Publishing who contributed to making this book what it is.

If you enjoyed *Seduced by a Rogue*, please look for the third book in the trilogy, *Tempted by a Warrior*, at your favorite bookstore in July 2010.

In the meantime, *Suas Alba!*

Sincerely,

Amanda Scott

http://home.att.net/~amandascott

Don't miss Amanda Scott's
next captivating
Scottish romance!

Please turn this page for a
preview of her next novel,

Tempted by a Warrior

Available in mass market
July 2010.

Chapter 1 _____

Applegarth, Annandale, Scotland, 1377

The traveler approaching the open kitchen doorway along the path that ran behind Spedlins Tower paused at hearing a soft feminine voice inside:

"'I expect I should be spinning, too, aye,' the maiden said sadly. 'But it would be to nae purpose. I could never finish so great a task in time.'"

The traveler took a step closer as the voice went on, creaking now with age, "'Och, but I could spin it all for ye, aye,' the old woman said."

"Gey good o' the auld crone!" cried several childish voices, as if they had many times heard the story and exclaimed always at the same place.

The traveler smiled, recognizing the tale from his own childhood. He moved nearer, trying to muffle the sounds his feet made on the loose pebbles of the path.

He saw the speaker then, seated on the stone floor of the scullery with her back to the doorway. Five small, fascinated children were gathered around her.

Beyond, in the darker kitchen proper, he discerned bustling movement and heard sounds indicating preparation of the midday meal.

The storyteller went on in her own soft, clear voice, "So the maiden ran to fetch her lint and put it in her new friend's hand. Then she asked the old woman for her name and where she should call for the spun yarn that evening."

One of the children, a lad of five or six, looked right at the traveler.

The tall, powerful-looking stranger put a finger to his lips.

Although the boy obediently kept silent, he continued to stare.

The storyteller continued, "But the maiden received no reply, for the old woman had vanished from where she stood. The lass looked long for her, and at last became so tired that she lay down to rest."

Three of the children eyed him now as a fourth, a lassie, piped up, "Aye, and when she awoke, it was gey *dark*!"

"So it was," the storyteller said. "The evening star was shining down, and as the maiden watched the moonrise, she was startled by an uncouth voice from—"

"Who is *he*?" the same lassie demanded, pointing at the traveler.

The storyteller, turning, saw him and scrambled awkwardly to her feet, saying as she did, "Sakes, where did you spring from?"

He noted first that she was black-haired, blue-eyed, and beautiful—and then, with unexpected disappointment, that she was heavy with child.

"Forgive me for interrupting you, mistress," he said. "They told me at the stable that I should come this way as it was quicker and none would mind. But if you will bid someone take me to Old Jardine, I will leave you to finish your tale."

"Nay, this is a good place to stop," she said, frowning and putting a hand to the short veil she wore over her long, thick plaits as if to be sure it was in place. "I can finish the story later."

To the instant chorus of indignant protests, she said firmly, "Nay, then, you must all go now to Cook and ask how you can help him. As for you," she added, turning her lovely blue eyes on the traveler again as the children obeyed her, "someone should have told you that Jardine of Applegarth sees no one these days."

"He will see me," the traveler said confidently.

"Mercy, why should he? Have you no respect for a dying man?"

"I doubt that that ill-willed old man is really dying. But he will see me because he sent for me. I am his heir."

Instead of the hasty apology he had every right to expect from a maidservant who had spoken so rudely to him, she grimaced and said scornfully, "You must have taken *that* notion from a tale of the same sort I've just been telling the bairns."

His temper stirring, he said, "Mind your tongue, lass, lest—"

"Why should I? Do you dislike being proven a liar?" she demanded. "For so you are if you claim to be the heir to Applegarth."

Doubt stirred. No servant of Old Jardine's would dare speak to him so impertinently. Despite their kinship, he barely knew Jardine. But if even half of what he had heard about the contentious old scoundrel was true, Jardine's servants would tread lightly and with great care.

"Who are you, lass?" he asked.

She gently touched her belly. "I am his heir's mother, or mayhap his heir's wife. Whichever it is, I can tell you truthfully that *you* are *not* his heir."

Stunned, he realized in much the same moment that the fact of Old Jardine's lie did not surprise him. In fact, he had expected a lie. He had just expected to learn that the old man was *not* dying. Suppressing the fury that had leaped at her words and attitude, he said, "I expect, then, that you must be Will Jardine's lady."

"Aye, of course, I am," she said. "Who are you?"

"Kirkhill," he said.

She frowned. "Should I know you? Is that all anyone calls you?"

"People call me several things, depending on who they are. Some call me Seyton of Kirkhill. As I am Will's cousin, you and I are clearly kin by marriage, so you may call me Richard if you like, or Dickon."

"I'll call you Kirkhill. I warrant it must be Lord Kirkhill, though."

"More to the purpose, my mother is that old scoundrel's sister," he said.

"Sakes, I did not know he *had* a sister!"

"I think she'd liefer not be one," he said with a slight smile. "But he did send word to us that he was dying and bade me hurry to Spedlins Tower."

"Then I expect I should go and tell him you are here and see if he will receive you," she said with a sigh.

"Nay, my lady. I did not come here to kick my heels whilst my uncle takes his time to decide whether he truly wants to see me. You will take me to him. First, though, I want to hear what happened to Will."

"So would we all," she said with a grimace.

"Sakes, do you not know? Jardine's messenger told me that my uncle was on his deathbed and that I was to be his heir, so I assumed Will must be dead. But as you've said you might be either the heir's wife or its mother . . ." He paused.

"Aye," she said, touching her belly again. "In troth, I do not know which. See you, Will was here and then he was not. He's been gone for over a fortnight."

"I hope you will pardon me if I ask if you and he were actually married. I am sure that no one told my mother of any such occasion."

"Aye, sure, we were," she said with an angry flash in her eyes. "If my good-father did not tell his sister, I am sure that is not my fault."

"Nay, it would not be," he agreed.

Looking away, she added, "My good-father has clearly called you here for no reason, sir. Doubtless, you would do better just to turn around and go back to wherever you came from."

"Do I look like the sort of man who would do that?" he asked gently.

She met his gaze again. This time he detected wariness in her eyes.

⁓

Seventeen-year-old Lady Fiona Jardine did not at all think that the man facing her was one who would cheerfully go away just because she had suggested that course. In truth, she was not sure what to make of him.

He was taller than she was by nearly a head, and looked

as if he might be twice as broad across the shoulders. He did not look much like the dark Jardines. His hair was the color of dark honey and curly, and his face revealed dark stubble, revealing that no one had shaven him for a day or two. But he moved with athletic grace, spoke well, and seemed very sure of himself. She envied him that confidence, remembering a time when she had enjoyed similar self-assurance.

But *was she actually married*? What a question to ask one! A true gentleman would never challenge a lady so. At least, she did not think one would, but the truth was that she had not met many gentlemen.

The only ones that came quickly to mind were her deceased father, her sister's husband, Robert Maxwell, and her cousin Jenny's husband, Sir Hugh Douglas. She scarcely knew the latter two, though, and she certainly did not count her cantankerous good-father as a gentleman. Nor would she count her husband so if Will was still among the living.

But gentleman or not, Kirkhill did not look like a patient man. And, if he was kin to Old Jardine and to Will, she would be wise to do as he told her.

"Come this way, my lord," she said quietly, and turned toward the kitchen.

They passed through that vaulted chamber and up the winding stairs to the hall, crossing it to the inner chamber behind the dais.

She paused then, glancing at her unwanted companion. "His chamber is no pleasant place," she told him. "And my good-father will be in no good humor."

"I'll bear up," he said, leaning past her to open the door and gesturing for her to precede him inside.

Grimacing, she did. The odors of Jardine's sickness were strong, and she wanted the business over quickly. Her companion, however, showed no sign of minding the noisome atmosphere.

The fat old man was awake, propped on pillows, glowering at her through his piggy eyes. His personal servant hovered over him, holding a cup in his hand.

Old Jardine waved him away. "What d'ye want, lass? I ha' told ye afore that ye must rap on the door and wait till ye're admitted."

"That was my doing, Uncle," Kirkhill said, urging her farther into the room with a touch of his hand.

"Richard! 'Tis yourself, then? Ye've come? By, but I'd scarcely know ye!"

"I warrant I was no more than seven when last we met, for I've not been next or nigh this place since then. And apparently I've come on a fool's errand now."

"'Tis no foolish thing to answer the cry of a dying man," Jardine muttered, his voice suddenly much weaker.

Fiona nearly rolled her eyes. She did not believe he was any weaker than he had been a moment before. Evidently Kirkhill agreed with her, because his voice took on an edge as he said, "But why did you declare yourself dying and me your heir? I expect the first part may be true, but the second is plainly false."

"D'ye think so? Only God kens the answer to that."

Fiona gritted her teeth. She would have liked to remove herself from the old man's presence, but curiosity bade her stay as long as they allowed it.

Kirkhill said, "Your good-daughter is obviously with child, Uncle. And she assures me that Will and she are married."

"Aye, 'tis true he did marry her, the young fool."

"From your message, I thought he must be dead," Kirkhill went on with a new note in his voice, a harder one, that made Fiona look quickly at him to try to judge what manner of man he might be.

Not that she counted herself a good judge of men, for she knew she was not. But she *had* learned to recognize certain important things about them. So she studied him carefully as he continued to gaze sternly at his uncle.

Old Jardine continued to look at him, too, as if he were also sizing him up.

When the old man's silence made it clear that he had forgotten the question or did not choose to reply, Kirkhill added softly, "*Is* Will dead, Uncle?"

"He must be."

"Even if he is, why did you say I was to be your heir? I don't like liars." As soft as his voice was now, it sent a chill right through Fiona.

Old Jardine said in his usual curt way, "Nor do I *tell* lies. We've no seen our Will now for weeks, so he must be dead, like I said. Nowt but a grave would keep that lad away this long without any word to me."

"The English have been restless, breaking the truce by sending raiders across the line just east of here," Kirkhill said. "Mayhap he got himself captured or killed."

"D'ye think he'd ha' kept his name to himself? He'd ha' told them he were my son straightaway, and I'd ha' got a demand for his ransom. I'd ha' paid it, too, for Will. He's naebody's prisoner," he added. "It has been too long."

"If he is dead, you *will* soon have an heir or an heiress," Kirkhill said, gesturing toward Fiona.

"Faugh," Jardine snorted. "I'll believe that when I see the bairn. Sithee, she'll more than likely lose it afore it be birthed. Her own mam lost more bairns than anyone else I've ever heard tell of."

"I won't lose *my* child," Fiona said evenly.

"Aye, well, whether the bairn comes or no, Richard, I want ye to find out what became of my Will. I thought if I let ye know that ye stand to inherit Applegarth, ye'd come here, and so ye did. I've also willed it that ye're to look after the place when I die if Will doesna come home. Ye'll do that right enough, I'm thinking, for a tithe from the rents."

"I will, aye," Kirkhill said. "I'd do that for anyone, tithe or none."

"I named ye guardian for the bairn, too," Jardine said, shooting Fiona a look.

"My child won't need any guardian but me," she said.

"Even an I believed that, which I do not, 'tis my duty to name someone *suitable* to look after his interest here, and to look after yours, too, aye," he said.

Wondering if that were true, she looked at Kirkhill.

He met her gaze with a stern look that somehow reassured her even as he gave a slight nod and added, "That *is* true, my lady. However, you should have someone you trust to look after your interest, a kinsman of your own."

"Should I?" Fiona said. "My good-brothers live at some distance from here, and my father is dead. I do have an uncle who served the Lord of Galloway, but I've not seen him these past three years, so he may be dead, too, for all I know."

"They ha' nowt to do wi' her, any road, and I dinna want

any o' them here," Jardine growled. "Get hence now, lass. I would talk wi' Kirkhill alone."

~

When the lady Fiona had gone, Kirkhill faced his uncle. "I expect you think I should just drop anything else I might be doing and stay here."

"Nay, I'm none so daft as that. Moreover, I'm good to look after things myself for a time yet. I just wanted ye to know how ye stand. Applegarth will be yours if Will be dead and the bairn also dies. I'd like a lad o' Will's to inherit, but I'm none so sure that I'd want one wi' that lass as his mam. God will decide that matter, I expect."

"He will, aye," Kirkhill agreed.

"Aye, sure, but I'll be damned afore I'll see any *daughter* o' hers taking Applegarth, so ye'll see to it *that* doesna happen," he added with a straight look.

"If I did not know better, I might think you mean me to do away with her."

"Aye, well, if I thought ye would, we might make a bargain o' sorts, for I've nae use for her. Too hot at hand for any man and doesna take well to schooling. Moreover, I've a strong notion that if my Will's dead, she killed him. Sithee, she were the last one to see him alive, and he were gey displeased wi' her."

Kirkhill concealed his distaste, saying only, "I'll gladly see what I can learn of his whereabouts, Uncle. Mayhap I should look for someone from his lady wife's family, too, in the event that she needs someone to look after her interests."

"Nay, then, ye'll look after Applegarth, so ye'll look

after her, too. Mayhap we'll talk more anon, but I'm tired now. Ye'll stay the night."

Mayhap he would, Kirkhill decided. He had little interest in talking further with Old Jardine, but he did want to learn more about Will's lovely lady.

She was waiting outside the door for him.

"He thinks that I killed Will," Fiona said without preamble, knowing the old man would have lost no time in expressing his suspicion of her.

"He did tell me as much," Kirkhill answered honestly. "I doubt that it's true, though. Unless Will was even weaker than my uncle seems to be now, I doubt that you could have managed it, particularly in your present condition."

"That is kind of you, sir, because I'm nearly sure I didn't," she said.

His eyebrows arced upward. *"Nearly* sure?"

"My good-father has accused me so often that I've almost come to believe him," she said glibly. "That is the real reason he invited you here. He wants to know the truth before he dies, so he can hang whoever is guilty."

"I can understand him wanting that, aye," he said, nodding.

"He will appreciate such easy understanding on your part, I'm sure. But mayhap, before you tell *him* as much, you should know one thing more." Pausing, she added, "I overheard him telling his man that he also suspects you, my lord."

THE DISH

Where authors give you the inside scoop!

♥ ♥ ♥ ♥ ♥ ♥ ♥ ♥ ♥ ♥ ♥ ♥ ♥ ♥ ♥ ♥ ♥ ♥ ♥

From the desk of Susan Crandall

Dear Reader,

After a good friend of mine finished reading one of my suspense novels, she asked my husband how he could sleep next to me at night, knowing how my mind works. After I'd given her a good dose of stink-eye, I really started thinking. Not about how dangerous it is for my dear husband—although that could probably be debated. Many of us do it every night without pause, but think about how much trust it takes between two people to fall into innocent, blissful, and completely *defenseless* sleep next to that other person.

But more important to this book is the question: When in our lives are we more vulnerable than when we're sleeping? I mean, it starts when we're children with the monster in the closet or the bogeyman under the bed. And for sleepwalkers, that vulnerability multiplies exponentially; their fears are real and well-founded, not imaginary.

Think about it. You go to bed. Fall asleep . . . and never know what you might do during those sleeping hours. Eat everything in your refrigerator? Leave the house? Set a fire? It would be horrifying. Even worse, you will have absolutely no recollection of your actions.

As they say, "From tiny acorns mighty oaks do grow." The disturbing vulnerability induced by sleep-walking was the seed that grew into SLEEP NO MORE.

As for my husband . . . the poor man continues to slumber innocently next to me while my mind buzzes with things to keep the rest of you awake at night.

Please visit my Web site, www.susancrandall.net, for updates and extras you won't find between the covers.

Yours,

Susan Crandall

♥ ♥ ♥ ♥ ♥ ♥ ♥ ♥ ♥ ♥ ♥ ♥ ♥ ♥ ♥

From the desk of Sherrill Bodine

Darling Reader,

You know I can't resist sharing delicious secrets about some of Chicago's best stories!

When I discovered that my friend, the curator of costumes at the history museum, was poisoned by a black Dior evening gown (don't worry—he's perfectly well!) and that it happened at a top secret fall-out shelter that houses some of the most treasured gowns in Chicago's history, I knew I had to tell the tale in A BLACK TIE AFFAIR.

After all, what could be more irresistible than a

time-warp fantasy place that houses row after row of priceless gowns that were once worn by Bertha Palmer, the real-life legendary leader of Chicago's social scene?

For those of you who may not be familiar with her, Bertha leveraged her social standing and family fortune to improve lives and to champion women's rights. So I thought, how perfect it would be if her gowns helped the women of Chicago once again, and one woman in particular!

It wasn't long before my heroine, Athena Smith, was born. I gave her two fabulous sisters who are just as devoted to fashion as Athena is—and, of course, as I am—and I determined that a couture gown would change her life forever. One of Bertha's gowns would poison Athena, just as that Dior had poisoned my friend, and that would throw her back into the arms of her first love, notorious bachelor Drew Clayworth. Of course, that's just the tip of the iceberg of this story because, as we all know, the course of true love never does run smooth.

Find out what other surprises and tributes to my beloved Chicago I have in store for you in A BLACK TIE AFFAIR. And never forget that I love giving you a peek beneath society's glitter into its heart. Please tell me *your secrets* when you visit me at www.sherrillbodine.com.

Xo

Sherrill Bodine

♥ ♥ ♥ ♥ ♥ ♥ ♥ ♥ ♥ ♥ ♥ ♥ ♥ ♥ ♥ ♥

From the desk of Amanda Scott

Dear Reader,

What sort of conflict between the heads of two powerful Scottish clans might have persuaded Robert Maxwell of Trailinghail to abduct Lady Mairi Dunwythie of Annandale, the heiress daughter of a baron who defied certain demands made by Maxwell that he believed were unwarranted? Next, having abducted the lady, what does Robert do when Lord Dunwythie still refuses to submit? And why on earth does Mairi, abducted and imprisoned by Robert, not only fall in love with him but later—long after she is safe and a powerful baroness in her own right—decide that she wants to marry him?

These are just a few of the challenging questions that faced me when I accepted an invitation to consider writing the "true" fourteenth-century story of Mairi Dunwythie and Robert Maxwell—now titled SEDUCED BY A ROGUE.

The invitation also came in the form of a question—a much simpler one: Would I be interested in the story of a woman who had nearly begun a clan war?

Since authors are always looking for new material, I promptly answered yes.

A friend had found an unpublished manuscript, dated April 16, 1544, and written in broad Scotch by

"Lady Maxwell." Broad Scotch is a language I do not know.

Fortunately, my friend does.

Lady Maxwell related details of how two fourteenth-century Dunwythie sisters met and married their husbands. ("Dunwythie" is the fourteenth-century spelling for Dinwiddie, Dunwoodie, and similar Scottish surnames.) SEDUCED BY A ROGUE is the story of the elder sister, Mairi.

Relying on details passed down in Maxwell anecdotes over a period of two hundred years, Lady Maxwell portrayed that clan favorably and Mairi's father as a scoundrel. The trouble, her ladyship wrote, was *all* Lord Dunwythie's fault.

So the challenge for me was to figure out the Dunwythies' side of things and what lay at the center of the conflict. That proved to be a fascinating puzzle.

Her ladyship provided few specifics, but the dispute clearly concerned land. The Maxwells thought they owned or controlled that land. Dunwythie disagreed.

The Maxwell who had claimed ownership (or threatened to *take* ownership) was just a Maxwell, not a lord or a knight. However, Dunwythie was *Lord* Dunwythie of Dunwythie, and that Annandale estate stayed in Dunwythie hands for nearly two hundred years longer. In the fourteenth century, landowners were knights, barons, or earls—or they were royal. So, clearly, Dunwythie owned the land.

Next, I discovered that the Maxwells were then the hereditary sheriffs of Dumfries. Sheriffs ("shire-reeves") were enormously powerful in both Scotland

and England, because they administered whole counties
(shires), collected taxes, and held their own courts of
law. The fact that Annandale lies within Dumfriesshire was a key to what most likely happened
between the Dunwythies and the Maxwells.

The result is the trilogy that began with TAMED
BY A LAIRD (January 2009) and continues now with
SEDUCED BY A ROGUE. It will end with TEMPTED
BY A WARRIOR (January 2010).

I hope you enjoy all of them. In the meantime,
Suas Alba!

Amanda Scott

http://home.att.net/~amandascott
amandascott@worldnet.att.net

Want to know more about romances at Grand Central Publishing and Forever? Get the scoop online!

GRAND CENTRAL PUBLISHING'S ROMANCE HOME PAGE

Visit us at www.hachettebookgroup.com/romance for all the latest news, reviews, and chapter excerpts!

NEW AND UPCOMING TITLES

Each month we feature our new titles and reader favorites.

CONTESTS AND GIVEAWAYS

We give away galleys, autographed copies, and all kinds of fun stuff.

AUTHOR INFO

You'll find bios, articles, and links to personal Web sites for all your favorite authors—and so much more!

THE BUZZ

Sign up for our monthly romance newsletter, and be the first to read all about it!

534 8724
Sherman Brown